SMUT

A ROMANTIC COMEDY

KARINA HALLE

First edition published by
Metal Blonde Books May 2016

For Scott and Bruce, the biggest dorks I know

PROLOGUE

AMANDA

New Year's Eve

"You look absolutely ravishing tonight," Alan says as he leans in to place a soft kiss on my cheek.

I pull back and eye him warily. "Ravishing? What are you, a duke all of a sudden?"

His blue eyes turn strangely shy and he averts them from my face, clearing his throat. In the background, the music seems to build as happy couples dance to and fro. "I'll get us another drink," he says quickly.

I frown as I watch him go, cutting across the dance floor and nodding at our friends. Ironically, Alan's family is so wealthy that I wouldn't be surprised to find out that somewhere along the line he's related to a duke. It would explain why he walks around like he's got a stick up his ass (hey, I'm dating the guy, I'm allowed to make fun of his posture. If he stood up any straighter, he'd be mistaken for a tree).

Still, he's been acting weird the whole damn night. I

know it's New Year's Eve and all, which has always been a rather big deal for us, but even so, Alan Kingston is normally smooth and unflappable. It's one of the reasons why we work so well together—I'm the (hidden) hurricane and he's the calm. Tonight, there's something a little bit off that has me, well, really wanting another glass of champagne. Or ten.

The winter storm isn't helping my nerves either. Outside, the wind batters the large floor-to-ceiling windows, causing them to rattle and shake. People let out little *ooohs*, coupled with nervous giggles as the rain pelts against the panes, like someone is throwing wet rocks. It's also completely black outside which adds to the uneasiness. Beyond the stately lodge you know the beach is getting absolutely pounded by the ocean—you can feel the vibrations every now and then, even if you can't see the angry waves.

Tofino has always been one of my favorite spots, even though I've only been to the sleepy surfing town a few times in my life, so naturally when Alan said we were doing our annual New Year's Eve party here, I jumped at the chance. Over the last four years I've been with Alan, we've done New Year's Eve in a cabin on Mount Washington, in the streets of Vancouver, on the beach in Mexico, and now at one of the most beautiful resorts on Vancouver Island, famed for storm watching in the winter, and surfing and whale watching in the summer.

Because last New Year's Eve down in Los Cabos was so quiet and intimate, I was kind of shocked that he wanted to invite not only every single friend of ours, but his parents too. That set off a few warning bells that I really should have addressed because now I'm standing here, watching him get champagne from the waiter, and

I'm deathly afraid of what's going to happen when he returns.

You know when you just get a feeling about *something*, and even if it's something you won't let yourself think about, it still festers somewhere inside you? I'm starting to feel as gnawed up as a rotten log.

"Amanda," Sarah Price says to me from behind.

I let out a sigh of relief, eager for the distraction, and turn around, smiling at her.

Sarah is a striking girl, tall and slender, with skin like polished marble and hair that flows like fields of silken wheat all the way to her waist. Her eyes are a rich, dark brown, shining like coffee. I know I'm going a bit purple prose over one of my oldest friends, but hey, it's what I do.

Tonight she's wearing a rather daring dress, a low cut black velvet gown that clings to her slight curves, giving her the appearance of an old-fashioned mannequin. She's turning heads as usual, even though we're pretty much around the same people here as we have been since high school. It amazes me that she's managed to stay single for so long. I know she says she's picky, but there's a world of guys out there that would give their left nut (and maybe their right one) to be with her. Sometimes I wonder how I might have turned out if I had stayed picky too. I'd be single...but would I be happy? It's something else that I don't dare think about.

"I haven't seen you all night," she says. "How are you?"

I shoot her a placating smile and run my hand over my updo, making sure it's all in place. It's true I haven't really said anything other than hello to her tonight, and over the last few months I've talked to her less and less. I still consider her a great friend, probably my closest one in some ways. But even though we come from similar families and were raised pretty much the same way, ever since I started university, I've felt this fissure between us. I'm sure this continental drift is natural when you're twenty-one and figuring shit out, but I'm becoming more and more aware of it.

And it's not just Sarah. It's everything, including Alan and this party that we're at. Once upon a time, these people were my world, but as time flies by, they're starting to feel like strangers, and this world seems less like my own and more like a cocoon I'm supposed to shed.

But lord knows with my parents, shedding anything they've brought upon me is next to impossible.

Still I say, "I'm good. It's kind of fun with this storm, eh?"

She wrinkles her nose. "Fun? It's frightening."

"Yeah, but being frightened is fun," I tell her. "Remember when we used to go on night hikes and I would take off with the flashlight and leave you alone in the dark?"

"Oh yeah, real fun," she says dryly. "You were the cruelest child, you know that? Scarred me for life."

I can't help but smirk. "Oh come on, that's why you liked me. Everyone else was too boring."

"Everyone else was *normal*," she says and then blinks, as if catching herself saying the wrong thing.

I'm not offended. I know that out of everyone in my private school for rich bitches and the silver spoon elite, I was the resident weirdo. I tried to hide it, and still do, lest I risk the look of utter disappointment on my mother's face every time I slip into geekdom.

"Well, normal is overrated," I say. What I really want to do is open the giant glass doors and run out on the deck and into the storm, letting the rain ruin my makeup and hair and dress. I want to feel fucking alive from my fingers to my toes

—I want to capture the lightning and hold it in my chest until I burst.

"Are you okay?" Sarah asks, putting her hand on my shoulder.

"Yeah, why?"

"You're crying."

I frown, and only then do I notice her face is starting to blur. I thought maybe it was her airbrushed foundation, but no, it's tears smearing my vision.

"Argh," I growl, and shove my finger into my eye. "It's these damn contacts."

I normally wear glasses for my nearsightedness but Alan insisted I wear contacts tonight. I rarely wear them, so my eyes seem to reject them every second, and it could be one reason I'm feeling out of sorts. With my glasses I almost feel like I have a persona, like Clark Kent. Without them, I'm exposed.

"I thought you were getting sentimental," she says, and after I blink a few times and my vision clears, I notice this strange twinkle in her eye, a devious slant to her mouth.

I swallow thickly, my gut all frothy again.

"No," I say slowly. "Over what?"

"No reason," she says, looking back to Alan who is gabbing with his father. The two of them both look my way and nod at the same time, like fucking robots. Out of the corner of my eye I can see Sarah nod to them and raise her drink.

There's something going on here. It's in the air and it's changing, and it isn't the storm at all.

Oh god, please don't let tonight be that night.

But you know it's coming, I tell myself. *You know he asked you what size ring you wear.*

"Oh god," I whisper, my stomach turning into a whirlpool.

"What?" Sarah asks.

I look at her, pained. "What do you know?"

"Huh?"

"What do you know?" I hiss. "Sarah. You're terrible at secrets. What do you know?"

She gives me a funny look. "I have no idea what you're talking about." But there's a warble in her voice, an uncertainty. She knows something. "I have to go to the washroom. Excuse me."

I watch as she quickly walks off.

Shit.

I take in a deep breath, trying to fight the nausea, my hands wrapping around my stomach. My nickname in high school, aside from Amanda Panda, Lord of the Geeks, and Tits McGee, was Sir Pukes-A-Lot. It didn't matter that I wasn't a sir. I still got sick every time I got really nervous, which led to many embarrassing moments during presentations, PE, and drama class. Clearly, having such a nightmare-worthy reflex defined my awkward teenage years, though I haven't puked in an awkward situation in a really long time, and I desperately want to keep it that way.

I wonder if I need to escape to the washroom to splash some cold water on my face, but before I can, Alan approaches me with the champagne.

"Here we go," he says, smiling at me with sparkling white teeth and handing me the glass.

I hesitate, afraid to take it, afraid I won't be able to grip the stem and it will shatter at my feet.

"You all right?" he asks in that gentle, sweet way of his, and I try and let the familiarity ease me back to normal.

I nod and grab the glass, taking a tepid sip. I can barely

taste anything right now, but at least it should help with the bile.

Deep breaths, stay cool, I tell myself as I meet his eyes.

"Guess the storm has me on edge," I tell him, watching him carefully. "You seem on edge too."

His eyes widen, brows pulled to the ceiling. "I do?" he practically squeaks. "No, no, not at all...I just..." He licks his lips and looks behind him at his dad who is now standing by a lectern that seems to have come from out of nowhere. His dad gives a barely imperceptible nod of his head.

Oh shit.

Alan turns back to face me. "Amanda," he says, voice soft and full of something that sounds like hope. My gut clenches. "Just stay right here. Don't move."

Oh god.

He walks over to the lectern. Someone turns down the music. The lights dim. People stop dancing.

I'm frozen in place. Stay right here? I couldn't even run, even if I wanted to, even if I needed to upchuck in the toilet.

Oh god, please, please don't puke, I tell myself. *Please don't let this be what I think it is.*

Alan picks up the microphone, tapping it.

"Testing," he says, his voice way too loud and crackly over the speakers. "Sorry, sorry everyone. I know midnight isn't for another hour, but I was wondering if I could have your attention."

Fuuuuuuuuck.

I glance around and see everyone either looking at Alan or looking at me. His parents, dressed in their finest and wearing expressions that only sun exposure and plastic surgery can bring, are watching me. So is Alan. So is Sarah, who is coming through the crowd, giving me an exaggerated thumbs up as she takes her place among everyone else.

"You see," Alan goes on, "tonight isn't just New Year's Eve. It's the fourth anniversary for Amanda and me. It's a special night, one we usually celebrate by ourselves, so you're probably wondering why I invited you all here to share in the night with us. I mean, other than the fact that we adore your company."

He flashes his smile at the room and some people chuckle. Lame asses.

"Well," he says, "I have an explanation. But it's not for you. It's for my shining star. My beautiful Amanda Panda Bear." He gestures to me, and I swear I can hear the sound of thirty heads swiveling at once.

I don't know how I paste a smile on my face, but I do, even though the room is starting to spin and my head feels like it's being put through an acidic spin cycle.

This isn't going to end well.

Then, to my complete surprise, he steps away from the lectern, the microphone going with him. Piano music starts tinkling and he begins to sing.

Sing.

"I remember all my life," he croons, wiggling his brow even as a drop of sweat rolls down. "Raining down as cold as ice."

Holy fuck. Is he singing "Mandy" by Barry Manilow?

Alan comes closer, gliding toward me like he's rehearsed this a thousand times, and then it occurs to me that it's Alan, of course he's rehearsed this a thousand times—he rehearses what he says to his parents before we roll up to their house every Sunday dinner.

I mean, never mind the fact that he can sing, which is something else I had zero idea about.

I've been with Alan for four years. I've lived with him for one. And I knew him for two years before that. I should be surprised that I didn't know this about him, but the fact is, I'm not surprised at all. Because I don't really know him. And he doesn't really know me. And that's why I know this whole evening, this whole horrible event flashing before my blurry eyes, is one huge mistake I'm going to have to deal with. Hopefully without tears or a side of vomit.

I'm standing in the middle of what looks to be an epic proposal to a man that I love but don't want to marry. Alan Kingston is the man my parents wanted for me. He's the man that most women want for themselves. He's smart, wealthy, sophisticated, loyal, good-looking, and kind. He's the reason my mother looks at me with less disappointment, he's the reason I'm treated with more respect by our peers, why we can get reservations at any restaurant, why I know I don't have to work a day in my life if that's what I choose. He's the reason I should be about to break down in happy tears, overwhelmed with joy over the life we're about to spend together, that he's picking me, Amanda Tits McGee Newland, over everyone else. He's picking the weirdo with her secret hopes and dreams.

But it's because of those hopes and dreams and every-thing that makes me tick that I know I can't say yes. Because a life with him isn't the life I want. I'm twenty-one years old. I'm young, so young, and I don't even know who I really am. All I know is the person I am currently doesn't want the life my parents have tried so hard to carve out for me. It wants something completely different. It wants to be free.

Calm down, I tell myself, swallowing the brick in my throat. *He might not be proposing anyway.*

Alan drops to both knees and actually *slides* toward me, microphone crammed dramatically against his mouth as he leans back, eyes closed, and belts, "Oh, Mandy! You came and you gave without taking!"

Oh for fuck's sake. I'm doomed.

It's my fault, really. I'd been feeling trapped and claustrophobic for at least the last six months, and I've just been too much of a lazy chicken shit to deal with the problem. Besides, the unhappiness has been really good for my novel. It allows me to live in that fantasy world completely and without any guilt. I'm not sure I could actually write if I was happy.

Well, you're not going to be happy after this.

I attempt to swallow again, my heart and lungs and stomach all doing a conga line inside me. My face is red hot and flushed. Everyone is staring at me, and I can't stop staring at Alan, who is singing with both so much cheese and sincerity that I just want to melt right down into the floor.

He finishes the song on his knees, down by my feet, and when it's over and the music turns off and the room comes to a hush, I know he's not getting back up.

This is happening.

He grabs my hand and I have to fight the urge to pull it away. He stares at me, but I'm not sure if he's really seeing me at all, if he ever saw me, because my eyes are begging, pleading, for him not to do this.

Don't make me break your heart. Not here, not now.

Oh, I've been such an idiot.

"Amanda Rose Newland," he says to me into the microphone, so I guess he's saying it to everyone else too. "When I first met you, you were this strange, strange girl with your glasses and your nose in a book, always reading on the sidelines or spending hours in the library." There are a few titters in the crowd, everyone clearly picturing *that* girl. "You had this ability to talk about characters in books and TV shows and movies like they were real, like they were your friends. You could spout random knowledge about trees and animals and countries like your brain housed an encyclopedia. I didn't know what to do with someone like you, but I was charmed by the beauty beneath your brains."

Surely he means the brains behind my beauty?

"And all the potential I could see deep inside. The real you. We've been together four years and you've surprised me day in and day out by turning into this intelligent, poised and proper young woman, the very lady I thought you would become."

Lady?? Okay, he must be out of his mind tonight because there's no way he'd ever declare me a lady. Nothing pisses him off more than when I let out a burp, but believe me, I can't help my acid reflux.

"I believe you'll make an excellent mother, that we will raise smart and beautiful children, that you'll be the best wife a dentist could have, by my side and through the thick and thin."

"Amanda..." He reaches into his pocket.

Our friends sob and gasp.

My stomach contents start moving up my throat.

Alan pulls out a ring with the biggest diamond I've ever seen. It catches the light like a disco ball.

"Will you do me the honor of marrying me?"

Everything inside me dies.

My hand flies to my mouth.

It's not from shock. It's to keep back the vomit.

"I think she's going to faint," I hear someone whisper in the crowd.

"This is so romantic," someone else says.

"She's crying," another person comments.

And I *am* crying.

My fucking contacts. Now the world is turning into a

blur, which you'd think would make things easier since Alan's eyes are nothing more than blue dots and I don't have to see any hurt or anguish in them.

But nothing is going to make this easier.

Just say yes. Just say yes and tell him no later. Save him this humiliation. Save yourself the humiliation.

Say yes!

I shake my head, the tears spilling down, bile filling my mouth.

"I'm so sorry," I whisper.

"Amanda," he hisses back, and I hear the warning in his tone. Don't do this.

I don't want to.

But I have to.

"I can't do this."

"Can't what?"

"Alan, I'm sorry," I manage to get out, trying not to open my mouth too wide. "I can't, I can't...I can't..."

And I can't finish my sentence.

Up comes the vomit.

My hand tries to hold it back, to hold my mouth shut, but it comes spraying out anyway, like a garden hose with a kink in it.

It lands all over Alan—his head, his face, his shoulders, even his shaking hand with the ring in it. The room seems to gasp as a whole.

And yet, somehow, somehow my mouth is still moving.

"I can't marry you," I say weakly, pulling my dripping hand away from my mouth.

The gasps grow deeper.

Someone whispers, "Sir Pukes-a-Lot."

I'm blinking back real tears now.

"I'm so sorry," I tell him, voice quavering. "I love you, but just not enough to say yes."

It's the most honest I've been in a long time. But it's too little, too late.

And though the last thing I want to do is be a coward, I turn away from the shocked whispers and Alan on his knees covered in puke, and the disapproving eyes of his parents, knowing I've disappointed my own parents as well, and I run.

I run through blurred vision.

Right into a table.

I cry out, the round side cutting into my hips, and the table tips over, drinks and food crashing into people's laps.

Some people are laughing, some are crying out in disgust. I think I hear Alan's mother full-on sobbing. It all fills my head, swirling around and around until it has a stranglehold on my heart.

Somehow I pull myself away from the table, from the wreckage, and make it to the giant glass doors before hurting anyone else.

I fling them open, the rain and salt-soaked wind pelting me in the face, and run outside.

It's cold. Dark. Wet. I am in the throes of this wicked winter storm.

But even as my heels slip and slide on the wood deck, as I grip the railing for dear life and run down the steps and onto the beach, where I plan to just run, run, run, I push all the feelings of humiliation and duty and shame aside.

I feel nothing but free.

ONE

AMANDA

THREE MONTHS LATER

RUNNING IS THERAPY.

At least that's what I tell myself. Over and over and over again.

This is good for you.

Don't quit.

Keep going.

This is hell.

I'm literally going to die.

Why am I doing this to myself?

Can I stop now?

I'm going to stop.

And I often do stop and try and catch my breath until some other jogger blasts past me and then my ultra-competitiveness kicks in and I end up running after them. Sometimes I can't catch up but at least it gets my legs moving again. Other times I run past them with a nonchalant look on my face, ponytail swinging behind me like running is super fun, super cool, totally no big deal for this girl, only to collapse around the corner in a heaving mess minutes later.

But somehow I keep doing it, every day. At first I started

running because it was the only way I could shake out my frustration. I tried taking kickboxing classes, but they kept conflicting with my class schedule and I accidently punched my instructor in the face, so that was a sign to move on. Running seems to be a better fit. I can go at my own pace, pick my times, and best of all for my inner hermit, I don't have to see or talk to anyone. It's just me and the ground beneath my feet. Well, and my stupid brain that constantly reminds me what *hell* running is.

And even though it clears my head—believe me, I've done a lot of thinking ever since Alan and I broke up—it just never seems to get easier. I'm waiting for that moment where it's painless, easy, and fun, and that just hasn't happened yet. Maybe it never will. Maybe that's why people run. They're chasing something they'll never get, the dangling carrot of promises that all hard things eventually get easy.

Today's run isn't easy, but at least it's beautiful. It's early March, and chartreuse buds are just starting to make their appearance on the tips of barren limbs. The ocean, slate grey and churning, foams against the rocky shoreline. In the far distance, Washington's Olympic Peninsula is hidden, shrouded by low, dense clouds that like to sit in Haro Strait between the two countries like some sort of tribunal council. It's still cold and damp, and the sun can barely penetrate the cloud cover, but I know in a few months, hell even a few weeks, our daylight hours will be long, the air will turn warm, and my usual jogging path along Oak Bay will start to swarm with the elderly out for their daily walk or happy couples making out on park benches. Hopefully by then I'll be able to handle couples, or just happy people in general.

After I turned down Alan's proposal, puked on him,

and made a general mess of things, we both decided we couldn't work it out. Alan was beyond humiliated, changing from the easygoing boy I loved to a stranger who hated the sight of my face. I hadn't been quite prepared for the split in his personality, especially as I only saw the nice guy over the last four years. I guess he'd been hoarding a whole lot of negative emotion toward me, and it all started coming out. Like vomit. But meaner and less gross.

(I promise I'll stop talking about puke, it's just so fitting right now.)

I can't blame him for being angry with me, because I was angry with myself. If only I'd confronted those feelings, the whole thing could have been avoided. But he was my first real relationship, my first love, the guy I lost my virginity to, all those big things, and I thought the feeling of boredom and complacency was normal. What I didn't think was that we would be in a pressure cooker. Even though we'd been together for so long, I was still in university for two more years, and we were young. I mean, Alan still had four years of dental school left. I really didn't think marriage was on his radar.

Of course there were all the clues. Asking about ring sizes and where we'd go on our honeymoon and how many children I wanted. Okay, so they weren't even clues, more like obvious signs that he was going to ask me. But I skirted around those questions and laughed them off, and well, no one is laughing now.

Naturally, after I publicly rejected him, I had to move out of the apartment we were sharing. But instead of moving back home like my parents wanted me to, I decided to find a roommate and get the hell out of Dodge.

It was the right choice. Not only is my current place super close to the University of Victoria, it has put some much needed distance between me and my parents (you can only hear about what a horrible choice you've made so many times). And I have a pretty awesome roommate.

Okay, maybe awesome isn't the right word. But she provides me with distraction and entertainment, and half the shit she says is slowly ending up in my novel in the guise of a hilarious sidekick.

When I first saw the ad for a female roommate on Craigslist, I somehow assumed that it would be another U-Vic student. The location was in Oak Bay, it was a two-bedroom basement suite...I assumed it was another twenty-something needing a roommate to save a buck. But Ana Vainola ended up being a forty-four-year-old Estonian woman who was as tall as an Amazonian with fake boobs that could poke your eyes out, Juvéderm-filled lips, a tan that looked like she was doused in Orange Crush even under the best light, and the loudest, rapid-fire laugh I'd ever heard. She was also a recent divorcée, and even though we're two decades apart and were raised in two totally different worlds, our transition from "taken" to the single life made us bond like nothing else. I've only been with her a few months, and even though she uses me as a guinea pig every night while she practices makeup for her beauty schooling, I can't imagine living anywhere else.

I suppose I could live by myself, but the thing is, even though I've been a self-proclaimed hermit my whole life, being alone right now scares me. Living with Ana lets me concentrate on my studies and my novel, yet whenever I need a break and a chance to escape from my head, she's right there, ready for a laugh or a lecture on how to prepare for the apocalypse.

At the moment though, she's at her beauty school and I have to shower and change and get ready for my writing class. When she's not here, I can usually get out the door in ten minutes. If she's here, I usually end up being sucked into a random conversation about pickles or rifles or uncircumcised penises (all of which came up over breakfast this morning).

When I'm done in the shower, I pull on some leggings, a long grey sweater that covers my ass (which hasn't shrunk from my running like I thought it would), and slick on just enough makeup to say I tried, then pull my wet hair back into a bun, put on my glasses, and head out the door.

I have a car, a Mini Cooper (a high school graduation present from my parents), and though I don't drive to school often because I feel like a douche, today I'm running late so I'm zipping over, hoping I'll be able to find a parking spot near the classroom. That's one of the reasons I don't drive—the time it takes to find a spot is about the same amount of time to take the bus, plus on the bus you're staying green, and it's a great excuse to listen to music and people watch. I think most of my best characters have come from dealing with Victoria's public transportation system.

Thankfully, I find a parking spot right by the building. My teacher, Professor Marie Dumas, may be carefree and encouraging and all sorts of weird (which I personally love), but she's a stickler for tardiness and academic excellence. When you're late, or you half-ass an assignment, she takes it personally. I've seen her tear up over giving a low grade before. But Writing Fiction 200 is one of my favorite classes and I give it everything I've got. After all, the writing program is my future, and a way to still get an education and my parents off my back while doing what I love. It's like a piggy bank for my dreams, ensuring that no matter what happens in my future, I'll always have this to back me up.

It's a reminder that I've fought to stay true to myself, even if my life doesn't go to plan.

After I park and run into the building, I pass my classmate Ali on the stairs, though she's running away from class instead of going to it.

"Where are you going?" I ask her.

She pauses on the stairwell and gives me a sharp look under her razor-cut bangs. "I'm not feeling well," she says, even though she sounds more pissed off than sick.

I watch her go and then shrug to myself before reaching the top of the stairs. My friend Rio is hanging outside the door to class texting someone, leaning against the wall and twirling her curly dark hair around her finger like someone out of a John Hughes film.

"Thought you weren't going to show," she says as I approach, snapping her gum between her teeth. "I just texted you."

I pull my phone out of my suede saddle bag and glance at the text blazing on it.

Where you at? We're getting our final assignment today. Also, I lost my bra last night so I'm wearing Saran Wrap instead.

You'd think I'd be shocked by a text like this but not when it comes to Rio. I glance up at her, my gaze going directly to her boobs. "Uh, what?"

"She's giving us our final assignment."

"Yeah, but more about the Saran Wrap in place of a bra..." I point out.

"Long story," she says, then leans in closer, her dark eyes dancing. "But it works. Just in case you end up sleeping with some guy who keeps comparing your vagina to the Rio Grande. I don't think he realized he was being insulting, especially after we finished off a bottle of Crown Royal while playing a Game of Thrones drinking game, but needless to say, I got out of his place and didn't think about the bra until now."

I frown, trying hard not to laugh. "But you have other bras, I'm sure."

"Oh, I didn't go home after that," she says, and I don't press her on it. If she wants to share the details, she'll share. "Anyway, I hope Marie gives us something more exciting than our last assignment."

"No kidding," I tell her, even though I'm lying. Honestly, I liked our last assignment, which was to write a short nonfiction story about ourselves without embellishing a word. My description of high school was like a less entertaining (and less murderous) version of *Heathers*. And even though this last project is the equivalent of our final exam, I can't wait to tackle it. I'm a total nerd, I know, but every assignment Marie has given us has really challenged me and keeps improving my prose. Plus, not to toot my own horn, but I have aced every project so far. Her edits and notes on my writing are like a drug, validation that I desperately crave, especially when no one else in my life seems to take my writing seriously.

I look around. "Hey, I saw Ali run off. Is she okay?"

Rio shrugs, adjusting her laptop bag on her shoulder. "I don't know. She stepped in the class, said something to Blake, and then ran off."

Ugh. Blake Crawford. Pretty much the worst human to ever grace this earth. No exaggeration needed.

"Were they dating?" I ask. Ali wears a permanent scowl, is super intelligent, and is pretty much the last person I'd imagine going after the fuckboy, manwhore, jackass that is Blake.

She rolls her eyes. "*Fucking*, Amanda, not dating. What else is new? He probably broke her heart and her vagina. Or vice versa."

"I wasn't aware Ali had a heart to break." I don't comment on her vagina.

"Guess she does. Serves her right. You can't play the player without getting played." She says this gravely, even though when it comes to Rio I'm not sure whether she's the ultimate player she seems to be or she's been screwed over once or twice. She has this bright, bubbly personality that masks anything that gets too close to heart. It's probably why, when I first met her in our writing program, we hit it off right away. She lightens me up and forces me to see the glass half full. At least, she's trying.

We take our usual seats near the front as I scan the room. Sure enough, Blake is in his corner, headphones on, and grinning at his phone. Probably watching a YouTube video on how to be a douchebag.

I can't stand his grin. In fact, I hate everything about him. I know, I don't really know him and hate's a strong word, but I have my reasons. He's the type of guy who would have made my high school years a living hell, only now I get to deal with his immaturity in university. Thank god I only have one class with him, otherwise all my time would be spent thinking of witty comebacks to his insults and insinuations.

I don't even know why he's in the class at all, mind you. He's a third year student and transferred from England last year, getting his business degree. Not sure how writing plays into any of it, but however it does, he doesn't take anything seriously. It's like writing and books and literature are one big joke to him, and I'm not the kind of person to take that lightly. Sure, maybe I get a bit too serious at times, whether it comes to writing or school, but that's because, well...I need to.

Then there's the fact that he's a self-proclaimed sex god that every girl seems to lose their damn head over. It's like the sight of him causes any vestiges of self-respect to evaporate, and girls practically throw themselves at his feet. I've seen it happen in this class—first with Monique, then Lisa, then Kendra, now Ali. The only upside to this continuous classmate walk of shame is that at least it makes class more interesting when every tragic poem and angry short story seems to be directed at Blake. It's like watching one of those train wreck reality shows unfold before your very eyes.

I just don't get it. Surely they can all see it's an act. Even if he's good in bed, how the hell does he even get you there?

Okay, well maybe it's because he's not exactly hard on the eyes. I'd be blind if I said Blake wasn't good looking. He is. I can admit it. I can find men attractive without actually being attracted to them (I used to think that about Brad Pitt, but he's changing my mind as he gets older). Blake is tall and lean with just the right amount of muscle, thick dark hair that's always a bit rumpled, and deep blue eyes that sometimes seem black. You know, the kind of looks that most girls want. Maybe even the kind that might blind you to the point of making a string of unhealthy decisions that ultimately help fuel their writing goals. I don't know.

Unfortunately, all of his beauty is spoiled by his shit-eating grin, which, as I said earlier, is probably his best and worst feature. Best because he flashes it all over the place and women spontaneously combust like matches are struck on their ovaries. Worst because I know what that grin represents: cockiness, arrogance, and one hell of an ego. There's nothing that bothers me more than guys who think you'd be lucky to have them, though now when I think about it, that's pretty much Alan to a tee. He was a lot subtler about it, but he did have this air of denigration that made me think he was taking pity on me half the time. Maybe that's why Blake bugs me so much.

Or maybe it's because he's an ass.

"All right everyone." Marie enters the room with a tepid grin, taking her place behind her desk, her long fringed shawl and beaded bracelets rattling as she puts her hands together and does this thing where she tries to look everyone in the class right in the eye. Marie is pretty much the stereotype of a creative writing professor. Her hair is waist-length and steel grey, she's always wearing some sort of heavy gemstone around her neck, and she smells vaguely of patchouli. Sometimes marijuana. As I mentioned before, she's a stickler for certain rules and can turn hard on a dime, even though she speaks with a fairy-like quality and her view toward life is one of both a free spirit and a bleeding heart.

"Who here is excited for your final assignment?"

"Me!" I say a little too loudly. I have to supress myself from raising my arm like some kind of keener. Still, I refuse to look sheepish about it. Everyone here knows that about me by now.

Especially Blake. I can't help but look over in his direction, and lo and behold he's rolling his eyes. He doesn't even glance my way to see if I notice; it's like an automatic reaction for him.

"Well," Marie says as she walks around the front of her desk. "I should let you all know that this assignment is a deviation from what you've been given so far." She leans back against the desk and folds her arms, her smile soft and somewhat pitying. Unease prickles the back of my neck. "Being a writer is hard work. Harder than you'll ever think possible. What makes it even worse is the fact that right now, for nearly all of you, writing is easy. You write down what comes from your heart. All struggle is rooted in the outcome, the fear of the grade, the pressure of the deadline. But not in putting down the words, not in telling the story. At this stage, all of you can just, as Hemingway once said, sit down at the typewriter and bleed. But for many writers, and to borrow a popular cliché, it's like getting blood from a stone. You have the want and the desire, but with experience and time, your self-doubt becomes louder and your inner critic comes out to play. It silences your creativity. You feel you aren't allowed to make mistakes."

Marie's tone is so serious that even Blake has stopped looking at his phone and is watching her with a furrowed brow.

"Writing is hard," she continues. "It gets harder when it becomes your career, your job, because it's no longer a hobby, it's no longer a manuscript hidden in your desk drawer. It becomes a platform from which the world can judge you. Your soul becomes target practice, and the critics hold the arrows. I'm not saying this to scare or discourage you, because I've been teaching this class a long time and I know nothing will discourage a wannabe writer more than harsh reality. I don't have to say a word. If it's in you, it's in you, and you will persevere no matter the cost, no matter how hard it is, because that's what you are born to do. To throw another cliché your way, the only way to fail is to quit."

She lets out a long breath of air and stares down at her wrists, adjusting her bracelets. "That all said, you need to know that this class, so far, has been a breeze. This has been about exploring your creativity without fear of judgement or mistakes. It's been about honing your skills, the craft,

about improvement. I have not touched on the actual chal-
lenges of writing in the real world...but with this last assignment I will do just that."

I exchange a quick glance with Rio. She looks just as
worried as I do. I hope we don't have to submit a story for a
contest or a newspaper or something that will be printed in
public because Marie is right, I don't think I'm ready for
that yet. Baring all to the classroom and sharing our work
with each other so far has been hard enough, even though I
know I write better than most of them.

"For this last assignment," Marie says, standing up
straighter, "I have decided to push you out of your comfort
zone. To force you to take risks. And most of all, to teach
you to embrace something, a skill that will become crucial as
you make writing your career, even though it seems to go
against every anti-social, introverted bone in your body. I
know a lot of you in here wouldn't classify yourselves as
such." She nods at Rio and Blake and a few others, who
don't exactly fit the image of a quiet, lonely writer. "But
when it comes to writing, we all shut down and internalize
everything. That's the nature of the game. We reach deep
within ourselves to pull up all the muck and the dirt and the
roots of who we are. But when you're working with editors
and publishers and marketers and librarians and whomever
else comes your way, you realize that though writing is a
lonely, isolating, primarily selfish profession, you need to be
able to work well with others in order to make this your
job."

"What if we don't want to make it our job?" Camelia
Parsons says, raising her hand. I swear this girl is half the
reason why book pirating is so rampant. "Making money
has never been an issue. It's not why I write. I write to bare
my soul, regardless if it sells or who reads it."

Marie shoots her a placating smile. "Then all the power to you. But if that's all you envision, writing for a hobby, then you can't truly care about bettering yourself, about learning the craft. We learn so that we may succeed, and that goes for anything in life, including the arts. It's a falsity that the moment we earn money or wish to earn money for our creations that it ceases to become art. If that's truly what you believe, that sales don't matter, then you need to question what you hope to get out of this. After all, art isn't just about creating. It's about sharing. And whether you want the sales or don't need the money at all, what you do need is all eyes on your work. You want to be recognized. You want to be seen."

"No disrespect, Professor," Blake says in his British accent, biting his lip for a moment. All eyes in the class swivel toward him. I know that he can't possibly be one of the artists that Marie is talking about—he's just another college kid looking for an easy elective to get his final grade. "But I'm curious as to what you're getting at. Just tell us. We can take it. After all, we've survived this long with you as our teacher."

Marie raises a bushy eyebrow but that's the extent of her reaction. How he doesn't get a rise out of her, I don't know. Marie is always a lot tougher on the guys in the class than the girls, but with Blake she seems to let things slide.

"Right you are, Mr. Crawford," she says. That's the other thing. Always calling him Mr. Crawford, as if he's not just another college student. Must be the accent. It gives him an air of respectability that fogs out all of his other shortcomings.

She clears her throat and eyes us all. "Excuse me. You know I'm prone to a tangent with the best of them. The point of the final assignment is this—to make writing hard.

To force you to think outside the box. And to ensure you learn to work well with others. Your final assignment is to write a twenty to thirty-thousand-word novella with another person in class."

There are a few gasps. I look over at Rio with wide eyes, hoping we can pick our partners. Writing with someone has never been on my agenda, but I think if writing with Rio were an option, we could really make it work. We're on opposite sides of the spectrum, but that might just bring out the best in both of us.

Marie goes on. "I know you have a short time span, but this will also help hone writing under a deadline. My hope for all of you is to share the work evenly. Whether you trade off chapters or point of views, or collaborate on each and every sentence, you should hope to contribute ten to fifteen thousand words each, which is about the same length as the last assignment. The only caveat here is..." She pauses, and this is when her sympathetic smile comes back into play. "That you don't get to choose your partner. I will choose them for you."

Ah. Shit. Rio grimaces, even though I know it's more for me than for her. She has this easy ability to get along with almost everyone, girls, guys, animals, plants. Me, on the other hand, I'm not so lucky. I'm not socially awkward, but to be honest, most people are total morons, and my tolerance for them isn't very high. Some have patience. I do not. And especially not when it comes to writing.

Marie twists behind her and picks up a piece of paper, clearing her throat before she starts going down the list. Rio gets paired with Ali, who of course isn't here. She's lucky though—Ali is one of the smart ones, and after whatever happened with Blake, she probably has enough emotional torment driving her to take on the whole project by herself.

"Holly McGuire, your partner will be Alice Oakes," Marie says, and while those two come to terms with it, her eyes meet mine, and not only do I know I'm next, I know I'm in deep shit. "Amanda Newland," she says, drawing out the pause, "your writing partner for this assignment will be Blake Crawford."

Silence sinks over the room.

Then someone titters.

"Oh, this should be lovely," Blake says from across the room, his voice dripping with sarcasm, his accent somehow amplifying it.

I can't even look at him though. I'm frozen in place, stuck staring at Marie with my mouth open a few inches. She can't be serious. There has to be some mistake.

But there is no mistake because Marie keeps going, listing off the rest of the partnerships while I'm left reeling. I can tell Rio is saying something to me, and I know that Blake is probably hurling British insults under his breath, but I honestly can't hear a thing because all I can think is that if this isn't a joke—and sadly, it doesn't seem to be—I'm not really sure what I've done to deserve it. Has Marie hated me this whole time? Maybe she has. Maybe she thinks I'm untalented, or a hack. Maybe all those As were just pity grades and now her real feelings are coming out. Maybe I've done something to her or said something or written something that she's found offensive, and this is her chance to get back at me. I mean, this is turning something I love into a living hell. I would rather get a bad grade than have to work—fucking *write*—with Blake.

I have to talk to her after class. I have to explain that there's been a mistake and I'm sorry for whatever way I've wronged her (is it possible she's telepathic and she's read my thoughts about her eyebrow hair? Because if so, I'm very,

very sorry). I will work with anyone else at all, but this, I don't deserve this. The art of writing doesn't deserve this.

But after she's spent the class droning on and on about the dangers of adverbs and passive sentence structure and I finally approach her, it's apparent she doesn't feel the same way I do.

"The pairings were entirely random," she tries to assure me as she gathers up her notes, the class quickly emptying, no one else apparently having issues like I do. "That said, I don't think there's anyone in this class that will impede your ability to tell a story."

"It's just that..." I'm searching for a way to say this without sounding like a total brat. "I take writing seriously. And for my final assignment, I really don't want to do this entire class—and you—an injustice by ruining everything I've worked so hard for."

She gives me a quick smile and places her hands, long fingers adorned with turquoise rings, on my shoulders. "You will not ruin anything, Amanda," she says, looking me dead in the eyes. "You're a great writer with a lot of talent. But you're young and you have a lot to learn. Writing isn't just about exposing ourselves. It's about learning. I think your partnership with Blake, with anyone really, will teach you things you never knew you needed to know."

And just like that she leaves the room and leaves me stewing over her mumbo jumbo.

I'm lucky I don't have any other classes after this one, so I get in my car and immediately head home. Well, first I stop by the liquor store to pick up a bottle of wine, then I head home, prepared to unleash all my pent-up rage upon poor Ana.

Only Ana isn't home. Then I remember she said she had a date after class with some guy she met on a dating app for divorcées. I should be relieved that I'm alone, and happy that she's seeing someone, but I'm not either of those things, and even though it's not dark yet, I open the bottle of pinot gris and pour myself a glass, then I open a can of cheese ravioli and heat it up. I sit at the small oak table in our kitchen that Ana has adorned with an embroidered coral and white runner, watch the sun go down through the narrow windows, and try and think my way through this while eating my single girl meal.

I decide to text Rio.

How much sadder can my life get? Not only am I paired with Blake, I'm drinking pinot and eating canned ravioli by myself. At least it's organic.

She doesn't respond right away, but that doesn't surprise me. Rio is currently going through a string of fuck-boys, and who knows, she might still be looking for her bra.

I shovel the ravioli in my mouth and sigh. Marie is testing me. She wants to see what I'm made of. She wants me to prove that I really can write and handle whatever is thrown my way. That's fine. I'll have to rise to the challenge. It won't be pretty, but I will get it done.

By the time I'm halfway through the bottle, I'm feeling more empowered and emboldened than ever. Not enough to answer a call coming through from my mother, the usual guilt trip over my life choices and a very detailed update on how poor forsaken Alan is doing, but enough to write an email to my new partner.

At the start of the school year, Marie made us all exchange phone numbers and emails with each other. I guess she wanted a community feel to the group, especially considering that we would all be sharing our writing. Naturally, I haven't used the contact info for anything since I've really only made an effort with Rio, but the time has come to reach out and make peace.

Be the bigger person, I tell myself. *Nip this in the bud.*

Hey Blake,

It's Amanda from Writing 200. Just wanted to touch base with you before the weekend regarding our writing assignment. I'm cognizant that we possess a lot of freedom with this byzantine project, but even so I think we need to discuss our intent and the subsequent strategy we need to follow. We only have so many weeks and I think the sooner that we establish a schedule, as well as all the normal logistics such as story, plot, and characters, the sooner we'll have a chance at success, ensuring this partnership will be an easy one. Providing, of course, that we remain disciplined and meticulous throughout the endeavor.

I'm available anytime this weekend if you want to get together to discuss our implementation. I think if we distillate on the main points during our initial meeting, we can complete the assignment on our own without much interference from each other going forth.

Amanda.

I sit back and read it over. Okay, it's a bit too wordy and I'm not sure if I've used the word "distillate" correctly, but I've just put it in there to throw him off, to let him know who he's dealing with. I also hope that by taking charge like this and setting the initiative, I'm creating a very professional—and very valuable—paper trail. AKA, when this project goes to hell, at least I have the proof to give to Marie that shows I tried.

Something tells me from now on nothing is going to be as easy as it seems.

I press send.

I wait.

And wait.

Open up a bag of pistachios and eat a few of them.

Nothing yet from Blake.

But a new text from Rio comes in:

You'll be fine, you know how to put him in his place. P.S. I'm in the process of getting my bra back right now. Turns out this dude hid it under his pillow for safe keeping. Not sure whether to fuck him again or just get the hell out. I'm hiding in the bathroom and I think the window is just big enough to squeeze through.

I can't help but smile at the phone. I actually wouldn't mind being in her situation for once. Juggling fuckboys and having endless sexual adventures (and misadventures) sure beats being Miss-Lonely-Hearts-Stick-in-the-Mud.

TWO
BLAKE

I'VE LEARNED A LOT IN MY TWENTY-THREE YEARS.

How to eat pussy like a champ.

How to lie through my teeth.

How to cook a brilliant spaghetti Bolognese.

And I've learned how to tell when people love me, like me, and when they genuinely hate me. You'd think this would be a pretty obvious and a basic skill to have, but you'd be surprised at how much of human fallacy comes from the inability to read each other. In other words, we're always reading in people what we want to see. Some of us want everyone to love us, some of us think that everyone hates us (and thus this gives us a valid reason to hate them).

Me, I have no delusions about who I am and what I am to people. I know I can be pretty callous as of late when it comes to women, and I know I deserve their wrath (although the whole replacing my conditioner with Nair trick that the crazy twat from the pub did went a little too far, even for me).

I know I can be worthwhile to people too, though maybe not always the right people and in the right way. All you need to do to know how people really feel about you is to turn off your ears and read their body language. It goes beyond the expression on their face, even though the eyes will rarely lie, and it starts to become something almost metaphysical. It's all vibe. It's instinct.

In other words, if a girl says she loves you and she's not looking you in the eye, it means she doesn't. Or she has intimacy issues. Or she's cheating on you. Either way, it means she's not flying halfway across the world to live with you anymore, that long-distance relationships aren't worth it, and you have a sad little problem on your hands.

So it's pretty easy to tell that my classmate in Writing 200, and my current writing partner, Amanda Newland, hates my bloody guts.

And, for once, I have no fucking idea why.

Well, that's not entirely true. I have some idea why. Because I don't particularly like her either. It's become something of a chicken or the egg situation. Her obvious dislike of me has led to my dislike of her, and my dislike of her has led to me, well, trying to get a rise out of her whenever I can.

It's a great way to pass the time in an otherwise boring class, even if I do feel like I've resorted to being an obnoxious teenager at times. But poking fun at how uptight she is and how she takes class—and I'm guessing everything in life —way too seriously is completely different than having to *work* with her. It's not that I have a lot of vested interested in this class or my final grade, but I do want to pass—no I *need* to pass—and get my bloody degree over with. Something that once seemed easy looks to be a whole lot harder.

As soon as class was over, I saw her make a beeline for our teacher. I knew she was trying to get out of it, but I'm pretty sure the professor has it in for me. More than that, she's stubborn and won't budge. So I let this be Amanda's battle while I resigned to having her as a thorn in my side for the rest of the semester.

In fact, knowing how seriously Amanda takes the class, and herself, I know she's going to be a total control freak over the project. That's fine. More control for her, less work for me. I guess the only good thing is that whatever we end up writing, I don't think it will be romance. What I've noticed from Amanda's writing in class is that she veers toward darkness, raw reality, and a lot of fantasy that's just one step away from playing World of Warcraft in her parents' basement and attending Comic Cons so that she can stalk her favorite wizard from a long ago cancelled TV show.

Of course I'm just guessing. I don't know much about her, but I'm also in no hurry to find out. The only appealing aspect of this girl is her hair and her arse. Her hair is the color of cayenne pepper and cinnamon, and her arse, well I wouldn't mind coloring it that way with my palm. It might take a few smacks, but they would be worth it. She'll pretend to be too virginal and stuck up to try it but I'll wear her down with the promise of my big dick. Not that I've ever fantasized about this scenario.

I'm about to text my friend Heath and ask if he wants to grab a drink at Spinnakers, my favorite pub (and thankfully not the same pub the Nair-wielding wench works at), when I get a call from my father asking me if I can pick up my stepbrother Kevin from school and drop him off at the shop.

I say yes, even though every time I step foot in my father's store, I end up running the cash and closing. I know my dad is prepping me for when I take over the business, and even though I'm pretty much getting my business degree just to keep him happy, I still have mixed feelings about the whole thing. It's like I haven't quite come to terms with the way my life is going, and I don't dare even think about it.

Kevin's elementary school is near the university, so I get in my Challenger (black, 1972, nickname: Mr. Mean), turn up Jack White's "Missing Pieces," and pull up to the usual spot. I smile broadly at the moms walking past, and even wider for the MILFs who ooze desperation and pent-up sexual frustration. They all know I'm Kevin's stepbrother by now and not some pedo, though I'm disappointed that I haven't been propositioned by any of them yet. Though there was that one time...

It's not long before I spot Kevin, and unfortunately I get to see his face fall the moment he sees me. It's not that Kevin doesn't like me, but we've only really gotten to know each other this last year. Despite our age and differences, I think we get on like Donkey Kong.

But I've been picking him up more and more these days, either from school or his friends' houses. My dad is always busy with the store, and because he's on the verge of bankruptcy, he can't hire any help. Angelica, my stepmother—Kevin's mum—seems to always be working late nowadays. She's a corporate lawyer who just made partner eight months ago, and even though her pay raise means my dad's store can stay afloat for now, it also means more hours.

I'm not sure if the situation is helping them much, but I try and stay out of their relationship. My dad and mum divorced when I was young. I was born here in Victoria and when I was six my mum whisked me back to her hometown of Yorkshire, England. I've been here a few times, and Angelica and Kevin have made it to the UK once, but until recently I wasn't exactly close with any of them, my father included.

"Hey, Blake," Kevin says to me as he opens the door, sounding like a despondent twenty-something stoner instead of a nine-year-old kid. Though with Kevin's long dark hair and his penchant for wearing a cape to school sometimes, he could pass the part.

"Hey, loser," I tell him, reaching over to muss up the top of his head. He wrenches away from me with a look of disgust. "You know, you think you could sound happier about being picked up from school in the world's coolest car."

He glares at me, so sullen. "It's not the world's coolest car. It's the world's *oldest* car."

I bristle. "Well it's better than your friends and their lame minivans."

Good one, Crawford.

"No," he counters with a haughty scowl. "Jill Carroll's mom drives a Porsche Cayenne. That's a *Porsche*. That's expensive and way better than this piece of shit."

"Hey," I snap at him. "No car is better than Mr. Mean. I bet Jill Carroll's daddy bought the car as a present, saying he's sorry for shagging the maid." I pause, Kevin's eyes widening as he takes this new information in. "Also, don't say shit. It's bad and I don't want another lecture from your mother about how your language is going downhill over the last year."

He flops dramatically against the seat, his head lolling on the headrest. "Whatever. She doesn't care enough about me to even notice."

Ah, fuck. The little bastard has a way of cutting deep.

"She cares, Kevin. A lot."

"Then why isn't she here?" he mumbles.

"You know she's working."

"She's always working."

"Well, maybe she's trying to buy a Porsche Cayenne of her own so you don't have to ride in this ancient piece of shit with me." I grin at him, hoping he'll return the favor.

"Maybe," is all he says, staying just as sullen as before. I start the car and we drive off, and I don't even have to look to know that Mr. Mean's engine is turning the heads of all the MILFs in the parking lot. Take that, Jill Carroll's mum.

"How is Fluffy?" he suddenly asks me.

My grip tightens briefly on the wheel and I exhale. "Fluffy is fine."

"Not giving you any trouble?"

"No," I say, then mutter under my breath, "thank god."

"Have you given him lots of cuddles?"

I laugh and give him a pointed look. "Kevin. You know I'm not the cuddling type. No exceptions for family or pets. Or girls for that matter."

"I used to cuddle him all the time. Till mom got mad." He looks at me, his features softening so much that I'm suddenly aware of how much he's aged over the last year. It's like he's been hit with the frying pan of adulthood way before his time. "Thank you so much for taking care of him. I swear, Mom will let him back at home at some point."

"No problem, kid," I tell him. "Though I'm pretty sure she wanted him out because you cuddled him *too* much. Ever hear about Lennie in Steinbeck's *Of Mice and Men*?"

Kevin's look tells me no.

"It doesn't matter. You'll read it in high school."

"Aren't we going home?" he asks me when I take a left and start heading toward downtown Victoria.

"Your dad wants me to bring you to the store," I tell him.

"*Paul*," Kevin says, that ever-present edge to his voice whenever he says his name. "I don't call him dad."

Even though he's been your dad since you were four

years old, I think, but I don't voice this to him. After all, Paul is my actual dad and my relationship with him is just as complicated. Who am I to talk?

Downtown Victoria isn't too far, especially as all the traffic on the Pat Bay Highway is heading away from the city, and pretty soon we're pulling up to Crawford's Books on Government Street.

Right. So my father owns a bookstore. It's been in the Crawford family for generations, basically since the city of Victoria was founded in the late 1800s. It's something of a local treasure, a spot that historians fawn over and tourists fall in love with. But at the end of the day, it's still a business trying to make money, and for the last five years the store has been taking a hit. Some, like my father, blame self-publishing and the rise of ebooks. Others, my mother included, blame the fact that my father never had a logical or business-minded bone in his body. Even the best intentions from the most passionate people can fail if they don't have a sound mind at the helm.

That's where I'm supposed to come in. I'm the supposed sound mind. My father, for a bunch of reasons he hasn't yet voiced to me, wants me to take over while I'm still young, but *only* when I have a business degree. He hasn't quite admitted that his lack of business and management skills have led to the store's demise, instead putting all the blame on the rising rent and real estate prices in the city and all the other things I've mentioned.

The store is one-of-kind, however, and that's the main reason why it's still running. Though the big commercial chain, Chapters, is up the street, those giant megastores seem to focus more on selling throw blankets, stationery, and prissy candles than books. People come to Crawford's Books because the store itself is an experience. At least that's what I gather from the hushed approval of the seniors that visit.

I park Mr. Mean on the street and pay the meter before we head into the store. The shop closes at 7pm, so I know I won't be working all night, but even so, the pub is still calling my name. I need a pint or two something fierce, especially after that class.

Despite Kevin's pouting earlier, he perks up when he sees the store. Kevin is completely obsessed with fantasy books and could—and has—happily spent days here huddled among the tall cedar shelves, reading everything he can get his hands on.

The bookstore itself is like one big giant room with a cathedral ceiling and a loft at the back that houses some of the rare editions. The floors are dark polished wood and everything is extremely orderly with each genre getting its own section—fiction and new releases at the front, history and non-fiction and local travel guides in the middle, fantasy, sci-fi, and young adult at the back. The only genre we don't carry is romance, which I think is yet another poor business decision on behalf of my father. Not only do women come in here all the time looking for romance, but from the research I've done, it's one of the biggest selling genres.

But dad is a literary snob—it was hard enough to convince him to stock more sci-fi and fantasy—and even though the books would sell, he won't even allow *Fifty Shades of Grey* in the store. I'm looking at this purely from a marketing perspective. Sex sells and we need more sales. We need more money coming in, period. But since he says smut and filth will lower our standards, it's just another smart idea that won't happen at Crawford's Books.

"Son," my dad greets me as Kevin and I step inside,

Kevin making an immediate beeline to the back of the store, his cape flowing behind him. Did I mention my stepbrother sometimes wears a cape and carries a stick of a polished wood that I'm sure is some kind of magical staff?

My dad watches as he goes and then turns to me, shaking his head as he pinches the bridge of his nose. My dad has always had a youthful appearance, a baby face that probably accounts for the way he used to win people over. You want to trust him, to believe him. But ever since I moved here, it's like he's aging before my eyes, faster than Presidents do once they get into office, all grey hair and deep lines and loose skin.

"Did you know that I caught him painting his nails the other day?" my dad says to me in quiet reproach, putting his arm around me and leading me over to the cash register in the middle of the room.

I raise my brow. "Pink?"

"No," he scoffs. "Black."

I shrug, not too concerned. I faintly recall trying on my mum's high heels when I was young, but I don't dare voice this to him. "Kids like to experiment."

"He's nine," he says as he smiles at a customer walking in, lowering his voice to me. "He's too young for that. And that damn cape. He's too old for that." His eyes drift to the back of the store. "Maybe it's my own fault. He's so wrapped up in fantasy books and those medieval video games we keep buying him for his iPad. You know he asked me if I'd take him in a couple of weeks to this event of sorts? A camp? A renaissance fair? I don't know, some place where kids and adults run around pretending to battle while wearing costumes."

"He wants to go LARPing?" I ask, trying not to laugh.

"LARPing?" he repeats.

"Yeah, it's an acronym for Live-Action Role Playing," I explain. "It's pretty much what he's doing on the computer. If Dungeons and Dragons is the gateway drug to World of Warcraft, then LARPing is pure heroin."

He frowns and shakes his head. "Then I'll definitely not be taking him."

I sigh, glad Kevin can't hear our conversation. As nerdy and weird as it is, I know being able to indulge his inner geek with likeminded nerds would really cheer him up. That's probably why he's retreating into the fantasy world so much. It's become so much more preferable than reality. I know after Rachel broke up with me, I dove into my work-in-progress like I was under fire in a foxhole.

"I can take him, if he asks," I tell him.

"Just like you've taken over Fluffy? Blake, I'm glad you're getting to know your stepbrother, but there's a difference between being a brother and being an enabler."

I narrow my eyes briefly. My father doesn't know me well enough to make that assumption. In fact, that sounds like something that Angelica would say. I can hear her influence in him all the time, which isn't a good thing since Angelica isn't my biggest fan.

The thought of my stepmother and how hard it's been to win her approval reminds me a bit of Amanda, and once again I'm hit by how annoying the next six weeks will be. At least when school is over, I can concentrate on work and what I have to do to get this place out of the red.

While I take over the cash, doing transactions with a handful of regulars, my dad goes around tidying the shelves and dusting the books. He does this at the end of every day, like putting the books back in the right order will put his life in the right order. It's therapy without much outcome.

I'm thinking of closing a little early—not for the sake of

the shop this time but because Heath just texted me wanting to grab a beer—when a stunning brunette strolls in. She's tall, almost my height, with lean limbs that glow with a tan she obviously didn't get here.

She's perusing the new releases at the front, her fingers tracing over the covers, looking every bit the casual browser.

I waste no time.

"Can I help you?" I ask as I approach her, shooting her a grin. I notice her fingers are resting on top of Stephen King's latest. "Fan of the King?"

"Huh?" she says, and then quickly looks down and shoots me a sheepish smile. "Oh, no. Actually, I've never read him."

I keep smiling at her even though my brain is detracting a point for that. But my brain also notices how perky her tits are, and that she's eyeing me with a kind of shy carnality that suggests I can take this as far as I want to.

"You know, he doesn't just write horror," I go on. I tap the book. "*Finders Keepers* is the second book in his crime thriller trilogy. You should start with *Mr. Mercedes*." I tap the book next to it, a paperback marked at twenty percent off. "It's witty, entertaining. I think you'd really enjoy it."

"Really?" she asks, looking back at the cover warily.

"Tell you what," I say to her, taking a step closer so that just the table is between us. "You buy *Mr. Mercedes* and read it. If you don't like it, I will not only give you a full refund, but I'll take you out for dinner."

I can sense my dad is somewhere behind me. His derisive grumble rolls through the store like a freight train.

"Oh, that's pretty smooth," the girl says, though the gleam of interest in her eyes is growing.

"I can be rough too." Another grin.

This time she giggles and looks away coyly. "Okay, well,

I was actually hoping to find another book. Do you have anything by Sylvia Day?"

I wince. Day is a prolific romance writer (with one hell of a rack). "No, sorry."

She shrugs, as if embarrassed she asked. "That's fine. I guess Stephen King it is."

I do an internal victory dance.

I pick up the book and hand it to her. As her delicate fingers take it, I hold on, refusing to let go. "But you have to promise to be honest."

"I will." She chews on her candy apple lip for a second, staring up at me through her lashes. "What happens if I like the book? Can you still take me to dinner?"

"You've got a deal..." I trail off, hoping my frown prompts her for her name.

"Samantha," she supplies.

Of course she's a Samantha. All the Samanthas I've met look and act like her. Sexual, sensual, but unusually bashful in the sack. Not that I mind. I like making them blush.

"I'm Blake," I tell her. "And I'll never lead you astray."

I ring her up at the cash register and write my phone number on the receipt. There's no point in getting her number—I know she'll be calling me soon.

She leaves the store and my dad follows her, locking the door and flipping over the "Closed" sign before whipping around to face me. "What the hell was that?"

I shrug, fiddling with the till. "What? I made a sale. Business as usual."

"Business as usual isn't propositioning the customers."

"Yeah, I thought you were with that other girl," Kevin says, and I jump, not realizing he's standing right behind me, a stack of young adult fantasy novels in his hands.

I give him a tepid look. "What other girl?"

"I don't know," he says, practically whining. "When you drove me home the other day, we saw her walking down the street and you covered your face so she wouldn't see you."

My dad shakes his head. "What's gotten into you, Blake?"

I take in a deep breath and keep my voice light. "Nothing at all. I'm twenty-three years old and I like the ladies, what can I say?"

"You weren't like this with Rachel."

My chest burns at that. "You didn't even know Rachel. You met her once." *Stop trying to act like you know anything about me at all,* I finish in my head.

He knows he doesn't have a leg to stand on. He comes over to the register, clearing his throat. "So, how much did we do today?"

Oh boy, the worst moment of the day. Bracing myself, I look over the numbers.

It's not good. It doesn't even pay the expenses accrued.

"Well?" my dad says, and I step out of the way so he can look at them.

I glance nervously at Kevin, and we both seem to hold our breath as dad closes his eyes, his fingers squeezing the bridge of his nose again. He holds it there, trying to compose himself. Then he swallows and shakes it off.

"Thanks for your help today," he says flatly, like he couldn't conjure up any emotion if he tried.

"No problem," I tell him.

He still doesn't look at me. "School is going well? End of the year is coming."

"It's going great," I tell him, even though that's kind of a lie. But I don't dare rock the boat. I know why he's asking me. He's reminding me that soon all of this will be mine, and if I don't know what I'm doing, I'll run the business into the ground. Just like he's doing.

"Good, good," he says absently. "I'll take Kevin home. Thanks for getting him."

"Anything for my bud." I eye Kevin. He seems unreadable right now. Maybe he's already fighting orcs or something in his head instead of watching his father worry about the money they're losing. "See you soon."

I get out of there and don't seem to breathe until I'm at The Bard and Banker pub on the next block. I text Heath and tell him about the change of plans, to meet me there instead. I need alcohol in my veins ASAP. My dad, Kevin, the business, the pressure, the mention of Rachel are all swilling through my brain.

While I'm waiting for Heath in one of the small semi-enclosed booths or "snugs" as far away as possible from the band I know will start playing later, I get an email in my inbox.

From Amanda Newland.

Oh yes, I can't believe I forgot to add her to my shit pile of worries.

I gulp down half of my dark lager before I can even look at it.

When I finally read it over, I can hear her voice in my head, throwing all these superfluous words my way, as if I would get confused and not understand her whole email. She must think I'm not only a total wanker but a fucking idiot. Actually, I get the impression she thinks that way about most people.

"You need to be taken down a peg, darling," I say out loud.

"Are you talking to your phone? Or on your phone?"

I look up to see Heath peering down at me with amusement. "Or just having a spat with Siri?" he goes on. "I agree she needs to be taken down a peg. Talk about a know-it-all."

"Ugh," I say, as he sits down. "You don't want to know the bloody truth of it."

"Well, there's got to be a reason why you're looking to get drunk on a school night," Heath says, then reconsiders it. "I mean, more so than usual."

Heath is in most of my business classes and is in a similar situation to me. Meaning, pressure from his parents is the main reason why he's getting his degree. With his carefree attitude and penchant for environmental causes, Heath would be much happier surfing his life away during summers in Tofino and snowboarding on Mount Washington in the winter. He's also a pretty good wingman. There's something about the shaggy-haired, perpetually tanned, surfer dude that the girls can't resist. Might be the fact that he's a pot dealer and they get their weed for free.

"There's this girl in my writing class..." I begin.

"Again? How many of them are there? I should have joined that class," he remarks, signaling the waitress for a drink.

"Definitely enough of them," I tell him, even though that's not why I'm taking the class. "But I haven't slept with this one."

"Hard to get?"

I grunt. "I have no doubt she is, but I'm not even trying. She drives me up the fucking wall."

"And you're saying you haven't fucked her?" The waitress drops off his beer, giving him a dirty look before she heads back.

"No," I say emphatically. "She's not my type."

"Anything with a hole is your type, Blake."

"Fuck off," I tell him, taking a swig of my beer. I can feel it slowly go to work, my nerves unkinking one by one. "Not this girl. You know those girls who refuse to smile or laugh at anything, who are born with a silver spoon in their arse?"

"I think you mean mouth."

"It's the arse with this one. Walks around with a sense of entitlement that they think they've somehow earned because they are so goddamn serious about life? Well, that's her. I bet she doesn't even need to wear glasses, she just wears them to try and look smart."

Heath grimaces. "Damn. Is she hot? You know I have a thing for girls with glasses."

I glare at him. "Listen brother, you just heard what I said. You don't want to go near her."

He takes a gulp of his beer and leans back in his seat, wiping his mouth. He gives me a lazy smile that I know all too well. "Just last week you were telling me about that annoying hostess from Earls you slept with, the one who started talking about her doll collection the minute you finished fucking."

"Yeah, and in order to get out of the rest of the date I had to pretend I was moving back to England the next day. Then I drove past her a few days later. I'm surprised Mr. Mean didn't get egged."

He points his glass at me. "You didn't answer my question. Is she hot?"

"No," I tell him, knowing that if I admit she's hot in the slightest he'll never listen to my plight. Oh, the fucking plight. So I decide to pull up the email and show it to him. "Anyway, I got paired with her for my last assignment and this is the email she sends me tonight."

He squints as he reads it over. When he's done, he looks almost impressed. "Thems some big words for a dummy like you," he says in his best hick accent. "Seriously though, sounds like the rest of the semester is going to be rough. Good luck with that."

"Nice to have your support."

"Well, I don't know. You going to answer her? You want me to write the email for you? I know this is the face of an innocent," he says, stroking his jaw between his fingers, "but I'm pretty good at putting people in their place."

"Heath, you can't get her stoned through the computer," I remind him, although I doubt she'd smile even if she was high. "It's fine, I got this."

And so that's how we spend the rest of the night. Several pints later, the band is blaring shitty Celtic punk, we're both sauced, Heath is high, and we've composed the world's most ridiculous response to Amanda.

"Do I press send?" I ask him, my voice slurring a bit.

He doesn't answer, just leans over and presses the send icon for me.

Whoops.

"Let's get another round," Heath says.

So we do.

THREE
AMANDA

I WAKE UP THE NEXT MORNING TO ANA PUTTERING around the kitchen and singing along to what sounds like an Estonian folk version of Mariah Carey's "Butterfly."

I groan and roll over, my head smarting a bit from the wine. It's been a while since I've drank a whole bottle. That whole first two weeks after the breakup, a morning hangover, and puffy eyes were pretty much routine, along with waking up among discarded tissues and melted pints of Ben & Jerry's, but I thought I was climbing out of the hole and finally getting used to being single. I guess not.

I check my phone, hoping to while away the time without getting up, but it's dead. Somehow I manage to drag myself out of bed and slip on my plush robe (it says "Hollywood Tower of Terror" on it—Alan bought it for me on one of our annual trips to Disneyland, something that hits me low in the gut, that pinch of knowing something you loved won't be a part of your life anymore). I sigh, trying to shake it off of me and then shuffle into the kitchen.

Ana is wearing my yellow apron and making pancakes, shaking her ample booty around to the song, which yes, is some weird foreign cover of "Butterfly." Odd how Mariah in Estonian is still very much Mariah.

She spins around, spatula raised like a microphone, and beams at me with squinty eyes overdone with mascara and purple eyeliner, her puffy lips stretched across her teeth. "Good morning, sweet one!" she says, giving another shake of her hips. "I'm making pancakes!"

"I can see that," I tell her, though when I walk over to the coffee maker and get a closer look at the frying pan, I'm not really sure what I'm looking at. "What are those lumps?"

"Oh, that is naeris and kaneel. Sorry, cinnamon. My grandmother's recipe. It's very good." She waves the spatula at the table. "Sit down, it's almost ready."

"I was just going to have my shake," I say, eyeing the cupboard where I keep my rice protein shake. It's bland, but it does the trick. I usually don't feel like eating a lot in the mornings.

"Sit," she says again. "You need your strength to hear all about my wonderful date!"

Ah, that's right. After I sent Blake the email last night, I ended up watching TV for a bit then passing out. I never got an email back from him before the phone died nor did I hear Ana come in last night.

"Okay, well, I'm going to need coffee for that," I say. I pour nearly the entire contents of the carafe into a giant mug that says Jamie Fraser's Sassenach on it, and sit down.

After a few sips, I start to perk up, and Ana slides one giant, fluffy yet somehow burnt pancake onto my plate. I poke it gingerly with my fork, a tiny puff of steam escaping like a bog of stench before smothering it in maple syrup.

"So how did it go?" I ask her, adjusting my ass on the

seat to get comfortable. I'm going to be here for a long one. Good thing I don't have class until this afternoon.

Ana practically prances to the fridge and back to get orange juice before sitting down across from me.

"He was a very nice man," she starts off by saying. "Very nice. Not exactly what I thought he would look like but pretty close. Maybe three feet shorter."

"Three feet? That's a big difference." Especially when Ana is like six feet tall.

"Yes, he could look my boobs in the eyes, no problem." She pauses. "Also, he was bald. And Nigerian."

"Was he not supposed to be a bald Nigerian?"

She shrugs and keeps smiling. "He said he was from Saskatchewan, but I guess you can be both. And the picture on his profile is of a tanned man with lots of dark hair. But looks change."

"Sure," I say slowly, cutting off a piece of pancake.

"He also wasn't a teacher anymore. He was fired after he was caught selling drugs to the students."

"Oh my god," I say, glancing up at her. "How did you find that out? Did he tell you?"

"No, not really. The cops told me."

I put my fork down on the plate. She has my complete attention now. I'm immediately trying to figure out how to write this into my book, but with, you know, a fantasy slant. "The cops? How were there cops? What happened, are you okay?"

"Oh yes," she says. She nods at the pancake. "Try it."

"I will. Just tell me why you were consorting with the police."

"They thought I was a hooker."

Now I've heard everything. "And why the hell did they think that?"

She tosses her blonde hair over her shoulder. "Mister Nigeria thought that maybe that was something I would be interested in. We discussed it on the street corner, and I guess we looked suspicious."

I raise my palm. "Hold up, Ana, hold up. Are you saying this guy was a pimp?"

"No," she says quickly, almost defensive. "He's *trying* to be one. He said he needed a new line of business since he can't teach or deal drugs anymore."

I blink, trying to absorb it all and come to terms with the crazy in the lives around me. First Rio, now her. "So then the cops busted you."

"Yes, but they believed me, of course. Well, first they thought maybe I was a Russian mail-order bride, but I was able to prove my beauty school and everything. I showed them my portfolio on my phone and I even offered to do one officer's makeup, but she said that would be against the law. They arrested Mr. Nigeria in the end because he had violated his parole."

"Wait, wait…I thought you said you had a," I make air quotes, "*wonderful* date?"

She grins at me, wiggling in her seat. "I did. Before all that happened, he took me out for dinner. I had the veal parmigiana. It was really good."

I slowly nod, trying to find the joke in all of this, but I know she's one hundred percent sincere. Which is sad. There's being an optimist and looking on the bright side of life, and then there's finding joy in a free meal because you haven't had that kind of attention in a long time.

"Well, that's good," I say, picking my fork back up. "At least you enjoyed yourself."

I pop the pancake into my mouth and take a tentative chew.

Very cinnamony. The syrup drowns out most of the weird flavor.

Then I crunch hard on something and pause, my gag reflex threatening me.

"Uh, what is this again?" I manage to ask, my hand coming to my mouth, the bits of pancake not sure if they should go down or back out.

"Naeris and kaneel. Turnip and cinnamon. Local favorite. Though I don't think I boiled the turnips enough, sorry."

I make a gurgling kind of noise in surprise but eventually chew and swallow. She's watching me as I finish it off with a big gulp of coffee. "Well, there's nothing worse than an overcooked turnip," I manage to tell her.

She nods emphatically.

"So," I say, pushing around the rest of the pancake and trying to eat around the turnip bits. "Do you think you're going to give up on online dating?"

Her head jerks back as if I've said something totally disgusting. "And where do you suppose I'll meet a man?"

"I don't know. Like a normal person, out in the real world."

She stirs sugar into her coffee and stares down at it with amusement. "Oh, sweet one. You're so young, you should know more about this than me. Why don't you give it a try? It has been some time since Alan, yes?"

I shake my head. "I don't have time for guys."

"Everyone has time for sex," she says, her eyes gleaming. "Especially boys your age who blast off like a rocket."

"Oh joy, what a pity I'm missing out." I get up and artfully throw half the pancake in the garbage when she's not looking. "Between hearing about Rio's adventures on

Tinder and whichever dating site you're finding these Nigerian pimps, I'm quite okay with being my single self."

All right, that's kind of a lie, especially since I was having a pity party for my singledom last night, but I have to admit it's sounding more appealing than Rio and Ana's love lives. At least my company is predictable, and my growing collection of vibrators never lets me down, even though as I was replacing the batteries last week, one did fall off the shelf, smacking me right in the cheek. Try explaining that black eye to your mother.

I'm still feeling in a bit of a funk though so I get into my running clothes before I can change my mind. Normally I run to an ever-evolving playlist, but I fear if I wait for my phone to charge, I'll lose my nerve, so I head out the door and start running.

I feel like mixing it up this time, so instead of heading onto Beach Drive as it skirts Oak Bay and the multitude of coves and waterfront houses like I normally do, I head in the opposite direction, running through winding suburban streets past the spires of the Victorian Craigdarroch Castle which was built by a coal baron in the late 1800s, which strangely doesn't look out of place in Victoria.

Victoria has always had a British slant to it, one of the reasons why I, and so many tourists, find the city so charming. Even today, a typical spring day with mild temps and a gloomy sky, there's something quaint and refreshing about it. All the lawns are manicured with perfectly trimmed hedges and crops of blooming bulbs. There's a profuse amount of brick that you don't normally find on the West Coast, and street addresses are done up in gold lettering. BMWs and Audis and the occasional minivan dot the tidy curbsides.

After the castle I head down Fort Street which is lined

with small shops and antique stores, dodging the usual bums and women pushing strollers. I've never understood those people who run through a city's downtown, especially when there are so many beautiful places that don't have vagrants and lights and traffic and endless people, but now I kind of understand it. It makes your run more of a challenge, like you're completing an obstacle course. It turns into a game, and I always have to win the game.

Usually when I run, I go my usual distance but never push myself to go further because running is already hard enough. But by the time I end up at the massive Empress Hotel that overlooks the harbor, panting, red-faced, and dripping with sweat, I realize that I've run six kilometers which is double what I usually do, and that's just one way. I didn't curse myself or my jelly legs even once.

With the seagulls wheeling overhead, I lean against the railing and stare down at the boats in the marina below, a few whale watching charters heading out hoping to spot our local orca pods. The tourists are all bundled in red raincoats that hang to their knees, chatting excitedly and taking pictures of everything, including me.

Against my better judgement, I wave at them, and they wave back before their attention turns to a seaplane making a very loud and low entrance onto the water.

I breathe in deep, my heart finally slowing down, and turn around to contemplate whether I should walk back or run back. I didn't bring any money, so I couldn't take the bus even if I felt like it. My mind during the run was blissfully blank, but on the way back I will have plenty of time to think. There's this anxiety, restlessness running through me lately, causing my gut to twist, my heart to kick it up a few notches, usually late at night. I thought it was attributed to being without Alan, but now I'm not so sure.

I stretch my arms above my head, twisting to the side, when I suddenly see something that makes me freeze.

It's Blake Motherfucking Crawford.

He's got his sunglasses on, aviators like all assholes wear, and is walking up the sidewalk with a neon yellow tote bag that says Crawford's Books. For some reason I'm focusing on the tote, which doesn't exactly go with his Converse shoes, black jeans, grey t-shirt, and black leather jacket. And as he walks toward me, seeming not to notice that I'm almost standing in his way, I'm putting two and two together. Is he somehow involved with the bookstore around the corner?

And there it is, the slight flash of recognition in his brows as they dart up, lines in his forehead deepening. Yet he keeps walking.

"Um, hello?" I practically yell at him, throwing my arms out to the side.

"Amanda," he says, stopping but taking two steps back. He clears his throat. "Nice morning." He says this so warily, like the sky is about to fall on us. Given the weather here, he's probably not that far off.

"Yeah," I say, wanting to bring up the email, but my eyes drift back to the tote. "You aren't by any chance related to Crawford's Books?"

"What?" He looks down at the bag and winces. "Oh yes. Yes I am. And I work there. That's my father who incongruously ordered neon yellow tote bags because he thought they would be more eye-catching."

"Hate to say it worked," I tell him, and part of me wants to chalk up the fact that his father owns one of my favorite bookstores as a plus to his character (also the fact that he dropped *incongruously* in a sentence), but my innate dislike of him won't allow it. Even though our conversation is going okay so far, I automatically lean back and fold my arms across my chest, on the defensive.

He nods quickly, and even though I can't see his eyes, I know they're darting all over the place. His hand goes to the back of his neck, rubbing at it, and he clears his throat, all signs of being uncomfortable. I would have thought if I ran into Blake outside of class he would have free douchebag rein with me, but maybe I've misjudged him.

"Did you get my email?" he asks quietly.

So he did respond. I nod, totally lying. "Yup."

His brows pull together. "Really?"

"So uh, where did you want to meet again?" I ask, taking a guess at what he could have possibly said in response.

He's still frowning, his head tilting slightly like he's appraising me. "The library...tonight...seven p.m."

"Right," I say, forcing a smile on my face. "Luckily I'm free."

"Yeah...well. I'm going to head to the store." He starts to walk off and then looks back at me over his shoulder. "So, you're sure about tonight?"

I give him a look. "I want to get this project over with as much as you do."

He licks his lips and nods. "Gotcha. See you then."

"Yeah, see you," I say, watching him walk off, my eyes briefly resting on his ass before I tear them away. Okay, so that was weird. He was the last person I expected to see and the last person I wanted to see, and yet he was acting like he was afraid of me. No jabs, no nicknames, no snide remarks. If it wasn't for the fact that he was acting so cagey, I would have said he was almost polite.

I'm not sure how I feel about it. Is it possible that I'm wrong about Blake? Maybe my email made him realize how

much I mean business. I might have intimidated conge-
niality into him.

What I do know is I need to read that email, and so even though my legs and lungs are protesting, I start running back home.

Luckily it doesn't take long for my phone to boot up and for me to access my emails.

I click on Blake's reply without much thought.

I wish I hadn't.

HEY SUGAR TITS,

I admit I didn't understand most of your email since you used all them big words and all. But heck, I like a woman who knows her right from her left. I can't promise I'll be a brilliant writer but I will promise to annoy the ever living fuck out of you every opportunity that I get. Seeing that I'll be monopolizing most of your time, because no I don't believe we should work on this separately, you better get used to my handsome face real quick. I can't promise you'll love it, but I certainly will. Maybe you can start doing me a favor and bringing a roll of duct tape to our meetings. I know you're probably too prudish to be tied up but it could come in real handy across your mouth when you start spewing all your high and mighty garbage. Then again, you are a girl and I've been programmed to tune most of your words out. We'll see.

Anyway, no need to use your pretty little brain as I already have several story ideas that I'm working on that you might like.

Cum for the T-Rex (a zany story about dinosaur sex and the women who go back in time to seek them)

Death by Farts (people die by hiccupping all the time

and it makes the news, so why not this? Could be an investigative journalism piece)

Ms. Know-it-all and Her Lonely Life (could be your autobiography but I won't get presumptuous. Oh look, I know what that word means).

I'm sure you'll find at least one of these suitable.

Look forward to seeing you, tomorrow at 7 p.m. at the library. Be there or be square.

Wait, too late.

Blake.

I'M FLOORED.

And then angry.

So very fucking angry.

No wonder he was acting that way earlier, he was probably expecting me to punch him in the face, and fuck, I really should have! Maybe gone for his overused nuts right afterward.

With my pulse thudding in my throat, I go back and read over the email I sent. Again, it's wordy, and yeah I was trying to make him feel like an idiot, so sue me. But it didn't justify his response whatsoever. And now, now he thinks that I just took it, that I'm totally cool with being addressed as Sugar Tits. Who does he think he is, Mel Gibson?

"Aaaargh!" I roar, bursting into the living room where Ana is sitting on the couch, totally engrossed with a soap opera that's been on since before I was born.

She cocks an eyebrow at me and it's only now that I realize she's at the "brow phase" of her beauty school, because it looks like two singed caterpillars have laid down on her forehead to die. I have a hard time staring at her eyes without my gaze drifting upward to the hairy, pencilled massacre.

"What's wrong?" she asks idly.

She means aside from her eyebrows.

I flop down on the couch next to her. "You know that asshole from my writing class?"

"Yes, the British babe."

I flinch, giving her a look of disgust. "Babe? What the hell are you on?"

"Percocet and vodka," she says cheerily. "Remember I met you after your class one day and he was there. Tall. Nice smile. Thick hair. A butt you want to bite." She clacks her teeth together.

My lip curls. "No." I shake my head. "He's not a babe or an anything except a fuckfart."

"Fuckfart," she repeats. "New word?"

I sigh. "Yes, but don't use it, it's patented. Anyway, I'm paired up with him for the final project in Marie's class. I have to write a novella with him."

I expect her to make a face but she's still smiling. Must be the Percocet cocktail.

"Oh, this is going to be fun," she says, wiggling her fingers, her prismatic gel nails catching the light.

"No," I admonish her, twisting in my seat to see her better. "It's not going to be *fun*, Ana. You know how important this class is to me. He's some playboy who thinks he's on an extended vacation. He doesn't take anything seriously. His email is proof of that, and he's going to sink my grade. On purpose now."

She doesn't look as worried as I feel she should. I mean, she does realize that if I fail, she'll have to hear about it until she ends up moving in with the Nigerian. "Have you talked to your teacher? Or him?"

"Both. Kind of. I bumped into him on my run, but at the time I hadn't read his email yet. I was actually nice to him. Nice!"

She turns back to the TV, the adventures of Eduardo the doctor enthralling her once again. "Maybe it's good. Let you be the bigger character."

"I don't want to be the bigger *character*."

Ana gives me an earnest look. "Do you want me to deal with him?" she asks in such a measured voice that I move back from her an inch.

"Uh no, that's okay." Whether she knows some old Soviet murder technique or just wants to yell at him while shoving her boobs in his face, I say hell no to her involvement.

"Suit yourself," she says with a shrug.

I head to my room and think about texting Rio, but she'll just tell me to pull up my big girl panties, put on some gangsta rap, and deal with it. I then think about writing the appropriate rebuttal to Blake, but I stop myself. He'll get an earful tonight at the library, and if he refuses to apologize or budge an inch, then I'm taking it to Marie with that email as proof.

Emboldened with my new resolve, I shower and get dressed and head to school to catch my back to back classes of Early American Literature and Journalism, even though I can't concentrate on a goddamn thing. When they're over, I've got two hours before I have to meet with Blake, and there's really no point in going home and coming back, so I take the time to get to the library early and do some writing of my own, on something that actually counts.

The Land of Tears and Bone is my fantasy novel, the secret pride and joy of my life, and a world where I'd rather spend ninety-nine percent of my days. I say secret because even though my family knows I'm writing it, they don't ask any questions about it and basically pretend it doesn't exist. Well, that's not true. The other day my mother asked if I was still writing about the occult. My mom goes a little nuts with her Christianity and thinks all fantasy novels must be derived from Satan somehow. Yeah, she's one of those people who thinks Harry Potter should be banned.

My sister, Dahlia, has a little more interest, but she's busy living on a farm somewhere in the British Columbian interior, rarely has access to the internet, and she doesn't have a cell phone for various reasons, some of which I totally get. She's a bit of a nomad and a hippie, and honestly always has been, but don't think my parents weren't disappointed in her when she announced she wasn't going to university and instead running off with her tree-planting boyfriend I call "El Beardo." I'm still not sure what his real name is, but he does have one hell of a beard.

It doesn't really matter in the end. Most people I talk to don't take writing seriously. If I tell them I'm an aspiring author, they get that "yeah right" look on their face, which is usually followed by "good luck with that." Then there are the people I went to high school with, the kids I grew up with, family, friends, anyone from that crowd. Writing isn't seen as something respectable, and that's something they, and my parents, still firmly believe in. So, when I can, I don't mention anything about my work-in-progress and I gloss over the creative writing part of my degree.

Thank god for the people in my program because I can talk to any of them about writing and they get it. Maybe our aspirations are all different—Rio thinks it will be a hobby for her and wants to teach English overseas when her degree is over—but our fears are all the same.

Except for Blake. Blake is the enigma, the person who

doesn't quite fit in. I feel comfortable baring my soul through the written word with anyone in that class except for him. It's like he's an intruder, someone to watch and spy and pass judgement without offering up anything of himself. That's not to say he hasn't written anything, but I truly doubt it comes from anywhere genuine. His work carries none of his soul.

The minute I step into the library, I exhale, closing my eyes for a moment to take in the familiar smell. There's a twinge of regret in my gut, and I wish Blake hadn't chosen one of my sacred writing places for our meeting, but I push on and ignore it. I go and find a table tucked away in the corner on the second level, and set myself up, opening my laptop, plus my one notebook for plotting and the other for world-building. The world-building one is a hell of a lot thicker than the plotting one. I get extremely carried away with the research aspect of the novel, and I have been filling up the tome for many years.

I haven't written for the last week, and while I'm eager to get back into it, I also stopped at a difficult part. I've written forty percent of the book and have hit a bit of a block. My character, Luthwen, is in the middle of his quest, and his ragtag group of characters, including a beautiful half-bird woman named Phenolope, are becoming integral to his journey...but I'm bored. There's a few scenes I have to go through before the first battle, and it's lagging. I know it's common for the middle of a book, but I haven't figured out how to keep my interest or the readers' that may one day read it, even though I've peppered the middle with exciting chapters.

Part of me thinks that maybe a romance between Phenelope and Luthwen could happen. It certainly feels natural, despite the characters butting heads. But I swore I wouldn't inject romance into this novel. First of all, far too many fantasies have them and they feel poorly written and unnatural, like they're thrown in there to keep the readers happy and not the author, or the authors think it will attract a whole new set of readers to their genre when it won't. Romance readers want romance, they don't want it with a plot about bird women and wizards and monsters that look like a giant ant crossed with a spider. They might not want it with a plot at all, so let's not pretend.

So I do what I always do when I'm stuck—research. That's probably why I've been writing this beast for two years. Every time I hit a road block I throw myself into something I can depend on. In this case, I get books about Greek mythology, the history of the Druids, and a Piers Anthony novel and bury my nose in them, getting as much inspiration and detail as possible while munching on garlicky kale chips and chocolate-covered espresso beans for sustenance (not at the same time).

I guess I'm so engrossed in reading rather than writing that time slips away from me. I don't even notice Blake until it's too late.

FOUR
BLAKE

I WAKE UP WITH A BRAIN FULL OF DRYING CEMENT, completely hung over, every pore in my body smelling like beer. I blink into the dim light, relieved that I managed to pull my shades shut before I passed out. Beneath my sour mouth and pounding head, there's this curious feeling, like a residue of guilt lingering deep inside me. This guilt is the manifestation of a hundred pins being stuck into a voodoo doll.

It comes back to me. Heath and I at the Bard and Banker, drinking our faces off and composing an email to Amanda. And I know I hit send. That's where the guilt comes in.

Fuck. What the hell did I say? What did we say? I know Heath was an accomplice.

Even though I'm hurting, I roll over and grab my phone, clumsily getting my passcode wrong a few times before it clicks. I check my email, and before I even see the message in the sent folder, it all comes back to me.

You know what would make a billion dollars? Some

kind of electronic retrieval system that will pull your impulsive and highly regretful texts and emails before anyone gets a chance to read them. If I were smart enough, I'd invent it, or at least be an early investor in said company because I think everyone everywhere has sent something they regretted. Usually while drinking.

I cringe as I read my email over, and I know, I *know* that this is bad news. If it were any other girl, she would maybe laugh it off—maybe—but since this is Amanda (and hence why I sent it to begin with), I'm giving her something she can take up with the school itself. The worst part, she hasn't even responded, so I don't know if she's not seen it yet or is just stewing on it and plotting a million ways to ruin me.

You're a grade-A wanker, I tell myself as I make my way into the kitchen. It's times like these that I wish I had a roommate, someone to bitch to in person, someone enabling who would pat me on the back and tell me everything's going to be fine. But I'm alone, which works most of the time, especially when I'm bringing chicks back here at night. No one wants a meddlesome roommate to interrupt the fun, and because most of the girls live in dorm rooms surrounded by people, having this level of privacy wins me extra points in their books.

Although I'm not completely alone. Down the hall, in the study, I have what seems to be a permanent houseguest —Fluffy. Luckily Fluffy is a low-maintenance boarder who only requires food, water, and shelter. Of course, Kevin mentioned there should be some cuddling involved, but I know where to draw the line. Love and cuddling don't work for me with humans, let alone pets—at least not anymore.

I pour myself a glass of water at the sink and slam back two Advil, a B-vitamin, and then chase it all with a Five Hour Energy drink just as my dad sends me a text asking me to bring some of the books I borrowed back to the store. I'm not supposed to, but if we have more than two copies of something, I usually take it home to read. I know my dad wishes they weren't science fiction novels about space and doomsday prophecies, but I honestly couldn't give a shit what he thinks sometimes. He's still my dad though and I feel obligated to help—it's my future after all—so after a quick shower, I slip on my clothes and dark shades and head out into the cobblestone streets of downtown Victoria.

My apartment, overlooking a colorful colony of floating homes, is located just beyond the ferries that head south to Washington State. If it wasn't for the fact that Angelica owns the apartment as an investment, there's no way I would be able to afford it on my own. All the money I saved back in England, the money I thought would see me on an around-the-world trip or two, is starting to run out, and there's no chance for me to get a part-time job when I spend so many hours working for my dad for free.

I head out into the gloom of the day, something that makes me feel at home along with the gardens (which, unlike back home, start blooming here in February), horse-drawn carriages, and high tea at the Empress Hotel.

It's actually just as I'm passing the massive façade of the ivy-covered hotel that I'm sure I've started hallucinating, because there's Amanda leaning back against the railing overlooking the marina.

I freeze for a moment like a panicked deer, unsure what to do and where to go. For one, it's her, and after that email, I should fear for my life, or at least find some way to protect my groin. For two, she looks bloody *hot*. I'm frozen in both fear and this shameful kind of desire because my dick is twitching and my limbs are growing heavy all because she's wearing these shiny blue skin tight leggings adorned with pink cherry blossoms that seem to accentuate every curve and muscle in her legs, hips, and arse. Then there's her breasts, impossibly firm in a sleek white tank top. It's like until this moment, I wasn't even aware that Amanda had much of a body, but fuck, there it is. And I'm going to have to figure out how to quickly forget it.

Before I know what I'm doing, my feet are moving and I'm hiding behind my sunglasses, hoping I can just walk past her and she won't see me.

But oh, oh shit. She does.

Feign ignorance Crawford.

"Um, hello?" she cries out in indignation.

Here it goes.

And then I'm sucked into a brief conversation with her, one that I'm certain will turn to bloodshed at any moment.

Yet, some fucking how, she doesn't freak out. She doesn't blow up at me. She doesn't try and kick me in the balls. She says she read the email, and yet I'm looking into her eyes, amplified by her fresh pink face, framed by cat-eye glasses, and they don't look any angrier than usual. Her dislike of me has somehow remained the same. Is it possible she has already reached her hate ceiling and is tapped out? Could it be she's had a sense of humor all this time?

Somehow I doubt it.

I decide to get out of there while I'm still unscathed and hurry off to the store. She still wants to meet me at the library at seven p.m., so I have no choice but to pretend that the email was never sent, and for both our sakes, I should forget she sent me one to begin with. I'm starting to think the only way through this is to just start the fuck over.

I can do that.

I think.

Later that evening, after being roped into working at the

store for a bit and muddling through a rubbish Ethics tutorial, I head to the library. I'm twenty minutes early. There's nothing that irks me more than being on time for something and finding out someone is already waiting for you. They're early, yet it comes across like you're the one that's late. Well, not this time. I can't let Amanda have the upper hand, even though I'm pretty sure she does.

I half-heartedly glance around the library. It's surprisingly busy at this time of night and devastatingly quiet thanks to the eagle eye of one of the librarians. I don't know her name, but she has a face you'd see speaking from an old tree in a Disney film, as well as a round, immovable build, and scaly hands. Her tongue will give you a lashing at ten paces if she catches so much as a laugh coming from your direction.

Quietly pulling out a chair, I take a seat at a table near the entrance, hoping to spot Amanda, but when it turns into 7:05 p.m., I'm starting to wonder if she'll even show. I check my emails, my phone, and there's nothing. I have a feeling that this morning was just a bunch of acting on her behalf, and she had planned to stand me up and go running to the dean.

Just in case I missed her earlier, I get up and look around again, this time going up to the second level. I'm just about to turn around when I see a flash of red hair in the corner. I go down the row and see her at a small table surrounded by stacks of books, a laptop open beside her though she's furiously scribbling in a leather-bound notebook that looks like its seen better days. She's got headphones in her ears, so she doesn't seem to hear me as I sidle up next to her.

"Hey," I say to her, waving my hand in her face.

She jumps in her seat, eyes wide, and lets out a yelp that comes out a lot louder than she probably realizes.

"Jesus!" she cries out, ripping the headphones from her ears and scowling at me like she's trying to set me on fire. "What's your problem?"

"Sorry!" I say, raising my palms while I hear the first "Shhh" of the librarian somewhere in the building. I lower my voice. "I was looking for you."

"You're late," she says, trying to catch her breath and compose herself. She angrily tucks strands of hair behind her ears and straightens her glasses, swallowing hard. I think I like her like this, slightly unhinged. A red flush appears on her chest, similar to the one I saw on her earlier today.

"I wasn't late," I protest quickly. "I was here at six-thirty, waiting for you."

"Yeah, well, I was up here. Ever think of looking for me?" Her eyes narrow, and even though I can't see her pulse tick along her jaw anymore, she looks like she wants to kill me. She probably does. I can't forget I've given her a good reason.

"Sorry. I didn't think you'd already be here." I force a smile and try to look as apologetic as possible, and gesture to the empty seat across from her. "Can I sit down or would you rather me stand?"

She stares at me for a moment, her mouth set in a firm line, her face blank. I can't read what she's thinking, but I know she's studying me like I'm a frog about to be dissected, and she's holding the blade, trying to figure out where to cut.

Maybe this is where I should turn and run.

"Yeah, fine," she says, and as I make a move to grab the seat she says, "No, wait. Hold on." She waves her hand at me, half out of her chair. "We need to talk before you even dare sit with me."

Here it comes.

"Something wrong?" I ask.

The glare deepens. I can almost see the pits of hell blazing in her eyes.

"Something wrong?" she repeats, giving me a brittle smile. "How about the email you sent me last night? Do you know how close I am to going to Marie with it?"

I fold my arms across my chest and peer down at her. "You didn't seem to mind much this morning."

She makes a small noise of frustration, her brows lowering. "I hadn't read the email yet."

"Really?" I ask, feeling the corner of my mouth tip up, unable to help myself. "Because I could have sworn you said you did."

Her chin juts out as she straightens in her seat, her attention going to the notebook in front of her. She quickly closes it up and slips it into her bag on the floor. "I think you owe me an apology and an explanation. All I did was email you wanting to work together on this and you responded by being the rudest, most misogynistic fuckface that ever was. I mean, I thought that's who you were, but there was some tiny, naïve part of me that hoped I would be proven wrong."

I should apologize. But I can't.

I sit down instead, hands splayed on the table as I lean in. "Why do you hate me so much?"

She looks shocked. "Why? How about the reason I just gave you?"

"Ignore the email for now," I tell her, and her eyes turn damn near satanic. "I'll explain in a minute. I just want to know. Before all of this. Why all the hate?"

She blinks, her mouth dropping just a bit so I can see

her run her tongue along the back of her teeth. "Because you're an asshole," she says, her voice so hushed and incredulous, it nearly makes me laugh.

Her admission doesn't sting. It just spurs on my curiosity.

"Granted. But what makes you say that? What have I ever said or done to you?"

But the moment those words leave my mouth—and the moment she levels me with her gaze—I know she has a list prepared.

She ticks off her fingers one by one. "The first day of class you asked if you could call me Big Red. I said no. Then you asked if the carpet matched the drapes."

I try not to seem ashamed. "In my defense, I was pretty sauced that first class."

"Then," she goes on, ignoring me, "we had to read our one-page stories out loud. After mine, you said that my stuff works better than Nyquil."

"Hey," I tell her, defensive and vaguely embarrassed. "I didn't think you heard that."

She cocks her head and shakes it. "Oh really. Then there was that time where I dropped my books right in front of you, and instead of helping me, you just stared at my ass as I bent over. Not only that, but I'm pretty sure you made a sound like you were coming in your pants," she adds, wrinkling her nose for added effect.

That vaguely rings a bell. "So you don't like being appreciated by the male species," I say, goading her.

"I don't want any species staring at my ass when they could be helping me," she says. "Not that I need help anyway."

I lean back in my chair, studying her. "Oh, of course not."

"What does that mean?"

I lick my lips and shrug. "I don't know, it could explain why anytime anyone has a critique about your writing, you just laugh it off, as if their opinions don't matter, don't count, and aren't warranted."

She stills. I know I've hit a sore spot.

A flash of pink tongue comes out, absently licking her lips. "That's not true," she finally says, though her voice is soft now, a whisper. "I can take criticism."

"Right."

"But, I mean, most people in that class couldn't string a sentence together if they tried."

I raise my brow. "You mean people like me."

Amanda thinks that over, like she's chewing it in her head.

"Why are you taking this class anyway?" she asks, and I know she's had a change of heart and doesn't quite want to call me an idiot to my face. I'm not sure if I like this sudden politeness, nor the change of subject.

"Because I want to."

She stares at me for a moment, still chewing, still digesting. I get why it's hard for her to believe, that she thinks there is some ulterior motive on my behalf, perhaps an easy grade, perhaps I just live to annoy her.

"Look," I tell her, feeling the need to explain myself, maybe just because of the way I've been acting. I half recollect the things I said to her in class and I'm surprised she noticed. Thank god there's no way she knows what I'm thinking most of the time. "I'm not taking writing because I think it's easy or a joke or I just need a credit. I'm taking it because I like it."

"But you're taking Business Management."

I peer at her inquisitively. "How do you know that?"

"Because during the first class, the one you said you were hammered at, everyone had to tell the class what they were taking at school, and I remember what you said."

I'm slightly impressed. "Well, then. I guess you were paying attention." I take off my leather jacket and hang it on the back of the chair, figuring I'm not going anywhere now. When I turn back to face her, I catch her eyes on my biceps. She quickly averts them, but she can't fool me. Is it wrong that I feel a strange sense of victory, maybe even pride, that she's noticed me in some way that doesn't involve me being a total asshole?

I clear my throat. "Anyway, not that it's any of your business, but I'm taking Business Management so I can properly take over my father's store. The bookstore. The writing class is for me. Maybe the only thing that *is* for me."

I'm surprised I've admitted that last part.

She tilts her head, eyeing me. She seems to spend a lot of time thinking me over, and yet the outcome always seems to be the same: fuckface. That was the term she used, right?

"So you want to be a writer?"

I don't answer her at first. "I want to get this project done and over with, and I want to graduate." All right, maybe it was a non-answer, but I don't feel like giving her any ammo. I sigh and lean back in my chair. "I'm sorry about the email. I guess you rubbed me the wrong way."

"Because you rub *me* the wrong way!" she says, and another "Shhhh!" comes from down the aisle.

"Quiet," I hiss at Amanda. "Do you want Treebeard to kick us out or what?"

A flash of worry comes across her brow and she nods, knowing exactly who I'm talking about.

"Regardless of who rubbed who first," I tell her, trying not to smirk at my innuendo, "we need to at least try and get along if this is going to work." I pause. "Or if anything, at least not kill each other until the novella is done."

"I'm not sure that's possible."

I shrug. "Well, a good start would be if you just accepted my apology."

She blows a strand of hair out of her face. "Fine." But of course she's not looking at me, she's pulling her laptop toward her, going into serious writer mode, just like in class. Whatever, I'll take what I can get at this point. Though I have to say, even though it was my idea, it's going to take a lot of discipline to not press her buttons. And no, that's not innuendo this time.

"So I've been doing some thinking," she says after a few beats, scrolling through something on her computer.

"Other than about turning me over to the dean?" I ask.

She glares at me over her glasses. "Yes. Since we both don't like this arrangement, I think one of us should do most of the work. Pick the topic, outline the plot and characters, while the other contributes a few chapters. Preferably in an alternate POV to make it easier."

"And you're thinking it's best if you do all the work?"

"Nope. If you want to do the work, that's fine with me. Just whatever has us seeing each other less."

I frown. She *really* has it in for me. "I foresee some problems with this. For one, we have completely different writing styles. I think it will be quite obvious who is pulling most of the weight. Two, how do I know that you're not going to throw me under the bus and complain that I didn't do any of the work? Or, for that matter, throw me under the bus and blame it all on me if we get a shitty grade?"

She eyes me over the top of her computer. "Because I could throw you under the bus right now if I wanted to. And I'm not."

I sigh and run a hand through my hair. "I'd rather just split the work and do the alternate point of view."

"You don't trust me?"

I laugh. "Do you trust me?"

"Fine," she snipes. "Then I'll work on the plot and characters."

"No. We both work on it. Together."

She gives an exasperated snort and cocks her head. "Why are you trying to make this more difficult?"

I honestly have no idea, other than it's kind of fun. "I just want an honest grade."

"Bullshit," she mutters under her breath. She clears her throat. "You know we're going to have to see more of each other this way. Might even take several days for us to plot this out."

"That's fine with me."

"Don't you have a store to help manage?"

I feel my jaw tighten for a moment before I manage my most charming grin. "I can do a lot of things at once. I'm very resourceful. Talented, some say."

She rolls her eyes. "We will let Marie be the judge of that. So, dare I ask if you have any ideas? Other than the ones proposed in the email, that is."

"Actually, I thought of several on the way over here," I tell her, which is true. "All based on different themes. Sex, death, guilt, betrayal, and deceit."

Her eyes widen, looking impressed. "Okay," she says slowly. "Are you serious?"

I nod. "How about you pick a theme and I'll tell you my story idea."

She bites her lip, and I find myself momentarily drawn to them and the light ruby sheen of her lip balm. If I let myself get carried away, I can almost—almost—see them wrapped around my dick. I squash the thought before it has any effect. Besides, I know the last thing she'll pick is sex.

"Betrayal," she says.

A little close to my heart, but she doesn't need to know that. "Betrayal," I repeat. "Where a husband ends an affair with a woman in order to make his marriage work, only to catch his wife cheating on him."

Those damn lips of hers form an o-shape. "Heavy. Personal experience?"

"No," I tell her. Not really. "But heavy is interesting. We could reverse it. Tweak it."

"I like it as it is," she says, though I can tell she hates to admit it. "What would you pick?"

"Do you really need to ask?"

"Right. Sex. Do you even need a plot for that?"

"Actually," I tell her, happy to prove her wrong. "There are plenty of erotic novels that have a plot. *Last Tango in Paris. The Claiming of Sleeping Beauty. Delta of Venus.*"

"The last was fifteen short stories," Amanda points out. "Should I wonder why you know all this stuff? Your father peddling smut at your shop?"

"My father has an abhorrence toward anything remotely sexual in literature. He doesn't even stock *Lolita.*"

"That's a shame," she says. "Good use of the word abhorrence by the way. If I knew better, I'd say you were trying to impress me."

What a peculiar girl. There's a tone of playfulness in her voice that I've never heard before. Maybe I *am* impressing her. About bloody time.

"So you want to hear the plot or not?" I ask.

"On second thought, not," she says, and she's back to being made of stone, cold and immovable. "I like betrayal though. Let's do that. You know, if we have to."

Little does she realize how easily sex works its way into the subject. But she'll find out soon enough.

We spend the next hour going over characters and hashing out the skeleton of the plot, as well as figuring out who is going to write what. Even though it was my idea, and even though Amanda said she didn't care if I did all the work, I can see the prissy control freak starting to come out and take over. It's tempting to let her to make things easier, but at the same time I want to battle her for everything she's got.

"So," she says, pausing as we exit the library just before it closes. "Treebeard, eh?"

"What about her?" I ask.

"A *Lord of the Rings* reference," she says, looking off across the dim lights of the parking lot. Night has settled in. "You do a pretty good job of keeping your inner nerd a secret."

I grin at her, throwing my head back. "I'm not keeping anything a secret. It's hard for girls to focus on anything else except my good looks and big dick."

Her eyes roll to the heavens, lips curled like she's about to spit something out of her mouth. "Pig," she mutters, turning away. "I'll see you later."

I'm tempted to yell "prude" after her but I know that's a total playground maneuver, so I just watch her climb into her Mini Cooper, another rich girl accessory. While she speeds out of the parking lot, I can't help but feel a strange tremor of excitement run through me. Not about working with her—*definitely* not about that. But this project, this idea which just a few hours ago was dormant in my head, is now a living breathing egg ready to hatch. I haven't felt that creativity, that drive, for a long time. Maybe it's the right thing to get my work-in-progress back on track.

Too bad I still have to deal with Amanda during this whole process.

And it's too bad that when I'm jerking off in bed later that night, the image that pops into my head is her wet ruby lips around my cock. I come so hard at that, it takes me a few moments to catch my breath, the room spinning.

Looks like the next month is going to be hell after all.

FIVE
AMANDA

"So how did it go last night?" Ana asks me the next morning as I settle down at the kitchen table with my coffee and a protein shake. No sign of turnip pancakes to be found, though this morning I think she's been practicing her contouring because her face is looking mighty Kardashian with a bit of 90's RuPaul thrown in there.

When I came in last night after the library, Ana was still out and I was absolutely zonked, even though the minute my head hit the pillow my brain started churning over and over the meeting with Blake.

"It wasn't as bad as I thought," I tell her before taking a timid sip of the scalding hot liquid.

And that's true. I mean, it kind of started out that way. There was no way I was going to let him forget the email he sent, even if I had to eat crow for a moment over that morning. Then there was the fact that he so clearly knew he'd been a total jackass to me in the past and yet pretended like it had slipped his mind.

Ana raises one eyebrow, a trooper fighting the Botox on her forehead. "You want to have sex with him now?"

I spit my coffee right out across the table and start coughing, my face growing red, tears welling. Ana calmly hands me a roll of paper towel.

"You can admit it, I won't tell," she says.

I shake my head furiously, tearing off the paper towel and wiping coffee off the table and my chin. "No!" I finally get out. "That's the last thing I want."

"But the first thing you need," Ana sits down beside me, palming her mug. Now her nails are white with flamingos painted on them. I have to wonder when she has the time to get them done and if she ever pokes a classmate's eye out. I know she's come dangerously close to me and that was before she was wearing the gel talons.

I give her my deadliest glare but it doesn't do anything to her. At least with Blake I saw him flinch a few times and I was using it on him a lot. "No one is having sex. He's still a pig. Maybe even worse than before." I pause and in some ways wish I had nothing more to say. "But he's not as stupid as he seems. At least, he's good at ideas and plotting. And realistic characters. We'll see if he can actually write."

"I thought you've heard his stuff in class, no?"

"I wasn't paying attention," I tell her truthfully. "I assumed it would be crap and turned off my ears."

"See that's why I had to leave my husband," Ana says joyfully. "I couldn't turn off my ears to his blah blah blah." She makes a talking motion with her hand. "And I couldn't turn off my ears to his ooooh, oooh, OOOOH!" And she's now making loud, high-pitched orgasm sounds that only an animal could hear. She gives me a wry look when she's done. "You know, because he was screwing our neighbor."

I've heard the story a million times before. It explains so much about Ana, yet I know if I were in her shoes, I'd have trouble mustering half the joy and energy that she has.

"Anyway," I tell her, "I don't think it will be the end of the world. If I can just focus on the story and not him, then we'll be okay."

"Because you want to have sex with him."

"Drop it," I warn her, getting out of my chair. "Just because a guy is good-looking doesn't mean that he's my type."

"Who is your type, then?"

That makes me pause. Alan's face flashes into my head. Memories of us in California, staying at romantic vineyard hotels, us laughing, drunk as hell, going swimming past pool hours. It's funny how every memory of us laughing and having fun and doing something exciting – dare I say sexual – are the ones that pop up the most, the ones I hold on to. And yet they only represent five per cent of the relationship. Even Disneyland was completely for me, he always went along willingly, having a fraction of the fun. That time I suggested having sex backstage of It's a Small World, like Ross Gellar did? Not only did he not get the *Friends* reference, but he flat-out turned me down.

Then a new memory bursts into frame, the one of Blake last night in the library, taking off his jacket, the way his biceps popped beneath his t-shirt, how his forearms seemed so massive, almost rough, in the library's austere environment. Like he knew how take charge of something, anything....me.

Nope, I tell myself adamantly. *Nope, nope, not that. Never that.*

"Well?" Ana prods.

"Tom Hiddleston," I tell her. "He's my type."

"Who? Is he your classmate?"

I laugh. "I wish. He's a British actor. Loki, from *Thor* and *The Avengers*."

She wrinkles her nose. "Oh, Amanda, you really are a *nerd*." She pronounces the word like she's proud to know what it means.

I shrug, learning long ago not to let that label bother me and making a mental note to never let her read my Harry Potter fanfic, nor my Benedict Cumberbatch erotica (in which, naturally, all the stories star *me*). "Then I'm a nerd who will know what she likes, wants, needs when she sees it. The moment I find someone like Tom Hiddleston, I'll let you know."

"And if you don't?"

"Then I give you permission to hook me up to one of your dating sites."

At that she starts tapping her fingers together at a rapid rate, her smile stretching across her face, making her cheekbones pop out and her eyes nearly disappear. "Oooooh, I can't wait!"

Yikes. Is it too early to add whisky to my coffee?

I DON'T HEAR FROM BLAKE THAT DAY, WHICH IS WHAT we agreed upon. We'd both work on our first chapters by ourselves and then make plans to read them over and discuss. But when the rest of the day turns into the next day and the next and then suddenly it's Sunday and I still haven't heard from him, I'm getting worried.

I hate to pester him. No, I hate to even talk to him, but I don't think I have a choice. Our class is tomorrow and the last thing I want is to go in there unprepared. Besides, I've written – and rewritten – my first chapter (which is technically chapter two, since his POV starts it off) a hundred times already and am itching for some feedback of any sort, even if it's from him.

So, while Ana sets out her makeup on the kitchen table and is about to attack my face with some new techniques she's learned, I send Blake an email (obviously we're not at the texting stage yet).

Hey Blake,

I have my chapter done and wondering when you want to get together to discuss. If it's easier, I've attached it here. Just wanted to touch base on the project and see where it's all fitting together, before class.

Amanda.

THERE. SHORT BUT NOT CURT. JUST ENOUGH FOR HIM to get the message.

Ana has just finished sponging on primer that feels like wet cement to my face when my phone rings. We both jump and stare at it while an unknown number with our area code flashes across the screen. I glance at her, brows raised. That couldn't be Blake, could it?

I turn away from her to answer. "Hello?" I ask gingerly, prepared to hang up if it's a telemarketer.

"Hello peach," Blake's British accent comes storming through. "Catch you at a bad time?"

Ana is already smiling like an idiot. I bet she can hear him through the speaker.

"Um, not really," I tell him, "though I'd appreciate it if you didn't call me *peach.*"

"You don't think it's fitting? I can always go back to Big Red."

"I think *Amanda* is fitting," I say crisply. "Why are you calling?"

"You mean why aren't I emailing you back or texting like a normal person?"

"Stop answering questions with questions."

He chuckles warmly, although I can hear his insincerity coming through. "Why email and text when I can call you direct and make a plan? Sorry...didn't mean to make that a question too."

Well I can't exactly argue with that. Must be his British genes coming through, doing things the proper way, even though Blake is anything but.

I turn away from Ana even more. "Did you read what I sent you?" I ask, trying to sound as blasé as possible over his potential opinion.

"No. Not yet. Wanted to wait. What are you doing right now?"

"She's getting a makeover!" Ana yells over my shoulder.

I push her away, trying to shush her while Blake asks, "Who on earth is that?"

"My roommate," I tell him. "And she's about to put a shit ton of makeup on me for beauty school practice."

"Is that a metric shit ton?"

Lord help me, I'm almost smiling. "Yes, a metric shit ton."

"And when do you think this will all be over?"

"An hour," Ana shouts before she goes back to rifling through her stuff. She holds up a brush like a serial killer wields a knife, and just as manic.

"Make that an hour and a half," I say to him. "It's going to take at least a half an hour to scrub it all off."

"All right, well give me your address and I'll come pick you up."

"And go where? The library is closed."

"But my apartment isn't."

I'm not sure how I feel about that. "How about a café?"

"How about a bar?"

"Caffeine is better than alcohol."

"That's not what Hemmingway said."

"Hemmingway shot his own head off," I remind him. "And I believe his quote was *write drunk, edit sober*. We're plotting and reading, practically editing."

"You're no fun, anyone ever tell you that?"

Ouch. That stings more than it should. In fact, I'm more pissed off by the fact that it hurt than the fact that he said it.

"I'm plenty of fun," I tell him, trying to sound flippant. "I just prefer a more intelligent way of expressing it."

"Of course, of course," Blake says, his tone bored now. "Just tell me your address and I'll come to you in an hour and a half. Figure it all out from there."

I give it to him and hang up the phone, pushing it away from me across the table.

"That was weird," I comment, staring at my cell.

"Mmmmm," Ana muses, wiping the brush across the back of her hand. "Weird but a good sign."

I sigh and stare up at her. "Don't tell me it has to do with sex."

"It's a good sign that he cares enough about your little project." She steps back and her eyes volley between my primer-spackled face and her platoon of makeup spread out over the table. "Though perhaps we'll put off my class practice for another day. Tonight, I'm going to make you look so beautiful you're not going to want to wash it off."

"Please, don't," I implore her. "I have no one to impress. Just do whatever crazy thing you were going to do. I'm your guinea pig. Go nuts."

But from the voracious gleam in her eyes, I wish I hadn't said that.

I'm not really sure what she attacks me with. After she removes my glasses, it's all kind of a blur of pointed, colorful instruments jabbing me in the face.

When she spills heavy duty eyelash glue all over the desk and then cries out what I have to assume are Estonian swear words, there's a knock at the door.

"What the hell time is it?" I say, fumbling for my phone but knocking it off the table. It's already dark outside but time couldn't have gone by that quickly.

"Oh, it's him, it's him," she says in a giggling hush. "He's here."

"Ana, go answer the door," I wave at her, trying to get up. "Stall him."

"But you look so beautiful sweet one," she's coos. I can barely see the devilish smile come across her face. "But if you insist."

Oh god no. There's no way I can let her talk to him alone.

"No wait, I'm on it!" I cry out, pushing her out of the way and running to the door. I fling it open and hope that whatever she did to my face looks somewhat decent.

Blake is standing there, laptop sleeve in one hand, cardboard coffee cup in the other. He seems somehow taller and manlier standing on my stoop with the dark of night behind him, a grey cargo jacket atop jeans and grey Vans. There's a peculiar twist to his dark brow and he seems surprised by my ambush but he's not looking at me any stranger than normal.

"Good evening," he says in an overly formal voice. "Is this where the brilliant author Amanda Newland resides?"

"Very funny," I tell him. "You're early."

"Actually I'm not," he says. He raises his coffee, gesturing to my face. "But I can see you're ready to go. Your roommate did a nice job, by the way. Very subtle. Suits you."

I watch him carefully. He at least looks sincere. "Okay, give me a second."

I hear him say "Sure," as I close the door on his face and run back inside. I scoop up my phone and grab my purse hanging from the back of the chair.

"You're really not going to invite him in?" Ana asks, hedging toward the door.

"No," I tell her adamantly. "There's no reason to and he's not meeting you. You'll be telling him how hot he is or how badly I want to have sex with him within a second."

"So you *do* want to hump like chickens."

My disgust turns to confusion. "What? Chickens?" I shake my head. "It doesn't matter."

Then I head for the bathroom because there's no way I'm leaving the house without seeing what she's done to me.

I flick on the light and a gasp escapes my lips. It really should have been a scream.

She's done the Kardashian contouring that almost looks passable when I'm looking straight on but the moment I turn my head, you can see the thick stripes of brown and white marking up my cheeks, my nose, my chin. I look like Lichtenstein pop art. It doesn't help that my lips have bright red matte lipstick shellacked on them, my cheeks look like they were splattered with coral sparkles and my eyes...my eyes make me look fucking crazy. My brows appear to have been whited out with concealer and then drawn on again in thick auburn arches and she's attached two false eyelashes to my lids. None of them match, not the brows and not the lashes, one of which seems to be climbing half-up my lid, making my eyes appear to be looking in two different directions.

"You like?" she asks, appearing in the mirror behind me. There is so much hope and worry in her overly-lined eyes that I don't dare break her heart or confidence.

"It's beautiful," I lie, flashing her a smile that makes my lips crack. "Thank you."

She beams at me and lets out a sigh of relief and I know that I can't take an ounce of it off my face until I'm out of the house.

Speaking of, somehow Blake was able to look at my face earlier and show zero shock or revulsion. I'm not sure if I should be worried that he's that good of a liar or impressed that he was able to hold back a millions barbs. Then again he did compliment me, which I now realize was layered with a metric shit ton of sarcasm.

I quickly grab my laptop bag and head for the door, ignoring Ana's gleeful noises. Blake is still standing where I left him and I quickly shut the door behind me.

"So I guess we're going somewhere," he says before taking a slow sip of his coffee. "I'm afraid I've surpassed my caffeine allotment for the day, so it'll either be a bar or my place."

I give him a pointed look – which has to look extra emphasized thanks to my runaway eyelashes – and push past him into the night, walking down the gravel path that goes through the backyard and up the side to where we have our own gate.

I can hear him following me, shoes crunching on the gravel, his presence at my back. Something about it all makes a nervous shiver run through me, as if I'm realizing that I'm alone with him for the first time. I'm not sure what it means, but since I know my face looks hastily put together, the feeling doesn't last long.

"So," he says, clearing his throat as we head up the

driveway. "How long has your roommate been studying makeup for?"

I glance at him briefly over my shoulder. "Don't even say it," I warn.

"What?" he asks innocently.

I roll my eyes and we stop by a black muscle car parked in front of the house. "This your car?" I ask him.

He nods, the streetlights illuminating a tiny smile on his lips. "This is Mr. Mean."

Judging by the car's round headlights and shark-like nose, the name suits the car. "A Camaro?"

"1972 Challenger," he corrects, going around to his side and smacking the roof with his palm. "Used to be my uncle's and when I moved here I snapped it up for a song. Eats gas like a motherfucker though but it's brilliant fun to drive. You don't get rides like this back in England."

He does seem like the type to drive an obnoxious car like this, vintage and all. Yet another reason why the girls must flock to him. Luckily I could give a rat's ass about cars.

I open the passenger door and eye the pile of textbooks on the seat, as well as an assortment of random stuff such as a large plastic sword that a knight would use, a baseball cap, a kit you'd get from a Halloween store with prosthetic elf ears, a half-full growler of beer, various fast-food containers and a small white cardboard box that seems to be emitting a chirping sound.

"Sorry," he mumbles and I stand there and wait as he quickly puts everything in the back seat. I don't even bother looking back there.

"So many questions," I comment as I step in and buckle myself, very aware of how close we are to each other. There's not a lot of room up here, at least that's what it feels like.

He leans in close, too close, and nods at my eyebrows. "You're not the only one." He squints at me and I try not to breathe in his smell. Too late. His scent is herbal and fresh, like sage and sea salt and for some reason it makes me happy, like it's conjuring up hot summer days by the sea, full of freedom and youth.

"Are you sure you want to go to a café like that?" he adds.

Ugh, he's right. I can't go out in public like this. I twist away from him in my seat, push my glasses to the top of my head and try to rip off the eyelashes. Only they won't come off. Good lord I hope Ana didn't use Krazy Glue. My eyelids are being stretched uncomfortably.

"Are you all right?" Blake asks and I'm so aware of him next to me and the fact that it looks like I'm trying to remove my eyeball.

"This fucking eyelash glue is like cement," I grumble, trying to not sound panicked.

"Guess I'll be taking you to my place," he says, starting the car. It responds with a roar and he waits till I'm done trying to fight with my eyes before he peels out onto the street. "I have to feed Fluffy anyway."

The Raconteurs "Broken Boy Soldier" starts playing but it's not loud enough to hide the silence between us as we head into downtown Victoria. I actually have no idea where Blake lives and this isn't making things easier. I want him to turn the car around and take me back home but I'm the one who sent the email and he's just doing exactly what I asked.

I think back to what he said last. "Who is Fluffy?" I ask.

"You don't want to know," he says gravely.

"Your cat?"

He tilts his head at me. "Why did you assume I have a cat and not a dog?"

"I don't know," I say, shrugging one shoulder. "You seem soulless."

He laughs softly. "Yeah, I suppose that might be true. Cats are wankers, too." He smiles at me and against better judgement, I'm smiling too. His smile is infectious.

Then again, so was the plague.

I quickly turn my face to the window and see that we're heading down toward the harbor, the lights of the bay sparkling in the night. We pass by various pubs and oyster bars filled with warm light and laughing people and something inside me pinches, a strange bout of loneliness that hits me sometimes.

"Not too late to grab a pint," Blake says, as if he knows what I'm thinking, though he couldn't, not quite.

I point to my face and don't say a word.

His lips press together, suppressing a smile. "Fair enough," he says. "But this is British Columbia after all. No one would bat an eye. Except for you."

"Ha," I say dryly. "Where do you live anyway?" As we leave the downtown core, we hook a right along the water, heading toward the ferries that go to Washington State. "Don't tell me you're in a houseboat."

"I'm not telling you anything, darling," he says with a smirk and a minute later he's parking on the street next to an apartment building that seems all glass, reflecting the harbor lights and the houseboat colony beneath. "Not quite a houseboat but I get seasick, so it works out."

We get out. It's a fairly new building and he takes me to his third floor apartment, my pulse beating against my wrist, my nerves coming into play again. Is it possible that I haven't been around a guy in so long that my body is freaking out over Blake against my will? I mean, sure his smile is charming...a little less shit-eating than I'd always thought...but he ain't Tom Hiddleston.

Though he does have one hell of a nice body, I can't help but think as we pause outside his door.

As if he hears my thoughts, he glances at me. I hope my cheeks aren't going red but then I remember the makeup and my cheeks are like two splotches of paint anyway. "You seem nervous."

"I have something in my eye," I answer deadpan.

"Well, don't worry, I'm not about to take advantage of a fair maiden such as yourself," he says, opening the door and gesturing for me to go inside.

"Believe me, if you even tried you wouldn't get very far," I warn him, gingerly stepping inside.

"Death by boring literature, got it."

I pause, shooting him a nasty look just as he flicks on the lights. The apartment is even prettier on the inside, all hardwood floors and stone grey walls, leather couches and a balcony that overlooks the harbor.

"This is sweet," I tell him in awe as I walk into the living room and look around. "Don't mind me asking, but how do you afford this?"

He grins at me as he shuts the door and hangs up his coat. "Would you believe me if I said I was Bruce Wayne?"

"The rich playboy part of it, yes."

His lips twist grimly for a second. "Definitely not rich. Just the playboy part, if you want to call it that. Oh and the incognito crime fighter after dark. Just another reason why you shouldn't be nervous around me." He walks over to the fridge in the kitchen, which, even though it's comprised of marble counters and stainless steel appliances, looks like it belongs to a college student. Dishes are piled in the sink even though there's a dishwasher and crumbs line the counter beside empty beer bottles and discarded cereal boxes.

"Fancy a beer?" he asks, opening the fridge.

I shake my head.

"Not a drinker," he surmises, bringing the beer out and shutting the door with his foot.

"Actually, I do have the occasional glass of wine but it's not exactly appropriate for what we're about to do."

And by occasional glass, I mean occasional bottle.

He bites his lip through a grin as he smacks the beer cap off the bottle, using the edge of the counter as leverage. "I haven't heard that one before."

I sigh, exasperated, and ignore him. "Where should we work?"

He motions to the leather couch with a nod. From the strange way he's eying me, to the vibe in the room, I'm getting the feeling that this is part of his whole seduction routine. I wonder if that's all that it takes. Bring the girls here, give them a drink, sit on the couch and pretend to watch Netflix. Next thing they know, they're getting screwed on the rug.

And probably liking it, I think to myself. I'm pretty sure that any girl that steps into this place knows exactly what she's getting into, even if she'll probably never see him again.

I take a seat on the armchair across from him, to make a point that I'm not like the rest of them and I'm here only because I have to be.

If he's insulted, he doesn't show it. He brings out his laptop while taking a lengthy swig of his beer. "It's my step-mother's," he says.

I glance at him, confused. "What?"

"The apartment. When I decided to move here and

finish my degree at U-Vic, my stepmother was able to rent the apartment for me. I basically pay for it by working at the bookstore."

"Ah." I look around. It all makes sense. "So you have a stepmother. When did your parents split up?"

"Oh ages ago," he says, leaning back on the couch and pulling one foot up across his leg. "I was born here but they split up when I was six or so. My mum and I moved back to England and she remarried. So did my dad."

"Only child?"

He nods. "I have a stepbrother though, here, Kevin. He's nine. My mother and Jenson, that's her husband now, they don't have any. What about you?"

Even though my curiosity is eager to learn more about him, I'm not about to share an ounce of myself. "I have a sister, my parents are still together."

Even though they should have divorced ages ago.

Even though they both take out their unhappiness and failed expectations on me.

But Blake doesn't prod or question me about them any further. He probably just doesn't care.

With both our laptops out, I decide to take control of the evening. It's the only way we'll be able to get through this and stay on task. There's something very distracting about sitting across from Blake in his living room and it has little to do with the way his eyes occasionally catch mine, the look of his broad shoulders beneath his thin olive-green shirt, the veins that rope around his forearms as he opens his computer.

"How about we read each other what we wrote?" I tell him, even though the idea of reading my work out loud to him makes me cringe. "That way we have a chance to really hear it and fix any errors."

He tilts his brow, looking at me uncertainly. "Are you sure? I mean, mine is total rubbish." He pauses. "But you'd know that, of course."

I raise my palm as a peace offering. "Going forward, this is a no judgement zone."

I can tell he doesn't believe that. Hell, I wouldn't believe it. It's hard as hell to turn off that side of me. Before he can protest, I tell him I'm going first and then plunge into it.

The other day we had worked out the characters while sticking to the main premise. Because the story has a slight twist, I'm writing the "other woman" for most of the book, only switching over to the wife at the end. We're doing it out of order but I'm too stubborn to correct it. In my chapter, the woman, Susan, is caught up in the "butterfly stage" of the affair, totally immersed in her attraction to the protagonist and giving very little regard to the fact that she's doing something wrong. In other words, the bitch is completely selfish but only has love to blame.

It's weird to read your stuff aloud, but it helps. I have to stop and start a few times because I keep coming across mangled sentences and skipped words. Actually there's a fair bit of them, even though I've gone through it so many times already. It's enough to make me feel like an idiot.

But Blake doesn't do anything but listen and I can't help but keep glancing up at his face as I read. He's frowning, like he's really listening to my every word but I can't tell if he likes what he's hearing or if he thinks it sucks.

I know one thing though—by the time I'm done, *I* totally think it sucks. All those feelings of entitlement, of feeling that my writing is better than most people's has been stripped away from me and Blake hasn't even had to say a word.

I rub my lips together before I let out a hopeful, "So?"

"It works," he says, then clears his throat. "Granted it was daft for you to go first when I have the prologue. I think we have some work to do to make sure the chapters match because what you're writing off of doesn't quite fit with what I wrote, but anyway."

And with that Blake launches into the prologue.

I have to admit, he's won me over with the opening lines, "I'm a liar and a thief. A thief of a heart that shouldn't belong to me. A thief of a heart that was easily taken. But I am one man, with two hearts, and none of them are my own."

His character—our character—Forrest is far more interesting and charismatic than I could have predicted. Somehow Blake writes him in such a way that he's almost forgiven for what he's doing—seeking out an affair with Susan. It's not perfect—some of the sentence structure is run on or doesn't flow and he has a load of skipped words and tense changes. But somehow I find myself ignoring all that, letting myself be swept away by his story.

When he's done he puts his laptop on the coffee table and steeples his fingers together, elbows resting on his knees. "That bad, huh?" he says with a wince, not meeting my eyes.

"What? No. Sorry." I sit up straighter. "That was really good."

He lifts his head alertly. "I'm sorry. Did you just... compliment me?"

I roll my eyes and wave him off with my hand. "Oh, come on. It's true. That was an excellent start."

"Go on..."

He wants an ego boost and while I certainly don't think he needs it in the package department, maybe he's insecure about his writing. I take a deep breath. "Well, Forrest was a lot more complex than I expected. You fleshed him out in just a few pages, without even interacting with Susan. The way you added in how his palms get sweaty when he thinks about her, what he's about to do, shows us that he knows the consequences of it all, without telling us he knows."

"And there was nothing you had an issue with?"

I purse my lips, thinking. "He might be thinking about sex too much. If you do a search for the word cock, I'd bet it comes up more than five times."

He leans forward, hitting a few keys on his laptop. "Four times," he says, rather triumphantly.

"Okay, well, it detracts from the story. Just a bit." I raise my finger as he opens his mouth to speak. "And no," I add quickly, "I don't have a problem with too much cock."

"I'm getting predictable," he laments with a smile.

Actually, your writing has proved otherwise, I think. But of course I don't tell him that.

"I'm bone dry," he says, waving the beer bottle at me before getting to his feet. "You sure you don't want one?"

I'm prepared to say no again, to set an example, even though I'm parched and a beer is sounding really good but he goes on, "I'm just saying, you look like you could use one."

My hackles raise. "What does that mean?"

"Have you forgotten about all that crap on your face?"

Shit, my makeup. Now that he mentions it, I can practically feel it seeping into my pores, trying to build a permanent bacterial colony.

"Can I use your washroom?" I ask him.

"Do you think I'm going to say no?"

"Just tell me where it is."

He points down the hall. "Second door on your left."

I'm surprised the apartment is big enough for a "second

door on the left" and when I step into the hall, I'm even more surprised to see four doors.

I know bathrooms are perfect for snooping but I manage to control every curious fiber in my body and just stick to going pee. I'm pretty sure if I opened his medicine cabinet I'd only find condoms and maybe herpes medication anyway.

It's when I'm washing my hands and contemplating putting his basil scented soap on my face, that I hear a loud thump from the other side of the wall, followed by a loud shriek.

I open the door and look over to the see the door next to me ajar and light spilling out into the hall. I peer my head around the corner. Blake is inside the room, standing beside a giant, and seemingly empty, aquarium.

"You okay?" I ask him, slowly coming inside.

Panic contorts his face as he quickly glances over at me. "Yes. Kind of. Fluffy just scared the ever loving shit out of me."

I stop a few feet away and peer at the glass, now seeing a few rocks, small logs, sand and a tree stump, as well as a shallow dish of water inside. "Uh, Fluffy? Your cat?"

Please say it's still a cat.

"If Fluffy was a cat, my life would be so much easier and I wouldn't have to change my knickers every time I come in here."

I keep walking over to him, slowly, though he raises his palm out to stop me. "You don't have a deathly fear of spiders do you?" he asks.

"Spiders?!" I exclaim and then I'm looking at the glass again and now, now I can clearly see a furry brown tarantula bigger than my hand working its way across the sand.

It's like bear, if it had eight legs, a million eyes and could fly across the room at you.

"Oh hell no!" I yell and I'm spinning on a dime, running straight of the room, down the hall and to his fucking door, my back plastered against it, one hand on the knob. The apartment is so austere and bright, it's hard to imagine I just saw that fucking thing in one of the rooms.

Moments later, as I'm catching my breath, Blake rounds the corner.

"So sorry," he apologizes, looking as white as a sheet.

"What the fuck was that?" I practically gasp.

"That was Fluffy," he says.

"He's a fucking tarantula!"

"I'm very aware of that."

"Why do you have a tarantula as a pet? Oh my god, what's wrong with you?"

A shiver runs through him which he tries to shake out. "And oh my god," I say, remembering his posture in the room, hearing that womanly shriek, "are you afraid of him?"

"It's true that I am deathly afraid of spiders," he says, heading right for the fridge and bringing out two beers. As he deftly pops the caps off both, he says, "But Fluffy is Kevin's and I said I'd take care of him. Turns out it's indefinite."

He strides over to me and hands me a beer, his fingers brushing against mine as he does so. I'm so on edge that my skin feels electrified by his touch.

"I don't get it," I say, softly now because he's nearly invading my personal space.

He runs his hand over the stubble on his strong jaw and nods, smiling to himself as he looks elsewhere. "I don't get it either. I guess Fluffy was an escape artist and Angelica, that's Kevin's mom, said he couldn't keep him anymore."

"I don't blame her," I say, feeling like a million spiders are crawling all over me right now. "And you willingly let an escape artist tarantula into your home?"

He sighs and leans back against the kitchen counter, legs crossed at the ankles and swigs his beer. "Yeah. Bloody brilliant, isn't it? But Kevin really loved that ugly abomination and he was in tears when it happened so I told him I'd care for him until his mum has a change of heart. And I'm pretty sure now that's never going to happen, so it looks like I'm stuck with the damned thing until Kevin forgets about him. Or loses interest. Or develops arachnophobia."

I have to admit, this is extremely sweet of him to do this for his stepbrother. "You must be close with him. Kevin, I mean. Not Fluffy."

He scratches at his cheek. "Not really. I'm trying. His mum has been working more and more, she's a lawyer, and I feel like I'm the only one he has lately that seems to care. My dad is so invested in the shop and trying to save it and..." He trails off and clears his throat, as if he's said too much.

And of course I can't help but bite. "Is the shop in trouble?"

"Nothing to worry your pretty little head about, peach," he says dismissively.

I raise my brow. "I told you not to call me peach."

"What's with your hatred of nicknames?"

"I don't have a hatred of nicknames," I argue. "I have a hatred of *your* nicknames. Believe me, I've had plenty."

Oh great, now I've said too much.

"Such as?"

"It doesn't matter," I say quickly. "We should get back to work."

"You can work after meeting Fluffy? It usually takes me a pint afterward to calm down. I'm supposed to feed him tomorrow and I usually have to get pretty bombed in order to work up the nerve."

So that explains the chirping box in his car. "Crickets?"

"Yeah, live ones. It's pretty barbaric."

"And how does your revolving door of women handle Fluffy?"

His head jerks back as he stares at me quizzically. "Revolving door of women? Who says that? And why do you care?"

"I don't care," I tell him, looking away. "It's just something you're very proud of. You've slept with nearly half the class."

"Not you," he points out.

"Because I'm not a fucking idiot."

"Not Rio either," he says.

"Because she's not stupid either."

"I don't think a girl has to be stupid in order to have a good time," he muses, tapping the top of the bottle against his lips. "Rio does seem like a lot of fun. It's a wonder the two of you are even friends, she's like sunshine and you're just this angry red windstorm that knocks down trees sucks the juice out of everything."

I can't help but grumble at him. "Rio is way too good for you." I don't need to point out if he pursued her enough, she'd probably give in. She does like a good time and she'd probably be the only one in class to not pen an anti-Blake poem. Still, I add, "You stay away from her."

"Forbidden," he says with a sharp nod. "I like those ones the best."

"I'm serious. She's not your type."

"You don't know my type," he says. "I bet you don't even know your own."

What is with this question lately?

I straighten my shoulders, raising my chin an inch. "I know exactly what my type is, what kind of person I need and want."

"Need," he repeats, lightly mocking. "Will you listen to that, the All Powerful Oz has just admitted that she needs things from time to time. I thought you'd be entirely self-sufficient."

"Oh I am," I shoot back. "You should see my vibrator collection."

His eyes widen and I refrain from clamping my hand over my mouth. I've said too much. Way, way too much.

I clear my throat, looking down at my beer. "Any smart young woman should always have a range of suitable man substitutes."

"Or you could just get a boyfriend."

"Not interested."

"Or a fuckbuddy."

"Not interested," I repeat.

"Eating carpet?" He snaps his fingers together. "Rio!"

I sigh, rolling my eyes. "Why does every fucking guy have to assume a girl is a lesbian because she's single and not sleeping around? I don't have to explain myself to you; you're nothing but an alcoholic with a tarantula. Go ahead and think I'm a lesbian if it appeases your ego, I don't care."

"Touchy," he surmises. "It's okay. I get it. We all have our issues. I think yours is the fact that your eyelids are nearly glued shut."

I ignore him. "Can we get back to work, because if not, I'm getting a cab back home."

"All right, we'll call a truce," he says, holding out his hand, a sly gleam in his eyes. I don't trust him at all but I'll pretend in order to get this done. I shake his hand quickly.

We both sit down on the couch, me beside him this time

and try to work through the changes to the chapters. We bounce ideas off of each other and even though I have Susan's POV, which is as interesting as I want to make it, I can't help but feel a bit envious over Blake. Not only does he have a phenomenal appreciation for Forrest's character, but he's got so much material to work with. His character is heavy, layered and complex and I can see the fever burning in Blake's eyes as he discusses him, like he's coming alive in ways I've never seen before. If I didn't hate the guy so much, I think I might be getting a glimpse of the real him— and liking it.

But he still drives me mad and when we're done for the night, he goes right back to pissing me off.

"Ali," he says as we head for his door.

"What about her?"

He shrugs. "Not much, but she got to meet Fluffy."

"Willingly?"

"He escaped. At a...*bad*...time."

My skin prickles. I can only imagine. "Well I'm glad you're telling me this now." I grab the front door and rip it open, happily stepping into the hall where big hairy spiders aren't potentially running amok. "No wonder she was so pissed at you in class the other day," I say under my breath as we get in the elevator.

"Oh, she wasn't pissed about that," he says, folding his hands in front of him and staring up at the elevator lights as they go down. "It's because I didn't call her when I said I would."

"Did you ever call her?" I ask.

He gives me a lazy grin in response.

"Once again, pig," I tell him.

And just like before, the insult doesn't seem to bother him. "They all know how they stand with me. I tell them from the beginning I'm just looking for a quick shag and nothing else. I can't help it if they all start planning our futures together the minute I get them to come. Though perhaps I shouldn't deliver so many orgasms in one session."

"You've got to be kidding me," I mumble to myself, shaking my head in disbelief as we head to his car.

"I joke about a lot of things, but not about sex."

Then it's too bad you don't take the rest of your life as serious as your sex life, I think as we speed away through the dark streets.

But soon, he won't be my problem anymore.

There's some solace in that.

SIX

BLAKE

"Something on your mind, bro?" Heath asks me, snapping me out of my haze.

Actually it's not so much as haze as a violent storm cloud that's kidnapped my brain, prodding it with lightning bolts. *The Heart Thief* —maybe not the most original title, but it's stuck —has taken over my life, and I'm pretty sure Amanda's as well. In fact, I've spent the better part of the last two weeks working either with her or by myself on the project, constantly writing and brainstorming, as well as reading as many good books as I can to help my prose along.

I haven't seen Heath once, haven't even gotten a good shag. The brunette with *Mr. Mercedes* called me the other day and I managed to go out with her for the sake of getting laid but she turned bashful by the end of the night and I was too distracted to try and take it any farther. We both went our separate ways and though I told her we should meet up again, it's getting harder and harder for my brain to focus on anything but the story.

The best part of all this shit is that working at the store now is something I look forward to. Despite my ambitions as a writer I had never really taken advantage of the fact that I have a world of books at my fingertips, that this world of books will soon be my life. Now I'm finding inspiration down every shelf and I'm interacting with customers more and more, rifling through their brains to figure out just how to craft the best work that I can, what exactly they're drawn to in the books they read. It's even made me more inspired for my own work-in-progress and I find myself gravitating toward that when I have nothing else to do.

"I'm here," I tell Heath, sitting back in my chair and watching the traffic flow down Wharf Street, the glittering blue harbor on the other side. In two weeks, spring has become an onslaught and even though it's late March, the cherry trees are in full bloom and everyone is wearing shorts. Right now it's t-shirt weather and knowing it could go back to being cold and rainy tomorrow, we've snagged a table on the patio in the square to have a few pints.

"You're not," Heath says. "You might as well be on your phone like everyone else." He glances around us and indeed, most people are staring at their phones instead of the view or their company. "Last time I saw you, you were present."

"I was drunk," I remind him. "We both were."

He studies me over his beer before taking a sip. "So then tell me, what's the real reason you've been holding out on me these last few weeks?"

I look at him frankly. "It's the truth. Sorry to disappoint you but there is no other reason. I've been writing. I'm caught up in it."

He doesn't believe me. "I've never seen you get so wrapped up in an assignment before."

"I've never had an interesting assignment before."

And, to be honest, I've never had an interesting work partner before.

I'm shocked at how much I've come to enjoy working with Amanda. Maybe enjoy is too plain of a word. I can do better: *challenging*. The whole thing is challenging. She keeps me on my toes. Not just in terms of writing and trying to better myself, because, let's face it, if she's competitive then I am too. We're both trying to outwrite each other, which is kind of working in our favor (though I'm sure Professor Dumbass will be the judge of that).

No, she keeps me on my toes because every time I'm with her I'm not quite sure what's she's going to say. She's completely predictable until she isn't. She's entirely too serious, uptight and while I retract anything prudish I've thought about her after she admitted she had a large stack of vibrating penises, she's incredibly stiff at times.

And yet, sometimes the strangest things slip out of her mouth.

Her mouth.

Which I can't help but focus on every time she speaks.

Those lips I keep imaging sucking my dick, slowly, loving every wet second of it.

Ignore it, Crawford.

Right. Where was I? Oh yes. She'll occasionally say something that makes me think I may have pegged her wrong. With her penchant for fantasy, I knew she was already on the nerdy side but I had no idea how deep it ran until she admitted she slept outside the movie theatre in order to be one of the first to see the new *Star Wars*.

"My boyfriend thought I was crazy but I did it anyway," she had said.

"Your boyfriend?" This was the first I had heard of him.

It turns out she did have a boyfriend, someone she was

with for four years but they'd recently broken up. I tried to get more info out of her but she clammed up, something I noticed she does a lot whenever the conversation becomes about something personal.

And fair enough. I'm not exactly opening up to her either. After all, we're just class partners and most of the time our conversation is entirely about the novella. It works for us anyway, at this rate we'll be done the project long before it's due, which will give me more time to work on my own stuff.

As if he can read my thoughts, Heath asks, "So have you pushed aside your book in the meantime?"

I take a long sip of my beer and tilt my head back to the sun. After a long and dark winter, the early spring feels good. "No, I'm writing it on the side. If anything I'm more motivated."

Heath is one of the few people who know I'm trying to finish my science fiction horror novel, *Blood Aurora*, something I've been working on for a few years now. When Amanda poked fun at my *Lord of the Rings* reference at the library, I had to laugh it off even though it's not something I advertise. Believe me, as much as women love a good fucking shag and a British accent, there's something about nerd boys that turn them off. I thank the *Big Bang Theory* for that.

He runs his hand through his shaggy hair and smirks. "I'm guessing it's the company you're keeping that's really motivating you." His head swivels as two fit blondes in yoga pants walk past the patio and take a seat at the bar adjacent. "Two for two," he comments.

The blondes don't interest me. I mean, they should. One looks like she does porn to fund her education, the other has small tits on alert and skin that gives off the "I spent winter vacation in Cabo San Lucas" glow. But it's Heath's comment that has my attention.

"You mean Amanda?" I ask, bringing his attention back.

"Maybe she's good for you. You still haven't fucked yet?"

I snort. "Right. Like that's on the agenda."

"Still a stick in the mud?"

"Uh, still something that hasn't even crossed my mind." Not really.

"I'm impressed," he remarks, his eyes going back to the blondies. "I think."

"She's become easier to be around," I admit. "But in this situation, we're strictly partners."

"Are you just saying that because you've already tried to get in her pants and you failed miserably?"

"Heath, dear, you know I don't try anything. I just do."

"That sounds borderline rapey."

I ignore that. "All I have to do is be myself and the rest is up to them. Why do you think I'm not making eyes at the girls over there? It wouldn't be fair to you otherwise."

"You're full of shit," he says, flipping around his coaster. "I think I liked you better when you were with Rachel."

"Of course, less competition," I say glibly even though his remark felt like a hot poker to my gut. There were a lot of things that were better when I was with Rachel.

Heath lowers his sunglasses and waggles his eyebrows and I glance over my shoulder to see one of the girls giggling behind her menu. "Seriously," I say. "You're going to woo her from afar?"

"Whatever works," he says, flashing her a grin before turning to me. "Hey I'm renting the cabin near Sooke again this weekend, Watchtower and Damon are coming. You in? You can borrow my spare drysuit again, you practically stretched it out last time." I open my mouth. "Not in the cock area," he quickly adds. "That would be impossible."

Even though I'm not as good at surfing as Heath and his surfer buddies Watchtower and Damon, I'm a fast learner and have been picking up the pace each time I go. The last time we packed up Heath's jeep with the boards and rented a cabin up north on the coast, we discovered a cabin of surfer chicks nearby. There was a bonfire, loads of booze and drugs, and things got pretty out of hand. I ended up having sex with two of the girls at low tide. It was pretty fucking magical – until one of the girl's boyfriends showed up. I'm not proud of my naked run down the beach and to safety but he was wielding a piece of driftwood like a fucking baseball bat.

"This time will be even better," Heath says, trying to tempt me.

"I'm sure it will. But I have to pass."

"Dude, what? Why?"

"I have plans," I say and hope he'll leave it at that but of course he won't.

"Don't tell me it's because of that bitch."

I'm surprised to find myself glaring at him. "She's not a bitch, she's just...prickly. And yeah, I do have plans with her. We've both got exams coming up – as do you, by the way – and we need to get together on Sunday to start finalizing things while we can. One more chapter each and it's almost done."

He groans and leans back in his seat, shaking his head. "It's like I don't even know you, man."

"That's because I'm Bruce Wayne."

His forehead crumples in confusion. "What?"

"Never mind," I say, picking up my beer. "I'll pay for

the drinks. You just go say hello to the blondes before they lose interest. I'll catch you later."

"Works for me." He finishes his drink and gets up. "Thanks, bro. See ya."

I signal over the waitress to get the check and she's halfway to my table before I realize her shift must have ended and there's a new girl on duty.

The Nair girl.

Bollocks.

"Blake," she says coldly, stopping by the table, one hand on her hip, a tray of beer in the other. "Didn't expect to see your face around here again." She glances at the top of my head. "How's your hair?"

"You're lucky I don't keep conditioner in my hair for very long. One minute and it's rinsed."

"I have no idea what you're talking about," she says, though I see the flash of anger and disappointment at her revenge not working.

I decide to push it. "In fact," I tell her with a grin, tugging at a strand. "I think it's shinier and thicker than ever."

I know I'm playing with fire here but I just can't help it.

"Do you even remember my name?" she asks, her tone pure ice.

"Do we have to go down this path?" I tell her, shooting her another smile that I know makes my dimples pop, one of the things she kept commenting on when I took her out. Because, no, I don't remember her name. Susan comes to mind but I think that's because she's the character in *The Heart Thief*.

She takes a few steps until her petite frame is right beside mine and brings the tray of beer dangerously close to my head. "Tell me my name or this beer is going all over you."

"You wouldn't dare," I say to her in a hush.

She raises her brows to say she would.

Cindy? Sandra? Cersei? I wish she was wearing a nametag.

"Stella?" I offer, wincing because I know it's wrong.

"Stella is the name of the other waitress you fucked over here," she seethes. The tray wiggles. I shut my eyes. "It's Magdalene."

You think I would have remembered that. "Like the biblical hooker?"

Her eyes narrow. The tray tilts. The pint glasses slant toward me.

Crash!

Beer goes everywhere, over my head, over my shoulders, my lap, my legs.

I'm legit sitting in a beer shower.

"Oh my god, I am *so* sorry," she cries out in a string of lies.

She pretends to fuss over me while I sit there, soaked from head to toe, the beer pints rolling on the table. She's lucky none of them broke and I'm lucky one didn't knock me on the head. The last thing I need right now is a concussion, though with everyone on the patio, plus onlookers, staring at me, losing consciousness would be preferable.

"Oh dear, I'm so clumsy," she adds, bringing her washcloth to my crotch and patting it there —*hard*. It's like she's playing Whack-A-Mole with my dick.

"Jesus," I hiss, trying to protect my balls. "Do you want me to report you for manhandling the customer?"

"I'll get Stella, the *manager*, to clean this up," she says smartly before turning and storming into the pub.

Stella too? Fuck me. I get up, absolutely dripping pale ale and porter, and yell after her, "Luckily beer is good for my hair too!"

I throw a few twenties on the table and get out of there before something worse happens.

"Dude!" Heath yells at me, laughing, as I pass by him and the blondes. "It's Karma, dude."

"Shut the fuck up," I growl at him as the blondes giggle and quickly head home to shower.

~

AFTER THE BAR ANTICS, I PLAY IT SAFE FOR THE REST of the weekend. Last I texted Amanda she was still down for our meeting on Sunday night, so Sunday morning when my dad says he needs someone to watch Kevin while he and Angelica go to a friend's for lunch, I volunteer.

When I pull up to the house, I'm not surprised to see Kevin sitting glumly on the front stoop, plastic sword in hand that he's whacking against the steps. With his glasses and cape sprawled around him, he looks like a nerdy and bored warrior waiting between battles.

I grew up in a small house in the woods on the Saanich Peninsula. It was up on a small crest, didn't get a lot of sun, though you could kind of see the ocean through the giant cedars if you squinted hard enough. It was an upscale neighborhood though, with lots of whitewashed mansions and groomed acreages, many waterfront with their own docks. Our house was this tiny little ugly dot, like a tick amongst everything fresh and healthy, but even though my mother was glad to get out of there when she took me to England, I was heartbroken. I didn't want to leave my dad and I loved that small, dark place with the mossy roof and the rain collection barrel where I'd watch bugs drown.

The minute my dad met Angelica though, he sold the house. Now they live in one of those sprawling houses my mother had envied and my dad is living the charmed life.

But I also know that not everything is as it seems. With Crawford's Books losing money, they're a single income family. They may have this giant house with the brick driveway and fruit trees in the garden, but Angelica has no choice but to work around the clock to keep it.

"Hey bud," I tell Kevin as I lock the car and stroll over. "Where are the rents?"

He shrugs lazily. He doesn't look at me. "I don't know. Getting ready."

"Feeling pissed off they didn't invite you?"

"No," he grumbles, then stabs the sword between bricks. "I hate the Chaunceys."

"That's a strong word," I tell him, sitting beside him. I practically have to shove him over to make room.

"Yeah well they're a bunch of turdburgulars," he says.

I can't help but smile. It reminds me of the insults Amanda lets loose every now and then.

"Turdburgulars are the worst," I tell him.

I totally get it though. In the time I've been here, I've met the Chaunceys on a few occasions and they're straight out of the Lord and Lady Douchebag sketch from SNL. The funny thing is, I lived in England all my life and I know just the kind of people they're trying to be. Sometimes when I look at Amanda I wonder if she was brought up by people like this, ones who think they own the land because they were part of the British stock who arrived here at the turn of the century. What they need to be told is that Canadian history is so short and minute compared to the

centuries we have going on overseas. If you have an important bloodline in England it's because you can trace your
family back to the bloody Dark Ages and beyond. Here it's
if someone's lived in the same house for a few decades.

"Ah, you're here," my dad says as he and Angelica open
the door, stepping out behind us. "Thought I would have
heard your car from a mile away."

"I still don't know what you were thinking letting him
buy that thing from Uncle Mike," Angelica says derisively,
flicking her long dark ponytail over her shoulder. Angelica
looks like a lesser version of Kate Beckinsdale and she's still
out of his league. Come to think of it, so was my mom.
There must be something to the Crawford charm.

I let her comment about the car slide. So does my dad.
His face goes red briefly but he keeps his mouth shut. "We'll
see you in a few hours," he says tersely and the two of them
slip past us, heading for their Lexus. I wonder if my dad
knows how silly it is to be driving a car like that while on the
verge of bankruptcy. With how crabby he is lately, I'm
assuming he does.

They've just driven out of sight, disappearing behind a
row of budding maple trees, when Kevin quietly
announces, "They're getting divorced."

It takes me a moment to process this. "What?"

He looks up at me and nods, mouth set in a firm line like
he's determined not to cry. "It's true."

"What? Kevin, what are you talking about? They aren't
getting divorced." Though the moment I say it, I know I'm
wrong.

"Yes they are," Kevin says, stabbing the ground again for
emphasis. "They fight all the time and when they aren't
fighting, they don't talk to each other."

"That's just marriage, buddy."

"No," he says sharply. "It's not. I keep hearing them talking about 'when do we tell Kevin?' and 'wait until school is over' and 'you're an asshole, Paul.'"

"But—"

"And then I found letters from lawyers. Two different ones. I googled them. They're divorce lawyers!"

Bloody hell, this kid is resourceful.

I shake my head. "Oh, Kevin. I'm sure there's some explanation."

"There is no explanation!" he yells at me, getting to his feet. "You're just like them! You don't tell me the truth, all you do is bullshit."

I get to my feet. "Watch your language, Kev."

"Blake! Fuck! You!" he half-yells, half-sobs, and then starts running around the house, the cape flying behind him. I stand where I am, completely gobsmacked. I'd never heard him swear like that before but I guess this is as good of a reason as any.

My dad and Angelica, getting a divorce. No wonder my dad has been so grouchy, why I've been watching Kevin and working at the store more and more. They've got a divorce in the works and my stepbrother will be caught in the middle, again, since he already had to go through a divorce when he was younger.

I can only hope that whatever agreement they have that my dad doesn't get completely screwed over. Angelica isn't the warmest, or nicest, person but she has to know that she's holding all the cards and my father has practically nothing.

I sigh, knowing I have to find Kevin even though he probably just wants to be alone. I walk around the house, hands in my pockets, feeling terrible that everything my dad wanted will once more be taken away.

I find Kevin sitting with his back against a blossoming cherry tree, playing a game on his iPad mini.

"Are you winning?" I ask him gently, trying to see over his shoulder.

He twists away, trying to not let me see. After a few beats he says, "It's not about winning in this game. There are no winners."

"Are there losers?"

"Yes. You can die."

"That doesn't sound like a very fair game." I pause. "Actually it sounds a bit like life, doesn't it?"

When he doesn't answer I crouch down beside him. "Look, I know you don't want to talk about it and that's fine, but when you do want to talk about it, I'm here for you, okay?" I put my hand on his shoulder and squeeze. "Okay?"

Finally he nods.

"Tell you what, we'll do whatever you want to do for the rest of the day."

He glances at me shyly before shoving his glasses up his nose. "For real?"

I hesitate, not sure what I'm getting myself into. "For real. I could dress up and we could wage a battle. You know I was thinking of you the other week and I bought some fun props for us to use. Elf ears, witch makeup, a new sword."

"Really?" Now he's excited.

"Just for you buddy," I tell him. "I was saving it for when my school quiets down but we can use them now."

He nods, chewing that over. Then he says, "No, we can save that. You know what I want to do today? Visit Fluffy."

I groan. "Kevin," I whine.

"Please," he says and then adds sternly. "You promised. Anything."

"Okay, fine," I say getting to my feet and hauling him up

to his. "I'll take you to see Fluffy. But you are not to take him out of the cage, you got it?"

"It's a terrarium," he corrects me.

"Whatever. It's Satan's playground is what it is."

He smiles gleefully and then takes off running toward the car, arms raised, waving his sword like he's about to battle an enemy. I can't help but feel the same way.

Luckily everything goes well and Kevin was just content to tap on the glass and feed Fluffy crickets, which I was forced to watch with him as he gave the gruesome scene some National Geographic worthy commentary.

When I got back to the house, Kevin was in a lot lighter mood, even though he started pouting when I had to leave.

"Please, stay for dinner," he whines as we stand in the hall.

Angelica pokes her head around the corner. "You're welcome to stay Blake." And if my eyes aren't failing me her expression is practically pleading. I guess she sees how much her son needs a friend right now.

I sigh, unable to say no. "Okay," I say and he shrieks with joy. "Let me just make a phone call first."

Even though I'm glad Kevin's happy I know Amanda isn't going to be. I dial her number—it doesn't feel right to text her this—and head outside to talk.

"Hey," she says, sounding surprised and I can't help but smile briefly at hearing her voice. I wipe it off my face right away.

"Hey, listen," I say and then I hear her groan over the phone. "What?"

"I know what you're going to say," she says flatly.

"Pretty sure you don't. I have to cancel tonight. I'm so sorry but—"

"Yup, I knew it."

I feel a twinge of frustration. "What does that mean?"

"It means I knew you were going to cancel. Let me guess, hot date?"

"Hot date?" I repeat.

"You're a terrible liar."

I press my palm into my forehead. "Why are you saying all these confusing things?"

"Rio saw you on Wharf Street a few days ago, hitting on some blondes with your friend."

"Did Rio also mention I had a heap of beer spilled on me?" Granted, I wasn't the one hitting on them, or even talking to them, so I don't know what the hell Rio is talking about but since Amanda is already jumping to conclusions, I have no need to correct her.

"She said something about that too," she says.

"And why do you care anyway?"

"Me?" she asks snidely. "I just don't want my grade to suffer because you can't keep it in your pants."

Oh that fucking does it. "Fine," I tell her. "I do have a hot date. Two blondes. Sorry I can't meet up with you but I think a threesome takes precedent over homework."

"Oh fuck off," she says.

"You're the third person to tell me that this whole weekend. It must be good luck."

She hangs up.

I stare at the phone for a while, the triumph over pissing her off slowly slipping away. I really should have told her the truth, but I just couldn't help myself. Let her think what she wants of me, what does it matter in the end? I'm no stranger to judgement and what she thinks of me should be my last concern. There are bigger things to worry about here.

I take in a deep breath and head inside the house.

SEVEN

AMANDA

"Seriously, fuck everyone," Rio says, swiping my phone from me. "You need to make my contact name 'Daddy Issues'."

We're in a tapas bar downtown, one of my favorite places to go since the food and wine are phenomenal and it's located down this narrow brick alley that makes you think you're in some quaint European city, but unfortunately neither of us are in the best mood. Rio has just finished telling me about the thirty-five year old single dad she's seeing, illustrating the time his ex-wife and child came home early and caught them both buck-ass naked in bed. Me, well, I've been listening to her but mainly stewing over the asshole maneuver that Blake pulled tonight.

I think what pisses me off more is not that I'm missing out on a night of finishing up the project but that I was actually looking forward to Blake's company. It pains me to admit it but for the last two weeks, I've started enjoying our time together, both of us working toward a common goal. It's like for once I'm with someone who understands the drive to write and the deep-seated perfectionist need to make it the best that it can be.

But then he blew off our meeting to go bang some chicks and so now I'm at the bar, drinking rioja like it's going out of style.

Rio hands my phone back to me and I check that she indeed changed her contact name to "Daddy Issues." "Anyway," she says, popping an olive in her mouth, "I'm not sure how much longer this will last."

"It's only been a week," I remind her quietly.

"Feels like a lifetime," she says, giving me a sidelong glance. "Hey, you better start smiling or keep drinking or I'm not going to sit with you anymore."

I roll my eyes and take a gulp of my wine. "I pick the wine."

She twists in her seat to face me, studying my expression. "I'm surprised you're this upset."

"I'm not upset," I reply testily. "I'm angry."

"That's called being upset, Amanda. And really, the question is, why are you angry? You knew he was like this. I mean, he's been your nemesis until recently."

"I think I liked him better when he was my nemesis," I say into my wine. Hating Blake was a lot more fun in some ways. At least I didn't feel hurt when he slighted me, just annoyed.

"People never change," she says, reaching for the sliced chorizo. She offers it to me but I shake my head. She goes on. "I mean, not really. It's not like I actually saw him hitting on them, it was mainly his friend, whom I've already nicknamed Johnny Utah."

I glance up at her sharply. "What are you talking about?"

"The other day," she explains between chews. "It was

Blake's Point Break friend that was hitting on them. He made the googly eyes and head nod and pelvis thrusts before he went and sat with them while Blake stayed behind and got a beer bath."

I try to form words. "Are you serious? Why did you tell me it was Blake?"

She shrugs. "I don't know, what's the difference? The point was, he's pissed off a lot of waitresses at that bar. I was by the window, inside when it happened and I heard quite the mouthful from some of the girls. They were actually clapping."

I rub my lips together, trying to think. The copious amount of wine is finally hitting me and thinking is getting harder. "He told me he was going out with them."

"Look, I'm not a psychic, I don't know what happened. But the fact is that Blake is a fuckboy you should never fuck and I've got daddy issues now and so the two of us are better off in here, with each other, getting drunk."

I eye her dryly, knowing very well that she'll be leaving this place with someone and it won't be me.

Half an hour later, I'm right. She's slowly applying pale lip gloss to her lips and looking over at three guys by the bar. The cutest one, slim, tall, tattoos, is going wild with eye contact. Another one, a trim beard and big arms, waves at her. Man, they're forward.

"Do you know them?" I ask her.

She grins slyly at me. "Dated them both. Not at the same time though but it's the same circle of friends."

This doesn't surprise me but still. "What?"

She shrugs and flips her crazy hair over her shoulder. "You want to meet men, go hang out at the marina bars. Those guys with boats sure know how to use their hands. They rigged me up six ways from Sunday. Once again, not together," she pauses, running her tongue over her teeth. "Though who knows tonight. Why don't you come over and I'll introduce you? You know you need to get laid."

"I'm not having any part of your exes or your orgy."

"The other guy might be single."

"I'll pass." I sigh and bring out my phone to call a cab and leave her to this wicked web she's spun. "Please don't bang two exes at the same time or I'm going to get confused."

She wiggles her fingers at me. No promises.

With my cab on the way, I make my way to the door, a light rain coming down and making the brick alley shine in the night. I look back at Rio inside who so easily sits at the bar with her exes and smiles like she doesn't have a care in the world and wonder why it can't be that easy for me.

I blow a wayward strand out of my hair and walk down the street to catch the cab.

~

"GOOD LUCK TODAY," ANA SAYS TO ME BEFORE SHE darts off to her school. "If you need his balls ripped off, you know who to call." She makes a clawing motion with her bright pink nails and heads out the door, her makeup case in tow.

I nod, wiping my brow on my sleeve. After waking up with an aching head and knowing I'd have to see Blake today, I went for a long run along the water, trying to get out my frustration. I'm exhausted now but still have this uneasiness in my stomach that I'm really hoping doesn't translate into me getting sick. The last thing I want is to puke in class. Or, really, ever again.

I haven't spoken to Blake since yesterday, nor have I

texted or emailed him and he's responded in kind. Because of this I know that class is going to be completely awkward and I have no idea whether I should address what happened or not. I mean I'm sure other classmates blow off their assigned partners too from time to time but this just happens to feel so personal and I'm not sure why.

Luckily once I get to school, I spot Rio about to head up the stairs.

"Hey," I call after her and hurry to catch up. "What happened with your exes last night, you never texted me."

She gives me a dry look and I realize she's still wearing not only her makeup from last night but the same clothes. "Ugh. I can't wait to shower all this regret off of me," she says, sounding wrecked. Then her eyes grow round as she looks over my shoulder. "Heads up, Hugh Grant Jr. is coming your way."

I turn to see Blake coming toward me. Shit.

I quickly whip around just as Rio is abandoning me, running up the stairs.

"You bitch," I mutter under my breath and try to inhale deeply.

"Amanda," Blake says crisply to my back.

I slowly turn around, raising my brow. "No nickname this time?"

His gives me a wary smile. "Oh I've got plenty but they're all very inappropriate during a proper grovel."

"This is you grovelling?"

He chews on his lip for a moment and looks away, his eyes shifting from dark grey to dark blue in the dim light of the hallway. "I'm sorry I cancelled last night," he says, focus on me again, brows raised in offering. "You forgive me?"

Shit. He's got one hell of a sweet face when he wants to

be sweet. Those dimples, the puppy dog eyes. He knows exactly what he's doing.

"Maybe," I say. "That really pissed me off. You're not the only who has a life you know, I put off things so that we could work together."

He runs his fingers along the stubble on his chin. His fingers are something else. I've only really noticed them as we've been working together but my mind has gone a few places imagining what else he can do with them.

And now I know I must be blushing. I clear my throat and stare at him expectantly.

"I know," he says. "Something came up."

"Two blondes with, I'm guessing, big tits is what came up."

He raises his finger. "Actually one had small tits and I never went on a date with them. Her or her tits. That was my mate Heath who did that. At least I assume he did, I actually never heard back from him."

I guess Rio was right. Not sure why that bothers me. "Then why did you lie?"

He coughs out an incredulous sound. "Because you assumed already that I was cancelling because of some girls."

"And you weren't."

"No," he says adamantly. "Look, darling, I know this may come as a surprise to you but I have a life that involves more than getting my dick sucked."

I flinch at his language though I'm not sure it's because of his crudeness or that it ignited a hot flare of interest inside me. I'm praying for the former. "Well you could have fooled me."

Some students brush past us, heading to the stairs. Blake reaches out and grabs my elbow, leading me out of their way and over to the wall. His grip on my arm is firm and gentle at the same time and what little intimacy this is surprises me.

He moves me so that my back is against the wall and peers down at me intensely. I've seen this look before when he's discussing his character and it makes me feel slightly off-balance. I swallow thickly.

"I just found out that my dad and stepmum are getting divorced," he says in a low voice. "It caught me off-guard though clearly I was missing all the signs. Anyway, my stepbrother Kevin was having a hard go of it all. They still haven't told him but the chap is smart, he knows. They asked me to stay for dinner and I couldn't say no. I'm really sorry I had to do that, I was looking forward to seeing you." He pauses, blinking a few times. "I mean, I was looking forward to working with you on the novella. But I don't mind seeing you either. Especially that arse of yours."

So many things flying through my head at once. I push the comment about my arse aside since it's not the first time he's made some remark about one body part or another. "I'm so sorry," I tell him. "You should have just said that."

"Well I obviously called you to tell you the truth but once you got all fiery like the barmy redhead you are, it was hard not to fan the flames. So I'm sorry for that." He holds his hand out. "Apology accepted?"

I put my hand in his and he squeezes it tightly. "Accepted." His brow quirks and I feel a smile tug at the corner of my mouth. "And I'm sorry for jumping to conclusions. You had a good excuse."

"You mean a threesome isn't a good excuse?"

"Not unless it's like your life's goal or something."

He puts his hand at my back and leads me away from

the wall to the stairs. "I'm pretty sure a threesome is every guy's life goal."

"Fair enough."

We head up the stairs and pause outside the classroom just as Ali slides past us, giving Blake the death stare. Clearly she's still not over him or the Fluffy incident and I'm not sure I blame her.

"My groveling isn't complete you know," he says to me.

"Well you haven't gotten down on your knees," I muse jokingly, tapping my fingers against my chin.

"Darling, when I get down on my knees I'll be paying it back in a different way," he says and I swear there's a change in his tone, like his voice got deeper, his accent huskier.

Don't even picture it, I warn myself.

He goes on. "Dinner. Tonight. After class. My treat."

My head jerks back like he just grew an extra ear. "Dinner? No way."

"We're friends," he protests.

"We are not friends," I remind him. "Partners. Classmates. Maybe POW buddies. But we're not friends."

"You're a very cruel woman."

"I'm a smart woman, but thanks for not referring to me as a girl like usual. Dinner is too intimate and we're supposed to work, not eat."

"What about working and then eating?"

"What about just working?"

"What about not being a stick in the mud," he volleys back.

"What about taking me for a drink," I finish, surprising myself.

It surprises him too. He grins and those dimples deepen. "All right, a drink. I'm buying."

"You sure are," I tell him. "But only after we get some work done."

"Fine."

"*Fine.*"

Interestingly enough, this is the first class where time seems to crawl past. Usually this class is over before I know it and I'm hanging onto Marie's every word. This time, all I can think about is Blake.

Blake.

Blake.

I've turned into the rest of them, feeling strangely satisfied that I'm going for drinks with him after class even though I'm sure it's what half the girls in here have done. I'm sneaking glances his way and when his eyes meet mine something in my stomach turns over, happily, like a puppy rolling over. But it's not surrender. It doesn't even have a name.

At least you're not thinking about Alan and the colossal mistake you might have made by not saying yes, I remind myself and damn it, it's like my mother takes possession of my brain every now and then.

By the time class grinds to a halt, I'm wanting a drink more than ever. I walk off with Blake and catch Rio giving me the *I knew it* look out of the corner of my eye.

"Where to?" I ask as we stride across the parking lot to his car.

"Ever been to Spinnakers?" he asks. "Brew pub out toward Esquimalt?"

I'd heard of it but never been there. Alan was always a fan of the fancier places downtown and certainly not brew pubs.

"Is this place safe?" I ask him as we get inside Mr. Mean, after clearing the usual crap from the passenger seat.

"Safe?" Blake asks leaning toward me, a piece of his messy hair flopping onto his forehead. I fight the urge to reach over and brush it off his face.

"Should I get a poncho for the beer spillage?" I explain.

He laughs, his smile wide and easy. "No, no. Spinnakers is sacred ground for me. I need some place I can go and not have to deal with someone's wrath."

"You do realize it would be easier for you to just not screw women over. Maybe just commit every once in a while or at least be honest."

His eyes darken, the smile fading a touch. "I've been nothing but honest."

There's something more there, something I want to poke and prod at with a stick, bring it out and examine it on a table. But I don't say a word, not yet anyway. It's not like I've been all that forthcoming either.

When we get to the pub I can't believe it's been here all this time and I'm only just going there now. Granted, I've only been of the drinking age for three years but still. I have a lot of catching up to do.

Spinnakers is located at the base of a cove just outside of the downtown core. With the sun hanging low and the weather back to being almost summer-like and perfect with a fresh breeze and blue skies, it looks like the perfect place to spend an afternoon having a few.

I follow him in through the entrance which consists of a bakery and a growler-filling station and we go upstairs where it seems less formal. There's a pool table and old teak tables tucked into nooks and crannies. The small upstairs deck is already full so we grab a table by the window, across from the fireplace.

"This is nice," I tell him as we sit down, grabbing the elaborate drink menu.

"I can't believe you've lived in Victoria your whole life and you've never been here."

"You wouldn't believe a lot of things about myself," I mumble, absently noting that every cocktail seems to have gin in it. How very English, just like Blake.

"Try me," he says.

I glance at him over the menu. "Try what?"

He sits back in his chair, all completely at ease and flashes me that smile. "Tell me something about yourself that I wouldn't believe."

I'm not sure if he's serious or not. "Let me get a drink first."

Only it's so very hard to choose. I settle on some raspberry vinegary drink called a "shrub."

"There's something you probably wouldn't believe," I tell him after the waitress takes our order (and doesn't seem to bare him any ill-will). "I like my drinks with vinegar in them." Though it's a first for me as well.

He cocks his head, seeming to think that over. "I believe it. Ever been to New York?"

I can't help but sigh. "No. I always wanted to. Even tried to last year, booked the hotel and everything but... things didn't happen."

"No money? The city is expensive."

I lick my lips, hesitating. "I had the money. I mean, my parents would have paid for it."

I can see a light going off in his head as he nods, the look of *this rich bitch.*

"Then why?" he asks and I have to give him credit for not saying anything about my privilege.

"Ex-boyfriend. The one I mentioned before."

"Alan?"

I'm impressed. "You have good memory."

"There's a lot of good about me that you don't know about," he says lightly though I swear there's a slight edge to his voice. "Anyway, in New York they have a pickle bar. Actually they have a few pickle bars."

"A pickle bar," I repeat.

"Just as the name says. I went a few years ago, got a cheap flight out from Gatwick and spent a week wandering around the city with no plans at all." He gets this dreamy, faraway look in his eyes as he stares at the fire. He shakes his head slightly, snapping out of it. "So the pickle bar is in East Village, I think, and it's nothing fancy, just a good place to get a drink except they serve their shots with pickle juice and you can even order a jar of pickles to eat on the side."

"That sounds..."

"Brilliant, right?"

Actually for my pickle-loving soul it does. "Who did you go to New York with? Family?"

"Ex-girlfriend," he says.

"When did you guys break up?"

He rubs his fingers along his chin and stares at the ceiling. "Um, maybe a year ago. No, less than that."

"She's still in England."

He gives me a simple nod. "Yes," he says, baring his teeth slightly.

"That can't be easy," I say, trying to put myself in his shoes. "Long distance and all that. I mean normal relationships are hard enough, I can't imagine how difficult they are when you're continents apart."

"Yes, well, lesson learned," he says quickly, smiling up at the waitress as she drops off our drinks. He gestures to me. "Did you want to order food?"

"What did I say earlier?"

"That we're obviously here to drink, then eat, then work."

I glance at the waitress and she's beaming down at us like we're some couple on their first date. I have the urge to tell her that I have to be here in order to graduate but I'm sure she's heard it all before.

I hold out my hand for the menu and the waitress hands it back.

"I don't know how I got roped into going to dinner with you," I tell him, trying to keep my focus on the list of farm-to-table food.

"Because I'm utterly charming," he explains, splaying his hands out.

"Well at least you didn't mention your cock. That has to be a first."

He doesn't say anything and I have to glance over my menu at him. He's staring at me with the intensity he had in the halls earlier, though his eyes look a bit lazier, languid, like they're drinking me in and loving it.

I swallow uneasily, not used to this attention from him, and pick up my drink. I take a timid sip, the vinegar a shock to my tongue but it quickly blends with the raspberry and other liqueurs. Before I know what I'm doing, I've finished half the drink and my body immediately relaxes.

"Thirsty?" Blake comments after a sip of his dark beer.

"It's a small glass," I say defensively.

"And I'm paying," he says. "And driving. Go nuts."

I push the drink away. "I'll behave."

He waits a beat, licking his lips, before he says, "I wish you wouldn't."

Oh boy. I meet his eyes and I'm held there for a moment. This whole thing was a mistake. I should have stayed mad at him. I should have insisted we work on this in the library like we have before.

"Hey," he says softly, breaking his stare and twisting in his seat to take out his laptop. "Let's get started."

And somehow, just like that, he moves into work mode which makes it easier to do the same. Over the next hour we go over our notes for each other and plot and plan the next steps to finish the story with a bang.

We also order more drinks and then when my head starts getting swimmy and we've done all we can, we put our order in for dinner. The sun has just set over the harbor, setting the grey water ablaze with pink and yellow and casting a glow to the walls.

"Your hair is glowing," Blake comments. "Like a bloody fireball."

I self-consciously smooth my hair back, making sure all the strands are properly tucked into the ponytail elastic. I'm feeling a bit unraveled myself.

He takes a slow sip of water, his eyes never leaving me. "Do you ever wear it down?"

I exhale noisily. "Yes. I do. But I prefer it back. And no, I don't want to wear contacts, I prefer my glasses."

"I prefer your glasses too," he says and I look at him, brows raised. He shrugs. "What? They suit you."

Funny. Most guys want me with the glasses off but then again Blake isn't most guys. And by that, I mean he shouldn't be thinking of me in a sexual way and I certainly shouldn't be entertaining it after two shrubs and an oyster stout which I tried at Blake's urging. It was surprisingly delicious.

"So tell me more about your ex," he says.

"Tell me more about your ex," I counter. "What's her name? You know mine."

He finishes off his water and stabs the lime with his straw. "Rachel."

"Are you pretending the lime is Rachel?"

He laughs. "This time last year, yes. Now, not so much. I don't really think of her."

I don't know how I know she broke his heart but I do. I wasn't even aware that Blake had a heart to break but I can see the undercurrent of pain there, one he's been trying to hide behind his dimples ever since.

"Water under the bridge," he adds, giving me a pointed look, the type that tells me to drop it.

And I really should. But there's something inside that compels me to keep talking. Maybe it's the shrub. Maybe it's the fact that I've already bared my soul to him through our story. He may not know it but there's so much of me in Susan, in her insecurities and failures. My characters are still me, even if they are masked by fantasy and fiction.

"Well," I say slowly, "Alan and I were together for four years. I lived with him for one. He was pretty much my best friend and always the nice guy, you know. He didn't really have any faults but there was something missing between us and I put up with it because I didn't know any better. I'd known him for so long and we started dating in high school and I think I was just so happy that a guy was interested in me, a guy that all the other girls wanted, that I jumped at it."

I'm staring at the wood patterns on the table as I'm speaking and finally look up to see him. He's listening, focused solely on me and gives me a little nod of encouragement. "Plus he was nice. I watched so many of my girlfriends get involved with the cheaters and the douchebags and I felt pretty lucky that I got a guy that wasn't like that." I pause, taking a sip of my drink. "But, after a while, I started to realize that he didn't really know me. And maybe that's my fault, maybe because I wasn't showing myself to him. I'd always been taught to hide who I was growing up, because my parents wanted me to fit in more than anything, maybe because my sister already gave the middle finger to conformity. Anyway, long story short, New Year's Eve Alan proposes to me in Tofino, at a party with his family and all our friends and I...I have to say no."

"Shit," Blake says softly. "How did that go?"

"Aside from puking on him seconds after he asked me?"

A smile spreads across his face, his eyes dancing. "You didn't," he says in hushed disbelief.

I nod and give him an embarrassed grin. "I did. It's a thing that happens. Anyway. I totally broke his heart and then I vomited all over it. Not the best way to leave a relationship."

He's laughing softly as he leans back in his chair, running his fingers over his jaw. "That's true but still. Damn. I guess it means I'm a horrible person that I find it all bloody hilarious."

"I'm sure I'll laugh one day."

He inclines his head, studying me. "Still not quite over it."

I give him a look. "I was with him for four years. He was my first love my first...everything."

"But you're better off now, you know that."

I shrug. "Depends who you talk to."

The waitress comes by just then giving us our food, a beet, hazelnut and goat cheese salad for myself, a meat pie for him. I'm thankful for having something to do other than spill the beans and after a few bites of the salad, my mind is distracted by my taste buds. By the time we're done eating, it's like we've both forgotten I opened up.

That is until he's dropping me at my house.

"Thanks for keeping me company," he says, large hands resting on the gear shift. "For the talk."

I feel my body grow hot as I meet his eyes. Man, I must be tipsy as hell.

"Thanks for getting work done," I tell him, keeping my voice level.

He gives me a tentative smile. "Well, what else am I here for?"

Our eyes lock and something deeper, wilder, passes between us. It causes my heart to pound so hard in my chest I think the only release is to open the car door and run, run, run into the darkness.

But somehow I compose myself, step outside and head down the driveway to my home, the night air cool and damp. I glance over my shoulder just before I go through the gate and he's still parked at the curb, watching and waiting.

EIGHT

BLAKE

I DON'T KNOW HOW WE DO IT.

But we do it.

The ironic affairs of Forrest Cosway in *The Heart Thief* are finished and handed into Professor Dumas on time. Actually, we had it ready to go a week before but Amanda wanted to keep on tweaking it, and while I would normally not fuss with a project this much, this one was special and I understood her need to make it all that it could be. Hell, I still think it could use another round of editing, but if there's anything I've learned from this class it's that you have to learn to let it go.

Now the manuscript has been handed over (as well as emailed), and there's a heavy sense of loss and confusion in the air, like the day after your birthday. For me it's double since this was my last assignment of my entire degree and I have no idea what's next.

No idea at all.

I try not to think about it.

"So," Amanda says as we leave the classroom, casually hanging her thumbs through the belt loops of her skinny jeans. With the April weather warm but temperamental, I'm seeing more of her skin lately, and right now my eyes rest on the dusting of faint freckles on her shoulder, showcased by her emerald green tank top. The freckles even lead down to the swell of her breasts, and I have an urge to find out where else they might lead.

"So," I say. She catches my eyes on her skin, and I'm in no hurry to move them away. "What next?"

"I guess this is it," she says, stopping by the foot of the stairs. She shrugs. "I mean, class is over, the year is over."

We're over, is what she wants to say next.

I knew this was coming. When the project was complete, we would cease to be partners and cease working together every other day. I didn't expect to feel this curious pang in my chest, but it's as unwelcome as a hemorrhoid so I swallow it down, push it aside, and ignore it.

"Hopefully Dumbass will take it easy on us," I tell her, trying to find something to say.

She rolls her eyes but smiles easily. "I can't believe I never thought about such an obvious nickname, even though Professor Dumas is not a dumbass."

"You were too busy trying to be the teacher's pet," I remind her.

"This is university. There are no teacher's pets," she snipes at me.

I rock back on my heels. "Hey, I said you were trying to become one. You didn't succeed." I pause, suddenly feeling awkward. "I'm sure we'll do great. I don't mean to get all cocky—" She lets out a derisive snort and I continue, "but we wrote the fuck out of it. And I'm not sure if you know this, but I'm kind of a big deal."

"Right, right." She sighs and looks around her, her body

language telling me she wants to get going. "Well, I guess I'll see you..."

"Come into Crawford's Books for a friends and family discount," I tell her with a wink. Bloody hell, that was lame. What's wrong with me?

"I promise," she says, yet I have a feeling she'll be avoiding the bookstore for the rest of her life.

She waves goodbye and heads down the stairs. It's exactly where I was going, but I don't want to do that weird thing where you say goodbye and then end up walking in the same direction, so I wait a while at the top of the stairs until I hear my name being called from behind me.

"Mr. Crawford," Professor Dumas says, waving her arms at me, the fringe on her shawl swinging. Her eyes are bright, a warm smile on her face. I love how she calls me Mr. Crawford, as if I'm distinguished somehow.

"Glad you're still here," she says as I walk over to her.

"Don't tell me you've read it already," I say.

"No, no," she says. "Just the first few chapters. You learn to speed read in this job."

I bite my lip, waiting for her to go on, praying it's not rubbish.

"It's wonderful, really," she says. "Complex. Layered. Not without its faults, of course."

"Of course," I say, though I can't believe how thrilled I am at the feedback.

"I'm sure the rest will be great," she goes on. "But I know you're graduating, and I wanted to tell you that you have talent. A gift, if I can use a cliché."

My grin is splitting my face in two. So much for being cool and composed. "You can use all the clichés you want."

"I just hope you don't stop. I know you've finished a business degree, and I know how important Crawford's

Books is to the community. Just don't let that side of things squelch your creative side. If you stay disciplined, you'll be able to write whatever you want and perhaps make a living off of it, as long as you make it a priority."

Obviously this is all music to my needy ears. But I still ask, "What about Amanda?"

She tilts her head at me. "Amanda? I'm not at liberty to talk about another student." She waits a beat. "But I will say that I was right when I thought the two of you would work well together. She's got a bright future ahead of her too, as long as she doesn't give up either. Writing is a hard profession, and it easily weeds out the dreamers from the workers, the ones who want a quick buck versus the ones who want to build a career. Stay with it and you'll both do great."

"Well, I'm pretty sure you can't really make a quick buck these days unless you're writing Fifty Shades of Grey Part Eight: Grey and Greyer."

"That's what I'm talking about," she says, her tone dropping with disapproval. "So many authors are popping up all over the place because of how easy it is to get rich writing self-published erotica. But real writers take the high road."

And I've totally tuned her out because now I'm thinking about what she said:

Get rich quick.

Self-published.

Erotica.

"So people are still buying those types of books," I say slowly. "I mean I know that sex sells and ebooks are taking over, believe me I hear about it enough from my father, but..."

"The romance market is bigger than ever," she supplies, and from the set to her jaw I can tell she shares my father's opinion. "And short, dirty, kinky books are leading the pack.

These so-called authors, all using pen names obviously, are uploading their trash, selling it for a buck, and yet bringing in hundreds of thousands of dollars. But that's just on Amazon. In the real world, literature rules, and that's definitely where you should be focusing your efforts."

"Definitely," I repeat absently. Hundreds of thousands of dollars? I'm starting to think working in a bookstore has blinded me to what's really going on in the ebook market.

"Anyway," she says quickly, giving my arm a squeeze with her dainty hands, "you have an honest and bright future ahead of you. Stay focused, make writing a priority, and you'll be displaying your own books in the store one day. If you need any advice, you know where to find me."

"Thanks," I tell her as she waves and heads back down the hall to the classroom.

A million wheels are spinning in my head, a million gears churning in my gut.

I run down the stairs and out into the parking lot, blinking at the bright sunshine and the few students milling about, the last stragglers after exams. Amanda and her Mini Cooper are nowhere to be found.

Calm down, I tell myself, heading to Mr. Mean. You don't need her to do this.

And I'm right. Even though I need to do a lot of research to see if what Professor Dumas says is right, Amanda doesn't need to be involved. Our partnership is over. Besides, erotica? She's the least erotic person I know.

Unless she has some dirty, kinky side hidden deep within, one her ex-boyfriend never let her indulge in.

This could bring it out.

I could bring it out.

I shake my head, trying to get my thoughts straight, to get those thoughts about Amanda far, far away.

I make a plan. I have to go to the bookstore anyway, but if my father catches me scrolling through Amazon books I can just tell him I'm doing merchandising research. Then I'm going to text *Mr. Mercedes* girl (what was her name again? Stella? Stephanie? Cersei?) and see if she's available for drinks tomorrow. I have some steam I need to blow off, and now that Amanda's steely presence is no longer unintentionally cock-blocking me, I need to jump back into the dating pool like a fucking cannonball where all parties get wet.

April marks the start of tourist season in the city. The flowers are in full-bloom and foreigners descend on the clean streets, looking to spend their money on tiny bottles of expensive maple syrup, t-shirts with moose and beavers on them, and slabs of smoked salmon. They also find their way to the bookstore, looking for a vacation read or just to admire the ambience, so when I get there we're already slammed.

We work non-stop, which is great for business, and even my father seems to be in a boisterous mood. He still hasn't mentioned the divorce to me, and I don't dare bring it up, but at least he's smiling more. The summer seasons have saved us in the past, but I'm not sure if this season will be enough to do it.

I end up staying late, putting all the books back in their proper places and tidying up the store while my dad jets off to an appointment that he seems awfully cagey about (I'm assuming it's with a lawyer). With the lights in the store off and darkness settling outside, I hop on the stool behind the counter and pull up the Amazon Kindle site on the work computer.

Amazon's Top 100 list is the best indicator of how books are selling, and the moment I peek at the Top 20, I'm a little mind-blown. Professor Dumbass is not such a dumbass after all.

About half the books in the Top 20 are cheaply priced erotica, ranging from $ 0.99 to $2.99. They all seem to feature the same guy, in various stages of undress. A few have Jesus beards and tattoos, more are cut off at neck level because I'm guessing their faces are hideous, and all are baring their steroid-pumped chests. Shit, I don't want to think about how small their balls must be to look so jacked up. If they're getting any pussy from being a cover model, I'm going to assume the girls will be sorely disappointed once they take off their pants.

The books also have similar titles, like *Bad Boy Being Badder* and *Sluts R Us,* and all seem to be written by Sassy LaRue and Lacey Lippes and I. Swallows.

And they're all selling well.

All of them.

Now I'm determined to find out just how well.

I do some Googling which leads me to the website of a best-selling author I've never heard of who blatantly states how much she makes from each ebook, how much she needs to sell in order to get to a certain place in the rankings, and how much she makes over the course of a year with a release nearly every month. It's tacky and probably unprofessional to boast about your earnings like that, but *I'm* finding it extremely informative, especially since her sales are in excess of three hundred thousand dollars.

I bring out a notepad with the store logo on it and do some math. A lot of math. My degree is coming in handy.

Basically, from what I figure so far, if I make up a pen name, find a stock image of a shirtless roid monkey, and write a twenty to thirty thousand word novella about some kind of romantic or sexual endeavour, and put it up on

Amazon for ninety-nine cents, I could stand to rake in some dough. If I released every month, I'd get even more dough. If I put some money into advertising and marketing, according to various other articles and websites, I could increase my sales even more.

Sales equals money equals saving the store. It means getting enough money to hire a manager who knows what they're doing, preventing my dad from going into bankruptcy, and giving me the freedom to do—and write—what I really want to.

It's win, win, win and all I have to do is write some smut.

But it can't be just smut. It has to be the clit-throbbing, panty-soaking, thigh-squeezing smut that gets women off again and again. Something plotless and easy to follow since masturbating all day has been known to delete a few brain cells. It has to be romantic too, just enough that while the dude is nailing the heroine, he's considerate (or whipped) enough not to go around nailing everyone else.

I only have a Kindle via app on my iPhone but it's a good enough start. In the name of research, I start downloading every bestselling erotic romance book I can find until my phone is full of them, and then I start reading. I also make a mental note to not let anyone look through my phone until I've read and deleted every one of these suckers.

It's nearly midnight when my eyes start to cross and my brain feels like rubbish. I've made my way through both *Big Balls*, a sports romance involving a well-hung tennis player named Rock Hardon, and *Begging for Seconds*, about Chevy Silverado, a billionaire chef who teaches his new cook how a turkey baster should really be used. Surprisingly, it worked a lot better in the book than it did in *Gigli*.

Maybe it's because I'm overly tired and my mind is trying to digest hours of explicit writing, but I'm feeling hopeful. If they can all do it, there's no reason why I can't. I mean, I actually know how to write, it's just the matter of finding the time and motivation. And maybe digging up some of that romance and tenderness that these books all seem to call for. I can write the dirty fucking kink pretty well, I think, but the whole lovey-dovey aspect of it is way over my head. I've only been in love once, and it ruined me, so I'm not sure my jaded point of view will be helpful.

But there's always Amanda.

Yes, she's also jaded and a bit of an emotional robot, but she's bound to be more sensitive than I am. I know she can at least write it. Her characterization of Susan and Bethany in *The Heart Thief* was honest and real and came from a soft place inside of her that I know doesn't exist inside me. She may hide it behind her glasses and resting bitch face and tendency to whip insults at you like she's shelling peas, but I know it's there.

And, to be quite honest, I want to see her again.

She's a bit much to take at times and I'm certain she still thinks I'm the world's biggest wanker—literally and figuratively—but I was getting used to her company. Writing with her was fun. Fighting with her was even more so. Maybe even hot. And hot is exactly what we need to bring to the table in order to rake in the dough.

But will she go for it?

That's a different matter entirely.

NINE
AMANDA

Phenelope walked into the clearing, the early morning fog dusting the tops of the yellow and pink leaved Galadrial trees, making it appear as though she was walking through a candy-colored dream. She wanted to get a head start collecting the peacock crickets from their flowery nesting places before the sun rose too high in the lavender sky, and the crew was on their way yet again.

Even though it was early and the land around her was still, she heard a rustling and the faint lapping of water from the thicket. She drew her bow, the wings on her back poised to spread at any moment. She crept forward, silent as a dolemouse.

There, through the branches, she saw a figure that made her entire body grow still. It was Luthwen, wading into the water, completely nude.

It was a jaw-dropping sight. His sinewy muscles and tanned skin gleamed above the surface like raw honey, the planes of his taut back rising from his firm buttocks. His hair seemed longer when wet, the color of copper, clinging to his shoulders as he surveyed the calm pond in front of him.

Phenelope swallowed hard, feeling a myriad feelings course through her. She had never thought of Luthwen that way and never once entertained the idea of him liking her. After all, she was part bird, and life was far too painful and serious to have physical relations, let alone to ever fall in love with someone else. But now, observing him in secret, she found her nerves sparkled with need, and the urge to strip herself naked to her feathers and join him in the water was nearly overwhelming.

But she couldn't.

She wouldn't.

She'd learned her lesson before.

I stare at the words on my computer screen, reading them over and over again, trying to get back into the flow of things, trying to figure out where to go next. But I can't. It's the most curious and frustrating case of writer's block ever.

Actually, the last time I'd written anything was when I fixed up the last few paragraphs of *The Heart Thief* before we handed it in the other day. Ever since then, my mind has been stuck, like slogging through mud. It's not even that the weather is gorgeous and the summer is laid out ahead of me like a warm, pristine blanket or that I'm distracted by life. It's not that at all. It's that the will to finish the story as I had planned it has whittled down to nothing.

When I was writing the novella with Blake, the words couldn't come fast enough, even though the easiest parts seemed to come with Phenelope and Luthwen's interaction. Just being in the habit of writing, of creating, spilled out into my other work. But now when I think about my next scenes and where I have to go after, it's like I'm dragging my feet. I can only write with a gun to my head.

The worst part is, the only time I do feel like writing a bit more is when I entertain the thought of turning the novel into a romance, or at least upping the sexual and romantic nature of the book. But I'm fighting it because Phenelope should be fighting it. We *both* have to stay strong. Luthwen may be handsome and brawny and oozing with sex appeal, but that doesn't mean Phenelope should sacrifice the mission by sleeping with him.

"How is it going?" Ana asks.

I look up over my computer to see her standing in the doorway, smiling warily at me. She knows, oh she *knows*, that the worst thing to say to a struggling writer is, "How is it going?" or "Get any writing done?" Bitch, if I've got writing done, you can fucking bet you'll know about it.

But I don't have the strength to get mad. I sigh, pushing myself back from the computer, and rub my forehead, trying to loosen the tension. "It sucks," I mumble. "I'm just staring at the screen, and when I'm not staring at the screen I'm staring at the walls and when I'm not staring at the walls I'm having a nap."

"Want to be my guinea pig again?" She waves a green lipstick at me. "I could use the help. I'm supposed to do space and fantasy makeup. You know, the nerd stuff you like."

That does sound more interesting than normal, and I know this time she'll probably nail it since her day-to-day makeup usually borders on the side of 80s futuristic prom queen, but I can't be bothered with doing anything. Even going for a run is a struggle. I fear my writer's block is slowly leading to life block. And then what?

"How about you do it to yourself and I'll watch," I tell her.

"Sounds kinky," she says.

"I'm pretty sure everything sounds kinky to you." Actually, everything has been sounding kinky to me lately, hence the pervy peeping Tom scene in my book.

Phenelope, you are a pervert, I think to myself.

Still, I get up and follow Ana out into the kitchen. I've totally resigned myself to the fact that makeup has permanently taken over the table. I often drink my coffee around mascara tubes and color correctors. The other day I found cream eyeshadow in my protein shake.

Luckily this is Ana's last couple of weeks of school, even though it means she's trying to practice on me as much as she can. I had Rio over the other day and watched Ana transform her into a pretty convincing drag queen, though I'm pretty sure that wasn't her intention.

Even though it's only three in the afternoon, I go and get a bottle of local pinot gris out of the fridge. Fuck it all—a prescription for the daily blahs.

I've just poured us both a glass—thank god for day drinking roommates—when my phone rings.

Thinking it's either my mother or a telemarketer, I fish it out of my pocket and glance at it.

It's Blake.

I have to admit I'm surprised to see him calling.

Surprised, and, well...I'll just ignore that little flip my heart did.

"Hey," I say as I answer, sounding more chipper than I mean to.

Ana watches me with a slow raise of her scarily arched eyebrow.

"Hey, Big Red," he says smoothly. "Catch you at a bad time?"

I stare down at the glass of wine. "Not really. Was about to get my day drink on."

"What a coincidence, so was I." There's a lengthy pause and I find myself sucking in my breath, not sure what he's going to say next.

"Did you want to join me?" he asks. "Beautiful day, a slow period at Spinnakers. We could grab a couple of shrubs on the patio."

"Last time you sampled my shrub you nearly spit it out on the waitress as she passed by."

"You know my luck with waitresses."

"And hostesses and classmates and most females. Yes, I do."

But beneath all the casual banter, I know I have to say no to him. The fact that we're both done working together and he still wants to hang out is nothing but bad news. I mean, what can we possibly offer each other anymore?

"Are you also saying yes to the pub?"

I can see Ana nodding anxiously at me.

"No," I tell him, and she groans loudly in disappointment. "I'm busy."

"Washing your hair?"

"Yeah," I tell him. "And not hanging out with you."

"You're kind of mean, you know that?"

"You've told me."

"Did I tell you I like that?"

"You have."

"And yet you keep doing it."

I sigh, even though I'm trying not to smile. "Anyway, I don't think it's a good idea. There's no reason for us to hang out anymore."

There's a pause. Am I being too harsh? Maybe.

I open my mouth to backtrack but he says, "But I have a reason."

"And what is that?"

"A proposition."

"Yeah, those never end well."

"This might. It might end with us being rich."

Now he has my attention. "What are you talking about?"

"Let me pick you up. I can be there in a half hour."

"But what is this about? I'm not going unless I know. My roommate had a bad dust-up with a Nigerian drug lord last month and I'm not about to follow in her footsteps."

"Tell him the chicken parmigiana was good," she whispers, gesturing to the phone.

"I hate to burst your bubble, peach, but you know I'm not a Nigerian drug lord. However, I do have a solution for that overactive imagination of yours."

"If I come, will you promise to never call me peach again?"

"No," he says, "but that's only because I'm nothing but honest."

"I'm still not sure that's true."

"Trust me."

"Not helping."

"See you in thirty minutes."

And he quickly hangs up before I can protest again.

"Is he coming here?" Ana asks excitedly. I'm not surprised to see her wine has been gulped down.

"No, we're going to Spinnakers again," I tell her, quickly marching into my bedroom to find myself something suitable to wear. I know my Lululemon pants and "Bazinga!"

tank top should suffice, but I'm strangely compelled to make myself look better.

Ana follows me. "A date?" she asks with cautious optimism.

"No," I tell her, adding a glare. "Not a date. I don't date guys like Blake, and he doesn't date girls like me. We've been over this."

"Not even if he's your fuckboy?"

I pause, rifling through my closet, and give her a look. "Where did you learn the term fuckboy?"

"Your friend, Rio," she says. "She talks a lot. I learned a lot."

I turn away from her and whip off my tank top, sliding on a mustard-colored flutter sleeve blouse that I know looks banging with my hair. Speaking of hair, I pull my elastic out and attempt to fluff it around my shoulders.

"It's so pretty. You should wear it like that," she says, coming up behind me and petting my head like I'm an exotic bird.

"On second thought, no," I tell her. I remember what he said to me about my hair. He would know it was for him. I pull it back into a loose topknot, slip on white capris and rose gold sandals, and I'm almost ready to go.

Oh, this part is going to be awkward.

I slowly turn around to see Ana staring at me, hopeful as all hell.

"I could just give you a light makeup. A dusting."

I manage a smile and nod. "Okay," I tell her, hoping I don't sound as scared as I feel. I mean, she's come a long way. Just because she was totally pumped to make me look like Groot a few minutes ago doesn't mean I'm going to walk out of here looking like I belong in a Marvel film.

I sit down at the kitchen table, and she spends a good

three minutes just staring at her makeup and then my face. Back and forth. I've never seen her look so determined before—I don't think the "natural look" is even in her vocabulary.

Then she gets to work. I drink the wine.

She's still finishing my face with blush when there's a knock at the door and I'm having severe déjà vu from the last time Blake came over. But luckily she kept her Krazy Glued eyelashes at bay, and when she hands me the mirror, lo and behold I actually look pretty foxy. The peach eyeshadow and winged eyeliner really make my blue eyes pop, and the blush blends naturally with my lightly freckled skin.

"Do you like it?" she asks, hands clasped by her chest, face already cringing at my potential reply.

"I love it," I tell her. And it's not a lie.

I give her a quick, albeit awkward, hug—maybe the first hug I've ever given her—and I quickly grab my purse and head out the door.

Blake is waiting in the garden that takes up the whole backyard of the house, one that the landlords have been toiling over ever since the first shoots started sprouting in March. Though they say we have free use of the yard and the quaint iron table and chair set situated among the lilacs, Ana and I are often intruding on their gardening whenever we use it. Ah, the joys of not having your own place.

"What are you doing?" I ask him, shielding my eyes to the sun while I bring out my sunglasses.

He looks up from a well-groomed patch of bluebells and grins at me, those dimples deepening in his cheeks.

With a ray of golden sunshine hitting him just so, he looks good. Really good. I know it's only been three days since I saw him last but I don't know. Maybe something has changed in those last few days. I'm noticing muscles I've never noticed before (which I know have always been there), the way he holds himself, the glint in his eyes when he's looking at me.

Fuck. Don't pull a Phenelope. If she can't have Luthwen, you *definitely* cannot have Blake.

"Honeybees," he says, gesturing to the bluebells. "I've been watching them."

"Okay. Why?"

He walks over to me, hands jammed in his pockets. "Because they're fascinating. Ever learn about them? Study them?"

Do I unleash more of my nerdiness or not? "When I was younger I knew a lot more. I'd read the National Geographics my dad had in the basement. There had to be a thousand copies. I read them all. I'm sure a few of them were about bees."

"Impressive," he comments, stopping a foot away from me. He cocks his head, studying me. "You look rather pretty today. Is that all for me?"

I roll my eyes and turn away before he can see me blushing. Fucking fair skin and overactive blood vessels. "You wish."

"Perhaps," he says with a quick grin as we stroll to the gate and he opens it for me.

"So why the bee fascination?" I ask him as we walk side by side. I don't know what it is, but in the last couple of minutes it feels like the dynamic between us has changed. Maybe it's because for once we aren't bound by anything. We're just together because we want to be.

No, I remind myself. *It's because he's promised to woo you with something secretive and you want to find out what it is.*

"My manuscript," he says as we reach the car. "To build a believable alien race I had to study the colony structure and instincts of the honeybee. They're bloody fascinating, actually. There's a whole world around us that we don't even get a glimpse of, all happening right under our noses."

"I bet you wouldn't say that about Fluffy," I point out, getting in the passenger seat. I'm taken aback by how clean it is. No pile of random shit to move into the backseat. Just last week he had a camping stove in here. I wonder if all this consideration is for me, but unlike him, I would never say anything.

"Fluffy is a monster from the bowels of hell," he says as he buckles himself in. "But believe me, he's made his way into the novel. Just picture him a hundred times the size."

Blake rarely mentioned his work-in-progress when we worked together. I didn't even know the genre. So to hear him talk about an alien race, I have to figure he's writing sci-fi.

Beneath his strong, lean build, big hands, cocky smile and gorgeous head of hair, it turns out that Blake Crawford is a closet nerd. A month ago I would have gone running to Rio with this information, but now I sit on it gleefully, knowing for all our differences, he's an awful lot like me.

"So I'm guessing you're writing science fiction," I tell him. Mr. Mean roars to a start and we speed off down the street, turning the heads of pedestrians as we go. I raise my chin, pretending I'm actually cool.

He leans in to look me over. "Sci-fi horror," he says matter-of-factly, his face inches from mine.

I instinctively suck in my breath, even though I ate lunch ages ago, and if anything I should smell like wine. I wait for him to go on.

"It's called *Blood Aurora*," he says eventually, turning

his eyes back to the road. "And I feel like I've been writing it since I was a wee one."

"How much have you written?"

"Maybe seventy percent. Not a lot."

I can't help but laugh at that. "Are you kidding me? Not a lot? I've been struggling at the halfway point with my book for ages now, and no matter what I do, I can't move past it. I'm stuck. It's driving me fucking crazy."

"Then maybe it's good that you agreed to come with me."

"Why, so I can drink my face off and forget that I have a book I need to finish?"

"Peach, I'd love to see you drink your face off. You're cute when you've had a few."

I shoot him daggers over that fucking peach nickname. At this point I'd rather be Tits McGee.

He only smiles. "Sorry. Bad habit."

Blake was right about Spinnakers not being too busy. We manage to snag a seat on the upstairs patio, both of us getting the Scottish ale from the brew pub, and I sit back, watching him curiously, waiting for the other shoe to drop.

Before it does though, I take a moment to drink in the scene and just...

Pretend.

It's what I'm good at.

I'm looking at Blake sitting across from me, paying attention to every little thing about him: the hairs on his sinewy arms catching the light, the way his thin shirt clings to his broad shoulders and ropey biceps, the thick slope of his neck leading up to his sharp jawline, the way his lips twist to the left, as if he's about to tell you a secret he shouldn't, his eyes that glitter with a million untold jokes. I feel like I'm sitting across from someone who is one hundred percent alive and ready to take on the world. For all his faults—and he has many—there's something almost enigmatic about him, something that makes you want to learn more. Something that makes you want to learn *from* him.

I finally, finally, understand why all those girls were throwing themselves at him. Because they believe he can make them better, just by being around him.

And so for this second I can pretend that I am here on a date with Blake, that we aren't both here because of some other opportunity, and that what we share is genuine and true.

It's all a lie. And it's so sad that I'm even pretending. But at least I'm not thinking about Alan. At least I'm for once not thinking it was all a mistake. At least I'm hopeful for the future because I know now that there is more for me —guys or otherwise. Especially everything *otherwise*.

After we get our beers, he raises his pint to me and looks me dead in the eye in such a way that reaches deep inside, disrupting something dormant.

"Here's to *The Heart Thief*," he says, even though we toasted over it the day we finished. "And to new endeavors. To the future."

I purse my lips for a beat before clinking my glass against his, the thick white foam spilling over the edge. "Cheers."

"Seven years of bad sex," Blake says before taking a sip.

"What?" I say, trying to wipe the side of my glass with a napkin. "I looked you in the eye."

"No, it's seven years of bad sex if you spill," he explains. "But don't worry, I can always bring you out of it."

As always, super inappropriate. God, I hope I'm not starting to like it. Regardless, I take a swig of beer, staring at him, unamused. "So, what is this new endeavor you're proposing? We write short stories for a living?"

I'm completely joking, but he tilts his head and displays his palms, like I'm totally right.

"What are you saying?" I prompt him.

"I had an idea a few days ago," he says, clearing his throat and putting on his extra-serious face which involves a furrowed brow and piercing stare, like he should be roaming the moors yelling for Catherine. "I did a lot of research before I decided to talk to you about it. Painful research. I think I may have spared you some of it. But I think we can make this work. I know we can. I just need you on board."

"Blake, I have no idea what you're talking about."

He licks his lips for a moment. "Okay. Okay, but listen to me before you make a snap judgement. Hear me out, hear all of it. Got it?"

The movie *Friends with Benefits* is flashing through my mind. He's not suggesting we have some sort of fuck-boy/fuckgirl arrangement between us, is he?

I don't even let myself think about it.

"Okay..."

"We work well together. Writing with you has not only been inspiring to my own work, but it's actually been a lot of fun. Who would have thought, right? Me, life of the party, and you, girl who sits in the corner and makes snarky comments about people."

"Blake," I warn him, making the signal for him to hurry up.

"Anyway, you can't deny we write well together. And that somehow we work well together too."

"Most of the time."

"Most of the time," he concedes. "But what if I told you

there was a way for the both of us to keep writing and make a hell of a lot of money."

"I hate to break it to you, but *The Heart Thief* was a project. No one is going to pay for a novella about an affair, especially not one that so reeks of Creative Writing class. I know enough about the market to know that."

He sits back in his chair, trying to move his face away from the ray of sun shooting through the patio. "Tell me what else you know about the market, then."

I exhale noisily and start flipping my coaster around. "Oh boy. Okay, well I've been subscribing to Writer's Digest for a few years, and I read Publisher's Weekly. I know what sells and what doesn't."

"And what do you know about the indie market?"

I'm surprised to hear him bring that up. I wouldn't think it would be on his radar, especially running a bookstore and all. "The indie market is all cheap romance and erotica."

"Below you," he says, more of a statement than a question.

"It just doesn't interest me," I tell him, trying not to sound like a snob. "I know what I want to write, and unfortunately high fantasy doesn't do well in self-publishing, so I have my sights on getting an agent and a publishing deal one day."

"But what if you could make more money than that publishing deal and you could make it *today*?" He presses his finger into the table for emphasis. "What if you and I write together? Under a pen name."

Though my first instinct is to just say no, I have to ask. "What would we write?"

"Erotic romance," he says without missing a beat.

I stare at him, face askew, not sure I heard him right. "Um..."

"Listen," he says. "The writers who are doing it are making a ton of money."

"They're also sell-outs."

"So? Maybe they have bills to pay, mouths to feed. You think it's so bad to want to make money? Greed is good, Amanda. Greed is good."

"That phrase doesn't really work with a British accent."

"And we wouldn't be selling out, per se. We can write well, but we're both beginners, really. It would be good practice, a way to get a foot in the door. We write what sells, what the masses want, need, crave, and then when we have their attention, then we can publish what we really want."

"Right," I say caustically. "Like the Fifty Shades readers are going to purchase my fantasy afterward."

"They might. Let's say three percent pick it up out of curiosity, or maybe there are open-minded readers who like a bit of smut to get off to, a fun way to pass the time, while they also read memoirs and history books and fantasy and who else knows what. You don't know. People have different tastes and like a range of different things, and having those three percent because of our smut is better than having zero, don't you think?"

He has a point but he doesn't need to know that. "You really think a publisher will want my book after I've written erotica? There's a stigma, in case you haven't noticed. Just ask your dad."

His eyes shoot to the ceiling. "Believe me, I know about the stigma. That's why we write under a pen name. Hell, look at everyone in the Top 100 on Amazon. I bet every dirty book is either ghostwritten, written by a duo, or maybe even an established author looking to game the system. No one is who they say they are. There are no rules here. We can do whatever we want. Put out a book a month, split the profits. By the end of the year, we'll be rolling in it."

"But what's in it for me?" I say.

He gives me a puzzled look. "Well, the money I just mentioned." He pauses, nods slowly. "Right. You don't need the money."

"It's not that I don't," I tell him quickly. "But I'm still in school and I have a student loan and my parents to support me until I graduate. I need money...I just don't need it badly enough to write *erotica* with you."

"You make it sound like a horrible idea," he says.

"It is a horrible idea," I tell him, letting a laugh slip. "Look, Blake...I agree that we work well together, but I just don't think this is the logical next step."

"But don't you want success?" he says, his voice lower as he leans across the table. "Don't you want to prove to people that writing can make money? Don't you want to feel like you've proved them all wrong?"

I rub my lips together, unable to look away from his eyes that won't stop piercing into me. "Not by writing erotica," I say softly. "I want that on my own terms."

His eyes briefly drop to my mouth. "This will be on your own terms, and everything you've ever wanted will be that much easier to get. Just...tell me you'll consider it."

I break away from his stare and busy myself with a drink. I hate that there is some part of me that is considering it and for all the wrong reasons. I'm considering it partly because if I don't say yes to this, I won't have an excuse to see him all the time, or even see him at all. I don't want to be *with* Blake, but I at least want to be around him.

"Let's just try it," he goes on. "One book. Same length as *The Heart Thief*. We'll come up with a pen name, a cover, and we'll write the fuck out of it. The premise needs to be ridiculous but the writing doesn't have to be. It's practice."

"For a career in the adult entertainment industry?" I say, my eyes focused on his hands as they grip his beer.

"For both our writing careers. We have nothing to lose right now. Nothing at all. And I'll front the money for the cover designer, the editor, the formatter, for Facebook ads."

Holy hell. He really has done his research.

He says, "Honestly, we just need to write the dirtiest, sexiest short story ever and I promise you if you want to quit after that we can, but I bet you won't want to."

"You're awfully confident," I muse.

He flashes me that grin. "Of course I am. Because I'm right. Do this with me."

I fold my arms across my chest and sit up straighter. "Why do you want me to do this with you? You could do it yourself and not split the profits. It sounds like you already know exactly what you need to do."

The waitress comes by at that moment and asks if we want more drinks. Blake orders more for us before I can say anything.

"It's on me," he tells me.

"Not necessary," I remind him. "Now, tell me. Why me?"

He chews on his lip, his eyes lazily raking over me. I would give anything to know exactly what he's thinking, what he sees.

"You can keep a secret," he says after what seems like forever. "You're ambitious. You're talented. And, well, I need your heart."

I blink at him, trying to process it all. "You need...my heart."

"You can't have the sex without the love."

I burst out laughing. "Oh man, what planet are you from, and what have you done with the real Blake Crawford?"

"I'm not saying it's true in real life, but I've done my research, and when it comes to romance novels, it's needed. No matter how dirty or nasty it gets, if it's a stepbrother screwing his stepsister," I wrinkle my nose at that, "or a teacher fingerbanging his student during class, there has to be love or it doesn't work. If you don't deliver the happily ever after, it doesn't matter how many holes she gets filled or how many orgasms she has."

"And you're saying you need me to write the romantic cheesy shit?"

"Fuck knows I can't do it."

"Well, I can't do it either!"

"Have you tried?"

"No," I tell him, my mind briefly flitting to thoughts of Luthwen and Phenelope. "And like I said, I have no interest in it."

"So fake interest," he says as the waitress brings our drinks. He gives her a quick wink, she smiles slyly at him, and it does something vile inside me. Is he hitting on her in front of me?

And, jeez, when did I think that was a problem?

His eyes dart over to me and he frowns. "Something wrong?"

I shake my head. "No. I mean, other than your proposition. You of all people should know how hard it is to write something you actually care about. I can't imagine how painful it would be to write about something you don't like."

"Funny," he muses to himself, looking away. "Thought you would have been up for a challenge."

"Writing with you was a challenge," I point out.

"Until it wasn't."

I inhale deeply, holding my breath in my lungs, trying to get some clarity. I don't want to commit to this idea that's really nothing more than a harebrained scheme, but at the same time...

"You don't have to say anything right now," he says. He brings out his phone and taps something out. My phone immediately beeps.

I frown and bring it out of my purse. He just sent me an email. "What's this?"

"I made you an official proposal. A business plan. About time I put those classes to use."

Jeez. He really is serious. Even with the hopeful gleam in his eyes, I don't think I've ever seen him so serious before, even when he was grappling with plot problems in *The Heart Thief*.

"I can't believe you made a business plan about writing smut," I tell him, putting my phone away and planning to look it over later.

He shrugs, squinting at the sun that has shifted again. "I'm serious about making money and potentially changing my life for good. What can I say?" Now he's shielding his eyes with his hand.

"Here," I tell him, bringing my cat eye glasses out of my purse. "They're prescription but they'll at least help with the sun."

He grins his thanks, and as he takes them from me, for a split second, our fingers brush together. But unlike the few times it's happened before, I can swear it's deliberate. His finger practically strokes mine, and his eyes pin me down. Fire travels up my arm, right into the thick of me.

I really should stop drinking around him. And, really, my reaction means I shouldn't write with him either.

He slips my sunglasses on and his mouth drops open. "Bloody hell, woman, are you blind as a bat?"

"No," I say defensively, even though the sight of him in my glasses is pretty ridiculous. "I'm nearsighted and only by a little bit." He doesn't have to know by how much. "That means—"

"I know what nearsighted means," he says. He takes the glasses off, blinking hard as he slides them back on the table. "I think I might be cross-eyed now."

"I'm sure you'll survive."

"You're going to have to write most of the book then."

I sigh. "Just...let me read over the proposal and I'll let you know."

"It would be better if you read it now."

"Why?"

He wags his brows. "Because I'm a lot more persuasive in person."

He's right, which is exactly why I need to be away from him to make a sound decision. Writing self-published erotica with Blake can only lead to one thing and I'm too afraid to find out what it is.

Blake is still staring at me, waiting for an answer. The drinks are getting to my head, making it easier to just give in, but I have to stay strong.

"I'll let you know tomorrow," I tell him firmly.

"You promise you'll read the whole thing and keep an open mind?"

"I promise."

"Okay..." He puts his hands behind his head, showing off his wide chest, the thickness of his biceps, and of course I'm staring at him like I've never seen a man before. He knows what he's doing. What an asshole.

"Get a good look?" he asks smugly, all damn dimples.

"Whatever," I dismiss him, averting my eyes and keeping them locked to my beer. Seems like I do a lot of staring at my drink when I'm around him.

"What should our pen name be?" he asks.

I shake my head. "You really are full of yourself, aren't you?"

"I refuse to accept that you might turn me down."

"And I refuse to accept that no woman has before."

"Oh, I've been turned down before."

"By who?"

His lips quirk. "You," he says pointedly.

I stare at him for a moment, my mind racing. "When did you proposition me?"

"I don't have to proposition you to know how you'd react."

"Oh yeah?" I ask, raising my brow haughtily. "And how would I react?"

"You'd kick me in the balls. You told me that once."

He sounds so sincere that I have to laugh. "I was just letting you know I could defend myself in case you wanted to take advantage of me."

"Amanda," he says, his eyes going soft. "I doubt anyone could take advantage of you."

"Too smart?"

"That and scary."

"I'll take both of those as compliments."

"Did I mention you're insanely talented and I need you desperately?"

A thrill runs through me at that thought and I don't even bother to ignore it this time.

"Seymour Butts," I say.

He stares at me blankly as I sip my beer. Eventually he spits out, "What?"

"Seymour Butts," I repeat, straight-faced. "Our pen name."

"*Simpsons* reference," he says with a knowing nod. "Well-played." He leans in, eyes dancing. "Does this mean you're accepting?"

"It just means I want to hear all our pen name options before I even think about it. How about—"

"Amanda Hugandkiss," he fills in.

I grin at him. "How did you know I was going to say that?"

"I think I know you pretty well, Miss Hugandkiss. What about Big Red?"

I roll my eyes. "No."

"Red but spelled read, like I read a book."

"Then people will call us Big Read."

He shrugs. "So picky. Okay, what about Patty Peaches?"

I burst out laughing. "You are terrible at this." I tap my fingers on the table, thinking. "Susie Dicksuck?"

Now he's laughing, head back, eyes shut. "That's brilliant! Please, *please* can we be Susie Dicksuck?"

I giggle. "We'll put it in the maybe pile."

And so we spend the next few hours going over potential pen names. By the time he drops me off at my place, my ribs hurt from laughing and we're acting like the biggest pair of dorks. I think our maturity level has dropped to reserve levels, which is totally new for me, but I'm liking it.

"So," Blake lists off as I unbuckle my seatbelt, "we've whittled it down to Susie Dicksuck, I.M. Hornay, T. Aint Licker, P. Ennis and Mike Hunt."

"I swear to god there was a teacher at my high school teacher called Mike Hunt," I tell him.

"And there was one at my high school called Dick Titball."

We burst out laughing again, tears running down my face.

I fumble for the handle. "Okay, I have to go to sleep."

I step out of the car as he says, "Amanda."

I stoop to look at him, leaning against the open door.

"Promise you'll really consider it," he says looking up at me, his voice gravelly. "I think it will be fun. I think it could change everything."

I promise him I will, and when I'm lying in my bed later, drifting off to sleep, I wish I made him promise that everything will change.

TEN

AMANDA

THE NEXT MORNING, BEFORE ANA EVEN WAKES UP, I pad into the kitchen and make myself a giant vat of coffee and find a free corner of the table to bring out my computer and look through Blake's proposal.

When I woke up, my first thought was to just dismiss last night as a drunken fun time and plan on never seeing Blake again. Writing erotica with him is a ridiculous move and totally the opposite of everything I stand for.

But slowly it's growing on me. It has legs. It has movement. And the more I read of his business plan, the more I realize he knows exactly what he's talking about. If we could pull it off, if we could somehow get readers and our foot in the door this way, this might open up a whole world for us. For me, if we're successful enough, I might be able to snag an agent. Actually, the more I read up about the self-publishing success stories, the more I realize that agents go after them, not the other way around. That would be huge for me and my high fantasy career.

I imagine the look on my parents face when I tell them I have an agent. They don't have to know about the pen names—in fact, I would make Blake swear to never ever tell anyone our secret because that's exactly what it would be— our secret. But I could just say that my fantasy novel (that they so easily dismissed) garnered the right attention. I could even tell Sarah Price and hope the news gets to Alan and everyone else I went to high school with, the ones who thought I wouldn't amount to anything besides a weirdo.

My only concern—other than selling out—is that I have zero experience in writing anything remotely erotic. I mean, I watch my little porn channel on the internet, I'm well-versed with my vibrators, and I know all of the kinky things I wanted to do with Alan even though he shied away from them for one reason or another. But I don't know how to write it. I guess that's Blake's part, but I don't know how to write romance and tender loving scenes either. My idea of romance is a guy who will take me to see an Avengers film and doesn't mind dressing up like Loki afterward.

Fake it until you make it, I tell myself. Maybe this way I can indulge the sexual storyline of my novel without having to change the story. I wonder if Blake will mind if I name one of the characters Luthwen.

Feeling nervous as all hell, I send him a quick reply to his email.

I'M IN. WHAT NEXT?
Kinkily yours, Amanda Hugandkiss

HIS RESPONSE IS ALMOST IMMEDIATE.

WE GET STARTED. YOU SHOULD PROBABLY BEGIN READING

*some of the stuff in the Top 20, at least the samples, just to
get a feel for the flow and prose. If you end up jacking off
over it, please let me know. With details.*

    Your place or mine?

    Dick Buttkiss

I ASSUME HE MEANS TO WORK ON THE EROTICA
together and not me jacking off. Speaking of, it's funny how
comfortable I am with him making remarks like that. I guess
he's slowly rubbing off on me, which is probably for the best
considering what we'll be embarking on.

*MY PLACE HAS AN INAPPROPRIATE ESTONIAN WOMAN, AND
your place has something from my nightmares. You pick and
I'll be there. And if I end up masturbating because of poorly
written porn, I'll save it for our book and describe it in full
detail. Sound good?*

    Yours sexually,

    Fannie Pounder

I'M GRINNING STUPIDLY AT THE COMPUTER, WAITING
for his reply, when Ana comes in all bleary-eyed.

    "What are you so happy about?" she asks, and when she
gets to the coffee maker she pauses.

    Wait for it.

    Her eyes light up.

    "Your date!" she says excitedly.

    "It wasn't a date," I remind her. "Get your coffee and I'll
tell you about it."

    She's going to get a real kick out of my new situation.

But as she's clearing her crap from the table, I get the reply from Blake.

I HAVE TO WORK AT THE STORE THIS MORNING, BUT I'll come get you at five. As much as I love inappropriate women, it's probably best we handle our secret project in secret, so I'll bring you here. We can order in and I'll make sure the Harbinger of Doom doesn't bother us.

Jack Goff.

RIGHT.

Secret.

"So what happened?" Ana says, her eyes probing mine for any information, preferably of the dirty kind. If she only knew.

And now, she can't.

"Uh," I stammer, backpedaling. "We went to the pub and it was fun."

"That's it?"

"Yup."

Her eyes narrow and she leans in close, her sun-damaged boobs mashed against the makeup on the table as she scrutinizes me. "I don't believe you. You know, in Soviet Russia, they taught you how to break your enemy and learn the truth. Very. Easily."

"Yeah, and you're from Estonia, which was free from Soviet Russia after 1991. Were you recruited to the KGB as a teenager?"

She purses her puffy lips. "I know things," she says finally, leaning back and slurping from her coffee.

"Well, it's the truth. We had drinks and a good time, and that's that."

"And it wasn't a date?" she asks suspiciously.

"Not a date. Just...it's good to discuss things with a fellow writer." And I shut my mouth before I say any more. I can't talk about this shit with anyone, I just can't risk it. I wouldn't be surprised if Blake made me sign a confidentiality agreement.

"You're a bit of a cockweasel," she says bluntly.

"A cockweasel?"

"You made me think something more had happened."

"I think you mean cocktease."

"Cock something. Cocks right in your face and you're just throwing them away." She demonstrates, though it looks like she's being attacked by flying dicks coming from all directions.

"Technically, Blake only has one cock."

"How would you know? You haven't seen it."

"And I don't plan on it," I remind her.

I have some homework to do before Blake shows up, so I grab my Kindle Paperwhite and notepad and head to Willows Beach down the road to do some light reading and note-taking. I lie down on the grass under an arbutus tree and decide to read the most popular book on Amazon, sitting at number three on the charts, called *Seduced by My Virgin Stepmother*, which is described as a "light and fun read that no one should take seriously." Well, at least they're upfront about it, and judging by all the five star reviews, it seems a lot of people want exactly that.

It's hard to read it without rolling my eyes every sentence. It's not badly written, per se, and if anything, it's entertaining. It's just not my cup of tea. But I'm trying really hard not to judge. I read to learn and think and to be challenged, but I also want to be entertained. I guess some readers just want a quick escape from their lives. I can't pretend that I don't find myself sometimes glued to those awful soap operas Ana is always watching.

And then I hit the first sex scene (which happens at the beginning of the second chapter).

And holy shit.

Now I think I get it.

Granted, the dialogue is unrealistic and cringe-worthy, and the dude is a crude alpha with a cock the size of a Subway sandwich, but hey, no one wants to read about pencil dicks either. The hero, Chet Texas, knows his step-mother, Paris Monroe, wants him bad (and through her POV we get a lot of "clenching" and "drenched panties" and "my sex was swollen with need," so we know she's equally as smitten), and after she spies on him in the shower, he corners her and...well, I hate to admit it, but I was feeling a bit swollen with need myself by the time he was done pounding her against the wall, using pumice against her nipples and a bar of soap between her legs. Her clit must have been sparkling clean.

By the time I'm done with the book, I'm looking around the park red-faced and slightly sweaty, totally convinced that everyone knows exactly what I've been reading. Thank god for e-readers. You can read the filthiest shit and pretend you're engrossed in *War and Peace*. The only problem is I'm turned on as hell and I'm not about to take part in public masturbation.

That said, maybe a character in a book would do just that. I scribble that down in my notebook, along with every-thing else I thought was either hot or important.

A text from Rio comes in: **I just paid my weed guy**

with a check. I think I've got the hang of this adulting thing.

I text her back: **Hey, random question, but have you ever read erotica?**

Her response: **Uh, yeah. I have a waterproof Kobo. Why do you think I take so many baths?**

Me: **Because you're a dirty girl. You walked right into that one.**

Her: **That's true. But yeah, you should get up on that shit, even though book boyfriends might ruin you.**

Me: **You don't need book boyfriends. Your whole life is one big erotic novel.**

Her: **That's true. I could write a book called Slammed by the Single Dad.**

Oh my god. Blake and I could totally write a book called *Slammed by the Single Dad*! I quickly write that down and hope Rio never finds out.

Back at home I'm compelled to read as many books as I can, but with Ana being home, I know I'll have to postpone getting off until later. Which means when it's almost time for Blake to come and get me, I'm wishing he'd really come and get me. I mean, how the hell am I supposed to read all this smut then write it with him? Him with his gorgeous eyes and devilish grin, and taut, muscled body, and those hands, those hands that could so easily pick me up by the waist and throw me on the bed before lavishing me all over with his tongue and...

"Sweet one, your man is here!" Ana yells, snapping me out of my torrid daydream.

Fuck.

It's like he knew I was thinking about him.

Fuck.

That means Ana is talking to him!

I scamper out of the bedroom and see him walking into the living room, looking around.

"I'm so glad we finally met," he's telling Ana, who is grinning at him like he's some kind of celebrity. I bet she thinks he's Tom Hiddleston.

"No!" I yell, and then stop as they both turn to look at me.

"Amanda," Ana says, pouting. "I'm being very good."

"She is," Blake says good-naturedly. "She only told me once in the last thirty seconds that you and I need to have the sex together."

"I said sex, not *the* sex," she says. "My English is better than that."

"Oh my god," I mutter. I quickly gather up my things, sliding them into my messenger bag. "Let's go." I grab his arm and lead him away.

"Nice meeting you!" Blake yells over his shoulder. "I promise I'll stay longer next time."

"You will not," I tell him as I march toward his car.

"Anything to see you all hot and bothered," he says. "Have you seen your face? You've got quite the glow going on."

I don't say anything and get in the car.

"Could this be the aftereffects of the big O?"

"No," I tell him quickly as the car starts and The White Stripes "Rag and Bone" starts playing. "Love this song," I tell him, turning it up and grooving in my seat.

He looks completely taken aback. "Since when?"

I keep grooving and raise my hand slightly. "Jack White fan here."

He reaches over and turns down the volume button. "Wait, are you trying to change the subject?"

"There is no subject to change. I didn't masturbate. End of story."

He laughs. "Fair enough. But I bet you were turned on."

"Maybe," I say, turning the volume up again as we take off down the street while I continue to do my silly seat dance.

Soon we're settled on his patio, our computers and kindles and notes crowding the table along with a growler of fresh home brew from Spinnakers. Sun fills the space, the breeze coming up from the harbor smelling of salt and the faint whiff of diesel fuel. I'm nervous because of what we're about to embark on but also completely at ease.

"All right, so we still need a pen name," he says. "And I have just the one."

He's trying so hard not to smile.

"What?" I ask cautiously.

"Amanda Lovecox!"

I roll my eyes.

"Unless you don't love cocks."

"I'm not going to answer that," I tell him. Then it hits me. "Blake Lovecox."

He shakes his head austerely. "I only love my own."

"Blake is a girl's name too."

"You don't have to remind me."

"So why not? I think it's perfect."

"Oliver Klozoff," he says, snapping his fingers.

"Do you want to get sued by Matt Groening?" I say. "Come on. This is just classy enough that people will believe it and it won't get caught by the Amazon censors. Believe me, I've been doing my research and that's an issue."

"Okay fine. Blake Lovecox. She'll make you love cocks too."

"Well, the best part is that Blake could go either way, so it keeps the mystery of who we are." I hold out my hand. "Deal?"

He shakes it, holding it for a second longer than he should. "Deal. I'm Blake and you love cocks."

"I can live with that. What's next?"

"We need a plot and then a title."

I frown. "Nah, I think we need a title and then a plot. Otherwise we'll never decide."

"Okay," he says, adjusting himself in his chair. He flips through his phone and pushes it toward me. "I've written down all the classic tropes and the elements the book needs."

I glance it over and read aloud. "Dirty talking alpha male. Extremely large penis. Built like The Rock. A millionaire is good, but a billionaire is better. Make sure he donates to Africa or does some charity work, even though he's an asshole with a damaged past. Must possess pillowy lips and intense eyes that gaze into your soul." I shoot him a furtive glance. "Sure you aren't talking about yourself here?"

He smirks. "Wait till you get to the heroine."

I continue. "Heroine is gorgeous but she doesn't know it. Perfect body even though she complains about having such a small waist and big boobs. Has a cunt that tastes like honey." I do a double take on that one.

"To be fair," Blake says, "I've had some tasty cunts in my day, but none of them have tasted like honey. Still delicious though."

I stare at him incredulously for dropping that but he just shrugs. "What? You better get used to this talk, darling, because you're going to be writing it. There's nothing but honey cunts and pre-cum and rim jobs from here on out."

I take a moment to digest all that before I read on. I clear my throat. "Must be a doormat and void of personality or any interesting characteristics so that the reader can interject their own selves. A virgin is preferred, but she must be able to get off on command. Condoms aren't necessary, but ropes and whips are. She must refer to her vagina as 'her sex' and be clenching constantly." I nod at that. "I noticed the clenching too."

"Also," he says, taking back his phone, "the hero should be in a position of power over her and take charge from the start."

"So degrading."

"But it's fantasy, so who fucking cares? You of all people should know what you can get away with in a fantasy."

"Yeah, but I make up worlds with orcs and bird people, not football coaches getting blowjobs from cheerleaders."

"Different strokes for different folks. And when I say strokes, I mean of the cock-handling variety."

"Yeah I get that, thank you." I sigh and take a sip of my beer, watching a seaplane take off in the distance. "You know, if we could actually make a career out of this, this wouldn't be half bad."

He grins at me. "Now you're talking. So we have those tropes. We just keep the books the same every single time. Change the character names around, and by the way, I have a list of those names as well. The books will all follow the same formula—sex within in the first couple of chapters. Then more sex. Then they fall in love. Then they break up. Then they get back together. Happily-ever-after epilogue with a massive sex scene."

"You make it sound so easy," I muse.

"It will be. Now we just need the title and the plot and we're good to go."

We put our heads together, and as the sun slowly dips down over the Pacific Ocean, we narrow our list down to a few with the most potential.

Falling for the Secret Male Stripper – Ford Titan is a nerdy high school teacher by day, a male stripper at night. When his eighteen-year-old barely legal student Shasta Black discovers this and threatens to tell the school, the two of them make a deal...a sexual one.

Riding Hard: a bad boy crime boss MC ménage forbidden second chance romance standalone – Outlaw Jones is one bad-ass biker dude, covered everywhere from his neck to his cock in tattoos. There's only one place where his body is bare—his heart—and he's saving that space for Angel LaRue, his best friend and the girl next door he last saw when he was a damaged teenager. But first, he has to rescue her from Dick Pounder, the equally sexy boss of the rival gang. Things get...sexual.

Spread Open: A Gynecological Love Story – Nelson Dunsmuir was one of the world's best Navy Seals. But when a mission goes wrong and he loses his best mate, he quits the Seals and decides to go back to his first career— gynecology. The moment Pender Galiano walks into his office needing a pap smear, Nelson knows he has to have the gorgeous virgin. But when old enemies rise up, Nelson has to protect Pender at all costs, even though loving her may cost him his life.

"Well, here we are," Blake says as we stare at our potential future on the notepad in front of us. "Really don't think we can go wrong." The night has settled, bringing in the chill of late spring. It would almost be romantic if we hadn't been laughing the entire time.

Not that I'm complaining. I need the laughs. Things between us have gotten so easy and I don't want that to change. If we're not laughing and goofing off, then...well...I notice things a little more. The way he stares at my lips. How he keeps touching me—a lingering hand on my shoulder, his fingers at my elbow to guide me somewhere. But mostly it's something I can't even define. It's a charged feeling between us, like the way the air pressure changes just before a storm. The hairs on my body stand up and my skin prickles in some sort of unseen anticipation.

"Are you cold?" he asks me. We're sitting next to each other, facing the harbor lights. It was just easier to work this way.

"Not really," I tell him, and before I can say anything he's getting up and sliding the glass door open and heading inside. When he returns he's got a blanket and two bottles of beer.

"Here," he says, gently placing the plush blanket around my shoulders.

"Thanks," I say, my voice barely registering. I cover myself with the blanket, close my eyes, and breathe in deep, his fresh, earthy scent filling my nose.

I feel him stiffen beside me.

Oh shit.

"Did you just smell the blanket?" he asks.

I open one eye to look at him. "I like to smell...blankets," is my flimsy response.

"You say the oddest things," he says after a moment. "Did I tell you I like that?"

I bite my lip and nod. He tells me a lot of things he likes about me, and the more I think about it, the more my skin burns, like it's begging for his touch.

I wonder how long I can blame it on erotica.

"So, what do you think?" he says, his voice lower as he leans in.

"About your smell?"

"About which book to write. But now I want to know how I smell."

"You smell like the opposite of Axe body spray. And I think we should close our eyes and point to one."

"Deal."

So with our eyes closed and our fingers poised above the pad of paper, we take the plunge and laugh when we open our eyes.

Falling for the Secret Male Stripper it is.

"Okay," I tell him. "But promise me you'll demonstrate some of his dance moves in the scenes."

"Only if I can demonstrate his other moves on you."

I brush him off, shaking my head. "You're terrible."

And I think I'm starting to like it.

ELEVEN
BLAKE

IT'S BEEN ANOTHER BUSY DAY AT THE STORE EVEN
though there's been quite a few returns. I've never understood people who return books after they've obviously read
them. "Oh no, that dog-eared page was there when I bought
it." Like hell it was. How about I punch you in the bloody
face and tell you that bruise was there before and then we'll
call it even.

I've got a meeting with Amanda tonight and every time
I think about it, I have to stop myself from calling it a date.
It's not a date, but I have to admit, sometimes I wish it were.
Obviously writing *Falling for the Secret Male Stripper* (or
FFTSMS or Stripper or Cock Book) has ended up being a
lot of fun, but it's almost too much fun. We've gotten
together every night this week, and by the time she leaves I
have blue balls the size of Donald Trump's head.

Honestly, I don't know what's happening. I've had to
cancel a date I had with the *Mr. Mercedes* girl (Sansa?)
because I'd rather be with Amanda instead, even though it's
taking every ounce of my goodwill to not make a move on
her. I mean, I don't want to think of her in that way since

she's my writing partner and I've made it this far without fucking up our strange little relationship.

But when we're dealing day in and out with hard cocks and slick holes and every romance cliché imaginable, it's nearly impossible not to be turned on. It doesn't help that Amanda is attractive. Her eyes are this vivid blue-green that light up every time she writes the word dick, and she has this smile, so beautifully cheeky, that sometimes takes my breath away. Okay, so that's a bit of a cliché, but I do feel breathless when the majority of my blood flow is heading straight to my pants. It's amazing she hasn't noticed my constant erection, though maybe she's just being polite about it. She's so humble she probably wouldn't assume it's for her.

Then there are her lips, which I've been a fan of since day one. If anything, they seem to get wetter, the way her mouth hangs open slightly and her pink tongue peeks out when she's thinking, and I really have to remind myself that she probably wouldn't appreciate me kissing her wildly while she's trying to write.

Probably.

That's what makes everything worse because I know, *I know*, she's getting turned on as she writes. Her eyes get this glossy glazed look and her cheeks flush and she squirms in her seat. She likes to laugh at the overuse of the word clenching, but damn I know she's squeezing her tight little pussy together in my presence, and so help me god, I want in on that.

I'm not made of stone.

And I know it's just a matter of time.

"Blake," my father calls to me, snapping me back to reality. It's almost closing time, and though the store is a mess, I have places to go and porn to write.

I look up to see him and Kevin coming toward me. I guess Angelica must have just dropped him off. And, shit, Kevin's eyes are all puffy and red under his glasses, while my dad's face looks etched in concrete.

"What's up?" I ask them cautiously. I look to Kevin. "Did you reread that scene again where Dumbledore dies?"

"Hey, spoiler alert!" someone among the stacks of books yells.

"*No*," Kevin replies in annoyance, wiping his nose. "We have something to tell you."

My dad comes over to the register and clears his throat. "This may be a shock to hear," he says, lowering his voice. "But Angelica and I are getting a divorce. We've signed the papers. We wanted to wait to tell Kevin so it wouldn't affect his school, but there's a small chance they might be moving over the summer."

I knew about the divorce part. I did not know about the moving part.

"Noooo," I say softly, looking at Kevin. "You can't go."

"I don't want to go!" he says, stamping his foot.

"Kevin!" my dad turns around to admonish him before leaning in close to me. "Don't make this worse, Blake. He's going to have a hard enough time as it is."

I glance at Kevin, standing there in his cape—silver this time—his knee high suede boots, his wooden staff, his glasses, and I know when he moves to another school the kids are going to be brutal. He's almost ten, and if I remember correctly, middle school is when all the world goes to hell.

"It would be nice if you came and had dinner with us tonight," he says.

My heart sinks. I look between the two of them. "I'm sorry. I can't tonight."

"Blake," my dad warns.

"I'm sorry, but I made plans and I'm not breaking them."

"Is it a girl?" Kevin asks in disgust.

"Yes, it is a girl," I tell him. "We're having a cootie convention."

"Seriously son, tell the girl you'll...woo her some other day."

"She's not like that. I mean...I'm not wooing her. I'm trying to woo her. But not in the way you think. I..."

The lines in my father's forehead deepen as he stares at me. "Are you saying you have a girlfriend? Is it serious?"

Well, I certainly can't tell them about the project because I'd be disowned in a second. Knowing my dad, he'd probably boot me out of his will, let the bank repossess the store, and send me back to England. I represent everything he thinks made him fail.

"It's not serious and she's not a girlfriend. She's a friend and maybe I want something more."

At least that's partially honest.

His eyes rake over me, not really believing it.

So I look at Kevin. "Honest. It's true. You know I wouldn't say no for just anybody."

Kevin, such a trooper, nods, even though it's obvious I've decimated his heart. "It's okay. I understand."

Shit. Now I feel like a right wanker.

"Look," I say to him, pasting a smile on my face. "A little birdie told me all about LARPing. What if I take you to one of the all-day events they have at Beacon Hill?"

My dad groans. I ignore him.

"Are you serious?" Kevin asks, his face lighting up like the fourth of July. "Will you dress up?"

"Of course."

"Will you bring your girlfriend?"

I tilt my head. "Um, probably not."

"I want to see you with your girlfriend."

I study him closely. Is it possible he actually doesn't believe me and wants proof? Am I that untrustworthy?

Well, Amanda *is* a giant nerd. She'd probably be thrilled. Maybe not about the fake girlfriend part, but the whole costumes and casting spells and pretending you're an elf necromancer named Whren the White, with ivory tits the size of hippos, who might wear nothing else under her corset. Hmmm. I may have looked up some LARPing porn while I was researching.

With a reassuring smile I say, "Sure. I'll bring my girl-friend. You just look into when it is and we'll make a plan. Okay? I promise."

Even though Kevin leaves happy, I leave the shop feeling seriously deflated. I hop in Mr. Mean and drive straight to Amanda's house, texting her when I'm outside.

She texts back: **You're early! Hey, Ana is out for the night on a date if you want to come in.**

Amanda is seriously inviting me in? I know she's talking about it from a work perspective, but even so, my cock twitches in my pants.

"Oh behave," I hiss at it as I get out of the car and stroll down the driveway to her basement suite.

She opens the door looking absolutely fresh-faced, her hair damp and pulled back into a low braid like she's just stepped out of the shower.

"Hi," she says, smiling broadly as if she's truly happy to see me.

Her smile creates a reflex in me, like yawning, and I'm grinning back at her. In fact, I think a few heady seconds swing past with us just standing in the doorway, staring at each other and smiling like dorks.

She breaks away first and clears her throat. "Come on in." She opens the door wider and gestures widely with her arms. "Your first proper tour of mi casa."

"You know, sometimes I miss having a roommate," I muse as I step inside. The basement suite is pretty bright considering and the walls are done up in yellow and lavender, a total chick pad. I'd been here briefly before, but now I have a chance to take everything in. The living room and kitchen are pretty typical, though the place looks a lot neater than I would have imagined.

"She's entertaining, that's for sure," Amanda says, heading for the fridge and looking inside. "I feel like I should offer you something, but all we have is orange juice and Estonian vodka."

"Maybe later," I say. "Show me your room."

A bashful smile curves on her lips. "This feels so high school."

"Don't worry, I won't try and fingerbang you while we listen to Maroon Five."

"Such a romantic," she mutters dryly, heading for her door.

"That's your job," I remind her, following right behind.

Amanda's room is exactly how I imagined it. And yes, I've imagined it. I've imagined it with the both of us in it in a hundred different positions. My favorite happens to be when she takes out a Harry Potter scarf and lets me use it as a blindfold before I plunge Draco Malfoy's wand inside her.

There's a Ravenclaw crest on one wall, and though I don't see any sign of a wand, she does have a plaque about muggles hanging above her bed. On her bedside table there's a TARDIS alarm clock and a giant Loki figurine made up in Tom Hiddleston's likeness. There's also a giant framed map of Middle Earth that must have cost a fortune, as well as what appears to be signed photos of the cast of *Firefly*, *Sherlock* (with my nemesis Benedict Cumberbatch), and one of George R. R. Martin.

"Ummm," I say, pointing at the photos before getting a closer look. "How did you manage to get these signed?"

She shrugs. "Ebay." Her eyes glance down and she smiles shyly. "So now you know how big of a dork I am."

"Peach, I already knew that the moment you first walked into the classroom. You were wearing a hoodie that said *Straight Outta Hogwarts*. Why do you think I took such a shine to you?"

"You were an asshole. That was you taking a shine to me?" She throws up her hands. "That's it. I really don't understand guys."

I take a few steps toward her until I'm just a foot away. Up close I can see her pulse in her throat, the way her eyes take me in until they're nearly brimming with something so vivid and wild that it's hard to look away.

"We're pretty simple creatures," I tell her, my voice husky in our proximity, holding her gaze, urging her to not be afraid. Because I know she is. I know she's afraid of so many things, most of all letting go. "We just want the pretty girl to like us."

She swallows hard, and I'm staring at the freckles on her throat, her collarbone, the creamy white of her skin. I wonder how she tastes, how she feels. I wonder if she knows just how alike we really are, how this is something we both *need*.

But she averts her eyes, as she always does when I get too close, when I stare too long, and brushes past me, leaving me cold. "We should get to work," she says briskly, heading out to the kitchen.

"Yup," I say slowly, taking a moment to breathe and compose myself before I follow her.

She putters about the kitchen table, clearing away the mounds of makeup and setting up her computer, Kindle, and notebook. She's become Robot Amanda again, her eyes gone hard, her lip stiff. I scared her, enough that she's regressed to the girl I knew in class, but I don't regret what I said. I'm tired of pretending that I don't want to do to her all the things we're writing about.

I'm still standing there watching her, so she pauses and looks up at me over her glasses. "What?"

I shake my head and exhale through my nose. "Don't worry about it."

She holds my gaze for a moment and something passes over her. Regret, maybe. Then she nods. "Sit down. Let's work."

And so we do. And for the first time in a long time, it's strained. I'm about to suggest maybe we need the Estonian vodka anyway when she lets out an exasperated sigh over something she's reading.

It happens to be something I wrote.

"What?" I ask, wondering what I did wrong.

She gives me an *are you kidding me?* look. "Okay, I was ignoring it earlier but I think you need to get a grip on some of this shit. This simply does *not* happen."

"Explain, please."

"I just think it's unrealistic for there to be so much talking, let alone the fact that the first time they do it it's in a public place."

"Too much talking?"

"Yeah." She scans over the document. "You know, give

me your cock, oh you feel so good, harder, harder, you're so big, fuck me harder, big boy."

"Have you even *had* good sex?" I ask incredulously.

She flinches. "Of course I have. And it's none of your business."

"We're writing about sex. It's completely my business. I'm not letting you interject your edits based on your personal experiences about sex, because believe me, if the sex is good, you're moaning my name."

She raises her chin. "Maybe all those girls were faking it."

Oh, brilliant.

"Excuse me?" I say, hands pressed to the table, nearly getting out of my chair. "You have no idea. I pride myself in giving a girl as many bloody orgasms as she can handle."

"Bloody orgasms don't sound like fun," she jokes softly.

"They can be if you're into knife play," I tell her, even though that's not exactly what I mean. Still, she scrunches up her nose. "Don't knock it until you try it, but that's neither here nor there. When you were with Alan, he must have made you come at least a few times."

If he didn't, I feel like finding the guy and showing him a thing or two for wasting four years of her life.

"Yeah," she says flatly.

"And in the middle of that orgasm, didn't you want to yell a few things?"

"Sometimes."

"And why didn't you?"

She looks at her nails as if they're suddenly fascinating. "It didn't seem right. It was...too intimate. I would have felt dumb. He didn't like any of that stuff."

The plot thickens. "Any of what stuff?"

"Sex that didn't involve the missionary position or the bed."

My mouth drops open. My brain and penis can't compute this. "I feel *so* sorry for you."

We must remedy this.

She glares at me. "It's not like I didn't want to do it. I did. And he did try it. Most of it. But it always went back to the same old."

I knew it. She's a nerd on the streets and a freak in the sheets.

"I don't mean to brag," I tell her in all seriousness. "But you do realize that I could give you an orgasm in thirty seconds."

Her eyes widen. I can't tell if she's horrified or intrigued. "I don't believe you and I don't want you to try."

She's not getting it. I frown, trying to explain. "If you're having good sex and it's with someone you're comfortable with, you won't worry about holding back. You'll cry out all the nonsense you want, you'll make noises like a pig, and scream like you're on fire because you truly can't have a good orgasm unless you're letting go on all accounts." I lean back in my chair and study her, running my fingers along my jaw. "I would venture a guess that every time you came with your ex, you were only experiencing half of what you should have been. How is it with your vibrators?"

I expect her to tell me to fuck off, that I'm getting too personal, but to my surprise she gives me a small smile. "It's better. But I do have a roommate with exceptionally good hearing." She clears her throat. "Anyway, so I guess I'm wrong. The heroine can make all the noise she wants."

"And have first time sex in public."

"I don't know..."

"Believe me, when you finally get a chance to fuck, you

don't care where it is. That's why I always have a condom in my pocket. And the more public the sex, the sneakier you have to be, the hotter it is."

"But in the book you would never get caught."

"You don't always get caught in real life either."

I can see she wants to ask me where I've done it, but she loses her nerve. "Okay." She looks back to the document. "I accept defeat."

But I don't want her to. I want to prove to her I'm right and not just have her take me at my word.

Is there a non-creepy way to show her just how good *good* sex can feel? I'm thinking not.

Or...maybe there is.

Might still be creepy though.

I chew on my lip for a few moments, thinking it over. Before she catches my eye, I furrow my brow in false confusion and sigh loudly, staring at my computer screen.

"What?" she asks.

"I don't know," I say carefully. "I'm kind of stuck."

"With what?"

"Well, I mean Ford and Shasta have been having sex for pretty much all of the book so far and I don't want to repeat myself."

She laughs dryly. "Blake, I don't think the average reader is going to notice how many times you use the word cock."

"Yeah, but you know. They might."

"You're being a perfectionist again."

"You should talk, you made me rewrite the classroom scene again and again."

"Because I don't think you can come standing up!"

I give her a withering look. She has so much to learn. "Anyway, so they go back to her place while her parents are out of town for the weekend and they're obviously going to fuck in her bed for the first time."

"According to the rules, it can't be missionary."

"Right. They screw in all directions. I'm just stuck by how to describe the motions in a new way. It's like, I need to see it for myself." I stare at her until she cocks her head at me.

"What are you staring at?" she asks, voice tight with caution.

I get up and walk over to her chair, pulling it out. "Get up."

"Huh? Why?" She looks around in confusion as I grab her arm and try to pull her toward me. Once she's on her feet, I take a firm grasp of her hand and lead her around the table to her room.

"I need your help," I tell her, closing the door behind us and flicking on the lights.

She's standing in the middle of the room, limbs stiff, a deer in the headlights. "With what?"

"My writer's block. Get on the bed."

"Excuse me?" Her voice goes so high I'm pretty sure only dogs can hear it.

I can only grin as I stride over to her, putting one arm around the small of her waist and throwing her back onto the bed where she bounces on her arse.

"Blake," she says, holding out her hand to me, palm out.

"Just give me a minute to show you," I tell her. "It's good for the both of us."

I know she has no idea what I'm about to do which makes it even more fun.

"Spread your legs," I tell her, and when she doesn't because she's looking at me in shock, I reach down and put my hands between her knees, prying her legs apart. "But Jesus, try to relax."

She clamps her knees shut, crushing my hands. "Tell me what the hell you're doing first!"

"Fine," I tell her, retrieving my hands and straightening up. I lower my voice and do my best Morgan Freeman impression. "Ford stares down at Shasta as she lies back on the bed in nervous anticipation. He has a hard time reading her but his confusion doesn't abate the throbbing need in his swollen cock."

Her mouth drops open, eyes nearly popping out of her head.

I continue my commentary. "Shasta's cherry red mouth drops open, anticipating his precum on her lips."

At that, Amanda snaps her mouth shut, though her eyes are still wide and wary. I put my legs on either side of hers, boxing her in. "Ford straddles her, wanting her so badly he can taste it, the honey flavor of her cunt from this morning still on his lips. But he has to take his time. He must." I lean over her until she's lying flat against the bed, her eyes glued to mine as I speak. "Shasta deserves more than having it over in a flash. He wants to make her come again and again and to make it painfully slow."

"Please stop talking like Morgan Freeman," she says softly. "It's making this weirder." But at least she's not telling me to stop in general.

I reach down and slowly slide my hand down her side, the thinness of her tank top betraying the heat of her skin underneath. Suddenly I have to swallow, my narration slipping away as the reality sinks in. I take a shaky breath in through my nose, trying to remember what I was going to say.

"His fingers trail down her stomach to the sensitive

skin of her waist," Amanda whispers, filling in for me, as she closes her eyes, putting her head back into the mattress.

Bloody hell. This is the most erotic thing I've ever seen.

My fingers do as she says, sliding to the bare skin between her top and the waistband of her jeans. I supress a shudder; she's so fucking soft and warm. I'm barely touching her, and she's undoing me. "He wants so badly to let loose, to ravage her with his lips and eager tongue."

"But he needs to take his time," she says, almost a murmur.

Testing my luck, I slowly take my hand to the button on her jeans. "He swiftly undoes her pants."

She stiffens. "But then thinks better of it."

I pause. "He wants to feel how drenched she is."

"But he knows she needs a little more foreplay," she quickly adds.

I can't help but grin. "So he brings his large, bear-wrestling hands up to her breasts."

"But before he does, he brushes his fingers over her shoulders."

And so I do. My hands look so rough and tanned against the delicate silk of her skin. Goosebumps erupt over her limbs while I slowly bring my palms down over shoulders, stroking carefully over her arms.

She arches her back slightly, her eyes still pinched shut but she's breathing harder.

Enjoying this.

I press myself against her leg and she lets out a small gasp.

I lower my mouth to her ear. "He presses his rock-hard cock against her hip so she knows exactly what she's doing to him." I pause then whisper, "How hard it is to hold it together. How badly he wants to come inside her, to feel her from the inside out."

I press my erection into her harder, sucking in my breath. Shit, it really is hard to hold it together. I close my eyes and let out a soft grunt that only makes her press herself into me in response.

I go on, my voice thick with desire. "His lips trail from her ear to her neck where he knows she'll be putty in his hands."

She inhales sharply. "But he knows she wants to be teased as long as possible."

"And yet," I whisper, my mouth hovering just below her earlobe, "she *has* been teased as long as possible. They both have. This was bound to happen sooner or later."

Gently, I press my lips to her neck. So soft at first. Barely making contact.

Her whole body goes rigid beneath me and the kiss hardens, my lips taking in more of her skin. My tongue snags a taste; she's so fresh, tart like lemons, and just like a lemon I want nothing more than to suck and suck.

She lets out a moan so close to my ear that it nearly sets me off. I drag my teeth along the length of her neck and I kiss her again, harder now, sucking in her skin while my dick gets harder between us, and slowly I'm rocking into her, trying to dissolve this maddening tension.

Her arms go around my neck, holding me in place, and I can hear her trying to catch her breath.

"She's not sure if they should be doing this," she says meekly, her voice cut off by a breathless gasp while I swirl my tongue down to her collarbone.

"Even though she's loving it," I murmur against her.

"Even though."

I lift my mouth away, shifting so I'm above her face, and

plant my elbows on both sides of her head. She looks so goddamn beautiful like this, the first time I've really seen her vulnerable. Wild. I've seen it in her writing, but I've never seen it for me. Her lips parted, her eyes closed, her neck arched and begging for more, her cinnamon hair spilling out from her braid.

I slowly take her glasses off her face and place them beside us. But she still doesn't open her eyes.

"He wants her to look at him."

When she doesn't, I run the tip of my finger over her lips. "He wants her to see him."

I watch her throat move as she swallows. "He wants to kiss her," I add.

I lower my mouth so it's just over hers and try to keep my voice steady. "He wants her to want it." I pause, very gently brushing my lips over hers. Electric. "Does she?"

Her eyes flash open, inches from mine. They're fearful and lustful and wanting, and she gives me a barely imperceptible nod.

Yes.

I close my eyes and kiss her, her soft, cushiony lips parting beneath mine. She tastes gorgeous, like mint and orange, and I could drink forever. Her tongue is wet and small and soft as it tentatively brushes against mine. It's good.

So good.

Too good.

I could kiss her into eternity if she'd let me.

A tight noise of want emits from her throat and everything inside me builds, my cock getting stiffer, needing desperate release. The kiss deepens and I want nothing more than to devour her, to let loose this wild, passionate hurricane I'm trying to hold back because if it gets loose, I'll ravage her until she can't walk, until she won't know her own name. I'll show her everything she's been missing and everything she'll be begging for after.

My hands slip down her shirt again, this time sliding under her tank top.

He feels her hot skin; she's nearly feverish with her lust.

My fingers trail up toward her breasts, skimming the edge of her bra.

Expensive lace, he absently notes, wondering if she was planning this.

Her hands come around my neck, holding me in place as she bucks up toward me.

She's desperate now, her pussy swollen and dying for sweet release.

I grasp the edge of her bra, pulling it down until her nipple is exposed. I run the pad of my thumb over it, feeling it harden into a pebble.

Fuck me. If I come in my pants, that's not going in the book.

"'Do you like that?' he whispers to her. I murmur this against her mouth.

"Yes," she says breathlessly, and as I rub my thumb over her nipple again, she stiffens all over, drawn to me, groaning loudly.

"Now that's what I was talking about," I smile, pulling back slightly.

She blinks at me, probably unaware of how loud she was. Luckily she can see well up close, so I know I'm not a blur, even if I might feel like one.

I want to hear more.

"Amanda!?" Ana's booming voice suddenly bursts into our living erotica. "Sweet one?"

We look at each other in fright. "Shit!" Amanda squeaks, pushing me off of her. "The Cock Book!"

Damn it!

We both scamper off the bed, adjusting our clothes before we go running for the door. Amanda flings it open as we burst into the living room.

Ana is frowning at the table, but luckily she's not within reading distance of our work.

"What did you do with my makeup station?" she asks, sounding annoyed, but then as she looks over and spots me standing in the doorway of Amanda's bedroom, her face lights up, going from happy to see me to jumping to all the wrong, yet almost right, conclusions.

"I'm so sorry!" she says in her thick accent, even though she puts her hand on her lips, thrusting out her breasts. Her finger zig-zags between the both of us. "I had no idea you were...here. Together. Like this. This is great!"

I swallow, glancing over at Amanda. She's going around the table, clearing it and closing laptops, and the more I stare at her, the more I realize she's avoiding my eyes.

"Why are you home early?" she says to Ana, trying to play it off. "I thought you had a date."

"I did. The food was excellent," she says with a smile. Then, as if remembering, she holds up a BC liquor store bag. "I bought some wine! Blake, please have some with us."

I scratch the back of my neck, my heart rate slowly returning to normal. "Thanks, that's lovely," I tell her. My eyes dart to Amanda. "But I should be going."

She looks at me, squinting, and maybe she can't see me very well without her glasses. She nods, expressionless. "Okay," she says, her voice clipped. "I'll, uh, see you sometime."

Holy fuck, she's just done a 360 again. The robot is back.

"Right-O," I tell her with a shrug, going to collect my things.

"Oh, don't leave because of me!" Ana protests, waving the bottle around.

"It's getting late," I say with an apologetic smile. "You two ladies enjoy yourself." I nod at Amanda. "Have a good night."

I go out the door just in time to hear Ana ask, "Were you fucking or fighting?"

Once inside my car I feel like I can finally breathe. I wait a few moments, thinking Amanda might run out after me and make plans for tomorrow but that doesn't happen.

Fuck. It was going so well. I came on strong but she was liking it and then...then we were interrupted and her stupid brain had to get involved and freak the fuck out.

Still, she was probably acting that way because Ana was there, and that lady is easily excitable on top of being completely barmy. I should be impressed she gained her composure so quickly.

I'll call her tomorrow. We'll make plans to write.

We'll see what happens in the next chapter.

TWELVE

AMANDA

WHAT THE HELL JUST HAPPENED?

It was my last thought before I fell asleep and my first thought as I woke up.

I lie back in bed, staring at the water stain patterns on the ceiling, as my head once again goes over everything. Only now it's the harsh light of morning and I still haven't figured out how to process it.

Last night...we got carried away. I should have known it was leading to that point. I mean, I kind of brought it upon myself. I shaved my legs. My cooch. I put on my fanciest lace bra and panties. I even wore my hair in a braid, which is one step away from it being down.

I knew Ana was gone (or was *supposed* to be gone) and I invited him over because I wanted him to see that part of me. I was only half-joking when I brought him to see my room—I wanted him to really know who he was dealing with here.

He didn't care. If anything, I think it endeared me to him. I'm sure if I suggested we skip writing and just play Fallout 4 instead all day, he'd totally be down for it.

Video games might have been a smarter choice. Video games don't lead to acting out sex scenes from your erotica novel.

I groan and cover my face with my hands. What am I going to do? We kissed. I felt his erection, how fucking large he is, and it was all for me.

Me.

I mean, how can we go back to just writing and pretending that didn't happen? I don't think I can.

You have to, I tell myself. Otherwise you won't be able to write a word, and throwing away a good thing for a quick fuck is the wrong choice here.

I'm right. I'm usually right. As well as we work together, as much as I've fantasized about Blake that way, sleeping with him would be a massive mistake. It would be good... hot...no doubt wild and sweaty and sorely needed, and god I'd give anything to wrap my hands around his cock, feel how thick he is and...

No. It would be a massive mistake. And he'd never commit to you, so don't even think about having a future together.

Fuck. One kiss and a hint at heavy petting and I'm spending my morning arguing with myself.

Luckily the smell of coffee and bacon brings me out of bed. After Blake left—and I felt kind of bad being so dismissive with him—Ana and I stayed up for a bit watching James Corden and drinking wine. She volleyed a thousand questions at me and I deflected them all with simple yes or no answers. I hope she doesn't start that today because I definitely don't have the patience before my coffee kicks in.

"Good morning," she calls out as I take a seat at the kitchen table. "I'm making bacon and *regular* pancakes."

"I'll just have the bacon," I tell her.

"But I've put the bacon in the pancakes," she says.

I sigh. "Then those aren't called regular pancakes."

"Wow, you're grumpy. I thought all the sex would have helped."

"Again, we didn't have sex."

"Well, you never said what you had."

"Does it matter?" I ask. She comes over and hands me a mug of coffee. "Thanks."

"Drink that and cheer up. This is a great day." She flashes her megawatt ivory-veneered grin at me.

I slurp back the coffee and close my eyes, taking it all in. "It's always a great day for you."

"I had a great date last night," she says. "Life is goooood."

"Do I want to know?"

"Yes," she says, sliding the pancakes onto two plates. "But I don't want to say anything about it in case I, how do you say? Ruin it all to shit." She brings me one, despite the fact I'm waving my hands for her not to. "Eat it, you're too skinny."

"Yeah right," I scoff. I feel like my ass has gotten wider ever since school finished. All this writing and sitting all day has made the excess fat and wine congregate in my butt cheeks. I figure it's my body's way of giving me a permanent seat—you're a writer now, here's your portable cushion!—but even so, it's not appreciated.

"Don't listen to me, then," she says. "Besides, your boyfriend seems to like your body."

"Not my boyfriend," I tell her quickly. "Never my boyfriend."

She opens her mouth but I cut her off. "Not my fuckboy either." Speaking of fuckboy adventures, I wonder if I should text Rio about this. I want to dish all about it but at the same time it doesn't seem right. She'll wonder why I'm spending all this time with someone I'm supposed to hate.

And I do feel like I hate him this morning.

Just a little.

For being so damn smooth.

And firm.

And good with his lips.

Tongue.

The hard length of his cock.

The way he made me moan, louder than I ever have before.

"Look at you," Ana coos. "So in love."

I let out a strangled cry of frustration. "Oh my god, I can't talk to you anymore," I tell her, getting up just as my phone rings. I expect it to be Blake with his ears burning but my heart sinks when I see it's my mother.

"Shit," I swear. "What day is it?" I've totally lost track after school ended.

"Thursday," Ana says.

Fuck. I promised to have lunch with my parents today. They've been hounding me about coming over for ages now and I've deftly avoided it. Until they brought up me being selfish and having no respect and blah blah blah.

"Hello, Mother."

"Don't sound so happy. You knew I'd be calling," her crisp voice comes through.

"It's early."

"Early to bed, early to rise, that's the life of a successful adult," she says, and it's loud enough for Ana to hear because she's already rolling her eyes, motioning that she's blowing her brains out with a gun. I don't know why parents always have to talk so loud on the phone, it's like they think they're underwater trying to talk through a tin can.

"Right," I tell her. "This successful adult is on vacation now."

"That may explain why you've been ignoring your parents. No need for school funding, no need to talk to us."

Ugh. The guilt trip. "I'm not ignoring you, I'm just…so what time is lunch?"

"Eleven-thirty," she says. "Your dad is making your favorite. Don't be late."

I assure her I won't and say goodbye. My parents are these real sticklers when it comes to punctuality. Actually, they are real sticklers when it comes to everything in life that is proper and safe and orderly. No matter how much I feel like I'm progressing and becoming an adult—on my own terms—they're always there to remind me that I'm still their child and most likely doing it wrong.

I show up at my parents' house at twenty after eleven, just in case, and to my surprise I see my Uncle Seth's 1980s hunter green Jaguar outside. Uncle Seth and Aunt Sylvia are ridiculous. When I was growing up I was taught to view them as eccentric, but now that I'm older, I realize they're dumb and kind of senile. I know everyone has relatives and family friends that embarrasses them for one reason or another but these two take the cake.

This is the house I grew up in. It's a large two-story built in 1912, which gives my parents an edge over their friends —at least they think so. "Anyone can build a new house. Not just anyone can buy something historical," my mother has stated. I mean, it is gorgeous and has been updated a lot and I loved how vast the property was as a child. I'd flit around, pretending to be a superhero, running from the nanny and interrupting my father's croquet game.

Yup. Some people actually do play croquet. My parents. Along with bocce ball and any other game that involves standing on the lawn in white pants with a drink in one hand.

Actually, that sounds kind of ideal. Except for the white pants thing.

Out front there's an iron gate flanked by a pristine brick wall that spans the brick driveway and stately columns on the front porch. At the back there is a clay veranda that overlooks the oasis and pond.

That's where I find my mother, Uncle Seth, and Aunt Sylvia, huddled around the table, sipping tea from fine china and snacking on scones and crustless cucumber sandwiches from a copper tiered serving tray. My mother likes to pretend her house is the Empress Hotel when guests are over.

"There you are," my mother says as if they've been waiting forever. "Your father was worried."

I roll my eyes and don't even bother pointing out that I'm early.

My mother gets up and gives me a light hug. She smells like Chanel and disappointment. Aunt Sylvia gives me a shy little wave and Uncle Seth just nods. He doesn't say much in general, which is just as well because the few times he does it's usually racist or sexist.

"There you are," my father says, coming outside, wiping his hands on his apron. At least his hug is more genuine than my mother's. I bask in the affection for exactly three seconds before he says, "You know, I had lunch with Alan's parents the other day."

Everything inside me freezes. "Great. Hope they're well."

No, I don't. I fucking *hated* his parents.

"Where is Alan?" Aunt Sylvia yells in that grating, nasally voice of hers. Think George Costanza's mother on crack. Uncle Seth can't hear that well and she assumes no one else can hear well either.

My mother gives her a look. "You know they broke up in January, Sylvie."

I look at my dad, dying for a change of subject. "Let's eat. I'm starving!"

There's a vague sense of awareness in his eyes before he heads back into the kitchen that perhaps I don't want to talk about my ex.

We head into the dining room and sit down at the table, all made up with layers of place settings like royalty is coming. My father serves my favorite salmon salad, and as usual there's more tea.

Aunt Sylvia gets an extra strong martini, as that's her thing. All day, every day. In fact, my father leaves the shaker beside her glass and a small jar of olives because he knows how fast she'll go through them. Saves time this way.

"So how do you feel having only one year of school left?" my mother asks as she picks at her salad.

Hmmm. A "how do you feel" question. I rarely get those.

"Great," I tell her. "I love school but I honestly can't wait to be done."

"Have you started looking for jobs?" my dad asks.

Sigh. I glance at him, keeping a smile pasted on my face. "Not yet. Next year."

"Do you still want to be a writer?" Sylvia yells over her martini.

Another sigh. "I'm studying to be one."

My dad puts his elbows on the table, folding his hands over each other in a near offering of prayer as he looks to my aunt. "With her degree, Amanda can work as a teacher if she wishes."

"But I'll be a writer," I remind him.

"Even though writers don't make money," my mom scoffs. "Who is going to pay for your place and your clothes and everything else? Once you're done with school, our help is gone. You'll be living on the streets." Here we go. Same old, same old. "You really made a big mistake breaking up with Alan." She throws down her napkin, genuinely upset.

"Um, I didn't love him," I reply testily.

"Why not?"

"Maybe she loves women," Aunt Sylvia yells.

I give her a withering glance before turning back to my mom. "Because I didn't love him. I don't know. He's a nice guy but..."

"The best guy," my mother finishes.

"Men like him don't come around very often," my father says, jumping in. "He'll make one hell of a dentist."

"I'm not sure that's a good thing," I mutter, spearing a piece of salmon with my fork.

"But he could have supported you," my mother says. "If you had just said yes, you'd be planning your wedding right now. I'd be planning it! Then you'd get married when you graduate, you'd be having children by twenty-five and learning what it's like to be a mother, a real woman, and then if you still have your flights of fancy, you could dabble in writing on the side. Maybe write children's books."

My face is burning with rage. I have a million things I want to say and yet my throat is so choked with anger I can't even say it.

"There's nothing wrong with being a lesbian," Aunt Sylvia prattles on.

My mother ignores her. "Amanda, you threw away the one good thing you had going for you. Alan would have made you a woman. Instead you broke up with him, humiliating him in the worst way, and you're back to the petulant child that you are. You'll never grow up now, you'll be lonely and single and chasing something that doesn't even exist."

I'm close to tears now and I *never* cry.

"I love writing," I manage to say, staring down at the salad. "It's what I'm good at. It's what I love."

"I love a lot of things too," my mother says. "And I never even dared to make them a career. You need to stop living in this fantasy land and start living in reality."

"Your mother is right," my father says, voice all low like he's really getting down to business and throwing his man of the house card around. "The minute you graduate, you're getting a steady, respectable job. I don't care where it is, but it's not going to be based on some half-assed dream of yours. Very few people in the world get to write for a living. You have to be pretty damn special to be one of them."

"Oh my god!" I cry out. "You haven't even read my stuff! You have no idea at all if it's any good."

"You know, it's pretty acceptable nowadays," Aunt Sylvia says, sloshing her martini around as it splashes over the side of the glass. "One word—Ellen Degeneres. She's a big deal. Oops, I spilled my drink."

"I'm sure you're good, sweetie," my father says, changing his tone. "But having talent and being good at something doesn't mean you'll get far in life. Stick to what's dependable. You know. Alan's getting pretty serious with a new girl..."

I frown at that. Really? Already??

"Apparently she's going to be a genetic scientist," he

says. "But you know, if you want him back, I'm sure I could put in a word for you."

"Jesus Christ, I don't want Alan back!" I yell.

"Amanda!" my mother cries at me. "You do not use the Lord's name in vain in this house. In any house." Her hand goes to her chest and she looks like she's having a heart attack. "You are just taking a turn for the worse. I think you better start coming to church with me again." She makes a faint sign of the cross.

"When I was in college, I had a very good girlfriend," Aunt Sylvia notes.

"Amanda," my father warns. "You better shape up or ship out. I'm serious. You need to get a hold of yourself and act like an adult, or we'll stop paying for your education. You won't survive very long on a government loan."

I try to breathe in deep but it's hard. My whole chest feels thick, like I'm drowning on the inside. No matter what, they still have this fucking noose around my neck.

"What did we do wrong?" my mother asks my father, shaking her head slightly. "After Dahlia threw her life away, I had such high hopes for this one."

"One night my girlfriend stole some barbiturates from her mother," Aunt Sylvia continues, finishing her martini. "Boy, did we have a wild night. I had rug burns on my knees for days."

I pause mid-chew. Now she has my attention.

"Amanda," my father says. "Just promise me that you'll think about it. About taking him back. Or at least letting us set you up with one of the Birmingham boys. All of them are going to law school now."

I don't say anything. There's no point.

Aunt Sylvia sighs dreamily. "Sometimes I wished I had

run off with her to Mexico like we'd planned. I would have never had to marry Seth."

"What?" Uncle Seth says.

"Yeah, what?" I repeat.

Surprised, Aunt Sylvia looks up at us with glazed eyes. "What were we talking about?"

"Never mind," my father grumbles. "Let's just try and eat the rest of the meal in peace."

And that's how lunch went with my parents. Not only do I think Aunt Sylvia and Uncle Seth are getting a divorce now, but I've learned just how much my parents don't believe in me.

It makes me realize how badly I want this book to succeed, to prove them wrong, even if in secret.

It also makes me realize that there's no guy I want to be set up with, none that I would be interested in dating. There's only one guy for me at the moment.

And after last night, the thought of him scares me more than anything.

By the time I get back home, I've pushed my parents out of my mind and Blake's found his way back in. I'm a nervous wreck again. Fortunately, I have the place to myself so I have time to stew over shit in silence.

Blake hasn't stopped texting me.

Let me know when you're free to talk — Turd Ferguson.

Give a shout when you can — Homer Sexual.

I just booked the editor for this weekend — Yuri Nater

Seriously, I'm not good at this game. We need to talk books. I promise I won't kiss you — Hugh Jass.

Call me for the sake of your future — Mike Rotch.

The last one has me laughing, even though I can't take a threat from Mike Rotch seriously.

I text him back.

What up?

He calls me.

I knew it.

I pick up the phone. "Why can't you just text me?"

"Why can't you use your mouth?" he answers smoothly.

Tread carefully. "I'm better at writing things out than saying them."

"Oh, you mean you're socially awkward and prone to saying the wrong thing all the time? You don't say."

"Shut up. What do you want?"

He snorts in amusement. "What do I want? As your business partner I'm here to remind you that we're on a deadline. We only have a couple of days to finish the book and then it's off to the editor and then it's uploaded to Amazon. Release day, baby."

"Did we figure out a cover yet?"

"The designer is looking. She knows the drill. Hot guy, shirtless, abs for days."

"Well, why doesn't she use a picture of you?"

"Riiiiight. You haven't even seen me with my shirt off. How would you know?"

"I felt your abs through your shirt last night," I tell him.

"Ah. She admits that last night happened."

"Fine, but it's over so please stop talking in third person."

"I'm flattered that you think I do steroids, but honestly I'm way too pretty to be on the cover of an erotica novel."

"I think your ego may be in some need of a boost," I muse dryly.

"So you've noticed? It's hard to stay confident when the main woman in your life won't return your goddamn texts."

"Well, you won me over with Mike Rotch, so what does that say about me?"

"It says let me come get you, let's write this bloody thing."

"Fine. At the library. The one at the school is still open."

"What? Why?"

"I don't think we should be alone together."

Silence. I can practically hear him thinking. "And why is that?"

"Because sex makes things messy."

"Messy is good."

"And according to you, so is greed and we won't even get a chance to be greedy if we're too preoccupied with sex."

"Believe me, you'll be greedy," he says lazily. "You'll have the greediest cunt around once I've gotten through to you."

My cheeks flame. Damn.

"You're speechless," he says after a beat.

I clear my throat a few times. "I'm trying to think of a witty comeback."

"Don't think so much then. In case you didn't notice, we didn't have sex. I just kissed you. *And* I asked permission."

"No you didn't, you just told me you were doing it."

"And you were totally fine with it."

"I was caught up in the moment."

"And there's nothing wrong with that. When should I get you?"

"I'm serious," I tell him, my resolve coming back. "Meet me in the library at six, the same corner we were in the first time we met there."

"Ah, memories."

"See you then." And I hang up on him before he can say anything else.

Lord help me get through this.

~

DESPITE NOT TEXTING RIO EARLIER, SHE ENDS UP texting me about wanting to go to the beach and smoke some weed, so I agree to spend the day with her on the sandy shores of Cordova Bay.

Though the sun is hot and strong and I have to apply SPF 50 every twenty minutes, it's still May and the ocean is only for the brave. I don't smoke a lot of pot but I have a toke or two, enough to just relax and get my mind to stop racing over all the Blake and my family bullshit. Rio, however, runs in and out of the water, shrieking as she goes, much to the annoyance of families nearby. She's actually quite the sight—even though it was her idea to go to the beach and she managed to pack a cooler full of cider and sandwiches, she's wearing mismatching bra and underwear in lieu of a swimsuit and you can totally see her nipples.

I really want to talk to her about Blake but somehow I keep it inside. It helps that when she gets high, she talks a mile a minute and about her own romantic endeavors. I learn that the single dad is gone, some foreign exchange student named Xan is in temporarily, and she's seriously considering abstaining from sex and chocolate for the rest of the summer.

"You're nuts," I tell her.

She shrugs, her dark curly hair falling over her shoulder. She's lying on her stomach on her ratty towel, reading the latest issue of *Travel and Leisure* with a dreamy look on her face. "I like a challenge. Don't you?"

I thought I did. It turns out that the erotica is the easiest part of our whole deal. It's Blake who is going to test me until the very end.

At just before six I get to the library and Blake is already there, the corner set up with his laptop and notepads, and it's like we're starting our night shift at the perv factory.

He looks up at me inquisitively, his hair rumpled, the slate grey sleeves of his shirt rolled up to showcase his strong forearms. He's so utterly gorgeous, I have no idea how I'm going to survive tonight.

"I was worried that you chickened out," he says quietly as I take the seat across from him. My eyes linger on his strong jaw, and I remember the way his stubble scraped against my sensitive skin last night and how badly I wanted him to keep going.

"We've got some smut to write," I tell him, taking out my computer. "A world of horny women is depending on us."

He stares at me for a moment, smiling faintly. There's no masking the sheen of intensity in his eyes, the way they hold me in place.

Please stop staring at me like that, I plead internally, ignoring the flash of heat between my legs. *Say something*.

He doesn't say anything, but he eventually looks away and starts typing. We both have our last chapters to write, which of course are pretty much nothing but sex, then there's the epilogue from Ford's POV, which again is full of weeping cocks and clenching pussies.

Only now I'm stuck, just as he was the other day. I really want this scene to pop, but once again I'm wary that I'm not saying anything new. You wouldn't believe how hard it is to find different words for dick and cock and pussy and cunt. After a while you just have to accept that erotica is going to always be a bit repetitive, even though you strive to be different.

"I, uh, need a new way to describe a cock," I tell him.

He giggles at that, brushing the back of his hand over his mouth.

"Oh, you're so mature," I chide him.

"Hey, I'm a twenty-three-year-old recent graduate. I won't become an adult until I'm forty, if I'm lucky." He pauses and puts his hand to his crotch, looking at me in all earnestness. "Want me to whip it out? Will that help?"

Yes.

"No." I glare at him.

His dimples deepen. "Are you sure? I'd think if you were writing about a thick, veiny cock it would help to see one."

Yes. It would.

"Keep it in your pants." I pause, trying to keep my eyes off his crotch. "Wait, are you saying you're hard right now?"

He scratches at the scruff of his chin, eyes dancing. "Pretty much, considering what I'm writing. Just say the word cock again."

"Fuck you."

"Well, what do you know," he says lazily. "The word fuck works too."

And the way he's saying it, the way it rolls off his tongue all slow and languid, works for me too. But he doesn't have to know that.

I look back to my work and do my best to ignore him, even though he's right there, so fucking close and representing so much I shouldn't have.

The chapters we have left are short and I'm a faster

writer than Blake, so I push through my writer's block by pulling out some secret desires and finishing mine within two hours.

While he's still writing, brow furrowed in deep thought, which I always find comical considering what we're writing, I go and get a bottle of Diet Coke from the vending machine. I normally don't drink anything with corn syrup and chemicals in it but I need something to stay awake.

Or do I? When I get back to the table, feeling the aspartame and caffeine leach into my system, I see Blake's taken my laptop and is reading my chapter. My heart somersaults and I know it's not because of the soda.

I stop by the edge of the table, tapping my fingers nervously along it until he eventually looks up at me.

"I can't believe you just wrote all this," he says softly. His voice is gruff and threaded with amazement.

"You like it?" I ask.

He murmurs an agreement, nodding as he looks it over again. "Darling. You're fucking filthy."

Is it strange to be proud of that? I give him a half-smile, feeling a little self conscious. "You said it needed to go out with a bang."

"Yeah, but I didn't think it would be an anal cream pie kind of bang," he notes, clearing his throat a few times after.

"Those are the best kind of bangs," I tell him, sitting back down. "Let's see what you wrote," I tell him, taking my laptop away from him and reaching for his.

"No way," he says, shielding it. "This is rubbish. I need to top you. You can't out-smut me."

"I think I did." I take a sip of my Diet Coke and grimace at the chemical soup. Felt like a good idea at the time.

There's not much for me to do while he fervently tries to up the smut in his chapter, so I get up again, tossing the almost full can in the trash and head down the aisles to my favorite section: *fantasy*. It's tucked away in the back on this level, and with the library being practically empty during these summer hours, it's like a ghost town. In fact, I think Blake and I are the only people up here and even Treebeard isn't anywhere to be found.

It's just what I need. Writing the anal sex scene between Shasta and Ford in the principal's office got me riled up enough, but now that I've seen Blake's reaction, that heat in his eyes, I can't pretend I'm not turned on. I need the peace and quiet and the wonderful smell of old books to calm me down, so I can regroup and refocus.

But even as I flick through a few Terry Goodkind novels I haven't read, my mind tumbles through the world of "what ifs." What if the book sucks and doesn't sell a single copy? Will we write another one together or is that the end of it? The end of us?

But what if the book does amazing? Am I prepared to keep writing more? Will we work as a duo still?

Will I be able to handle being around Blake over and over again without anything more happening between us?

What if I can't?

I have no answers.

What I do have is his sudden presence at my back. I feel his heat, his height, his strength, his build standing right behind me. I was so wrapped up in my thoughts that I didn't even hear him approach.

I swallow hard, gripping the worn copy of *Sword of Truth* in my hands like it's a life raft. I'm too afraid to turn around because he's right there, waiting for something, for me. I can hear his raspy breath, smell the sage and salt, and feel the electricity thrumming between us.

He doesn't speak. I hear him shift and his hands are at

the back of my head, fingers carefully sliding the elastic down the length of my hair. I close my eyes and try to steady myself as he runs his fingers through my loose strands, spreading it out on my shoulders and breathing it in, before pushing it to the side, leaving the back of my neck bare and exposed.

I inhale sharply, my skin prickling in nervous anticipation.

He places a soft, warm kiss at the back of my neck and my limbs immediately want to turn to jelly from the current of his touch running down my spine.

Stop him, I tell myself. *This wouldn't happen otherwise. You're both just getting high on your own supply.*

Yet I want to get higher.

I want to stop thinking.

I want to be free.

And I want him to show me.

Carefully, as if I'm made of glass, he slips a finger underneath the straps of my camisole and bra and slides them down my shoulder, his lips moving along, his kisses become harder, deeper, hungrier as he goes. I shudder, unable to hide what he's doing to me.

I try to turn around, to meet his mouth, but he holds me in place with a hand at my waist before it slides slowly down my side, over my hips, and down to the hem of my skirt. He slips his fingers underneath the fabric and starts bringing his palm up along my thigh, so large and warm against my sheltered skin.

I have a hard time swallowing. Thinking. I want this so badly, but I know we shouldn't and we shouldn't do it here, but as his fingers curve in between my legs and brush my cleft, I nearly fall over, almost delirious.

"Fuck," he hisses at my back, withdrawing his hand. "You're bare."

"I was at the beach earlier," I tell him, as if that's a reason why I'm not wearing underwear.

"That's even hotter. I'm imagining grains of sand in all those places." He grabs both my wrists, the book dropping to my feet, and raises them above my head so I'm gripping the bookshelves, my back still to him.

"Just hold on," he whispers gruffly.

I don't need to ask him what he's about to do.

I could give you an orgasm in thirty seconds, he'd once said. I smile to myself, resting my forehead against a few copies of Patrick Rothfuss novels, grateful for their soft spines. Even if his claim was all bullshit, I want him to try.

I feel him drop to his knees behind me, his hands running along my ass, squeezing and kneading until they slip under my skirt and gently tease the bottom curve where my cheeks meet my thighs. I stiffen, my skin so fucking sensitive, like a hair-trigger. Yet I'm wanting more, afraid for more, knowing that things are moving so fast and needing them to move faster.

"Patience," he whispers, his voice choked as his fingers slide between my legs. "Do you realize how wet you are?"

I do now. Slowly, deliberately, he drags his long fingers over my clit and I gasp as the bundle of nerves threaten to shatter me.

"God, you're like silk," he murmurs, groaning. "So perfect." He presses the rough pad of his finger over the swell and makes a small circle.

Over.

And over.

Again.

Fuck.

Everything inside me tightens and I feel like a rogue bomb that could go off at any second, right here in the fucking school library. He keeps moving his finger, adding more and more pressure until the tension is nearly unbearable and my skin feels licked by flames.

My skirt lifts up higher and he's adjusting his position behind me. Suddenly I feel his nose, the scruff of his chin on the back of my thighs and I nearly yelp from shock.

"Just relax," he says huskily. "Bite on a book if you have to."

I might have to. He parts my ass with his hands, firmly squeezing my sensitive flesh and I grow rigid in anticipation, waiting, waiting, waiting before I feel his wet tongue snake out between my legs.

The shock makes me shudder.

He's licking my cunt.

From behind.

His face practically buried in my ass.

I hate to be one of those virgin erotica heroines that say oh gee golly but...

Oh. Gee. Golly. And fucking then some.

But before I can come to grips with it, with what's actually happening to me under the bright lights of the library, one of his hands goes to the front of me and his fingers start tapping along my clit, sensitive beyond belief, as his tongue keeps fucking my cunt and I am going lose my fucking mind.

He growls into me, muttering something animalistic, about how I taste like the ocean and his tongue is relentless, and I can feel excess dripping down my legs. My thighs start to shake, trying to keep me upright as my body tenses and tense and tenses and...

Spills.

I grip the shelves for dear life as the orgasm slams into me, and if I weren't holding on I'd be writhing and rolling on the floor. A scream claws up my throat and I bite into the top of a paperback, trying to muffle it. Even though we'd just talked about being vocal the other day, I'm still aware we're in a public place.

He just tongue-fucked me.

From behind.

In the fucking public library!

I don't even know what planet I'm on because I'm not even feeling the slightest bit ashamed. It's like all my dirty fantasies about this place have finally come true.

"That was so fucking hot," Blake says with a groan and I hear what sounds like the crinkle of foil. I have to blink hard to come back to reality, and then he's trying to turn me around, only my hands are gripping the metal edge of the shelves so hard it's nearly impossible to unclench them. I also think I'll fall on my face if I don't have the support. I'm lightheaded and my knees want to give out on me. The orgasm has rendered me into dust.

But somehow I do turn around, pressed against the shelves for support, and the sight before my eyes nearly makes me delirious again. His jeans and boxer briefs are down to his ankles, his cock is protruding out in front of him, and he's preparing to slip on a condom.

I don't have much experience, but it's seriously the largest, thickest, most intimidating dick I've ever seen. In person. And totally on par with what I've seen in porn. The sight of it in Blake's hands, the way his fingers wrap along the thick base and slide up to the darkened tip, precum glistening in the lights, makes my head spin, my body immediately hot with need once again.

"Want to do the honors?" he asks, his voice choked with desire as he slowly slides the condom over the tip.

Jesus.

"It looks like you've got a good handle on it," I practically squeak. I can't tear my eyes away—it's fucking hypnotizing. Still I manage to say, "You're pretty presumptuous."

He grins at me and comes forward, pinning me back against the shelves. "We can quit for today," he whispers against my throat before nipping it between his teeth. "But I felt you squeeze my tongue as you came, like you were milking it. My cock is jealous." He licks up behind my ear and groans. "Don't you want to feel me deep inside you? How hard and thick I am, stretching you, making you full?"

"Yes," I pant, my head going back.

He bends slightly at the knees and his hands go under my ass. Like I weigh nothing more than a feather, he hoists me up and my legs hook around his waist. At first I'm worried he won't be able to hold me up, but there's no sign of concern from him at all except for the faint sheen of sweat on his forehead. He's staring at me like I'm something to be conquered, so much desire and determination in his eyes, a primal need to claim.

He positions his cock at my entrance, teasing it against my clit slowly. A low hiss escapes from my lips, my body wanting to tense up and give in at the same time.

"I'll take it slow," he murmurs in my ear. "At least I'll try to."

He slowly pushes himself in, taking ragged breaths, trying to control himself as I stretch around him. I can't even exhale. All the air, the tension, it's trapped inside me as he works himself in, one wet inch by wet inch. Thank god he already made me wet as sin earlier, otherwise I don't think this would work. He would fucking break me in two.

"Amanda," he whispers, my name urgent on his lips. "Fuck. This is better than I imagined."

"You imagined this?" I manage to say, gasping lightly as he pushes in another inch.

"All the time," he says between groans. "All the time. I've been wanting to do this from the very start. When I first laid eyes on you. I wanted to see how damn dirty you could be. Oh, *fuck*." He pushes himself to the hilt and all the air leaves my lungs. I've never had someone so deep, like he's embedded himself inside me.

"You okay?" he whispers, his hooded eyes searching mine. His fingers brush the loose strands of hair from my face, already damp with sweat.

I nod, trying to swallow, my hands going to his shoulders, trying to hold on. They're rock solid and taut as he strains to hold me up. "I'm good," I say breathlessly.

He gives me the laziest half-grin and slowly pulls himself out. The drag feels incredible, but when he's almost fully out, I immediately crave the fullness.

"How good?" he says huskily, teasing me as he holds back.

I dig my heels into his ass, pulling him back into me.

We both moan and after my breath returns I say, "This good. Keep going."

"Wasn't planning on stopping, peach," he says in a raspy voice, his accent thicker with pleasure.

He plants kisses along my jawline, his stubble razing my skin until his lips join with mine. Our mouths are moving together in a deep, searing kiss unlike the one yesterday, unlike any I have ever had. Our kiss, frantic, hungry, all-encompassing, leads into a rhythm that his body matches with mine as he thrusts his hips forward, his cock driving deeper and deeper inside me. Every nerve in my body is being pulled inward, swirling into a hard knot, live wires tangled, begging to be set free.

He pulls his mouth away, damp from our kiss. "You feel so fucking beautiful," he whispers, staring into my eyes, fevered with desire, and I can hardly believe these words are coming from his lips, that those lips were just kissing me. I can't believe he's just fucking me, here, now, so strong and thick and hard and making my body and soul feel like I'm about to step over the edge of the universe.

I run my fingers down his forearms, feeling the sinewy muscles as he holds me in place, then I brush my hands back up to the hard planes of his shoulders. I dig my fingers in, needing more, wanting more. He growls unapologetically with wild lust, slamming in harder while one of his hands slips down to my clit.

He knows exactly what he's doing.

We're both on the verge, on that precipitous edge, and one of us has to jump.

He strokes his finger along my clit, swirling once, twice, and then that's all it takes.

I'm an earthquake and the world, my world, breaks in two, and fire and light and everything that is explodes from within me. I'm crying out, the whimpers escaping me, and as I hold on to him, as he starts coming inside me, I don't care.

I've always wondered what Blake would sound like when he comes. It's animalistic. It's guttural and primal and he's fucking, fucking, fucking me, the shelves rocking back and forth, his hips thrusting into me until I'm sure they'll leave bruises, until there is nothing left of him.

He sucks in a breath and slows, his hips coming to a lazy stop.

"Well, that happened," he says, his voice broken. He

tries to get better footing and then slowly pulls himself out of me.

I don't even know what's going on. My world is still shattered, spinning on its axis, and all that's left is a warm glow inside me that shines greater than the sun.

He slowly lowers me to the ground and I have to hang on to the bookshelves to stay upright, stacks of books falling out and tumbling to my feet.

"What's going on up there?"

A shrill voice breaks the spell.

I have to blink my eyes a few times to figure out what's happening. The sex has melted my damn brain.

"Bloody hell, it's Treebeard!" Blake exclaims, trying to pull up his jeans.

"You still have a condom on!" I whisper.

"There's no time!"

And there isn't.

Because his pants aren't quite up yet and his sheathed cock is hanging out when Treebeard comes around the corner. It doesn't help that my skirt is still hiked around my waist in bunches.

"What are you two doing?" she exclaims, frozen at the end of the hall as she stares at us.

"Run," Blake whispers to me as he finishes buttoning his jeans.

He grabs my hand and we run down the aisle as Treebeard starts coming after us.

Then we dart up the next aisle, leading her around. "You grab the computers, I'll lead her astray. Meet you outside," he says, and then he's taking off in one direction and I'm going in another.

I hope to god she doesn't come after me because we've been working in a corner, but luckily it doesn't take me long to gather up our stuff and start running down the aisle and to the stairs.

I don't know where Blake is at first, but then I see his dark head disappearing behind the history section and a few seconds later Treebeard (good lord can that woman run). With both messenger bags slung on me like a pack mule, I make a run for the doors, bursting outside into the night just before Blake does.

"Keep going!" he yells, and all my days of running are finally paying off because I plow over to Mr. Mean. But Blake is even more fit, like a superhero, and catches up in seconds.

He runs around and gets in, unlocking my door just as I see Treebeard emerge from the library, shaking her fist at us like something from a cartoon.

I jump in the car but I don't even have a chance to close the door before he drives away, squealing out of the parking lot.

"Do you think she's going to report us?" I ask him breathlessly, watching in the side mirrors as the gleaming glass walls of the library disappear. My heart is racing so hard I can hear it.

"Well," he says, letting out a little laugh. "Let's just say you should avoid that library next year. Or wear a disguise."

"That was my happy place, you know!"

He raises his eyebrows suggestively. "And yet somehow I just made it a hell of a lot happier."

I can't think about that right now. I'm not even over what we did. My skin is hot and flushed, not just from the escape but the damn sex. I'm still aching inside from where he just was.

"Holy shit," I finally exclaim, leaning back into the seat. "I can't believe we just did that." My head lolls to the side and I stare at him, wide-eyed. "I'm not sure that was smart."

"It was the smartest thing we've ever done," he says, turning up "Fur-Lined" by How to Destroy Angels on his stereo.

The jury is still out on that.

"Shit," I swear. "My car is there."

"You can get it tomorrow," he says.

I look out the window as we approach the downtown core. "Where are we going?"

"My place," he says.

He gives me a sidelong glance, razing his teeth over his lower lip. "You know I'm not fucking done with you."

"You're definitely not done with yourself. I believe you have a condom somewhere in your underwear," I point out.

He looks back to the road. "Okay, maybe not my finest moment. All the more reason to get it right the second time."

Despite the muffled protests from my brain, like someone yelling behind a bank vault, my legs are still weak and my lips still remember the taste of myself on his tongue, and my body knows just what it's like to come with him inside me.

There's no going back.

I push my brain aside. My body rules tonight.

THIRTEEN
BLAKE

Holy fucking shit.

That's the only phrase that keeps running through my head as I drive us through the streets of Victoria, heading to my apartment.

That, and bloody hell can Treebeard run fast!

One minute I was sitting in the library, reading over some of the filthiest shit my mind has ever had the pleasure of processing, the next minute I'm watching the creator of it disappear around the library stacks and it's like every single nerd-boy fantasy I've ever had decided to come out to play.

The other day, with her body hot and soft under my hands, that loud, uninhibited moan, the way she pressed into my cock, I knew we were seconds from fucking. If we hadn't been interrupted. I mean, I'm sure Amanda would have had a little freak out at some point because it's taking all of her willpower and stubbornness to pretend she's not attracted to me.

But I know she is. She just needs to shut off the part of her brain that thinks too much, and I refuse to believe that's all that exists in her. I mean, her imagination so far has been as dirty as they come, and her real life fantasies can't be that far behind.

So I followed her down the stacks. Dropped to my knees and gave her pleasure like she's never had before, in a setting I'm sure is dear to her darkest fantasies.

I planned to stop it at that, but she was so wanton and needy and I was beyond turned on from tasting her like that, sinking into her from that angle, that I was ready to go.

And I still am. I'm not about to let her get away, to go back to her home and feel ashamed and pretend this didn't happen. It happened. We both know it's going to happen again.

I park the car in the garage and we ride up in the elevator, the tension between us shimmering and raw. I want to kiss her again, to taste her, hold her, bury myself so deep inside I don't know where she ends and I begin. I know what she feels like now and you can't let go of that too easily.

Once inside, I flick on the kitchen lights, giving the room just enough glow. I head to the bathroom quickly, getting rid of the condom and washing up.

She's still standing in the kitchen, looking around like she's never seen this place before.

We don't say anything. There's nothing to say with words.

I grab her hand and lead her to my bedroom, a place she's only poked her head in before. It feels strangely sacred now, as if I haven't had hundreds of lovers in this bed, as if it's been pure and waiting for her—a blank slate.

She goes to the bed and sits on the edge of it, kicking off her sandals and staring up at me with big eyes while I slowly disrobe. I unbutton my shirt first before tossing it across the room, and I see her eyes drink me in, gazing hungrily at the hard ridges of my abs, the firm pecs on my chest. She even seems to appreciate the light dusting of chest hair and the treasure trail leading from my navel down along the sleek planes of my hips. I've always had good genes from my mother's side, and my daily trips to the gym downstairs have paid off.

My pants go next but she's seen this show before. That doesn't mean she doesn't drink me in though, thirsty for it as my cock juts out in front of me, hard as it'll ever be. She's practically breathless and wide-eyed as she stares, looking a trifle intimidated despite everything.

It's exactly what my ego wants to see.

"Lie back," I tell her gruffly as I get on the bed and crawl toward her, my thick shaft bobbing between us. I put my hands on her shoulders and nudge her back while I settle over top of her. I run my thumb over her lips, pushing gently until her lips wrap around the tip. She sucks softly and I feel the jolt right through me, all the way to my toes.

"I don't think you realize what you do to me," I murmur to her, one hand moving her skirt up around her hips. I remove my thumb and pull her tank top over her head as she arches back to let me. I toss it beside the bed as she deftly undoes her bra.

I stare down at her full breasts, so perfect, spilling to the sides. They seem to glow in the room, pure and flawless, her dark pink nipples hardening before my eyes. I can't help but grin and gently blow air across them. She arches her back again, and I watch her skin prickle as I trace the goosebumps across her chest with my tongue.

She makes this breathy, gaspy sound and I press my body down on top of her so she can feel how hard, long, and ready I am. Her eyes widen but they aren't afraid. She knows now that she can handle it and handle it well.

I reach over to my bedside table for a condom packet, my pulse racing in my wrist, and I spread her legs apart with my knee. I breathe her in, the smell of our sex earlier hitting me like a fucking tonic.

I pause, even though my body is like a bomb ready to trigger, and take it all in. Amanda. Here in my bed. Not groping with our clothes on at her place, not fucking in the library, but here in my bed, naked and vulnerable below me. I know that few men have seen this view before, to have this trust from someone who holds her cards so close to her chest.

This means a lot more to me than I first thought it would. It means a lot more than she could possibly know.

I rip the condom open, sheathing the thin latex over my length. My eyes are drawn to Amanda's as she watches freely in fascination, no rush here now. There's nothing but time and the two of us as she slowly removes her skirt until it's dangling from her foot.

Once the condom is on, I take a shaking breath and lower myself down to her, keeping all my weight on one arm as my free hand snakes between her legs. My eyes close at the feel of her warmth—she's like a hot summer night and I could drown in her headiness.

I bury my head into the crook of her neck, making small, quick bites along her delicate skin until I find the soft, delicate lobe of her ear. I lightly tug on it between my teeth until she moans, her fingers digging into my shoulders, just like she was earlier.

Trying to steady my breath, I slide my hand up to her cunt and a low, guttural groan rises up from my chest. She feels like heaven—just as plump and silky as before, and absolutely wet.

"You're so perfect," I tell her as I push two fingers inside her tight little hole. The way she squeezes around them, holding me, makes my eyes momentarily roll back in my head. My cock swells to the breaking point and I'm not sure how much longer I can hold back. I'm practically panting, working her like this, and she squirms, her head rolling from side to side, that mouth of hers wet and open. Wanting more.

Her breath catches, and her round, pale breasts heave upwards. I run my tongue over her nipples, hard pebbles that respond to my every touch, every smooth lick, and she groans again, louder this time. I want to take her to the limit, I want her inhibitions stripped. I want to watch it all. I push my fingers in further and the groan deepens. Her hips jerk upward, again and again, nearly desperate. Watching her writhe and moan underneath me, from just my fingers feels better than any drug.

I can't take much more. I make a fist around my rigid shaft and position it at her entrance. Her eyes flutter open as I slowly rub my swollen head up and down her silky cleft, taking my time to tease her, to tease myself.

Keep it together Crawford, I tell myself. *Go slow.*

It's the hardest thing. Every nerve in my body is ready to slam into her sweet depths and fuck her until we're off the bed. It takes all my strength to slowly ease my way inside her. She's so hot and wet as I slowly push my way in that I begin to shake. I pause and take in a deep, wavering breath before I continue.

Her face contorts as I push. She's so fucking tight, like a vise. Both of us are breathing hard, sweat building on my brow, our skin damp. When I'm in deep, I slowly pull out again, watching my cock as it withdraws, glistening with her juices.

Heaven. Simply put.

She lies beneath me, her legs hooked around the back of mine, looking too gorgeous for words. Seeing her on the verge of ecstasy like this is part of the problem. I can't take my eyes away and the more I watch her, the more I want to explode.

I slowly pull out and then reach down and hook my arm under her.

"Up," I whisper roughly as I flip her over so she's on her stomach. "Hips up, peach."

She moves back slightly so that her hips and stomach raise off the bed, and she grabs the edge of the blanket, curling her fingers around it.

The sight of her like this gets me even harder, that perfect arse that I've lusted over all year now bare and round in front of me. I can see a small freckle on the left cheek and I dip my head down to nip it.

"Ow," she cries out softly.

"Sorry," I say. "Couldn't help myself there."

I reach down, arcing over her stomach, and place my finger on her clit and rub it around, her juices spreading. I work at her until I feel her widen, her legs spreading more, and then I push in again from this angle. Here she's even tighter. I can plunge deeper and I know I'm hitting all her sweet spots. She gasps and I grab her arse, holding on tight, my fingertips sinking into her soft skin.

She's so wet and lush, I could lose myself in her forever.

But I don't have forever.

My pace becomes quicker as my balls rise, tighten, threatening to let loose inside of her. They smack against her skin, the slapping noise filling the room as I pound her in and out, in and out, quick and relentless, bringing me to the edge.

I groan loudly, unable to keep quiet. The need in me to

come is too sharp, too hard, too much. I slide out slowly and watch my thick shaft, shiny with everything she has, then I plunge back in. My whole body shudders.

"Come for me," I growl at her, knowing I wrote a line like that earlier, but I don't fucking care. I want her to come with me, again and again.

I work my fingers into a frenzy, her face sinking into the blanket and her muffled moans get louder and louder while I slam into her harder and harder.

"Oh my god!" she cries out, followed by a string of nonsense that sounds like poetry right now.

The bed is shaking.

She's shaking.

I'm shaking.

Then I'm coming.

Hard.

I take in a deep breath and let out a low, guttural cry as my coiled muscles let loose and the orgasm rips down my spine, shooting out through every vein. I see the fucking stars. The moon. The light that lives in the back of your head.

Then there's nothing of me left.

I'm empty. Sated.

Boneless.

I lean against her, trying to feel my limbs, my grip on her hips slick with sweat.

She's collapsed into the bed, not moving but breathing hard, her back rising with each breath.

Carefully, I pull out and then through my haze, I tie the condom and toss it into the trash. I lie down on the bed next to her and pull her to me, rolling her over so we're face to face.

"Hey," I say to her, still breathless, propping my head up with my elbow.

She swallows, her face flush and damp, her pupils dark like stones. "Hi."

"So how was round number two?" I ask lazily.

Her lips curve. "Better than round one."

"How so?"

"No librarian running after us?"

"Really? I thought that made things special."

"There are different kinds of special," she says.

I bite my lip and then reach over, playfully dragging the tip of my finger over her nose. "You hungry?"

"For what?" she asks warily.

I roll over and get up, not caring that I'm hanging out in front of her partially erect. "Food," I tell her. "That's happening again by the way" —I gesture to the bed— "but I need my strength."

I grab her hand and pull her up to her feet.

She's immediately bashful, standing there completely naked and awkward, trying to hide her body from me.

I walk over to my dresser and toss her a shirt.

"Here, put that on," I tell her. "Unless you want to be naked. No complaints from me."

She slips the shirt over her head. "This is good, thanks. What's for dinner?"

"Cold pizza," I tell her as we walk to the kitchen.

"Cold pizza? That is so college student circa nineteen eighty-nine," she tells me, leaning against the island counter, as if we were alive then. "Do you have Pepsi too?"

"Well, tonight it's college student two thousand sixteen," I tell her, opening the fridge. "And Pepsi? What's wrong with you?" I pause and peer around the fridge door at her. "You might want to avert your eyes. I have to bend over."

She averts them by way of rolling them up to the ceiling. Good enough.

I get the pizza out and start divvying up slices onto plates. "Ever see that Seinfeld episode where Jerry has that girlfriend that's always naked?"

"Yes," she says. "Please don't open any pickle jars around me."

"No promises." We sit down on the stools at the kitchen island and nibble on our slices. Amanda keeps blushing, and I can't tell if it's because of the good sex, the fact that we're having sex at all, or the fact that I'm naked. I have a feeling her prat of an ex-boyfriend never walked around naked in front of her. She probably only saw his penis in the dark. Might have been a good thing.

I'm staring at her like a total dork, probably with a goofy look on my face, when she stops chewing, her mouth open, the pizza hanging limply from her hand. Her eyes widen, focused on a spot beyond me.

Then her hand starts shaking and the pizza is shaking, and it's like I'm watching that scene with the Jell-O in *Jurassic Park*.

I stiffen. "What is it?" I'm already whispering, preparing for a raptor behind me.

Her eyes dart to mine. "Um," she says, voice squeaking. "Just how dangerous is a tarantula?"

Oh no. Oh no.

No.

My head whips around to see Fluffy on the counter behind me.

I swear he lifts one of his hairy legs and waves it at me, giving me a wink with one of his many dark shining eyes.

There's a split second where everything freezes. Fluffy in mid-wave. My heart. My lungs.

And then Fluffy suddenly moves.

And I don't know if he's flinging himself at me or just running away or what's going on, but I scream bloody murder and I jump to my feet, running clear to the other side of the room. Somewhere in this display of utter cowardice I remember I'm with Amanda. And I'm naked. And still I'm hoping she's a bigger man than me.

But she's also screaming, running down the hall.

"Are you okay?" I yell at her, shudders running through me.

"Yeah!" she cries out from around the corner. "Ahh, I feel like he's crawling on me!"

"Me too!" I slap my hands all over my body. My eyes dart all over the living room, the kitchen, expecting to see that fuzzy rose gold body anywhere.

"What are you going to do?" Amanda yells.

"I don't know. Kill him?"

"You can't do that, it's Kevin's!"

"Fucking Kevin," I mutter. "Fine. I guess. We'll. Capture. Him."

I let out an embarrassing cry.

Amanda cries out too. "Okay. Okay. We'll do it together."

"We better or I'm calling the fire department."

"I can't believe you have a fear of spiders!"

"Why? So do you! And it's a bloody tarantula! It's as big as my hand!!"

"Yeah, but you're a man."

"Well, I'm sorry, I didn't realize you needed tarantula-wrangling skills on top of a massive cock and orgasms to go. Want me to go into the jungle and wrestle an alligator, too?"

"Let's just...get it."

I sigh, trying to gather the courage. "Okay. You come from that direction and I'll come from this one and maybe we can corner him."

I take a few steps, taking stealthy glances around the room. At the moment, everything from the remote to a coaster to a shoe looks like Fluffy.

"Is he actually dangerous?" Amanda yells.

"I did a bunch of research," I yell back. "Once I got him, I wanted to make sure he wasn't a stowaway from *Arachnophobia*. I didn't want to end up like Bill Pullman."

"That was Jeff Daniels."

"Or was it Bill Paxton? Anyway. He's a Chilean Rose tarantula and they're supposed to be docile. But I've seen him eat those crickets, I mean snap their bloody heads off. And I know he looks at me like he's going to do the same."

I creep forward until I'm just past the couch and I see her head peek around the corner of the hallway.

"Are you carrying a weapon?" I ask.

She has a toilet plunger in her hands, holding it like a baseball bat. "I had to grab something."

Damn.

I should have a weapon.

I grab a magazine from the coffee table and roll it halfway into a scoop.

We both edge forward.

Peer over the island.

There he is.

Sitting in the middle of the kitchen floor.

But I swear he's on his haunches and hissing.

Like the bastard is waiting for us.

Come closer, he seems to say. *Come closer, my friend.*

Since he's from Chile, he has the accent and everything.

"Now what?" Amanda asks, gripping her plunger.

"Well, I guess since we can't kill him, we can't manhandle him either."

"So I can't bat him across the room? Because that spider in *Home Alone* put up with a lot."

"No," I tell her with a disappointed sigh. "They're delicate. If you were to handle him and drop him, he could die."

"Accidents happen," she says slowly.

Man, do I love this woman's brain.

I'm smiling but I shake my head and quickly wipe it off my face.

"No. Think of Kevin." I'm saying it more for myself.

I creep forward.

She creeps forward.

Fluffy turns to her.

She freezes.

He turns to me.

I freeze.

Amanda makes her move.

She comes at him with the plunger from behind, getting him moving.

He comes scuttling toward me on those fuzzy eight legs.

Somehow I lower the magazine and he crawls right onto it.

Now I'm holding the magazine at eye level and Fluffy is sitting on it and I'm screaming silently, mouth open and everything.

A living nightmare.

"Get him to his cage!" Amanda yells.

I'm naked, with Fluffy balancing on a magazine, and somehow I make my way down the hall, to the study, and place the entire magazine inside, my hands shaking nonstop.

I withdraw my arms in shock and Amanda quickly puts the lid back on as Fluffy scampers into one of his logs to hide.

"Okay," she says, taking in a deep breath, "you say he's an escape artist, but you left the damn lid off."

I blink. "Shit. I guess I was too preoccupied to pay attention." I give her a look. "With you."

She frowns. "If you're trying to be sweet..."

"It's true. I normally don't forget to put the bloody lid on. If anything, it's all your fault for being enticing."

She rolls her eyes but grins. She takes my hand. "Come with me, naked and afraid man."

Right. The naked thing.

Everything that's happened post-sex hasn't been my finest moment. No wonder the women are only around for one night.

But Amanda leads me back into the bedroom.

And even though I swear I'll never be able to shake what happened, she's pretty good at making me forget.

FOURTEEN
AMANDA

IT TAKES ME A FEW MOMENTS TO REALIZE WHERE I AM. There's a cushiony duvet wrapped around me, and under that, a warm, heavy arm around my side.

Blake's arm.

Oh my god.

I wasn't even drunk last night but it's all coming back to me now in flashes.

Hot, filthy flashes.

Jesus O'Malley.

I feel like I've been hit by a big giant sex bus.

The things he did.

The things we did.

His tongue.

His cock.

Getting caught by the librarian.

Speeding away from the school, laughing, nervous, the stars above us, feeling so fucking crazy.

Coming back here, having him fuck me mercilessly again until I thought I was a prism, shattering with colors.

Then of course Fluffy.

I try not to think about that.

I turn my head to look at Blake, his face smashed into the pillow next to me, deep asleep. Like most people he looks different when he's sleeping. Younger. Vulnerable. Sweet. Though I know Blake is anything but sweet. Sexy, funny, crude? Yes. Sweet? You must be mistaken.

Still, I like seeing him like this and being this close I can observe all the details without those eyes of his watching my every move. He's got two small moles on the left side of his cheek, near his dimples, a smattering of faint freckles across his nose that I don't think were there last month. They must come out with the sun. I lean in closer. There's a faint scar above his upper lip that I bet he got in a fight or from some embarrassing childhood accident.

"Get a good look?" he mumbles.

I gasp in surprise and jerk my head back. He opens one eye and looks at me.

"Were you just pretending to be asleep?" I say softly, my heart thudding in my throat.

Half of his grin is buried by the pillow. "I wanted to see if you'd pull the cliché staring at your sex partner maneuver."

"Sex partner?"

He closes his eyes and tries to shrug. "It's early."

"Well, now that you're awake, I have to go pee," I tell him, prying his heavy arm off of me. I crawl over him ungracefully and scamper to the bathroom, aware that I'm buck naked as I go. I can hear the bed squeaking lightly and he is so obviously turning around to watch me go. Thankfully I remember which door is the bathroom and I don't disturb Satan's hamster.

Once inside, I breathe a sigh of relief, taking in the cool

masculinity of his bathroom, the privacy. I sit on the toilet and put my head in my hands and try to think.

But all I can do is smile.

I just had sex.

A lot of sex.

With someone other than Alan.

And it was the best fucking sex of my life.

And the guy who did it is lying in his bed, with his golden, toned body, all male, all in charge, and it's the guy I never thought it would happen with.

I know I have two choices now. I can go back in there, tell him it was a mistake, and for the sake of our careers we shouldn't do it again. Or I can go back in there and get royally, beautifully fucked again.

Decisions.

But a knock at the door brings me out of my thoughts.

"Are you decent?" Blake asks from the other side. "Or trying to climb out the window?"

I flush the toilet. "Just a minute," I tell him, quickly washing my hands.

I open the door and he's standing there completely nude, his dick looking spectacular even semi-hard. More images from last night flood my brain and I'm surprised at how fast I'm turning into a horny perv at the sight of a half-hard peen.

Of course I'm so distracted by that, that I forget I'm nude too. His eyes rake over my body, probing and relentless, and he gives me a lopsided grin. "I can't believe I have you standing here naked in my bathroom," he says, shaking his head. He then brushes past me. "I have to piss. Give me a second, then we'll take a shower."

Showering together? I quickly get out of the bathroom

and find myself hovering in the hallway, unsure of what to do with myself. Again, I could tell him no.

Or I could shower with him.

I've never actually showered with a guy before. I'm not even sure if it's supposed to lead to sex.

Might be good practice for the next book, I tell myself.

Or I could just run like hell.

The door opens a crack and he peers at me through it. "Good. Thought maybe you left."

I didn't even get a chance. "I'm not going anywhere," I tell him.

He opens the door wider and strides over to the shower, and even though I saw his ass a million times last night during the Fluffy escapade, it's still a sight to behold.

What a fucking wonderful ass.

He turns around, the water running.

And an even better cock.

I mean. Damn. Seriously.

I could write an entire book about his cock.

In fact, I might have to.

I step into the shower, trying to shed any ounce of insecurity.

It's all gone the moment he lays his hands on me.

Soap works its way over my body, over every crevice, his hands gentle with just enough pressure, sliding over my breasts, my stomach, my hips, my thighs.

When I'm slick as anything I return the favor.

I soap up every inch of him as I take it all in, marveling at this fine specimen, his body belonging to a Greek god. Not kidding. Even the overlooked male body parts like calves and feet are perfect. His feet are huge and well-groomed with clipped toenails and no toe hair. His calves are long and broad with the right pop of muscle. No chicken legs, which is such a rarity on guys his age.

Then there are his thighs, looking like they could be sculpted out of gold and on display in a museum as some sort of feat of athletic prowess.

His abs? Zac Efron worthy.

His ass? I can't even go there. I could bounce quarters off it though. And I really, really want to sink my teeth into it, just to see what it feels like.

His back looks like he could rip a door off and throw it fifty feet.

Then again, his chest, shoulders, arms, all say the same thing.

He's not what he would call a "roid monkey," but I say he belongs on a book cover anyway. He's fucking perfect, and way, way too hot for a girl like me.

And I'm going to take complete advantage of it.

He's completely covered in foam from head to toe now.

"Rinse," I tell him, hanging the sponge back up.

He raises his eyebrows, wiping the water from his face. "Bossy."

But he steps into the stream, washing it off.

You see, I don't want soap in my mouth.

And I've been wanting to do this for a while now.

I get down on my knees, ignoring the hardness of the tiles and focusing on the hardness of his cock as it bobs in front of me, water rolling off the broad tip. I wrap my fingers around the thick base of his shaft, tentative at first. I can't remember how Alan wanted to be touched when I gave him head, and Blake is so much more experienced. I don't want to do it wrong.

I take in a deep breath, trying not to choke on the water, and slowly, carefully slide his tip through my lips. I let my eyes fall closed at the sound of his moan. The taste of him, mild in the water but still one hundred percent man, hits my tongue and spurs something deep inside of me, making me crave him even more.

"Shit," he murmurs, voice breaking into a groan, placing one hand against the wall to keep himself upright, those abs of his straining.

I slide my lips to the end then stroke along the underside of his shaft with my tongue, feeling how hot his skin is, smoothing over every vein and rock-hard ridge.

"Look at me," he whispers. "I want you to watch me watching you."

Boldly, I look up and our eyes meet in a current of lust until I put him in my mouth again. It's just too much for him. He pinches his eyes shut, forehead wrinkled, mouth dropping open as he sucks in air.

I want to take my time, watching him slowly succumb to me. There's so much power in my hands and nothing more intoxicating than knowing you're bringing a man to the edge. Blowjobs are not only underrated, they're addictive, and I can easily see myself having a bit of a cock craving when it comes to him. Or a lot of a cock craving. Whatever.

The moans that come out of his mouth now as I work him steadily with my hands, lips, and tongue, are becoming lower, like they're rising from a deeper, more animalistic side of him. I saw parts of this side last night and I want more of it. I want to see Blake surrender to me completely. I want to see him change into an animal with just one craving: me.

His legs stiffen and his body becomes strained, the tension building inside him. I glance up and our eyes meet briefly and his glazed expression tells me that he's in awe, that at least for now, he's mine and at my mercy.

I should be gentle with him.

But I'm not.

If anything, I'm emboldened.

My fist moves faster, slick and wet over his hot length, and my free hand moves up his legs until they find his perfectly groomed balls. I tug lightly, testing him.

"Fuck!" he cries out hoarsely. "I'm coming. I'm coming."

I try not to smile, knowing now what triggers him. His cock becomes hotter, his skin stretched under my lips, and I keep going as I feel him change in my grasp.

Every muscle in his body stills, frozen, as the orgasm hits him, then suddenly he's panting, his breath rough and ragged, and his cum is shooting into my mouth, almost to the back of my throat.

I swallow almost immediately, even though being in a shower is the perfect excuse to spit. But fuck it, he has no problems ingesting me, and when I'm all in, I'm all in. I want every part of Blake, not just some.

"My fucking god," he rasps, leaning against the shower wall, the water still spraying on us.

I carefully get up, my knees aching, trying not to slip on the slick tiles.

I place a soft kiss on his rounded shoulder.

He slowly turns to look at me, his eyes sated, his hair wet and flattened over his head, looking so goddamn beautiful.

"You," he whispers, sounding amazed. "Look at you."

I'm not sure what I look like, my lips swollen from suck-ing, my skin soaked, my hair sticking down my back.

But whatever he sees, he makes me feel like I couldn't be more beautiful.

When we're all clean and dry, it's tempting to just fall

back into bed again. But Blake has to go to the bookstore to work for a few hours.

"You could keep me company," he offers as we get in Mr. Mean.

"I'd love to pop in for a second," I tell him, very conscious of not being that girl who gets clingy after sex. I've learned some things from Rio. "But I've got some errands I have to do in town. I can take the bus back to the school to get my car after."

He frowns. "You sure? I can drive you home when my shift is over."

I smile reassuringly, giving him a dismissive wave. "Don't worry about it. But thank you."

"So," I say to him as we cruise down the busy streets of downtown, looking for parking. "What do you think your dad would say if he knew what we were doing?"

"He'd say, way to go, Son, she's gorgeous."

"I meant about the books. And would he really say that?"

He gives me a look. "Let's not go there. But books? He'd say I'm contributing to something that ruined his life," he says glibly. "What would your parents say?"

"They'd say I'm dragging the family name through the mud. Then they'd say that they're terrible parents and don't know where they went wrong and wonder why both their children ended up being such nonconformists." I pause. "Then my mother would tell me I'm going to hell."

"Tall order," he says. "Another reason to keep Blake Lovecox a secret until the end of time."

"Or at least until we get a movie deal."

"Agreed."

Despite how busy the city is with tourists, the bookstore is actually pretty quiet.

"I thought summer was your busy season," I say.

"It is. Usually when the Clipper ferry or the cruise ships get in. Give it another hour." He leans in close to me. "If it wasn't for that, this store would have gone under long ago."

"You're here," a voice booms from the counter.

I look over to see his father, who could be Blake's double, albeit shorter, rounder, and with glasses. It's funny, I'd always known him as the owner, and now to know him as Blake's dad makes things a lot more interesting. I'm pretty sure he yelled at me once when I was in high school for trying to read "A Feast for Crows" without buying it. As you can imagine, I was here for a long time.

"And on time," Blake says, flashing that charming smile of his on his dad. It doesn't seem to work on him though. Then again, it barely works on me...no, really.

Oh, who am I kidding?

"Who is this?" his father asks.

"Dad, this is Amanda," he says.

"Your girlfriend!" A kid's voice fills the air, and after a few thumps of feet running on the hardwood, I see who I can only assume is Kevin emerging behind a row of books and running toward me with a plastic sword drawn. "You exist!"

My eyes dart to Blake and I raise my brows in question. Girlfriend?

"Yes, my girlfriend," Blake says through a strained smile as he tries to pat Kevin's head.

Kevin shies away and comes right over to me. "You're his girlfriend. I'm his best friend," he says proudly, poking his thumb into his chest.

"This is my stepbrother Kevin," Blake explains.

"Did you tell her about LAIRE?" he asks excitedly.

"Laire?" I repeat. I'm still having problems with the girlfriend thing. Why would he tell them I'm his girlfriend?

"It's an acronym," Kevin explains to me, as if I'm dumb. "Live Action Interactive Role-Playing Explorers. There's a battle at Beacon Hill Park and Blake promised me that the both of you were going to take me there."

Obviously, this is the first I've heard of this. My gaze goes to Blake, amused. "Are you going to dress up like Loki?"

Blake frowns. "Um..."

"Because you know I'll go if you dress like Loki."

He wiggles his lips for a moment, trying to get out of it. "I'm not really sure that dressing up as other characters is allowed..."

"Yes it is!" Kevin says, waving his sword through the air. "That's why this one is so fun! It's like Comic Con but with fighting. I'm going as my own character, Betoolamous the Brave but you can wear whatever you want."

"Still think this is a mistake," their dad says with a sigh, turning back to the cash register. "Why can't you go to a Justin Bieber concert like other kids your age?"

"Dad!" Blake says in horror. "No. That man is no longer child-appropriate. He has a lightning bolt tattooed on his *face*."

"Cool, I want a lightning bolt on my face," Kevin says with a wondrous look. "Just like Harry Potter."

"See what you did, Dad?" Blake says.

"Actually, I think it's a cross on his face," his dad points out, glaring at them both. "But no one is getting any face tattoos!"

I watch them volleying back and forth for a moment before I realize I don't really belong here, and the longer I stand here, the more I have to pretend that this whole girl-friend label isn't weird.

"Well, it was nice meeting you, Kevin," I say, giving him a slight bow since he's holding a sword and all. "Nice to meet you, Mr. Crawford."

"Likewise," he says absently, not looking up from the register.

"Call me," I tell Blake quickly before turning on my heel and leaving before things get weirder.

I'm halfway down the street when I hear Blake calling after me.

I turn to see him dodging a man on a unicycle before he catches up.

"Sorry about that," he says, putting his hand on my shoulder. The unicycle guy pedals past, muttering obscenities.

"About what? Volunteering me for LARPing or telling your family I'm your girlfriend?"

"Both," he says. "Come on, you know how I am. I had to tell them you were a girlfriend to get them off my back. I couldn't tell them you were my writing partner." He runs his hand through his floppy hair and looks off for a moment. When his gaze returns to mine, he flashes me a smug smile. "You know that we're just fucking. That's all we are, all we will be. It's just good fun."

Damn. I have to pretend that doesn't hurt. For all intents and purposes, it *shouldn't* hurt, but it does. C'est la vie.

"Right," I say flatly.

He studies me. "You agree, don't you? I mean that's what you want. To be partners that fuck on the side."

I manage a stiff smile. Sometimes I forget how crude he can be. "As long as writing is the priority."

"Good, yes. Of course it will be," he says, nodding quickly. He shoots a glance over his shoulder. "I have to get back to the store. Send me your files tonight and I'll turn them over to the editor."

"Sounds good," I tell him. "Talk to you later."

I turn away from him and head down the street as a force field comes over me, the one I used to have before I got all caught up in him. I don't have any experience with casual sex, but if I want to keep having my fun, I'm going to have to learn to rein all my feelings in before things get complicated.

Then again, I'm having hot sex with my writing partner. I'm starting to think it's complicated already.

FIFTEEN
BLAKE

I swear I don't understand women.

I never will.

After I shagged the hell out of Amanda and she shagged the hell out of me, she totally lost the plot. And I don't mean that in book terms. I mean, things got weird. I think it was because Kevin called her my girlfriend in front of her. And me. And my father. I could practically see her jumping out of her skin in horror.

But then after I explained to her that we were basically fuck buddies who worked together—an office romance, if you will—that didn't help either. If anything, she seemed to shut down in front of my eyes, completely withdrawing.

If she were any other girl and this were any other situation, I would have just said "see ya, I have no time for your daft bullshit." But because I do like her, you know, as a person, as well as her being a good shag, and I work with her, that really wasn't an option. We had to see each other whether we wanted to or not.

Actually, it ended up being for the best that we couldn't ignore each other.

So we kept on meeting up to work on the book.

And we would put all that weird shit aside and we'd write.

We went through edits together one night.

And then I ate her out on the couch.

The next day we did more edits.

She sucked me off in my car when I dropped her off.

After that we tried our hand at formatting before I took her doggy-style on her bed, not even caring that her room-mate could hear us.

Needless to say, we got the book professionally formatted instead.

Which left us more time to screw.

Fuck.

Shag.

Bang.

Basically anything that involved getting off.

Anything to loosen her up.

Anything to take advantage of her kinky side which was very slowly coming out to play.

And then...

Then we pressed publish.

And we sat back.

Waited.

Until the book was live.

Falling for the Secret Male Stripper, with its pithy blurb and headless model on the cover (holding a Photoshopped ruler, because of course he's also a teacher) popped up on Amazon, ready to purchase.

We did it.

All systems are a go.

Amanda is curled next to me on the couch, her feet pressed up against my side, nursing a glass of red wine. Her glasses are off and her hair is down and her face is flushed for so many reasons, but I know one of them is because I just went down on her moments ago. I can still taste her on my tongue, something I don't mind lingering.

We both have our laptops out, and we're both on Amazon's KDP page monitoring our sales. The Facebook ads just started running, so we're waiting to see if that translates into results because at the moment, we have zero.

I glance at her. "You sure the ad is running?"

"Yup," she says, flicking over to the tab. "But I don't think it's been viewed yet. What about the bloggers you contacted?"

"They said they'd leave their reviews on Amazon today."

"And they're five-star reviews?"

"The ones I saw on Goodreads were," I tell her. "But then there were a few one-star reviews from users who hadn't even read the book."

She scoffs. "Why would people do that?"

"Who knows. Maybe they saw the word "stripper" in the title and got offended."

"Or maybe they read the blurb."

"Or looked at the cover."

"Maybe it's my mom."

"Maybe a stripper broke their heart and it's a trigger book for them."

"Any sales yet?"

"Nope."

After a while, the waiting game gets pretty boring. And tense. And I know what we're both thinking: we've made a huge mistake. The whole thing has gone tits up. Really, who were we kidding?

"Let's go for a drink," I tell her, desperate to get us out

of this funk. We hop in Mr. Mean, cruising around Oak Bay before we head to Spinnakers. When we get to our usual table, Amanda brings out her phone and I can tell she's going straight to the KDP site or the Top 100.

I hold out my hand. "Give it to me."

Her head snaps up, a guilty, pleading look on her face. "Oh please, I have to know."

"Nope." I wiggle my fingers. "Give it or you're getting a spanking later."

A wicked grin spreads across her face and she holds the phone close to her chest. "Promise?"

"Fine. If you don't give it, no spanking."

She grumbles, rolling her eyes, but it works. She hands it over. I take her phone and slip it in my pocket.

"The ads are running," I remind her. "The bloggers are promoting. If we had friends and family to tell, I'm sure they'd be spreading the word but we don't, so this is the best we can do. Let's just see how it does. Tomorrow, if there's nothing, we'll try something else. Maybe more money into ads or try contacting other bloggers. Have a giveaway on our Blake Lovecox author page."

"We have no followers," she points out.

"Maybe tomorrow we will. Hope for the future, live in the moment." I say that just as the waitress delivers our drinks. "And this moment includes drinks."

We say cheers again over our release day.

To being fucking done.

To potential sales.

We clink glasses to us.

We say cheers to letting go.

And we say cheers to good sex because when all is said and done, at least we have that.

I guess we're just a pile of nerves, brimming with weeks

of work and worry and strain because we end up drinking our faces off.

I mean, we got bloody obliterated. I think I start dancing on the pub's pool table at one point, while Amanda rides the cue stick like a horse.

We take a cab back to my place where we promptly pass out on the bed. I have to wonder if all authors go through this on their release days.

When the next morning rolls around—actually it's closer to noon—we can barely remember our names.

It's a good thing.

There's just the both of us, naked, gazing at each other with sloppy smiles, living through the hangover.

Then Amanda remembers the sales.

She stumbles out of bed and staggers to the living room, and I can hear her flip open the computer. I've nearly fallen back asleep when I hear her gasp.

"Oh. My. God. Oh my god!"

She's either having a self-induced "Big O" or something brilliant has happened. I quickly fumble out of bed and join her, blinking hard at the light from the living room windows.

She's kneeling on the floor, pointing to the laptop screen on the coffee table and grinning like she's lost her bloody mind.

"One thousand," she whispers, her mouth dropping open in a contained scream. "Ahhhhh!"

"What?" I'm sure I've heard her wrong.

"One thousand!" she shrieks.

I drop to my knees beside her, resting my hands on her shoulders and holding on tight.

"Open the Top 100, open the Top 100!" I tell her, eagerly peering over her.

Her fingers can't move fast enough.

We both hold our breaths in unison as she clicks along each section until...

Eighty.

We are number eighty.

The fucking eightieth bestselling book in all of bloody Amazon, in all of the millions and millions of books.

Eighty.

I look at her, wide-eyed.

She looks at me.

We burst out laughing at the same time.

"Eighty!" I cry out. "Bloody hell! We fucking made it!"

"The book works!" she says. "The ads work! It all works!"

"We work," I tell her, grabbing her face in my hands and kissing her softly, sweetly, a mix of emotions pouring through me. It only occurs to me then that I normally don't kiss her like this—it's always a part of foreplay or something that happens during sex.

But fuck, it feels good.

It feels right.

I slowly pull back and her eyes slowly flutter open, gazing at me with thoughts I'm too afraid to read into. Something serious beneath all the laughter. Something that strikes me hard in the gut.

I swallow hard and clear my throat. I need to get my head back in the game. "You know," I say teasingly, running my hand down her neck, down her chest, cupping her breast. Her nipples immediately harden as my thumb brushes over them, circular and slow. "I owe you a spanking from last night."

"A celebratory spank?" she asks deviously.

I've never spanked her before so I'm surprised to see her open to it.

"I'm not joking," I say, raising my hand. "Eighty for the eightieth spot."

She wiggles with anticipation and then closes her eyes, mouth open, neck arching back as I pinch her nipple hard.

"Will you pretend to be Ford Titan?" she says huskily, head lolling as I bring my mouth to her nipple and suck. Slowly, gently.

"If you'll be the naughty school girl," I murmur against her breast.

"Do we have a ruler?"

I raise my head, mouth going for her neck. "I have measuring tape."

"Good enough. But you can only use twelve inches. Otherwise it's not fair."

"That's what she said."

"That's what you wish she said."

She's got me there.

~

"We have our first one-star review," Amanda grumbles from the patio.

I pad out of the bathroom, towel wrapped around my waist, and spot her with the computer out, looking like a pile of shit has just been dumped on her.

I mean, she's still stunning wearing one of my worn U-Vic t-shirts, with the sun lit behind her, her face devoid of makeup, the freckles coming through. But her teeth seem to be grinding against each other and I think she's about to toss the computer off the balcony.

"Well, we both knew that was inevitable," I tell her as I

walk up to her, reaching across the table to take a long swing of her coffee. "Not everyone likes every book, and the internet breeds assholes. It's a wicked combination."

It's been three days since the book released and we've spent nearly every moment together watching it climb and climb to the number eleven spot on Amazon's list. It's funny how excited we were with eighty, but now that we're almost in the top ten, it's a letdown to be on the cusp of it. We got spoiled pretty fast, and the fear that we'll fall from our new height is building.

That said, sales are steady, the majority of reviews have been positive, and we've even started getting fan mail sent to our joint Blake Lovecox email account. I know we're supposed to be writing new stuff to keep the momentum going, but the thrill of release week and marketing is taking over. The marketing never bloody ends! We have to pay more attention to our social media feeds—Facebook groups and blogs and Twitter and Instagram and Google Plus (just kidding—no one uses that), and we even got our cover designer to come up with a logo for us. Our tagline? "No gimmicks, just smut."

"I get that people are jerks, but this is different," she says, jabbing her finger at the screen. "This is from a blogger who writes her own books on the side without disclosing it, which is some really shady stuff. All this time she's had a blog and leaving authors all sorts of nasty reviews, then gives her own books five stars. It's not fair and now she's being a total cunt to *us*."

I can't help but laugh every time I hear her use that word. It sounds so wonderfully wrong coming from those sweet lips. "Maybe she was having a bad day."

"Yeah well, we're her biggest competition now so obviously we're on her radar."

"Take it as a good sign," I tell her, coming around and rubbing her shoulders. "This just means we've made people stand up and take notice. The more popular we get, the more arrows will be fired our way, and I bet a few of those reviews come from other authors anyway. But who cares? As long as we keep being honest and doing what we're doing, their own desperation will ruin them. Just ignore them. And stop reading reviews."

"I've tried, I can't help it," she cries out.

I slam her laptop shut. "There. Stop reading them. They will ruin you."

"You haven't even read it!" she protests. "All you've seen are four and five stars."

"And I'm taking the five stars with a grain of salt," I tell her. "Just as you should. Look, we've done the best we can with the subject we had. The book is done. It's released into the world. You can't control how people feel about it so reading reviews is absolutely pointless. Just ignore them and let's move on."

She pouts, looking absolutely adorable. "When did you become such a criticism guru?"

"Darling, I went to an all-boys school in England. You only heard criticism. You learn to handle it."

"And somehow your ego survived intact and grew bigger than ever."

I grin down at her, slipping my hand down the soft skin of her chest. "What can I say, it was overdue."

"Seriously though," she says, putting her hand on mine to stop me. "We have to keep going. With the writing," she adds.

"All right, well, back to the drawing board." I sit down across from her and steal her coffee again.

"Hey," she chides me.

I shrug, wiping my mouth with the back of my hand and pushing it back to her. "Sorry, darling, I'll make you another cup. Okay, so we still have those other ideas we came up with."

She rubs her lips together in thought. "We do. But I think we need more. Our tastes have evolved since then. At least our aspirations have. This book did really well. We have to come up with something that will do equally amazing. We don't want to be a flash in the pan."

"We really should have written in some characters that could have been spun-off of."

"Nah, not in erotica. I say we do a tried and true staple with a twist." She smiles to herself. "What about *Slammed by the Single Dad?*"

I laugh. "That could work," I concede. "I'm guessing it's self-explanatory."

"Yeah...but never mind. Let's put that aside for now."

My mind starts flipping through all the books I see bloggers using all those eggplant emojis for (eggplant equals cock, by the way).

"I've got it," I announce. "*Dirty Broken Bad Boy Billionaire*. About a billionaire with a big cock who loves to eat pussy but can't commit."

"It's been done."

"The title?"

"The concept."

"Yeah...but there's a twist! You see, the heroine is the nanny of his child. And she uncovers a secret about him."

"Sounds a lot like *Falling for the Secret Male Stripper*."

"Well, we can't stray too far from the formula that works."

"All right. *Dirty Broken Bad Boy Billionaire* is up next for Blake Lovecox." She pauses, looking me up and down.

"Can we put you on the cover, wearing a suit? I think that would be really hot."

"Hot for the readers or hot for you?"

"Both."

"I'm okay with that," I tell her, flattered that she wants me on the cover. I flip her computer back open. "Let's leave Ford Titan and Shasta Black in the past for now. Our new hero and heroine need names."

Let the brainstorming begin.

AMANDA

I USED TO THINK ONE OF THE MORE COMPELLING reasons authors write together is because they have someone else to cheer them on, someone to be accountable for besides themselves. If you slack off, you have someone to tell you to pick up the pace, to hit you upside the head, to force you to work. After all, it's harder to let two people down rather than just one, especially if you're used to disappointing yourself all the time.

But the more I write with Blake, the less I get done. Somehow when we hated each other we were able to get a lot more writing done. Now that we've tried to actually make this a career, now that we're actually making fucking money, the words have stopped flowing and writer's block is forever rearing its ugly head in my life once again.

Oh, who am I kidding? I can't pretend I don't know why we've been slacking. It's not the pressure of trying to top *Falling for the Secret Male Stripper* (not entirely). It's the challenge of choosing writing over fucking. Because, Jesus, for once in my life I've got every single sexual fantasy I've ever wanted, everything that my ex never was, all at my fingertips. It's instant access to an orgasm whenever Blake is around, and when he isn't around, I'm getting hand cramps from masturbating so furiously. It's not just the smut that we're writing. It's the smut that we're doing.

Every spare second.

Obviously the only solution is to avoid each other and try and write separately. That was my plan anyway, and I knew just the place to do it. My parents have a cottage on a nearby island that's been in the family for at least fifty years. It's small, nothing fancy, though some of my fondest memories were being young and running amok there with my sister. Usually our nanny Karen would take us there when my parents wanted peace and quiet in the house, but sometimes, some lucky weeks during the dog days of summer, it would be the four of us—Dahlia, me, Mom and Dad. For once I could actually feel what it was like to have a family, and since the cottage is small, we really got to know each other. Even my mother, who never drinks anything other than wine now, would drink beer on the porch, wear flip-flops and no makeup, and take us for walks along the beach while I entertained her with stories.

The minute that I told my parents I wanted to use the cottage for a few days to "relax," the more I realized I wanted Blake there with me. It's a completely stupid idea to invite the very reason why your work ethic is non-existent. But I can't really explain it. It's not that I want his company, I mean the guy drives me crazy outside of the bedroom, but some tiny part of me wants to show him something of my past. Besides, a change of scenery will probably do us some good, and even though it's scary to take the two of us and remove us from the world we're used to, I think it will work out.

If it doesn't completely blow up in our faces.

But we'll see.

First, though, I have to work up the nerve to ask him. And the fact that I have to work up the nerve, that I'm actually nervous, that I'm actually worried, says a lot of things I don't want about me. Mainly that I care what Blake Crawford thinks of me.

Because, shit. I do care.

A lot.

On Wednesday night I send him a text. I'd just seen him yesterday for another writing session turned sex romp, and I'd casually mentioned that the next time we saw each other we had to get something done besides each other.

Totally fine if you say no, but did you want to get away for a few days to write? I was going to go to my parents' cabin on Salt Spring Island this weekend for inspiration. Thought it might help.

I stare at the phone and lie back in bed.

Just staring.

Waiting.

I spy on a few Facebook profiles.

Still waiting.

Paint my nails emerald green.

Still waiting.

I hear Ana opening the fridge so I scamper out into the kitchen, looking for a distraction.

"Busy writing?" she asks me before pulling out a jar of mayonnaise and closing the fridge door with her ass. I watch, mystified, as she unscrews the lid and then dips a spoon inside of the jar. She leans back against the counter, that dollop of mayo resting on the spoon, her dark purple gel nails like dinosaur claws.

God, I hope she doesn't eat that.

"Uh, no," I say. "I'm having a hard time concentrating."

"It's all that penis you're getting," she says, the spoon going to her other hand.

"Cock," I tell her. "It's always cock. Maybe dick. Never penis unless you're talking about someone related."

She scrunches up her nose. "Why would you talk about the penis of someone you're related to?"

"I have no idea but from now on its cock."

She shrugs. "I can deal with cock. I can deal with a lot of cock. This, you know." I watch as she opens her palm and plops the spoonful of mayo into it. She puts the spoon down and starts rubbing her hands together, like she's putting on hand cream.

"What," I start, pointing at her, "uh, what?"

"What?"

I nod at her mayo hands. "What are you doing?" I hiss.

She looks down and grins. "Oh, you've never seen this before?" she asks, seeming pleased. She then starts rubbing her mayo-covered hands over her fucking face. "It's great for your skin."

I raise my brow. "Yeah. I'm sure GMO-filled canola oil does as much good for your face as it does your immune system."

She makes a dismissive sound. "My grandmother used to rub fresh goat's milk all over her face and she had skin like a baby."

I don't bother pointing out that fresh goat's milk and canola oil are like comparing apples and poisonous oranges. Instead, I try not to stare at her in revulsion as her face turns an oily white. It must be the erotica writer in me because all I can think about is how much it looks like an epic cum shot. Cream pies all over the place.

"Well, tell me how I can help you," Ana says as she washes her hands in the sink. "Need me to be firm with you, like a dictator? I have experience."

I shake my head, unable to take her seriously as a dictator with a face full of mayonnaise and/or cum. "No, that's okay. Actually, I may go away for the weekend, you know, for inspiration."

"Oh yes? Where?" She frowns quickly, looking hurt. "Am I too much of a pain?"

"No, no," I assure her, even though she is around an awful lot now that her makeup schooling is over. "It's not you. I just can't think. I can't concentrate and I'd rather be doing everything else except writing. Procrastination is at an all-time high."

"And you're sure it's not me?"

"Nooooo," I say again. "My parents have a cabin on Salt Spring Island, just a thirty-five-minute ferry ride from Swartz Bay. It's small, cute, with a little wood stove and a big deck overlooking the ocean. It will do me some good. Recharge the batteries."

"So you're going all alone..."

"Well..." I say slowly, studying the linoleum pattern on the floor. "I may have just invited Blake."

A lengthy pause falls over us. She takes a moment to think that over, pursing her lips. "I see," she eventually says, her expression growing disarmingly suspicious.

Don't take the bait.

"Interesting."

Don't do it, Amanda. You don't want to hear it.

But I can't help myself. "Why, why is it interesting?"

Damn it.

She shrugs. "I might not know many things, but I know things about people, particularly men."

"Do tell."

"This isn't about writing."

"It is!" I exclaim. "A change of scenery, fresh air, all of that will be good for me!"

She wags her pointed nail at me. "You do not jet off to some island somewhere with another man if you're not interested in him."

"Hey, it's not like I'm not interested at all. I mean...I'm only human."

"Mmm-hmmm."

"I mean..." I bite my lip, wondering how much I should say. "The sex is just...incredible."

Her eyes roll to the ceiling. "I know, I live here, remember?"

I ignore the heat in my cheeks. "But just because I like to have sex with Blake doesn't mean I like him. More than a friend. I mean, I guess it is more than a friend. But we're fuck buddies and that's pretty much it. You know. A fuck-boy, like Rio would say."

"Which makes things kind of complicated when you go away together, don't you think?"

Shit. Will this make things complicated? Maybe I'm scaring him off. Maybe he won't want to write with me anymore...or have sex. I'm not sure I could survive without either.

Then again, the other week we both agreed to get tested for STDs. I mean, that's a pretty big commitment in its own way. It said we weren't sleeping with anyone else. And luckily, the tests came back negative. I've been on the pill forever, so it's just been that much easier, and the sex has gotten that much better. There's *nothing* like the feel of his raw, hard cock inside me.

I just hope I haven't scared that cock away.

"Well, he hasn't responded yet so maybe..." I trail off, wondering if I should quickly send another text, telling him I've changed my mind and would rather go alone. But what if that makes him feel rejected? Wait, can Blake even feel rejected? I'm not sure that's an emotion he's capable of, along with empathy, sympathy, or shame.

"He'll say yes, don't worry," she says with a sigh, heading into the bathroom. "Time to wash this off."

I watch her go and then nervously head back into my room, eyeing the phone as it sits on my pillow, like it's going to lash out at any moment.

You can fix this, I tell myself.

I gingerly pick up the phone and peer at it.

Blake finally texted back, for once not calling.

Sounds great. When do we leave?

Ah.

Shit.

It's Friday morning and I'm standing on the curb outside my place, waiting for Blake. The sun is just starting to peek out over the maples, streaming through in columns of golden light. There's always been something magical about summer mornings. I guess because when I was younger, the summer meant vacation, and if you were up early during the summer that usually meant you were going somewhere fun.

That's true today, but even though I'm excited about heading to the cabin for the weekend, I'm also flat-out nervous as fuck. I woke up before the sun even rose, taking my shower and spending extra time on my appearance, like I'm going on a date. And in some ways, it is a date—a really long one. I also went through my duffel bag for the millionth time, packing and repacking my clothes. I want to stay comfortable, earthy and sexy, which is somewhat of a tall order. The girls in the Free People catalogs can pull it off, but I'm another story.

Even though I'm the one who invited Blake and we're going to my family cabin, he insisted on taking Mr. Mean. Can't say I have a problem with that. The Cooper is cute, but Mr. Mean is a sexy beast, just like its driver.

Butterflies toil in my stomach, heating up my spine and cheeks. I suck in a deep breath and somehow manage to hold it in as I hear the roar of Mr. Mean's engine and see the black car coming around the corner.

Blake pulls up alongside the curb and gets out, shooting me a grin that I wish didn't weaken me in the knees.

"Madame, your chariot awaits," he says, sliding his aviators on top of his head. "Sorry I'm late, I literally rolled out of bed fifteen minutes ago."

"It's fine," I tell him, coming over with my bag. To my surprise he takes it from me and puts it in the trunk, then opens the passenger door, gesturing to it. "After you."

I shoot him a wry look. "How very gentlemanly of you. You feeling okay?"

"Darling, you should know I'm not a morning person by now," he says, going around to his side while I get in. "And you should know that they make me delusional. Appreciate the gentleman while it lasts." He starts the car and slips his shades back down, the corner of his mouth quirking up. "I'm certain all vestiges of decorum will vanish the moment I get you alone."

"Number one," I say to him, holding up a finger. "We're alone right now, and two," I tick off another finger, "you need to stop reading the thesaurus. It's good in a bind and that's it."

He leans over and snaps his teeth at my finger, trying to take a bite out of it.

I shriek, a little too loudly, and then dissolve into nervous giggles, also a little too loudly. I need to calm my panties, stat.

"And you, my peach," he says, "need to relax a little."

"I have been relaxing. Too much. Hence this trip."

"No," he says with a quick shake of his head as we cruise down the tree-lined street, passing by folks walking their dogs and a kid delivering the paper. "I said yes to this trip not because we're going to work."

"What?"

"Let me finish. I said yes because I think the problem you're having with so-called writer's block isn't that you're not inspired. After all, you're getting my dick, how much more inspired can you get?"

"You think that's the solution to everything."

"It's never not been," he admits, and I can tell he believes it. "Your problem, Amanda, is that you're succumbing to the pressure of success."

"The pressure of success?" I repeat. "You really are delusional in the mornings."

"Hear me out," he says, licking his lips. "Look, when we wrote our class project together, we were so focused on just getting it done and producing something and fucking surviving it that neither of us really thought too much about the final grade."

"Speak for yourself," I tell him, even though he's somewhat right. Even though I cared deeply about getting an A and acing it, I also knew I would be graded on how well my part was done and the act of completion, rather than the quality of the story as a whole.

"Then," he continues, "we decided to have a go at Stripper and see if we could really do the whole erotica self-published ebook thing. There was no pressure at all—it was, for all intents and purposes, an experiment. It was for fun. It was a challenge. And it led to some pretty amazing discoveries. Like you're phenomenally good at not only writing about cock but getting it too."

I let out a snort.

"And you're incredibly cute when you make those noises," he adds.

I try not to take that as a compliment. "Anyway..."

"Anyway, now that we've proven we can do it, now that we're committing to do another book, to make the fucking big bucks, to make this something real...the pressure is on. And I don't think I've ever met someone who takes on pressure like a job itself. It's like if you don't feel the weight of the world on your shoulders, if you're not grim and serious and suffering, then it's not real."

I swallow and gaze out the window, wishing I made coffee to go. The coffee at the ferry terminal is heinous and I'm going to need some sort of stimulant to handle all of this. "I can't help it if I take it seriously," I say quietly. "If it's going to be my career, I have to take it seriously. Stephen King said that writing isn't something to be approached lightly."

"Stephen King is also a liar." I frown at him. "He's a liar for a living, all authors are. So are we."

Except we're acting out our written fantasies, I can't help but think.

"Look," he goes on, his tone softening. "I'm not saying we can't take this seriously. I think we already are. We're going about it the right way. But at the same time, we're writing about billionaires and strippers. Respect for the written word and all that, but you have to have fun too, find the joy, and most of all, forget about everything else. Forget about the books. Forget about the future. Writing is about the now, is it not? It's about putting down words and creating worlds and really, that's it. Worrying about how the book will do, how it will be received, whether it will all be worth it is just a waste of time and takes away from the creation of it all."

He pauses and I can feel his eyes studying me underneath this glasses. My face, reflected in the lenses, looks tired and pained. "I agreed to this trip because I think it's a great chance for you to let go. To forget that the whole world exists. Let's not use our phones. No internet. We won't talk about the future or the past. It will just be about you and me and the book and that's fucking all."

Wow. I know he was just telling me not to take things so seriously, but I don't think I've ever seen him look so serious. I wish there wasn't something so incredibly attractive about this, the way he's taking charge and acting like...an adult.

"Okay," I say, my voice soft. I attempt to smile and lighten the mood. "I thought maybe you agreed to this weekend because of sex."

"There are more things to life than sex," he says. "I think writing might be one of them."

I try not to look shocked that he actually just said that. I hate to admit it but this man is doing a pretty good job of keeping me on my toes.

Thirty minutes later we end up at the ferry terminal in Swartz Bay, barely squeezing onto the ferry with our heinous BC Ferries' coffees in hand, one step up from gas-station garbage. There are some giant cruise-ship sized ferries that head to Vancouver and the mainland, but the one that goes to the island is like an open barge. There are some small indoor lounges at the side where walk-on passengers can sit, protected from the elements, and there are some seats above that on the upper deck, but for the most part the ferry is a raft topped with parked cars.

AKA there is no privacy.

AKA anyone can walk past your car at any given time. Or just be parked beside you and look inside.

AKA it's extremely inappropriate that Blake's hand is currently sliding over to my denim shorts, slipping between my legs.

"What are you doing?" I hiss, looking around us to see who could be watching. The ferry is on the move and the people in the truck next to us have left to go sit on the deck. The rest of the cars around us also seem empty, except the sedan on Blake's side. There's an old couple in that one, the woman reading the newspaper, and if they were to even look in this direction they would clearly see what he's doing.

Or attempting to do.

"Relax," he says. "No one is going to see." With his hand he deftly undoes the button of my shorts and works the zipper down.

"Those seniors reading the free newspaper might see!" I tell him.

He looks over his shoulder and grins back at me with those bloody dimples. He really does wield them like a weapon. "I really doubt it."

He leans over a fraction more, his hand slipping down into my underwear, down into my cleft. Surprise, surprise, I'm wet as hell already.

"That's a good girl," he murmurs, his languid eyes

taking me in, watching me, as he glides over me, his fingers long, hard, slick.

Fuck.

I know I really should keep my eyes open, pretend this isn't going on, act natural.

But I want to feel it. Every inch of it.

I close my eyes and rest my head back, melting into the seat and into his touch.

My body prickles with need, so aware of everything. The diesel smell of the ferry exhaust, the salt air coming in through the window, Blake's heavy breathing, the faint, wet sound of his fingers slowly working me. It's not long before the car smells like sex.

"You're so gorgeous," he tells me. "Just like this. Just taking what I'm giving you."

His fingers continue in the lazy motion, like he's beckoning me, but I want more, so much more. My hips start to rock into his hand, my own hands gripping the seat and armrest.

Friction. I need more friction.

For once in my life, I'm too fucking wet.

He groans, withdrawing his hand for a beat and then easing it back in. Teasing me.

I whimper—soft, eager little noises.

"Tell me," he whispers hoarsely, and even the sound of his voice is a turn-on. "Tell me what you want."

I normally don't tell guys what I want in bed. But I think that's Blake's point.

He drags his fingers down, teasing at my entrance.

"Tell me," he repeats.

"To come," I moan breathlessly. "More pressure, your fingers inside."

He slides his fingers inside me and I gasp, my body

clenching around him, holding on, wanting more, so much more where that came from.

"You like that?" he asks, and I know he's watching every inch of my response but I don't care. I like it. I love it. I fucking need it.

"More," I whisper just as he slides his fingers out and comes back in, thicker, with his thumb now rubbing my clit. All the tension inside me spreads and tightens and glows and I know I can't hold back any longer.

I want to tell him to keep going.

But I can't speak.

It doesn't matter that this is happening in plain view of the people on the ferry, it doesn't matter that I feel so bare and vulnerable with Blake once again. It's been this way from the start, from our first encounter in the library. Hell, even before that. When I was writing my heart out, baring my soul for him.

None of it matters because I'm in the here and now and all I feel is a part of him inside me, moving through me in a way no one has.

I come in an explosion, a firecracker, a bomb.

I cry out, soft at first and then louder as the waves grip me, shake me, loosen everything inside me that wants to hold on. My fingers squeeze the seat and armrest until they cramp up, my body jerking with each spasm until they slowly fade away, leaving me in a puddle of bliss.

"You came just in time," Blake says, clearing his throat. "The ferry is docking."

And just like that he takes his hand away and quickly zips up my shorts.

I open my eyes, trying to get my bearings, to see the couple from the truck walking toward us. I button the top of my shorts and straighten up in my seat, shifting toward Blake like I've been talking to him this whole trip.

He bites his lip and grins, his eyes roaming over my face. "Never done that before," he admits.

I raise my brow, still trying to catch my breath. "I suppose I should be honored that I'm the provider of so many firsts for the famous Blake Crawford."

He shrugs. "I'm honored you played along."

We both stare at each other for a moment until the ferry docks with a lurch and the cars start offloading. The lane next to us goes first, and just as the seniors in the sedan pull away, I swear the old lady looks right at me and winks.

SEVENTEEN
BLAKE

Even though I've been living in BC for the past two years, it always surprises me how little of the bloody province I've actually seen. I guess I can't really be held at fault when I've gone home to England every summer and over Christmas, but even so you'd think I would have taken advantage of some of the stunning scenery and destinations from time to time. Don't get me wrong, I love Victoria, even if it tries too hard to be "Little Britain" at times (and nowhere near as hilarious as the TV show), but the warm, Mediterranean climate makes up for it. Still, I hate feeling like there's a whole world out there that I'm turning a blind eye to.

That's one of the reasons I didn't hesitate when Amanda texted me about the weekend. The chance to get away was one I wasn't about to pass up. Plus, she would be there. Plus, she really does need to relax. Plus, well, I have to admit that the pressure is getting to me, too.

I don't want to tell her that though. If I acted anything less than confident, I know she'd put even more weight on her shoulders, and we all know serious Amanda isn't a lot of fun to be around. It's one reason why I can't help but piss her off when she gets that perma-scowl on her face. Relaxed Amanda is a fun Amanda, and fun Amanda is this heady mixture of sexy and adorable, something I can't get enough of, no matter how hard I try to rein it in.

And I have been. Even though my immediate answer was that the trip sounded great, all the warning bells were going off in the back of my head, the ones that are loud and blaring and telling me that I'm veering into unwelcome territory. It's not new to want to keep shagging a girl—if the sex is good, how can you not? But when she's all you think about, every moment of every day, well then, buddy, you have a problem.

I'm determined not to have a problem. But after seeing her come in public, in Mr. Mean, surrounded by people and the ocean and salt-tinged air, I'm starting to think wanting Amanda might not be a bad problem to have.

Then there's the fact that when we pull off the ferry and onto the island, Amanda directs me where to drive, and her whole demeanor changes right before my eyes. She's sitting up in the seat, leaning forward and gazing out all the windows, looking like a child on Christmas morning.

She's beautiful, I think to myself, and the thought catches me off-guard. It's not that I've thought of her as anything but, but for once she's not sexy with eyes full of lust or bitch-hot, like when she's calling me a pig (and god, do I fucking love it when she calls me a pig). She's beautiful in this wholesome, pure, wild way, like she's becoming the sum of all the beauty she sees.

"Wow, I remember that old church!" she cries out softly as the road winds past a small stone Catholic church flanked by old headstones, some draped with what looks like Mardi Gras beads.

The road curves away from the waterfront and sailboats moored out in the bay and heads inland toward an impressive monolith of rock presiding over the valley. "That's Mount Maxwell," she points out. "We'll have to go up there later, if Mr. Mean can handle potholes large enough to swallow him."

"We'll see," I tell her, knowing full well that potholes are my nemeses. As is Benedict Cumberbatch.

"Oh, and the vineyards," she says dreamily as we coast up a hill, vineyards and olive groves flanking us on either side, cascading down the slopes of sun-bleached grass. So far this place isn't at all what I was expecting. It looks more like Tuscany than Canada.

"We have to do a wine tasting one of these days. There are three wineries, a beer brewery, a cider house, and even a lavender farm," she says, her eyes dancing as she takes it all in.

"I thought we were supposed to be writing," I tease.

"It's inspiring."

"Drinking? Of course. Spoken like a true writer."

"Well, you said I needed to relax," she says. "I say we play tourist in the afternoons, you know, as a break. Or a reward."

If I can pull myself off of you, I think. Let's not kid ourselves, writing and wine and sightseeing are all good, but we both know we're spending this weekend with me deep inside of her, everywhere she'll take me.

But none of that seems to be on her mind just now, even though my fingers still smell like her cum, something I want to keep sniffing but don't want to seem like a total pervert, not when she's in this rare joyous element. Talk about a mood changer.

So I keep my dodgy perversion to myself as we wind our

way across the island, past bucolic farms and stately houses hidden among towering trees. I swerve around swaths of bike riders who are pedaling their hearts out on the narrow road, something that looks like total hell, until we finally turn off the main road and head down toward the water.

"Can you imagine living there?" she says, sighing as we go past waterfront houses, their backyards a beach.

"I think you easily could," I point out as we come to the end of the road and head down a bumpy gravel driveway until we stop at what can only be her family cottage. "I mean, this is your family's, right? You'd live here during the summer, be in the city in the winter." I pause. "Naturally I'd have to live here too. Is there an outhouse I could reside in?"

She manages to tear her eyes away from the scenery and looks at me curiously.

"What?" I go on. "You would go crazy here without me."

Maybe that seems too forward, but I don't care. I park the car at the end of the driveway and she opens the door and steps out, her body drawn toward the cottage like a tractor beam.

The cottage is not at all what I was expecting. Given Amanda's family and their wealth, I was expecting something grand and obnoxious, even though she had told me numerous times it was small and modest. Well, she was definitely right. It is small, can't be more than two rooms, and it's a step beyond modest. The first word that comes to mind is *quaint.* Which is one step above "rustic" and "dilapidated."

It's pretty awesome.

"Wow," I say, stepping out of Mr. Mean.

She pauses on the stone path, the squares cracked and

worn, periwinkle and grass running between them, and looks back at me, her brow raised saucily. "Is that ever-present sarcasm I detect? Have I let you down?"

I close the car door and stride over to her, shaking my head. "Not at all. Honestly, the fact that this is your beloved cottage makes me like you just a little bit more."

"A little bit more? That means you must like me somewhat."

"You know I like a lot of things about you," I tell her, running my fingers under my nose and grinning at her. "Why don't we step inside and I'll show you more thoroughly this time."

She rolls her eyes, even though there's a hint of a teasing smile on her hot pink lips. I'm suddenly hit with a strange, almost guilty realization that I haven't kissed her today. I should have her magenta lipstick all over my face, my neck, but instead I got her off on the ferry without touching anything more than her pussy. There's something crude about that, and though that's a feeling I never shy away from, it just doesn't seem right anymore.

"Okay, so maybe the cabin is nothing special," she says as she continues down the path and stops in front of the wide covered back porch along a high bank of grass that overlooks the harbor. She spreads her arms out proudly and throws her head back. "But how can you not be impressed by this view?"

I *am* impressed. I briefly take in the family of quail running from the low hedges and toward steps that must lead down to the beach, the wooden stairway flanked by tall cedars. I notice the covered deck with Adirondack chairs and woven blankets, perfectly set up for the sunrise or star gazing, the stack of firewood in the corner.

I also take in her arse, perky and toned from her crazy

(yet well-appreciated) addiction to running, her legs, her back, that gorgeous red hair of hers, forever bound in that ponytail, and finally, when she turns around to look at me because I've remained suspiciously silent, those lips again.

Before I know what I'm doing, I'm moving down the path like a ghost and grabbing her face between my hands. Her eyes are wide and wild beneath her glasses, and her mouth drops open, so sticky sweet, and I press my lips against hers, inhaling her taste, her scent, the lush softness of her mouth.

For a long, agonizing second she stiffens, unsure of what to do next. I know I've caught her off-guard with this kiss—it's caught me off-guard too. But before I can regret it or second guess it and step away, she's melting against me, her hands wrapping around my waist while mine drift from her face to her hair, to the back of her neck, holding her there while our tongues dance languidly against each other.

I press myself against her, my cock as hard as concrete and straining against my jeans, ready for release. She gives a soft gasp as I dig into her hip, a throaty sound that only makes me thicker. Getting her off on the ferry was one of the hottest things I've ever done and I'm surprised my dick has survived that case of blue balls.

But it won't last much longer.

"Let's go inside," I whisper to her, taking her hand and leading her to the front door.

She fishes a key out from under the mat.

"Really?" I ask.

She waves the key at me and puts it in the lock, opening the door. "Anyone who wants to break in has to hitchhike out here. Believe me, all the riff raff is in town and they're harmless for the most part."

We step inside. The cabin smells like old cedar and

memories, and from the look on Amanda's face, they're all hitting her at once.

She walks to the middle of the small room by the wood stove and sits down on the couch, staring at the board games that are at least as old as she is.

Aside from a small dining table, two couches facing a coffee table, the wood stove, the kitchen, the bathroom, and the bedroom there isn't much to it. It's just enough for one or two people. But I can tell it's more than enough to Amanda.

I sit down on the couch next to her and let her take it in.

After a while I brush the hair back from her face and ask, "What do you want to do?"

At first I'm not sure if she's heard me, she has such a faraway look in her eyes, lost in a memory somewhere. Then she looks at me, blinking back to reality. She takes me by the hand and leads me to the bedroom. "I want your cock inside me. Everywhere."

I gulp, swallowing hard, more than ready.

I follow her, standing in the doorway before the twin bed covered with flannel sheets. She slowly strips in front of me until she's this pale glowing goddess, beckoning me to join her.

Where she goes, I follow.

I strip quickly, feeling fire running through my veins, a sense of urgency unlike any before, and then I'm climbing on the bed after her, prowling like she's the prey and I'm the hunter, or maybe it's the other way around because I'm in her pull, her power, and there isn't anything I can do about it.

She lies beneath me, her hair loose now and spilling around her like a red halo, looking so flawless and pure and soft against the thick flannel. My cock juts out between us, bobbing as I move above her body, and the need to drive myself so deep inside her is more dominant than ever.

It's the need to claim.

To make her mine.

That primal, animalistic instinct to take and hold and possess. As alpha as it sounds, it's real and raw and it's an ache in my chest, clawing its way out of me.

It has been for a long time.

I lower my body onto hers, relishing the feel of her skin against mine, the heat we're already creating. Her legs open wider, parting for me as she raises her hips, but I'm not ready for her now, not yet.

I kiss her, electric, fast, and she slows me down, turning the kiss into something like satin, soft, drawn-out, and deep. Heat slides through my veins, my pulse quickening with lust.

"Turn over," I tell her, and she does. My words come out thick as I face this desperate, trembling kind of hunger.

With the smooth mounds of her arse facing me, I move down the bed and place my tongue on her cheek, making long, wide licks up and then down, back and forth, while I'm squeezing the other cheek. I switch places, paying attention to her signs, how much she wants, if she wants it.

Her hips are rising into me, her arse pressing into my mouth.

She wants more.

Even with my cock almost painfully rigid, everything swimming with this heady infatuation, I slide my finger down her arse cheek, parting them gently.

"Do you like that?" I whisper. Everything is wild and tense.

She makes a sound, tight and breathless, that sounds like "yes."

I draw the finger back up, and she stills for a second before relaxing.

It's the "no, I shouldn't like this" and then the "but I do."

I lower my head and gently blow on her.

She stiffens again, then presses herself back.

More.

I slide my tongue in slowly, my heart intent on climbing out of my chest.

Amanda sucks in her breath sharply; the exhale is a low groan I feel rumble through me.

I slide my hand around, finding her clit and lightly petting it until she's moaning again, her hips circling for more.

Her legs spread wider, giving me greater access in all ways and I'm experiencing her in a way no one has before. If this is akin to claiming something, then I'm planting my flag. But more than that, she's opening up to me, putting her pleasure in my hands, and offering herself. She's vulnerable, something so rare for her, and I want to drown in the feeling.

I can feel her close to coming. She's panting, her body growing warmer, on the verge.

"Oh my god, Blake," she says hoarsely, and I nearly lose my fucking mind. "Keep going."

I do. My tongue plunges in, so tight, and my fingers stroke and circle. She's panting, breathless, needy.

She's incredible like this, about to throw herself over the edge.

And then she goes. It happens quickly, and I feel her unravel under my tongue, my lips, my fingers. She tenses for a split second and the world seems to still, tipping on its axis, and then she's shattering, arching her back, crying out my name.

I lift my head and get off the bed, standing at the end.

I don't give her any time to recover. There is no time. I'm that close.

I grab her hips and flip her over, then reach down around her waist, my hands so large against her, and yank her down toward me until her arse is at the edge of the bed. She stares up at me in a daze, and I know her cunt is still pulsing, the orgasm slowly abating.

Her legs go up along me and I grip the back of her thighs. She manages to reach for my cock, just her touch causing my eyes to close, the breath to leave me.

With a firm grip, she expertly guides me to her entrance, and when I open my eyes she's staring at me with wonder and need and then I'm pushing inside...

Losing myself.

I'm losing myself.

And I don't care.

I groan, the fire building inside me as I push in to the hilt, the pressure reverberating through me.

She's so tight.

A fist of raw silk.

So good.

So good.

And that look in her eyes, the way she won't look away. It holds me captive as I work her, sliding in and out, deeper and deeper the higher she raises her hips. My body gets warmer, tighter, and that coil builds inside, layer by layer, until I know I don't have long.

"Oh, keep going," she manages to say, her head rolling to the side, her mouth open and gasping.

I wish I could go on forever.

I wish I had her forever.

Because being inside her now is different. It's not just fucking. It's becoming something else.

I'm starting to know her in so many ways, inside and out.

My lower back tightens, and everything inside me cracks.

I come, back arching, pushing into her so fucking deep as I grunt loudly, sounding more animal than man.

She's coming again with me, her noises so soft compared to mine, and we're rocking together, joined, until everything inside me is gone.

She has it all.

I collapse on the bed beside her, the flannel scratchy against my cheek, and I pull her into my chest. Even though it's early in the day and we have a weekend ahead of us, there's nothing I would rather be doing than lying right here, listening to the waves, with her in my arms.

EIGHTEEN
AMANDA

Crazy as it seems, the time away with Blake actually seemed to help my writer's block. Ever since we got back, the words have been coming a lot easier. I'm not only working steadily on *Dirty Broken Bad Boy Billionaire* (try saying that five times fast) when I'm with Blake, I'm spending time with Phenelope and Luthwen when I'm not.

Ironically, I don't feel the push to put my characters in a sexual situation anymore. If anything, it's a sweetly romantic one, held back through loads of tension and unrequited feelings as they soldier through their fantasy world. But when it comes to sex, it's pretty much the last thing I want to write when I have scene upon scene of my erotica focused on double penetration with dildos and sixty-nining and anal beads.

I can't say that the increased productivity in our writing has led to a drop in our sex life because that's simply not the case. We've just somehow found a rhythm and made it work. Apparently, exhibitionism seems to be a theme. We made love on the beach, in the car, deep in the vines of a vineyard.

At least, I think it's all working.

The sex is amazing.

But...there's something else.

Something I can't put my finger on.

Something I don't want to put my finger on.

I've noticed it since we got back.

When we fuck, there's this tenderness on both our parts that keeps coming out, wrapping around us like it's second nature. When we're done, we no longer just get up and go back to work and move on with our lives.

We linger. We stay in bed forever. Just talking. About everything. Relationships, childhoods, books, films. We laugh.

We laugh a lot.

And each time this happens something in my heart aches. Because I'm experiencing everything that a relationship should be, but it's not a relationship at all. No one even knows we're together except for Ana, and she doesn't know about the books so the actual whole truth has never been laid bare.

I want to be honest with him. But I don't know how I feel and I don't know where to start.

I really like what we have and I don't want to ruin it.

But I want more.

Not more books, not more money, not more work, not even more sex, as good as it is. I just want more of *him*. I want all that he is and I want to be able to call it mine and dive in and possess every part of him. I know I sound no better than the possessive alphas in our books, but it's true.

He's becoming something more to me, something very real but all we're surrounded by is fiction.

We take a break from each other for a few nights. This is mostly my doing. I need to talk to Rio, need to go out and lift my head out of the sand. I need to see the life around me, the world that exists without the books and Blake. I need to know that no matter what happens, there is always more out there, even when Blake feels like all I need.

"You look like you need another drink," Rio says to me.

We're back at our favorite place, the Tapas Bar, managing to snag a table on the small patio that ducks out into the middle of the alley. The weather is beautiful, a welcome respite after a week of rainy gloom. We're in the heat of summer again.

She pours from a near-empty jug of sangria and it splashes noisily into my cup, spilling a bit onto the table. "Shit, we need more," she says, signaling to the waiter for another. She gets half out of her seat and yells after him, "And napkins too, please!"

I fish the orange out of my glass and suck on it with a sigh. "I'm fine."

I'm not really sure how to tell her I've been sleeping with Blake for a month now. She'll definitely be hurt that I didn't tell her earlier, and when she gets hurt, she likes to hurt others. Like, physically.

"I'd say you need to get laid," she muses, eyeing me over her gigantic sunglasses, "but I'm not sure that's it. Either you've been hitting it hard with your battery-operated boyfriend or you've managed to snag dick elsewhere. You seem a bit...spent."

"Well, I have been running a lot," I tell her, taking a long gulp from my glass. That's still true. When I wake up in my own bed, I try and go running, and sometimes when Blake hits the gym in his apartment building, I'll jump on the treadmill.

Just like fuckbuddies would do, I tell myself dryly.

"That's not it," she says. She leans in closer, her layers of brass bracelets rattling on the table. "Are you doing hard drugs?" she attempts to whisper. Very loudly.

I jerk my head back. "What? No!"

Tell her. Tell her now.

"So, whatever happened with that guy you were seeing?" I casually ask her.

Damn it, Amanda!

She cocks her head, studying me. "You're trying to change the subject. You never ask me about any guy I'm humping."

"Because you always tell me, whether I want to know or not. Anyway, the last text I got from you, you said that God was testing you with copious amounts of brownies and dick."

She shrugs and sips her drink. "Both were enjoyable. But you know what? I'm over men."

"Again."

"Yeah. I mean, what's the point? What can they offer that my fingers can't?"

"Fingers cramp up."

"As do hands when they're giving a hand job for the millionth time."

I give her a look. "Hand job? Who have you been with lately, a sixteen-year-old?"

"Ugh. Even I wouldn't do that. No, seriously. After I get my degree I'm blowing this popsicle stand—"

"Too bad you've already blown everyone in it," I mutter under my breath, just loud enough for her to hear.

She narrows her eyes at me. "I heard that."

"Well, I said it loudly," I retort.

"Don't use *Friends*' references at a time like this. I'm telling you my life plans. This is serious business. Once I'm out of here, I'm traveling the world and teaching English and I'm probably going to go stay at a yoga commune in India and learn to be one with myself, then go to Bali to surf and maybe fall in love."

"That's the plot of *Eat, Pray, Love*."

"It was a good book."

"Yeah." My stomach growls even though I'm not hungry. Nothing like second-guessing your current quasi-relationship to kill your appetite. But I know drinking sangria on a hot day without food is asking for trouble.

I pick up the menu and start considering the options.

Olives?

Fried potatoes?

Rio taps me quickly on the hand. "Oh my god, Amanda," she whispers harshly. "Look but don't look."

Of course I follow her gaze to the alley and look.

Walking on the sidewalk amongst the many people out for dinner and drinks is Blake.

He's wearing black pants and that slate grey dress shirt he wore when we had sex in the library, the shirt that unbuttons just enough to see a hint of chest hair, that showcases those shoulders and large forearms on which I've memorized every freckle and hair. It's one of my favorite shirts on him, and when he wore it the other day for the cover of the Billionaire book, I couldn't help but throw myself at him. As usual.

His hair is shiny, disheveled, catching the evening light and he has this cagey look in his eyes, making him look brooding and intense and all the things I want to see in him.

He looks like mine.

I want him to be mine.

I swallow it down though, prepared to just sit there and watch him move past, his long legs taking easy, casual strides.

Then I realize there's some guy with him. Shaggy hair to his shoulders, tanned, wearing skate shoes, board shorts, and a Quiksilver tank top. The guy probably smells like surfboard wax too.

The two of them look like men on the prowl, and a pang of horror runs through me when I imagine what their plans are. After all, Rio and I are out and I'm keeping an open mind about the guys I meet. Why would I expect less from Blake?

They're almost gone, Blake's gaze now directed at the bricks on the ground beneath them. I almost exhale the breath I've been holding when Rio stands up in her seat and yells.

"Hey, Blake!"

"Oh my god," I hiss at her, grabbing her dress and trying to pull her back down. "What are you doing?"

"It's water under the bridge, isn't it?" she tells me, waving at them.

I dare to look over to the alley. Blake's eyes light up when he spots me. Even though I've never met the guy he's with, he doesn't look too confused. He probably assumes that Blake has slept with one of us.

His assumption would be right.

"Hello ladies," Blake says, hands thrust casually in his pockets as he strolls to the railing between us. His eyes linger on me and they're nothing but warm. "How are we this evening?"

"Where are you guys going?" Rio asks. She gestures to the seats. "Here, sit with us. It's been ages since we've seen you, Blake."

"Yes," he says, smiling at me. "Ages.

I try to show nothing on my face, but I can tell his friend

is studying me very closely. I wonder what Blake has said about me, if anything.

"We'd love for you to have drinks with us," Rio says, finally sitting back down. "And I just ordered more sangria!" She pretty much yells that last part. People in the alley turn to look at us.

I give Blake a withering look. "You better sit with us or she's just going to get louder."

He holds my eyes for a moment saying nothing and saying everything. He nods, biting his lip in that way he does while still smiling.

"Heath," he says to his friend and gestures to the table. "Might as well."

Heath looks at us eagerly. He's definitely game.

"We'll be right in," Blake says, and they disappear inside the front door of the restaurant.

Once they're out of earshot I grab Rio's hand, squeezing it painfully hard. "What are you doing?"

"Ow, you wench," she says, ripping her hand away. "Like I said, water under the bridge. When's the last time you saw him? When you handed in your assignment? That was ages ago. So he was an asshole in class, he's not in class anymore."

"You can't fuck him," I warn, shoving my finger in her face.

She looks completely taken aback.

Just then the boys show up.

"Hey, thanks again," Blake says, taking the seat across from me. "We were looking to get a few drinks somewhere, but every place is packed."

"It's the weather," I tell him.

"What a small town Victoria is," Rio muses.

"Very, very small," Blake says, grinning at me.

I can't help but smile back. Yeah, that smile? Still horribly infectious. Every part of him is horribly infectious. Once you have his cock inside you, that's pretty much all you'll ever want for the rest of your life.

"Amanda," Rio repeats, and I realize she's been talking.

"Huh?" I ask, tearing my eyes away from him.

"I asked you if you had fun working with Blake," she says.

I raise my brows. "Uh, yeah, it was fun."

"She's very smart, you know," Blake says.

"You're not so bad yourself," I tell him lightly.

Heath's eyes are volleying between us. "Wait a minute. Is this the Amanda you had to work with on the book? For school?"

Blake gives him a warning look.

"Yeah, that's me," I say quickly. "Why? What did he say about me?"

"That you were a stuck-up bitch," Heath says.

Blake pounds him hard in the shoulder. "You are such a wanker!"

"That's okay," Rio speaks up. "Amanda hated your guts the whole semester."

"Oh, she told me that," Blake says.

"You thought I was a bitch?" I ask him, surprised, but not exactly insulted.

"Peach," he says, "I've told you I thought you were a bitch."

"No, you said I was a dork."

"And a nerd."

"And a prude."

"And a stick-in-the-mud."

"And a lot of things."

Rio and Heath are watching us. I shrug, trying to act

causal. "Luckily we were still able to work together. We ended up getting an A on the project."

"You know, she's not a prude," Rio says out of the blue, or maybe her mind is just ten steps back tonight. "She just doesn't sleep around."

"That's good to know," Blake says, leveling me with his gaze.

"Wish we could say that about old Blake Dawg here," Heath says. "I'm pretty sure there's a waitress here that wants to kill him."

"What else is new?" Blake and I say in unison.

We both grin.

Eyes twinkling.

And I'm realizing how damn hard it is to sit across from him and not touch each other. Even when we're working, I usually have my limbs draped over him or he has his hands in my hair, or he's stroking his thumb over my shoulder. There's always contact.

"I guess you two really got to know each other, eh?" Rio says carefully. I'm wondering if she's picking up on anything.

"A bit," Blake says lightly. "Wouldn't mind knowing more though."

I feel like I've got something lodged in my throat. I try to swallow.

Then the waitress comes by, and while she doesn't appear to know Blake—thank god—the rest of the conversation eases off of us and onto other topics. All the while though, as the drinks flow and the tapas come out, I feel locked in Blake's force field. From the depth in his eyes, to his easy smile, the way his hand is across the table, so close to mine—he's all I can think about.

It's fucking unbearable.

"I've got to go to use the toilet. Excuse me," Blake says later, getting out of his chair. He turns around, and I see something in his eyes, a beckoning.

I chew on my lip, looking at Rio and Heath who are in deep conversation about travel. And by deep, I mean they're discussing the significance of full-moon parties in Thailand and what drugs to do.

"I'm going to go get a drink from the bar," I say after a minute, but they barely hear me.

I get up and head to the washrooms at the back.

There are only two private stalls and I have no idea which one Blake is in, and now I'm wondering if that look he gave me meant anything at all.

"Blake?" I whisper, looking between the doors.

Nothing.

I decide to try the women's one.

It's not locked.

But there *is* a woman on the toilet, pants around her ankles, doing her business.

"This is occupied!" she yells at me, and I quickly slam the door shut.

"Sorry, sorry, sorry!" I cry out, feeling all sorts of embarrassed even though it wasn't my fault at all. Why do people do that? Just lock the fucking door.

I turn to go for the men's but there's already a man going for it, turning the handle.

He opens it wide and Blake is in there, just standing there in the middle of the washroom.

Luckily he's fully dressed.

"I'm sorry," the man says curtly.

"I was just leaving," Blake explains quickly, coming out of the bathroom and standing beside me. "Hi," he says, peering at me.

"Hi," I reply, smiling like a goof.

The man eyes us suspiciously before closing the door and locking it. The door thumps on its hinges, the man making sure it really is locked.

Then the women's washroom opens and the occupant comes out, glaring at me as she goes.

"You know her?" Blake asks as he ushers me into the washroom.

"Making all sorts of friends tonight," I tell him.

He locks us in, and before I can say another word, he's grabbing my face, lips devouring mine, tongue pushing into my mouth, stroking every pent up desire.

I grab him in kind, my hands in his hair, at the back of his neck while his hands grab my waist, my ass, pinching, groping. We grapple together in a frenzy of heat and lust and something unbelievably real.

I'm pushed back against the tile wall, pinned there, and I'm his, completely his. My body operates on pure instinct, throwing myself into him with no inhibitions, no caution. It craves him as much as my mind and soul do. As he presses against me, breathing hard and kissing me, messy and wet, I put my hands around his shoulders and relish the lean, taut muscles of his back as I pull him in.

One of his hands is lost in my hair, tugging on it the way I like, and I let out a breathless gasp from the sweet pain. The other is lifting up the hem of my dress, shrugging it up around my waist. He slides the satin of my underwear aside and lets out a deep moan that I feel vibrate through me as he explores me with his fingers.

"So wet," he murmurs. "You get so fucking wet for me." He sticks three of his large, long fingers inside me and I clench around them, begging for more.

"Hurry up and fuck me," I tell him.

No, seriously. Someone's going to knock on the door at any minute.

He laughs, low and rich, reaching down to lift me up so my legs are wrapped around his waist. I reach down between us and frantically try to undo his belt. He stares at my frenzied hand for a moment, clearly enjoying just how much I want him.

"Hold on, peach," he says, pulling down his pants and boxer briefs until his cock bobs freely, so dark and rigid. I love him like this, so raw, thick, and all for me.

He holds himself at my opening and waits for a few beats. I can feel the heat coming between us, the way his eyes burn into me, until his gaze drops to his cock as he's about to push its stiff length inside me. Before I can urge him in, my fingers tightening their hold on his back, he pushes with one large, powerful thrust.

I can't help the cry that escapes from my lips, and then the soft, "Oh," as he slowly, agonizingly, pulls himself out, his cock absolutely drenched.

He eases himself back in, a few inches at a time, his lips brushing over mine.

"You're really something, you know that?" he whispers against my mouth, his words breaking off into a groan. "I don't know what I'd do without you."

My heart catches high in my throat. I can't speak, I can only feel, and the intense gaze of his eyes tells me that something is happening, something new. His eyes continue to burn as he pushes himself in and out, pumping steadily. He grabs my chin lightly and holds my face, making sure I can't break eye contact, can't look away. It's nearly embarrassingly intimate, the way his stare feels like he's stripping me bare.

Our moans are hushed, our breaths rough and ragged as

he moves inside me, his hips circling so he hits each and every tightly wound nerve.

It's so fucking good.

It's everything.

We are joined, connected, and the more he thrusts in, deeper, deeper, the warmer he feels, like barely contained fire. A bead of sweat rolls off his nose, and finally his eyes pinch closed as he approaches his climax, his mouth going for the crook of my neck where he bites and sucks and grunts as he pounds me, each thrust getting faster than the last.

"Fuck, fuck, fuck," he hisses, inhaling sharply. "I'm coming."

Before I even have a chance to try and catch up, he lets go of my waist and slides a finger over my clit, petting it twice, and that's all it takes to set me off like dynamite.

I explode outwardly, until I feel like there is nothing left and he explodes into me. I can feel him inside, hot and potent as I throb mercilessly around him, my nails digging so hard into his shoulders as I ride him out that I know they're going to leave marks tomorrow.

My heart is huge, filled with stars and bliss.

This man. This gorgeous specimen of a man, who fucks me with all he has.

I want this man forever.

"Blake," I whisper, trailing off because I can't catch my breath, because I know what I want to say but I don't know how to say it.

He's breathing heavily into my shoulder and I run my fingers through his hair, loving the feel of it, loving everything he is.

"That feels so good," he murmurs.

"Better than the sex?"

"Nothing is better than that." He lifts up his head and gazes at me with sated eyes. He gently brushes his thumbs over my cheeks. "I don't know how to top that."

He's got that look I love in his eyes, the one only I bring to him. Sleepy, relaxed, happy. Absolutely satisfied. But there's tenderness brimming underneath, something rare and beautiful, like a key that makes my heart want to burst free like a bird from a cage.

I smile shyly, suddenly feeling like it's all so much, too much, and if he wants to he can just reach into my soul and walk around in it, examine every inch of who I am and then just walk away.

"We should get back," I tell him.

He nods, brows knitting together for a moment. "Of course." He gently lowers me to the ground and then takes a wad of toilet paper, running it up the inside of my legs where I can feel him drip down. It's such an intimate gesture and yet quite crude at the same time. Pretty much like Blake himself.

We give ourselves the once over in the mirror. He smooths down my dress, I straighten his shirt. We head back outside.

Heath and Rio are still talking and barely look up at us when we return. I know it has to look pretty obvious—the two of us have flushed faces and dilated pupils—but I don't really care anymore.

Later, while Heath goes down the alley to smoke a joint and Blake goes with him, Rio tugs at my hair, much like Blake did earlier. Only this time it's not fun.

"You guys," she says, tugging with each word, "are totally fucking."

"Ow," I tell her, ripping my hair out of her hand. I smooth it back, pouting at her. "Well, it was hard not to be obvious about it. Though I suppose I could have said we were at the bar doing shots or something."

"No, not now," she says. "I mean, of course you just had a bathroom quickie. I'm talking about before this. You guys have been seeing each other, haven't you?"

"We're just friends," I assure her, having a drink of water.

"Friends with benefits?"

"Something like that."

"I don't believe it. It's something more. I've seen the way he looks at you. I've seen the way you look at him. You guys aren't just friends."

I feel my cheeks flame and hope the low lights of the patio hide it well. "I don't know what else to tell you."

But I do.

I could tell her the truth.

I'm falling in love with him.

NINETEEN
BLAKE

"You were in the bathroom for a pretty long time. Food poisoning?" Heath asks all too innocently.

We're walking back from the bar to my place. I really wanted Amanda to come home with me, but Heath is staying over since he got a new apartment in Langford, out of the way, and getting a cab was proving to be way too difficult tonight. God I wish they had bloody Uber in this city.

I don't say anything to Heath. I assumed he was preoccupied with Rio because it was pretty obvious why Amanda and I disappeared for a while. And honestly, I don't want to get into a discussion about her. She's way too personal of a topic now. I want to keep her as close to my heart as possible.

"Dude," Heath goes on. "I have to commend you. She's pretty fucking hot. I'm amazed you've been able to keep it in your pants all this time."

I suck on my teeth loudly and his eyes flit to mine. "Have you been banging her this whole time?" he asks.

"We're just friends," I try and explain, even though I know we're anything but. Even though having sex in a public restroom is nothing new to me and by no means romantic, that meant something. That said something about *us*. How badly we want each other and need each other. It nearly killed me to be at the same table as her and pretend like she wasn't more to me than a casual fuck. She's not that at all, and I don't know how to process it other than to screw her silly.

Maybe that's been our problem. Every time some inkling of a feeling pops up, we jump right into bed with each other and fuck it out of our systems.

But you can't ignore something like that forever.

I fear something like that only comes along once in a lifetime.

I was hoping the fresh air from the harbor on the walk home would help, but Heath's yapping mouth is muddling up my thoughts.

"Just friends," he muses. "A fuckgirl. Have you had any other fuckgirls while you've been giving her the D?"

"It doesn't matter."

"It totally does. You've been fucking the same girl. And only that girl. On more than one occasion. Right?"

"So?" I shove my hands into my pockets and shrug my shoulders up. There's a chill in the air tonight which is odd for summer. Maybe it's because my nerves have me on edge and my gut is churning like I've got razor blades in there.

"So," he goes on, obviously not yet done with this, "you haven't done that once since you and Rachel broke up. I seriously thought you'd fuck the entire city before your dick fell off or something."

"You should talk."

"I should," he says. "But I'm not trying to run away from my problems. I have no problems."

I stop and stare at him. "What does that mean?"

"Other than my life is sweet?" he says, tucking his hair behind his ears. "It means that ever since Rachel cheated on you, you've been having your revenge on her by sleeping with everything that moves. You've been a total dick to them all because Rachel was a dick to you. And you've tried to prove to yourself, over and over again, that you don't need relationships or commitment, or even *love* to have fun."

My mouth drops open. Is Heath seriously lecturing me about love?

"Don't pretend I'm not right, dude," Heath says, kicking at a stone. "We all get screwed over at some point in our lives. It's part of the great circle. The circle of life. You remember *The Lion King*, right? Simba's father dies, so he has to avenge his death by killing Scar, and he becomes so focused on that he nearly messes things up with Nala, the one true thing that will save him more than revenge ever will."

He continues walking down the street and I can only blink at him for a moment before catching up. "Are you sure that's how *The Lion King* went?"

"You know it was based on *Hamlet*, right?"

I'm surprised *he* knows that. "I still don't think..."

"Anyway, Amanda might be your Nala, and that's okay. But don't throw it away because you hate Jeremy Irons."

I shake my head, falling into step beside him. "I'm not throwing anything away."

"You're just stuck and don't know how to take it to the next step. What you really need is to take her on a walk through the jungle, preferably while Elton John—"

"Will you stop with *The Lion King* analogies?"

"Fine. But you have to admit they're helpful."

I'm not too sure about that.

But I do have "Can You Feel the Love Tonight" in my head for the rest of the walk.

Thanks, Heath.

~

"It's enough for this restless warrior," Heath sings from the kitchen, "just to be with you."

I groan and roll over. I thought the song had invaded my dreams.

I get up and stagger out of the bedroom. Heath is fully dressed and belting out the song into a half-empty glass of pineapple juice.

"Hey, you're finally up," he says, stopping his singing mid-lyric and finishing the juice. He pounds the empty glass on the counter. "I'm just about to jet off. There's a good swell off Point No Point."

I eye the microwave clock. It's only eight a.m.

"All right," I tell him, glad to be alone to get my head on straight.

"By the way, I fed Fluffy for you," he says. "I love that little dude. The way he munches on those crickets is so cute."

I raise my brows at him. "Well, one day that little dude might just be yours."

"Awesome," he says with a goofy grin, heading for the door. He pauses. "Oh, and remember to go get that little lion, pound her until she purrs, and tell her how you feel."

"Right."

He gives me the hang loose sign and heads out the door.

I sigh, going straight for the coffee maker. He made coffee and he fed Fluffy. Not a bad guy to have around sometimes.

After I have several cups of liquid gold on the patio, watching the seaplanes take off and the water taxies ferrying people from the taco stands and houseboats at Fisherman's Wharf, I try and go over what to say to Amanda. I might not have to say anything at all. Or that's just wishful thinking since I have no clue what I even want.

Do I want a relationship with her?

I'm not sure if I can open myself up like that again.

Do I want to just keep sleeping with her as is?

Of course. But the feelings are only going to get worse.

Stronger.

Deeper.

Wrapping around me like vines until there's no hope of being cut loose.

What I do know is that she's more than just a writing partner. She's become everything to me. And the last time I had someone be my *everything*, I lost everything when she left me.

I head back inside, the heat already strong this morning, and put on The White Stripes to get Elton John out of my head. I pick up my phone from the charger on the wall, hoping Amanda has texted me.

An email displayed on my lock screen puts my heart in my throat.

It's from Rachel.

Funny how life works like that. Like when you have a dream about some random person and then happen to see them the next day.

I breathe out slowly, trying to expel the tension in my chest, and sit on the bed, taking a moment before I open the email.

Here I go.

Bollocks.

There's a lot to read.

I scan over it, blinking hard at what she's written and going back over it again.

It's not a friendly "hi, haven't talked to you for a bit, how is life?" email.

It's the "I made a huge mistake and I'm alone now and I realize I still love you and miss you more than ever, please come back, we can make this work" kind of email.

The love of my life, the love that ruined me, is admitting she was wrong, is asking for a second chance.

And now.

Now of all times.

Bloody fucking hell.

I drop the phone, my head swimming, trying to process it all, trying to think.

It's enough to make kings and vagabonds believe the very best.

Fucking song.

I think I'm going to need to add a little something to my coffee.

I'm about to get up and rummage through my rapidly-depleting liquor cabinet when the phone starts to ring.

Shit. Don't tell me she's calling me too.

I cautiously pick it up and see Amanda's name flashing across the screen.

Seriously? She never calls me, I'm always calling her.

"Hello?" I answer urgently.

"Hey," she says, sounding small and far away.

"You never call."

"I know."

"How are you feeling after last night? Did you guys stay long? Did you go somewhere else? Did you have fun?" I'm totally rambling like a runaway train here.

She laughs. "You goof. Of course I had fun. I'm good. I just went home after." She pauses and it's obvious there's something on her mind.

"So..."

"Blake, uh, I'm not sure if this is appropriate or not, but my friend from high school, Sarah Price, she invited me to her engagement party tonight. I just saw her back when, well, months ago, and now she's with some guy and anyway, I was wondering if you would go with me."

Oh. *Oh.* Not at all what I was expecting.

"Of course I will. Why wouldn't I?"

"I don't know," she says quietly. "Maybe it's weird."

"Hey, you ask me to do something, I'll do it."

Please don't think something like this is weird.

"Do you still have that suit you wore for the cover?"

"Of course. I'll wear it." I pause. "Are you going to wear your hair down?"

"I'm not fucking Rapunzel," she scoffs. "Anyway, uh... do you mind picking me up? Maybe around seven?"

"You don't want to do some writing today?"

She lets out a dry laugh. "I'm going to a party where all my old high school friends will be. I need a dress, badly. Something to make them look twice."

"Now I see why you need me," I joke.

"Well, that's part of it."

"I'm flattered."

"When aren't you? See you at seven?"

"See you."

I hang up and stare at the phone, going back to Rachel's email and reading it over again.

~

At seven I'm knocking on Amanda's door and swatting at a moth that's taken a liking to my face. I have to admit, I'm actually nervous. I feel like I'm taking a date to the prom or something. My palms keep getting sweaty, and I have to wipe them on my pants.

The door opens a crack and part of Amanda's face peeks out.

"Hey," she says, and even though I can only see her eyes, lips, and cheeks, she looks bloody gorgeous. She isn't even wearing her glasses. "You swatting at invisible elves?"

"There was a moth," I explain.

"Insects just love you." She looks me up and down and smiles. "You look pretty good."

"Pretty good?" Damn. I thought I looked fucking amazing.

"You look more like a business man than you do James Bond."

"James Bond?" I repeat, shaking my head. "I was going for the Bad Boy Billionaire who's about to sweep you off to the opera in his Lotus."

"So Richard Gere in *Pretty Woman*, then."

"I don't know what you're talking about," I tell her, putting my hand on the door and pushing it open.

She steps back and does a little swing of her hips, arms out in open display.

"What do you think?" she asks hopefully.

What do I think? She looks like the most beautiful woman I've ever seen. Her dress is simple, a golden yellow strapless number that sweeps the floor, but it pushes up her breasts and makes her curves stand out while her skin absolutely glows against the color. Despite her Rapunzel comment, she's worn her hair down in loose waves that spill over her shoulders.

I'm immediately hard.

"You can feel exactly what I think," I nearly growl at her, stepping forward through the doorway and pulling her toward me.

"You like it!"

Ana's voice breaks through just as I groan into Amanda's neck, my erection pressed firm against her hip. Damn this bloody woman.

I look up and do my best not to glare at her. "I didn't realize you were here."

Ana smiles, holding up a glass of wine. "I'm always here."

I pull back and give Amanda a sheepish look. "Well, you did a great job on her makeup."

"Thank you," Ana says. "I also did her hair. I'm trying out a new career." She takes a gulp of her drink. When she finishes swallowing she says, "It was either hairdresser school or become an anesthesiologist."

"That's makes no sense," I tell her. I glance at Amanda expectantly. "Shall we go?"

She nods quickly as Ana chirps, "Have a good time, sweet things!"

We hurry up to the car and get in. The moment her door closes, I lean in, running my hands through her hair, the thick, silky feel of her strands causing something inside me to loosen, like all the tension from earlier is finally being released.

She stares at me, her eyes searching mine in the dark, probably wondering what I'm doing.

"Is that lipstick kiss proof?" I ask quietly, focused on her hot pink mouth.

She shakes her head gently, her mouth parting slightly.

"Too bad." I lean in closer, closing my eyes as I very

gently press my lips to hers. She inhales sharply before she gives in, opening her mouth just so, just enough to gently tease the edge of her lips with my tongue.

At this point I've probably kissed Amanda a hundred different ways, but this kiss is different. This kiss reveres her. In this kiss she should know she's a goddess, a fantasy priestess, a ruler of my world.

I slowly pull my lips away and press my forehead against hers while she lets out a small breathless gasp.

"What was that for?" she asks after a beat.

"For you," I tell her before breaking apart.

I buckle up my seatbelt and start the engine, Mr. Mean roaring to life.

The party is located out at a winery in Saanichton, so we have a half an hour drive ahead of us. She's strangely silent for most of it, staring out the window at the darkened highway.

"Will it be good to see your friends?" I ask her lamely. It sounds like small talk and I hate that, but the dynamics between us keep on changing and I can't even keep up with my own feelings.

"Maybe," she says, running her fingers absently down the window. "Like I said, I haven't seen Sarah in forever."

"And the rest of them?"

"Well, actually, I saw the rest of them the last time I saw her."

"Which was..."

"New Year's Eve." Something in her voice catches.

A light goes off in my head. "You mean when you chundered on your ex during his marriage proposal?"

"That's the night."

I exhale loudly, gripping the steering wheel. "Wow. Okay. So tell me why we're going to this again?"

She finally looks at me. "I told you. I just want to...show them that I'm okay."

"But, *you* turned *him* down. Doesn't this situation usually call for the other way around? The jilted lover shows up with something to prove? I mean, maybe Alan will do just that."

Her mouth pinches together.

"Oh," I say, finally getting it. "He's going to be there. Your ex-boyfriend."

She nods, looking sheepish. "Yeah. I asked Sarah. He'll be there. With his new girlfriend who is supposed to be a genetic scientist slash supermodel. Apparently they exist outside of sitcoms."

"So you're taking me to try and make your ex jealous?" I can't seem to keep the annoyance out of my voice. The fact she's pretty much using me makes a hot and bitter coal burn in my chest.

"Kind of," she says. "You don't mind, do you?"

"The fact that you're using me, or the fact that you want your ex to care?" I pause while she doesn't say anything. "Do you seriously want him back?"

Bloody hell, she better not say yes. My heart starts to spin in my chest.

"No," she says quickly, shaking her head. "Not at all. I told you. I didn't love him and breaking it off was the right thing to do. Believe it or not, I'm a million times happier now."

But do I have anything to do with that?

"I just want to show them all that I did okay, that's all." She sighs and starts examining her hands. "I was the nerd in high school."

"You're still a nerd, geek, dork, and a hundred other things that make you *you*," I point out. "Own it."

"I do. But I mean, people only liked me or put up with it in my final year because I was with Alan. I wasn't bullied or anything like that, but I was never the one people wanted to hang out with." She seems to think that over. "Maybe it's because I never wanted to hang out with them."

"You think?"

"Anyway, you wouldn't understand."

"Hey, peach, I get it. You want to prove that you're still a catch or cool or whatever on your own and that it had nothing to do with that tosser. But these people...they don't matter. Nothing that happened in high school matters. That was a different world, a different planet. It doesn't matter who you ate lunch with back then or what your nicknames were. Like it or not, act like it or not, but you're an adult now. You've almost finished university. You're living in a great place with an older roommate and getting all these life experiences you can't buy. You're being you and you're doing your thing...and you happen to be a motherfucking bestselling author with a huge career in front of her, as well as one hell of a paycheck."

I put my hand on top of hers and squeeze. "And you've got me."

She rolls her eyes.

"No," I tell her, my voice rough. She blinks at me in surprise. "I mean you really have me. If you'll have me."

She worries her lip between her teeth, staring at me with wild eyes. I don't know what she's thinking, but I need her to say something, anything, because for the first time I'm putting my heart on the line here and I have absolutely no idea how she's going to take it.

I look back to the road, turning off on the exit that leads to the winery.

The silence is too thick.

"I got an email from Rachel," I tell her.

"What?" she asks, her voice sounding raw. At least that got her attention.

"Yeah, this morning. Strange timing considering."

"Considering what?"

"Heath and I were talking about her last night."

"Oh," she says, her voice becoming small. She looks out the window again. "What did she want?"

"She wants me back."

She stiffens, her fingers paused before they go back to playing with the pleats in her dress. "I see."

"She said that she made a huge mistake, that she regrets cheating on me. Her own heart was broken, karma, of course, and she knows the pain I went through. Apparently I was the only loyal, dependable thing in her life, if you can believe that." I let out a caustic laugh. "She said she still loves me with all her heart, that she never stopped loving me and wants a second chance."

My eyes keep darting between the road and Amanda. She's gripping her dress, her knuckles going white, but she won't face me.

"Are you going to take her back?" she asks quietly. "Try long distance again?"

The fact that this so obviously bothers her is like a tonic to my soul. It means she has to care.

"Do you think I'm going to take her back? Do you think I'm still in love with her?"

She shrugs with one shoulder.

"Amanda," I say, grappling for the words. When I don't say anything else, she slowly turns her head to look at me. Fearful. Hopeful.

"I told her it was too late," I admit. "I told her I didn't love her anymore, because I don't. That ship sailed a long time ago. And I told her I wished her the best of luck but the truth was, I've met someone else." I give her a faint smile, aware of everything riding on this. "You."

"Me?" she repeats, her voice barely audible.

"I didn't mean it as a work partner. I didn't mean it as someone I'm casually sleeping with. I meant in a completely jumping the gun, getting ahead of myself, answering for you when I shouldn't, I want you to be my girlfriend kind of way. She doesn't have my affection, my future, or my heart. You do, Amanda. You do."

There. I've laid it all out on the table.

No regrets.

Except she's still not saying anything. She's just staring at me incredulously

And I'm pretty sure one of Fluffy's crickets is loose in the car and chirping on cue.

Finally she says, "That is the cheesiest thing I've ever heard you say. Honestly, I'm shocked."

I sigh. "You know what? It's true. You don't have a romantic bone in your body." I raise my finger. "And don't make a joke about the romantic bone in my pants because I walked right into that one."

We lapse into an uneasy silence.

"So," I say, eyeing her. "You're just going to let me tell you that shit and you're not going to say anything?"

"What do you want me to say?"

"What do you want me to say?" I repeat, raising my voice, nearly taking the car off the road. "How about anything? How about, oh Blake, I want to be with you too, you have the biggest cock I've ever seen. Or how about, Blake, you're a fucking wanker and I hope you get on the next plane to Yorkshire."

She cocks her head, her brows knitting together. "I think it's been pretty obvious how I've felt."

I feel like my fucking head is exploding. "Obvious? I don't even know what you're going to say or how you feel, so no, not obvious. What the hell is with you girls? You think every man is a fucking mind reader." I give her a look. "It's called communication."

"Well, you could have told me your revelation earlier."

"I could have, if I had realized it."

"Men," she says, shaking her head. "You think with your dick so much you never once stop to check in with your brain."

"Look, I think we both can agree it's hard to think when you're not only peddling smut but acting it out like a full-time job. Writing has become the day shift, fucking has become the night shift."

"Agreed."

"So now what?"

"I guess I'm your girlfriend," she says, the corner of her mouth turning up into a smile.

"Are you going to laugh? Are you taking the piss?"

"Kind of," she admits, and breaks into a warm grin. But that's when I see it. It's not humor, its happiness. I have to assume she can see the same thing on my face.

Finally we pull up to the winery, a slew of cars parked outside, the stone building done up with sparkly lights. I feel like we've arrived in so many more ways than one.

I unbuckle my belt and twist in my seat to look at her, taking her hand in mine.

Her hand that's mine.

I stare at it for a moment, sliding my thumb over the faint hairs, her porcelain skin, her hand that feels nothing other than perfect when I hold it.

I feel like there's a sunrise in my chest, burning hot, while everything about the world is brighter and anew.

I swallow thickly. "I hope you realize that the last place I want to be is at this party. I want you in my bed, and I want to pleasure you until dawn, hard, long, fast, it doesn't matter, but that's all I want to do for a very long time. But because this matters to you, I'm going inside. We're going to make the rounds, say hello, maybe have a drink and a dance and then this thing" —I bang the steering wheel with my free hand— "is turning into a pumpkin and I'm taking you away. Got it?"

She grins at me, leaning forward to give me a kiss. "Did I ever tell you how much I love it when you get forceful?" she coos.

I can feel the blood rushing to my cock. "No. Why did you have to tell me now?"

Her eyes twinkle slyly as she reaches over and rubs her hand along the length of my erection.

I groan sharply and go to press her hand into me harder.

But she gives me a wink.

"Come on," she says.

And quickly gets out of the car.

Damn it.

TWENTY

AMANDA

I was completely nervous about the party up until about ten minutes ago. Which was good because if my nerves kept up like that, I could totally see myself having another Sir-Pukes-a-Lot moment in front of these people, which would pretty much seal my fate as that girl that is literally always vomiting (or chundering, as Blake calls it).

But now, now everything is different. Everything has changed. My nerves are dancing for an entirely different reason.

When Blake first mentioned Rachel, I could have sworn he was going to say he was going back to her, maybe even going back to England. And no matter how hard I tried to convince myself before that I could handle losing him in that way, the fact is that I couldn't. It slammed into me like a rock, the very thought that he might still love her, that he might not be mine after all.

But then everything swung around, and in the most adorable, dorky (adorkable?) way, he told me he wanted something more from me. Like, a girlfriend, boyfriend, this is an actual relationship kind of thing. No more just casual sex, no more just writing partners. He wanted more and I...

I didn't know what to think. I know I'm falling in love with him, that I have been every time I see him, every time I catch the dimples on his cheeks, the gleam in his eye, the way he makes me laugh like no one else in this world. God, he fucking makes me laugh.

Yet committing is scary, especially to someone who spent the better part of his time here sleeping with everyone in town. He's a manwhore, but I know he was also deeply committed to Rachel, and I'm not quite sure how safe my heart will be in his hands. I know he likes me, and I know everything he's saying right now is coming from his heart.

But will he mean it later?

That doesn't really matter though, because every relationship starts off with fears. It's about a leap of faith and I'm leaping with him just as he's leaping with me.

My boyfriend.

I hold out my hand for him as we walk toward the steps of the winery, the music and laughter drifting out from inside.

He grasps it in his, looking ever the gentleman in his suit, and he steadies me, giving me strength. In the distance comes the faint hoot of an owl. The moon is low on the vineyards, bathing the rows of grapes in traces of silver, and there's the fresh scent of lavender rising on the warm breeze.

"We could just stay out here," he says, looking around wistfully. "Two for two with vineyard sex."

I want to stay out here too, and yeah, some dirty sex in our fancy duds would be pretty hot. In fact, now I regret coming here at all.

I didn't really mean to use Blake in the "hey look, I'm

with a hot piece of ass right now" way, but at the same time I didn't think he, of all people, would mind being arm candy. When I got the email from Sarah, she sounded so sweet and happy, and she'd always been that one friend who I should have kept in touch with more. Besides, she had come to every single party that Alan and I had, so it was only fair I attend her engagement party.

But my pettiness and competitiveness came out to play, as usual. Once she told me Alan was coming with his girl-friend, I knew I couldn't go alone. I've mentioned that I'm petty, right?

Luckily Blake's been a good sport, and now that we're actually together as a couple—as of a few minutes ago—at least I know that nothing of who I am will be a lie.

Except for the writing part. As much as I wish I could tell them that I'm a big deal now in some circles (they don't have to know which circles), I know I can't. The word would spread so fast and both our lives would come crashing down. It wouldn't be worth it just to have them be impressed for a moment.

"Here we go," I say to Blake, raising our joined hands in the air in a show of bravery before I take a deep breath and we head inside.

"Amanda, you came!' Sarah says to me almost immedi-ately, running up from the crowd.

She's looking stunning as usual and she pulls me into a hug. Wow, she's drunk, too.

She pulls away, holding me by the shoulders, and looks me up and down. "You look fantastic. Have you lost weight? My god, your boobs." She looks over my shoulder at Blake and raises her brows, seemingly impressed. She leans in and whispers in my ear, "This is your new man? Damn, he is cute. Where on earth did you find him?"

"Hi, I'm Blake," Blake says, offering his hand, over-hearing it all.

She shakes it, smiling coyly at him. "And he's English, too."

"Yes, he is," he says. "You must be Sarah."

"I am." She looks around her. "My fiancé David is some-where, I'll have to track him down. I'll come find you in a bit," she says before she hurries away into the crowd. Many people are now stealing glances my way. I recognize most of them, offering them a timid smile but nothing more. I'm not sure if I should be the stand-offish, shy girl they knew me as before or go out of my way to be extra nice, to make up for the whole New Year's Eve fiasco.

Blake places his hand around my waist and pulls me to him. "Remember," he says in my ear, shivers running down my spine, "they aren't important. They don't matter. Let's just do our thing and go."

I nod, licking my lips. He's right. These people never liked me, not the real me. Just the me they thought was acceptable once Alan was with me.

Speaking of Alan.

Oh shit.

Shit. Shit. Shit.

He's walking toward me, wearing a grey suit, no tie, a beer grasped casually in his hands. I'm not sure how it's possible, but he seems to have extra swagger.

Where the hell did he get the swagger from?

I paste a stupid fake smile on my face while the rest of me stiffens.

Blake notices. "This the cold fish?" he whispers at my back.

I don't say anything. My mouth is locked in this ridicu-lous grin.

"Amanda," Alan says smoothly, stopping a few feet away. "What a surprise. Really didn't think you'd show after what happened last time."

"Well, nothing says engagement quite like my vomit," I tell him.

Blake bursts out laughing behind me, while Alan seems stunned. Actually, I'm stunned. I can't believe I said that though I guess acting poised is a bit of a stretch for me.

"Ha," Alan says slowly and now he's wearing the fake smile. "You still have that way about you, don't you?"

"Hi, I'm Blake," Blake says, offering his hand and what I assume will be his phrase of the night.

Alan eyes his hand, eyes me, eyes Blake. Then the fake smile is back and they shake hands.

"Alan," he says. "I assume Amanda has told you all about me."

"Only the bad parts."

Blake is totally deadpan and Alan frowns at him.

"*Ha*," Alan says again, more unsurely now. "You found someone as equally dorky as yourself. So where did you two meet?"

"Dorks Anonymous," says Blake. "We're in recovery but it's a tough road." He winces in mock strife.

This time Alan can barely offer up a smile. "Uh huh." He covers his mouth with his beer, and I swear he's muttering something under his breath.

"Sweetie?" A tall leggy Megan Fox-type woman comes slinking over.

"Oh!" Alan exclaims, putting his arm around her. She's at least two feet taller than him in her heels, and in her short Grecian white dress she looks like she just strolled off the Victoria's Secret runway. "This is Georgia. She's my girlfriend."

I smile at her as we shake hands. I feel like her bones are light enough to belong to a bird, and I immediately think of Phenelope. "I'm Amanda."

"Oh I know," she says with a small smile. She looks at Blake. "And you are?"

He gives her the long head nod. "Blake."

"Amanda and Blake. Well this is awkward," she says, and we all laugh, even me. At least she knows how to break the ice.

"Where did you two meet?" I ask her, partly out of conversation, partly out of curiosity.

They grin at each other. "Well," Alan says, his chest practically puffed out, "I met her at a conference. Doctor Ron Teethington was in town doing a lecture. If you don't know, he's one of the leading health experts on gum disease and how it manifests itself into long-term illness. He's one of the reasons why we're fighting to include dental work into BC's health care plan."

Blake snorts. "Wait a minute, wait a minute," he says, waving his hands. "He's an expert on teeth and his name is Ron *Teethington?*"

Alan frowns, exchanging a wary glance with Georgia. "I'm not sure what the problem is," he says.

Yup. That's the Alan I remember.

"Are you shitting me?" Blake exclaims, laughing now. "Teethington!"

"Easy, Sterling Archer," I warn Blake, elbowing him in the side.

"Doctor Teethington is the leading expert in his field," Georgia tries to explain, not appreciating our lack of reverence for her beloved dentist.

Blake looks at me as if to say, *you were with this guy for four years?*

I paste another smile on my face, aiming it at them as I grab Blake's arm. "Well, it's been really nice to see you."

"Did you know that Georgia is in med school?" Alan adds quickly. "She's going to be a genetic scientist. She's going to cure the world of all diseases. How about that for a career?"

We're not even together anymore and yet he still has to take a shot at my writing.

"Wow," Blake says drawing out the word and widening his eyes in mock shock as he looks at Alan. "That must mean your dick is a lot bigger than mine. Congratulations."

I have to clamp my lips shut to keep from laughing as I haul Blake toward the bar and away from their confused faces.

"Oh my god!" I exclaim as we get to the bar, swatting him across the chest. "Now he's not going to get the joke *and* he's going to think he has a larger penis than you." I look over at them across the room, yelling, "Which is so not true!"

"Two beers," Blake says to the bartender before turning to me. "I cannot believe you were with that guy for four years. Oh my god. How did you not go bloody insane?"

I shrug sheepishly. "I settled. I was flattered and then I settled."

"Don't you ever fucking settle for me, you promise?" he asks, holding out his pinky finger.

I roll my eyes but shake on it. "I'm not settling for you. I'm practically pining for you."

"Oh really?" he asks, folding his arms and raising his chin. "And this is you pining?"

"I've been showing my pining through blow jobs."

"Hmmm. I guess I approve."

The bartender slides us our drinks but Blake motions to

him. "And a shot of Jameson for the lady and me. Make it two." He winks at me. "Open bar."

"You're driving," I hiss at him.

"We can cab it if we have to," he says. "Something tells me we're going to need a lot of booze to survive this cock up."

"What happened to just going home?"

"Eh, now that I'm here I want to get my money's worth." He takes the shots from the bartender and hands me mine. He holds his up. "Here's to open bars."

"To open bars," I say.

"And to us."

And even though that perpetual smirk is on his lips, I can see the depth in his eyes, the warmth, the need, the want. The fact that he absolutely has my back through all of this.

"To us."

We slam back the shots—both of them—and then the beers. And then rinse, repeat.

It's not long before I'm completely wasted. I should have eaten something beforehand, but I was just too nervous and Ana's dinner of cold beet soup and rye bread wasn't exactly appetizing.

Blake seems to have my back though. He's with me nearly every step of the way, even indulging me with a drunken dance, until Sarah sequesters me by myself, introducing me to her fiancé David, whom I think seems nice but looks like the type of guy who would wear an ascot (if those even exist anymore) and get weekly manicures.

While Sarah blabbers on and on about David, in front of his face, I get more and more drunk.

One of the last things I remember is seeing Blake across the room talking to Georgia and Alan of all people. He seemed to be passionately explaining something and then all their heads swiveled my way.

I think I smiled and waved.

I'm not really sure.

Then all the world went black.

"It's okay," Blake says soothingly.

It's *not* okay.

It's never been less okay.

I'm on my knees in his bathroom, hunched over the toilet, vomiting my guts out.

At least it didn't happen last night but I can't be sure of that.

Meanwhile, Blake is holding my hair back for me, even though I've tried to push him away a few times.

God this is embarrassing. No one wants to vomit in front of the guy they're sleeping with.

Or their new boyfriend, I remind myself.

"It's okay," he says again.

I want to tell him it's not okay at all but I obviously can't speak. I heave and heave and heave until I don't have anything left to upchuck.

Then Blake scoops me up, flushes the toilet, and leads me to the shower where he strips the both of us naked and steps inside with me.

My legs are shaking, and I taste nothing but stomach acid and leftover Jameson, but the moment the hot water hits me, I feel some of last night dissolve.

I moan loudly and place my hands on the shower wall, trying to hold myself up while my head hangs down.

"Darling, don't you dare moan in here like that," he says

to me, squirting body wash into his hands and rubbing them together. "I'm not about to take advantage of a hungover wreck. Just as I didn't take advantage of you last night."

"How noble," I mutter.

"Well, it's kind of noble when you were attempting to give me a blow job the entire cab ride back here. Poor cabby, I had to tip him extra, even though I think he enjoyed your effort. Even when we went to bed, you didn't pass out like I thought you would. Instead you kept at it again."

I manage to look at him, the water running down the strong planes of his face. "Really?"

He nods, sliding his hands over my shoulders. "Yup. I've never seen you so horny. I've also never seen you so smashed before."

When I woke up this morning I felt like I was lying at the bottom of a grave filled with dog shit and vomit and had to climb my way out. But Blake was in bed with me and already had water, Gatorade, Advil and a B-Vitamin booster on the bedside table ready to go. Too bad it wasn't long after that I had to run to the bathroom.

"Did I make a fool of myself last night?" I ask him. It almost hurts to speak.

"No," he says. "You were quiet. You kind of went inward. Everyone else was drunk though, so we weren't the only ones, and I made you leave before the party was over."

I breathe in deeply, closing my eyes, water running into my mouth. "Thank god. Did you behave yourself?"

There's a beat of hesitation before he says, "Of course I did," and continues soaping me up. "Want me to shampoo your hair?" he asks, and it reminds me of our first time in the shower together.

"Okay," I tell him, relaxing into him as his strong fingers work through my hair. It feels so good to be attended to like this. I know Blake is naked in the shower with me, but I still appreciate how non-sexual it is. Granted, I can feel his erection poking my hip, but still. He's being tender with me, with every touch of his hands, each caress of his eyes as they gaze at me. All that and after puking in front of him, too.

When we get out of the shower, he slips his robe on me and leads me to the living room where he feeds me jasmine tea and organic soup and dotes on me in a way I never thought possible. I mean, beneath my raging headache and queasy stomach, my heart feels as if it might burst.

This is more than falling in love.

Fuck it.

I *am* in love.

And I think he can feel it.

Even when I try to talk about work, he tells me we can discuss that tomorrow and that today is a vacation, a day to recuperate. He's practically doing everything short of feeding me grapes.

"Don't you have to feed Fluffy?" I ask him, my feet on his lap as he squeezes them, giving me a foot massage.

"Heath took care of that yesterday," he says, visibly shuddering.

"I hate to bring this up, especially as I'm not in the right frame of mind to talk about hairy arachnids" I say, "but how long do you plan on keeping Fluffy?"

He tilts his head to me, a piece of dark, thick hair flopping over his forehead. "Is this your first step as my girlfriend, to get rid of Fluffy and maybe my Lionel Richie records?"

"First of all, Lionel Richie is a god."

"*All night long,*" Blake belts out.

"*All night,*" I sing back. "And second of all, no. If you're cool with having a giant, ugly, hairy, yet surprisingly delicate tarantula in your apartment, then I'm fine with it, too. But he does seem to cause you permanent anxiety and he's not exactly yours."

He sighs, closing his eyes as he leans back against the cushion. "I know. With the divorce and all, Kevin might be moving, I'm not really sure. I hope not. But if he does, he for sure won't be able to take him. Luckily I think Heath may want him. Crazy bugger."

"That's going to suck," I tell him, knowing how close they are. The way that Blake acts around Kevin, talks about Kevin, is one of the sweetest things I've seen. I know girls get all soft in the uterus when they see a man with a baby or a puppy, but this is kind of the same thing. He's a good older brother and it makes me realize the depths he has inside him, the ability to really love.

"Tell me about it," he says. "You know I never had a brother growing up, and even though I'm so much older than Kevin, that's who I see him as. And when he told you I'm his best friend? That's not a lie. I'm the closet friend he has. I worry for both of us if he has to move." He gives me a pleading look. "That's why this LARPing thing is so impor-tant. You sure you'll come?"

"When is it again? I'd come even if I wasn't officially your girlfriend."

"Next Sunday."

"That works. Just remember, you are dressing up as Loki."

He glares at me. "Fine. If you dress up for me."

"Fine." I pause, not sure what I'm agreeing to. "As what?"

He taps his fingers against his lips in mock thought. "Hmmm, I better choose wisely, this might be a once in a lifetime experience."

"Don't you dare say Princess Leia in the gold bikini."

"Awwww," he groans loudly in disappointment.

"I'm not wearing a bikini to a glorified renaissance faire slash comic con battle."

"But your body is amazing. And you didn't mind showing it off when I was pounding you on the balcony." He jerks his head to the glass door.

"No," I tell him.

"Okay. Fine." He ponders over it. "Jean Grey. As Phoenix. The spandex suit. And you better wear your fucking hair down, Rapunzel."

"Deal."

He sighs, looking at his phone. "I better go get the car back from the winery." He gets up, stretching his arms above his head, and my eyes go to the hard planes of his hips, the slice of washboard abs.

"You sure you don't want me to come?" I ask.

"Stay here and rest," he says. "I'll be right back."

He heads for the door.

"Blake," I call after him, my heart thudding in my ears.

He pauses with the door open and glances at me over his shoulder.

I fucking love you.

"Thanks," I tell him. "For taking care of me."

He breaks into an easy grin. "Of course. You're my girl."

His girl.

His girl who is brutally afraid to hand him her heart.

He leaves and I let out the longest breath, collapsing back into the couch. I lie there for a moment, almost being lulled into sleep, when my phone beeps.

I reach for my iPhone and hold it above my face.

It's a text from Sarah.

Is it true what they're saying? Is this really you?

And then there's an Amazon link.

Oh my god.

Everything in me freezes, ice cold.

I click the link, hoping, hoping, hoping…

It takes me right to the Amazon page for *Falling for the Secret Male Stripper*.

Holy fuck.

HOLY FUCK.

NOOOOOOOOOOO!

The phone drops right on my face, clocking me right in the nose.

"Arrrgh!' I cry out in pain. I sit straight up, my head spinning, everything spinning, and fuck my life, is that blood coming out of my nose? I wipe my finger underneath and stare at the red smear.

But that's the least of my worries. I frantically try and open the phone and text Sarah, my fingers shaking as I try and type.

What are you talking about? Where did you hear that?

I see the three dots flashing. They disappear.

Then come back.

Then disappear.

"For fuck's sake, write what you were going to say!" I scream at the phone, shaking it.

Finally: **Blake told Georgia and Alan. He said you were really successful now and you wrote together. I just wanted to let you know it's cool. I just bought both your books. I had no idea you were that slutty lol.**

I stare at the screen, dumbfounded.

He told them.

He told them our secret.

He's going to ruin my life.

I text her back: **Please don't tell anyone. That was supposed to be a secret.**

Again with the flashing dots.

Then: **I'm sorry, I think everyone knows. It's all over Facebook.**

"WHAT?!" I scream out loud and instinctively toss my phone across the room.

I cover my face with my hands and rock back and forth on the couch, trying to breathe.

It's on Facebook.

My parents are on Facebook.

Maybe there's still time, I think to myself. *Delete every tagged post!*

I bring out the laptop and go on Facebook.

It's everywhere.

Some posts are genuinely trying to be helpful: "Hey I went to school with this girl and now she's a successful author, check it out." Others are mocking: "Dude, who knew Amanda Newland was such a pervert?" And some are just straight up posting on my page: "Is this true? Is this you?"

I immediately start untagging my name from the posts, praying my parents aren't still friends with anyone from my high school, but it's too late.

My phone rings.

I don't even have to look at it to know it's my mother.

I shouldn't answer. I should just ignore it and try to do as much damage control as possible. But what's the point when all the people I was trying to hide this from already know?

The damage is done.

And I'm so fucked.

I answer it.

"Hello?" I ask innocently, pretending that my head isn't on the chopping block.

I just hear heavy, ragged breathing, like one of Khaleesi's dragons figured out how to make a phone call.

Then, "Guess what I found out today?" my mother says, her voice so icy and eerily calm that it chills me to the bone like only she can.

"The world is round after all? Dinosaurs are real?"

She ignores that. "I found out that my daughter is not at all the person I thought she was. I found out that she's a cheap fraud, a charlatan. A hack."

"You heard the news," I say flatly.

"The news? What is wrong with you?" she screeches over the phone. "Do you realize you're going to hell by writing this stuff?"

"I'll probably see Aunt Sylvia there."

"How dare you," she says. "I haven't told your father yet about your, your...*hobby*. But when I do, I don't know. Amanda, I seriously don't know what he's going to do or say. He might cut you out of the will."

I can barely form words. "Seriously?"

"Oh, now you're worried? You don't give a damn about your parents until the money stops flowing, is that it? Is that why you think you can write this trash?"

I groan loudly, pressing my fingers into my forehead. I can't think.

"I don't care about the will," I cry out, feeling my defenses come down. "But why can't you guys just be supportive without going to extremes? Why can't you just accept me for me? That's all I have ever wanted."

"As a daughter who writes porn?" She makes a sound of disgust.

"It's not just porn!" I yell, so sick of this argument. "I'm writing my fantasy just as I always have, the book you don't even care about, but do you know what? Even if I only wrote erotica, I wouldn't care what you have to say. I make people happy! Blake and I provide readers with fun and entertainment and an escape from their lives, which is a damn good thing because life is hard and really sucks some-times. Life isn't a fairytale and not everyone gets a happily-ever-after, but in our book world they do. And believe it or not, it's made me a better writer." I pause, breathing hard. "I don't want to be ashamed of it. I'm not. So take it or leave it."

Silence.

I almost think she's hung up.

Then I hear a faint sniff.

"You know," she says venomously, "I had a hard time being proud of you before, for turning down Alan and your bright future with him and continuing on with your silly degree. But I tried. I did. But now? Now it's impossible. I don't even want to tell people you're my daughter anymore."

I can't handle it. I burst into tears and hang up the phone.

Then I collapse to my knees, trying to hold it all together.

Kind of seems impossible now.

The cab to the vineyard seems to take forever, traffic clogging up the highway, and once I get to the winery it's busy with people.

It's a gorgeous day though and I've got a gorgeous girl waiting back at my apartment.

My girl.

I start humming that tune as I stroll through the tasting room and end up buying a bottle of pinot gris and a bouquet of yellow flowers. She probably won't want to drink the wine for a few days, but the flowers should at least cheer her up.

As I head back to the car I look around, remembering how completely weird last night got. Amanda was absolutely bombed, and while I was drunk too, I had to keep it together for her sake. She was open and vulnerable, surrounded by all the sharks of her past, and I wasn't about to let anyone take advantage of her. She may act like she's got a coating of armor around her, but I know how deeply she feels things sometimes.

That's why when I ran into her prat of an ex and his

legs-for-days girlfriend, I couldn't help but defend her. She may have not needed me to be her knight in shining armor and I hope to god it never gets back to her because I'm pretty sure that would be the end of us, but I couldn't let them make fun of her and her ambitions. I had to let them know just how successful and talented and smart Amanda truly is.

So I fought her battle for her because I know she would do the exact same thing for me. I have her back. She has mine.

Another reason why I love her.

Bloody hell. My own thoughts make me pause, a kick in the chest.

Love.

I didn't even think it was fucking possible after Rachel. I swore I would never give myself to another girl, that I would keep everything in my heart cold and wrapped up, with not a thread loose.

It had worked so well.

Until she walked into my life and pulled on a string I had never noticed.

And I unraveled.

Slowly.

But surely.

Fucking pansy, I tell myself, starting the car.

But even if I am, it's all still true.

I am a pansy.

And I'm madly in love with her.

I sigh heavily and drive off down the highway. Because the world works in strange ways, "Can You Feel the Love Tonight" comes on the radio. I turn it up, roll down the windows, and start belting it out with a huge shit-eating grin on my face. It's just like that scene in *Jerry Maguire* where

Tom Cruise is singing "Free Falling," except much, *much* lamer.

When I get to the apartment, the bottle of wine in one hand, the bouquet of flowers in the other, I still have that Tom Cruise grin on my face. I'm not sure I'll ever be able to stop smiling.

Until I open the door.

And see Amanda standing in the middle of the living room, her hands curled into fists, her eyes blazing into me with fire and brimstone.

"What's wrong?" I ask her. She looks like she's near tears, but the fury in her expression has me staying back and close to the door in case I need to run for my life.

"You told," she seethes.

Bollocks.

"Told what?" I ask cautiously, stepping over to the kitchen to put the wine and flowers on the counter. I feel like I'm a bomb diffuser and it's about to go off at any second.

She shakes her head slowly, her fists opening and closing. "You told everyone at the party that we write erotica together. You told them our pen name. You told them about *everything*."

Her voice is thin and reedy and stretched by the anger I know she's barely holding back.

I raise my hands and inch backward. "I can explain."

"You asshole!" she yells, running at me, pounding her fists on my shoulders, arms, chest. Damn she has hands like rocks.

"Ow, ow, ow," I say, trying to shield myself, holding up my knee to keep her back. "Please just listen."

"You told them our secret!" she yells, her face as

crimson as her hair, a vein ticking in her forehead. "Do you know what you've done?"

She breaks away and walks back into the living room, her hands grasping her head. "How could you do this?" she whispers.

"Hey, I did it for you," I call after her, keeping the kitchen island between us just in case.

"What?" she snaps, slowly turning around and coming back to me. "You did what for me?" she asks, leaning against the counter, eyes flashing.

"Look, that tosser of yours and his girlfriend were saying mean things, okay? You know, those underhanded comments about how weird you are and how you're a dreamer and the usual, good luck with being a writer, you'll never make it, so what was I supposed to do?"

"They said that?" she asks, horrified.

"Yeah, but it doesn't matter."

"It does matter! Now they know I'm an erotica author! Do you think that made them respect me? You should have just punched him in the face."

"I wanted to!" I yell at her. "And it did make them respect you, as they should! You should have seen their faces when I told them. I may have dropped how much money we make too, and believe me, in the long term, it's more than they'll ever know. They were impressed, Amanda. I shut them right up in their tracks. Words work better than fists."

Her face softens with worry, and for a moment I think the anger is fading but then some kind of wall goes back up again and her eyes turn hard and mean. "That wasn't your secret to tell. Now everyone knows. My parents." She shakes her head, looking away. "You have no idea what it's like to be a constant disappointment in your parents' life. Now I'm practically disowned because of you."

"Amanda, it doesn't matter."

"Oh, fuck you!" she yells, spinning around and jabbing her finger in the air. "Fuck you, Blake. You keep telling me what matters and what doesn't, and guess what? Some things do! Some things do and you don't get the right to comment on what things matter to me because it's personal and you should know that. You should know that about me. How do you think your father will feel when *he* finds out?"

I still and swallow hard. "He doesn't have to find out."

"Oh really? Because I've already gotten an email from someone at the Victoria Times Colonist wanting to interview us both for being secret successes."

Fuck. "You didn't say yes..."

"Of course I didn't! I wouldn't betray our trust like that. I'm not like *you*."

Now I'm angry. "Hey, I was defending you!"

"And I didn't need you to defend me. I just needed you to keep your stupid mouth shut for once!"

"You could be a bit more grateful, you know," I tell her, unable to keep the edge from my voice. "It wouldn't kill you."

"Grateful? You ruined everything for the sake of your ego."

"*My* ego?" I practically roar. "What the fuck? You're fucking daft, you know that!"

"We had an understanding. We were in this together. And to think I trusted you. I trusted you with my heart!" she sobs.

I stare at her, gobsmacked, as the rage boils within me. "Your heart?" I repeat incredulously. "You've never given me your heart!"

She swallows hard, her chin wavering. She quickly rubs the makeup out from under her eyes and part of me wants to rush over to her, to hold her and tell her I'm sorry and that everything will be all right.

And the other part of me is breaking apart and coming back together, hardened. Not understanding how easily she can flip like this, how she can just say these things like I haven't meant anything to her, like she's never trusted me at all.

I *had* to have meant something to her. It couldn't have just been in my head.

"You're right," she says with a sniff, looking away. "I never gave you my heart." She shrugs and gives me a sad smile. "It was probably for the best."

She grabs her purse and starts to head out the door.

I should stop her.

I shouldn't let her go.

I should make her stay.

There are a lot of things I should do. But all I can feel is my heart dissolving in my chest like someone's poured a vat of acid over it.

So I watch her go.

"By the way," she says, pausing before she closes the door. "I may have fed Fluffy and forgot to put the lid back on. Have fun."

"Argh!" I cry out, immediately feeling like he's on me already.

The door slams shut behind her.

I can't believe what just happened.

I've lost Amanda.

And Fluffy is somewhere loose in this apartment.

Look at you, you sad arse, I tell myself, trying to steady my nerves and repair my heart all at the same time. I make my way out onto the balcony, the only place in the apartment I figure is safe from the monster, so I can think.

Fuck.

I am an idiot.

And not just for telling her ex about our secret. I seriously regret that now and I was sober enough to know what I was doing. I just got so caught up in the moment, I needed to say something. And she was right. I didn't need to defend her.

But god it felt good.

Maybe it was my ego talking after all.

I lean back in the chair and look across the harbor. It's far too beautiful of a day to break up. The clouds need to come in, the rain needs to come down, a cold bitter wind needs to carve right through me, matching how empty I feel inside. Instead, there are birds chirping from the trees and children playing happily on the grass below by the seawall.

I get out my phone and call her.

It goes straight to her voicemail:

"Hi, this is Amanda Newland. I don't check my voicemails ever, so please hang up and text or email me. If this is a telemarketer or my parents or someone born before 1961, better luck next time."

I know she doesn't check these, but I leave a long babbling message, apologizing, and ask her to call me back. Then I call her once more.

Again.

And again.

Text.

Email.

Wait.

Nothing.

I decide to head to the store and see if Kevin is there. If

he is, I'm totally borrowing him and bringing him back here for a Fluffy hunt. At least that's one problem I'll be able to solve.

Meanwhile, I wonder if I can talk to my father and break the news to him before the word gets out. Amanda's old friends and my friends don't run in the same circles, but it's a small world and obviously if a journalist has already caught wind of this supposed story, there's a chance that word could travel down the grapevine to the bookstore. I mean, it is pretty ironic. Son of the city's most elite bookstore is a randy smut peddler.

Except I really don't want to do it. I'm dragging my feet to the store, opting to walk because it will take more time. But it's time to be a man and own up to it. If I was prepared to throw Amanda under a bus, I can throw myself under a bus too.

"Dad," I say as I enter the store.

He looks up from the register in surprise. I wasn't supposed to come in today. Luckily it's quiet in here.

"What is it?" he asks, frowning at my grave tone.

I guess that's a good sign. I don't see any signs of torches and pitchforks. He obviously doesn't know yet.

"I have something to tell you," I say to him.

"Can it wait?" he asks, gesturing to a few people lingering in the store. They aren't paying us any attention. The usual casual browsers, not sure what they're looking for.

"It can't." I stand on the other side of the counter. I learned something from Amanda this morning. Always keep your distance between yourself and potential injury.

The line between his brows deepens. "Okay...did you get someone pregnant?"

"No," I tell him. "But I'm not sure if this will be worse to you or better."

"Great," he says dryly. "Okay. What is it?"

"Dad, it turns out that I don't really want running this bookstore to be my full-time job."

He stares at me blankly. I'm not sure if he's heard me or not.

I go on. "The thing is, I do have a full-time job, and it's one that's making me a lot of money. More than I could have ever dreamed of at this age."

"Are you running a prostitution ring?"

"No," I say warily, trying to read his face. "But sex does sell."

"Blake..."

"Okay, well I love this store and I love you and I want to help, I really do, but the only way I can help either of us is if we hire a full-time manager for the store. A financial whiz. Someone who knows what they're doing."

"But you have a business degree," he says gruffly. "You're supposed to use it."

I scoff. "No one uses their degrees anymore. Welcome to the new generation, Dad."

"And how do you propose we pay for the manager? With what income?"

He's taking this surprisingly well so far. Maybe he's thought of hiring someone too.

But the other shoe is about to drop.

"I told you," I remind him. "I have money. The money will go toward that, and I promise the business will go back into the black."

"Son, if you don't start explaining where the hell this money is coming from..."

"Dad." Here goes nothing and everything. "I've secretly

been writing books on the side and self-publishing them. Under a pen name."

"What?"

"They do really well. Really, really well. Amanda is my writing partner and we write them together."

"I don't..." He blinks dumbly.

"Our pen name is Blake Lovecox."

His head jerks back. "That's a terrible name."

"And we write smut."

Now he's speechless. "What?" he growls.

"We write smut," I say with a helpless shrug. "Erotica. We've released two books already and we're working on our third. The reviews are great. The money is better."

He's slowly shaking his head and I can practically see the steam escaping from his ears. "This better be a joke." His voice is practically choking with anger.

"No joke," I tell him, pulling out my phone and showing him. "These are our books."

He takes a quick glance. "That's disgusting," he seethes.

"Yeah, sometimes it is. But I didn't want it to be a secret anymore. I'm not ashamed."

"Well you damn well should be!"

"Why?"

"Because it's not real writing. It's not literature. It's garbage."

"That's what people said about Shakespeare back in the day. His plays were just entertainment. But what's wrong with that?"

"That's what movies are for."

"That's what all art is for. Your creations can become anything to anyone. I've realized there's nothing wrong with letting people escape for a few hours. Plus, you should hear about all the sex lives I'm saving."

"Other than your own?"

"Dad, I know how you feel about the genre and that's fine. But really, if you want to save the store, the first thing you need to do is start carrying smut. Or at least romance."

"I would never," he grumbles, his face growing red. "And I would never carry that junk of *yours*."

I knew he would be like this. I don't even bother taking it personally.

"Dad," I tell him, pulling up the calculator and entering a few numbers. "I get my first check from Amazon very soon." I place the numbers in front of his face. "This is how much I'm giving to the store. The rest is going into savings."

He stands there, stunned.

"And that's from one month of sales from one book." I enter more numbers.

He's speechless. He licks his lips, eyes darting to me.

"Are you serious?'

I nod.

He clears his throat. "Well then. Congratulations on your new career."

He pats me on the back, and I watch nearly all his worries lift away.

I wish I could say the same about mine.

TWENTY-TWO

AMANDA

It's been a week since I last talked to Blake.

He's called, texted, emailed me every single day.

I ignore them all.

I mean, it's ridiculous the way I'm acting. I know I'm being a brat. I know I said a bunch of things I didn't mean because I was just so hurt and vulnerable. And I know I can't keep ignoring him forever. Even if we weren't writing partners with two books out and a third in the works, even if we didn't have paychecks coming that we'd have to divide between us, I'd still have to talk to him because I'm in love with the asshole and that feeling isn't going away anytime soon, no matter how hard I try to crush it into the ground.

But I'm stubborn, way more stubborn than he is, and when he finally stops messaging me, then I feel the pinch. The real fear. It never was about our secret coming out and that people might judge us. Losing him has always been my number one worry.

I know he cares for me. I know, especially after talking to Sarah, who told me just how wonderful he was at the party, the things he was saying about me, that he would

354

never intentionally do anything to hurt me. And I know that the manwhore is gone and what's left is one hell of a sexy man who makes me laugh, makes me come, and worships the ground I walk on.

But I worry it's too late.

Because it was so easy for me to close myself off again. And after everything that has happened with Rachel, I'm not sure he'd be willing to open up and give me another chance.

I just don't know anything anymore.

So I go for a run.

It's Sunday morning and Ana is making turnip pancakes once more, so I head out of the house and decide to run into the city and dodge tourists. She's been very supportive of my new career. After I was outed, it was only a matter of time before I had to tell both her and Rio. They were shocked, no doubt, and Rio made me promise to write *Slammed by the Single Dad* one day and that she'd give me detailed descriptions of their escapades. I told her I'd think about it.

Ana, of course, wants some sort of credit in my books for being the world's best roommate. I told her I'd think about that too.

Then there are my parents, who haven't called me since that day. I'm fine with it. They're blood and family, so I know that eventually we'll reconnect. But I'm in no hurry. I can get by without their money, at least until I graduate and my loan runs out, thanks to the Amazon payments, and I think it's about time that I put some distance between them and myself. I can't grow, can't become the person I am with them holding something over me. Besides, after talking to Dahlia the other day, I know that they'll come around and be more meddlesome and involved than ever, so I should enjoy this break while I can.

For once the run isn't burning up my thighs and knees, and the city is still a bit sleepy in the morning sun. I cut down across the Empress Hotel and start jogging along Wharf Street when I hear someone yell my name.

"Amanda!"

The voice belongs to a kid.

I turn around and see a tall, stately looking brunette, very Kate Beckinsale circa her romantic comedy days and Kevin, Blake's stepbrother. While she's dressed in a white pant suit like she's about to board a cruise ship, he's dressed head to toe in plastic armor and carrying a flag with a yellow crest on it. He waves the flag at me.

"Hi," I say, feeling awkward as they come toward me.

Kevin looks up at his mom. "Mom, this is Amanda, Blake's girlfriend."

I force a smile on my face, not sure if I should correct Kevin or not.

"Hi," I say, giving her a wave. "Sorry, I'd shake your hand but it's sweaty."

She smiles. "I'm Angelica, Blake's stepmother."

"Nice shirt," Kevin says to me with a big smile on his face.

His mother peers at my chest. "Is that Benedict Cumberbatch?" she asks incredulously.

"Mom loves him," Kevin says, shoving his glasses up on his nose. "Our whole house is a shrine to him."

"Oh, it is not," she says, putting her hand on his shoulder and giving me a quick smile.

"Yes it is. Remember when Blake broke your Sherlock shot glass set and you got all mad and made him buy you a new one?"

Oh my god. I see where Kevin's nerd genes come from. I can also finally see why Blake hates Benedict Cumberbatch so much.

She keeps smiling, nervous now as she tucks her hair behind her ears. "They were a gift, sweetie, that's the only reason why I was mad."

"And then you wouldn't let him touch that mug that says 'seductively deductive.'"

"That's enough, Kevin."

He just keeps smiling, turning his attention to me. "Hey, guess what day it is?"

I frown. "Sunday."

"No, why I'm dressed like this." He pats his armor.

"Still figured it was just a Sunday."

Angelica looks at me. "I'm taking him to Beacon Hill Park to do his...what is it again? Comic con?"

"LAIRE," Kevin says. He frowns dramatically at me. "Did you forget, Amanda?"

Oh shit. The fucking LARPing shit.

"Blake is doing it with you, right?" I ask him.

"Yeah, he's meeting me there in a few hours," he says. "But you also promised."

I wince, giving Angelica a look. "Well, the thing is..."

They both stare at me. Obviously Blake hasn't told them anything.

I sigh. I really, really don't want to go there dressed as Phoenix from X-Men and potentially be shunned by Blake. But I'm not sure I have a choice. "Do you mind if I bring my friend?" I ask him. "She's really good at fantasy makeup."

"Sure!" Kevin says. He stabs his staff into the ground, the flag waving. "Come on, mother dear, our kingdom awaits." He then turns around and starts strutting away.

"Thank you for doing this," Angelica says to me. "It will

be really good for Kevin. And for Blake." With that, she turns around and trots after her little king.

Hmmm. Blake. Maybe she knows something after all.

There's no time to think about it though. I continue on my run all the way to a costume shop just outside of downtown where I manage to snag a Phoenix costume that's straight from a cosplay sex catalog. Then I run back home and break the news to Ana.

"I'll bring the wine," she says excitedly.

Two hours later, Ana and I descend on a scene of utter pandemonium. All of Beacon Hill Park is awash with fellow freaks and geeks from all walks of life. There are children and adults, men and women, and a few people who could go either way since they're dressed like Groot or an orc of sorts. Everyone seems to be split into groups, battling each other with weapons and shields, the air filled with cries and the dull thud of foam against foam. There's even a beer garden in the distance and a few food trucks that I have no doubt are serving up Game of Thrones style meals.

My Phoenix costume makes me look slightly out of place—there seem to be a lot of people here dressed up as their own creations, and barely any of the women are dressed in such a form-fitting manner. Ana blends in a little more, wearing a full-length red and white Estonian folk costume she pulled from her closet, albeit with a makeup case in one hand and a bottle of opened wine in the other.

"Hello, fair maidens." Two men are walking toward us, one round like a potato and dressed like a medieval squire, the other looking like Zaphod Beeblebrox from *Hitchhiker's Guide to the Galaxy.*

"I am Randy the Retiree," the potato man says. He gestures to his friend. "And this is—"

"Zaphod Beeblebrox," I fill in.

"No," Zaphod says, frowning, tossing his straggly blonde hair over his shoulder. "I am Darth Star Lord from the planet Clorox, guardian of the galaxy."

I cock my head. "I think you're getting a bunch of things confused."

"We are from the Senate of Calgon," Randy the Retiree says and gestures to the field with his arm. "We put on this affair for many to enjoy. All are welcome. Especially the fair ladies."

"I brought makeup and wine," Ana says with a wide smile, totally in her element.

"Very good," Randy the Retiree says. "Your services are needed here." He puts his arm around her and leads her away.

Zaphod peers at me. "And what is your warrior name?"

"Um, Jean Grey, turned into Phoenix."

"Peculiar name, Jean Grey Turned into Phoenix" he says. "Come, let us retire to my tent up on yonder hill so we may properly get acquainted away from prying eyes. Everyone is always watching the Senate of Calgon."

He tries to put his arm around me but I shrug away from it. "I'm not here to battle, or whatever you're suggesting. I'm here to find someone."

"Ah," he says, folding his arms. "And who is this warrior you seek?"

I try and think. There are hundreds of people here fighting in a blur. "He's British..."

"Everyone here is British," he says. "Doth not hear thine accent?"

"Right. He should be with a kid. His name is Kev...I mean Betoolamous the Brave."

"I'm afraid I can't help you, for there are many brave ones here." He takes a step closer to me. "As am I. Did you know I've been called the best bang since the big one?"

"All right, Zaphod," I tell him, going around him. "Go back to your Pan Galactic Gargle Blaster."

"My what?" he asks as I start jogging across the field toward the beer garden, figuring that's where Blake probably is. That's where I'd be.

Unfortunately, I have to head right through a battle to get there.

Foam weapons are coming at my head from all directions and it doesn't seem to matter that I don't have a shield and I look like I'm trying to go somewhere, because I am hit absolutely everywhere. Foam to the face, shoulders, boobs, gut, ass. Then the ass some more by some medieval pervert with a very large sword.

"Ahhhh!" I cry out, trying to run and shield my head and ass at the same time when suddenly the pervert is struck on the back and he falls to the ground in dramatic fashion.

"Death is such a pity," he ekes out, reaching for me with his hand before he mock dies.

There is no pause in the battle before the hits start up again, but there is a hand grabbing mine and leading me out of the chaos and clamor.

When we're a few feet away from the action and I can breathe, I look up to see who my rescuer is.

But I already know from the feel of his hand.

Except this isn't Blake at all. It's Tom Hiddleston. I mean, Loki.

Don't ruin my fantasy.

"You saved me," I tell him.

Blake's face is far too serious for the battleground and far too serious for playing Loki. But it's him, dressed from head to toe in his armor, from the green cape and gold-plated shoulders, to the horn helmet atop his head. He looks menacing.

Badass.

And fucking hot.

"What are you doing here?" Blake asks as the battle rages around us.

"Kevin didn't tell you?"

He shakes his head, his helmet starting to tip over. His hand shoots up to steady it. "No."

"Oh," I say, feeling stupid. "Um, well I ran into him today. He was with your stepmother. You never told me about her and her Benedict Cumber—"

"Don't even say his name."

"Anyway, he expected me here today and your step-mother seemed really grateful when I said I'd still come so... here I am."

"And that's the only reason?" he asks softly, peering intently into my eyes.

"No," I tell him. "I came here for you. To tell you I'm sorry."

His brows come together. "For what?"

"For being a twat. For not returning your messages. For blowing up at you like I did."

"Amanda," he says. "You had every right to be mad. I knew it was our secret and I wasn't thinking. Clearly. I get it."

"No," I tell him. "I shouldn't have freaked out and left you. I just didn't know what to do. You know...being with you...it scared me so much to imagine losing you, I couldn't handle it. It's almost like I made it happen so it wouldn't have to happen down the line."

"That is such a guy thing to do," he says.

"Don't be sexist," I tell him, punching him in the armor. It kind of hurts. "Girls are allowed to do stupid shit too."

"I don't know if you're allowed to do them, but you do them anyway," he muses.

I raise my fist. "Don't make me punch you again."

"Hey, you're Phoenix. You can change the whole damn world with your mind, just as you can with your writing. Why do you think I wanted you to come dressed as her? You can do anything you put your mind to, whether it's making a fortune on erotica or writing something very dear and personal to you. You're practically a superhero. And you're really good in bed."

I swallow hard, the butterflies in my chest taking off. "So...it's not too late?"

"For what?"

"For us," I say feebly. "You stopped calling me."

"Just because we write about stalkers doesn't mean I am one. I wanted to give you space and time to figure your shit out. I wasn't going anywhere. We're writing partners."

"And sex partners."

"And friends."

"And dorks."

"Speak for yourself," he says, raising his head high. "I'm the king of mischief."

"Well, the queen of mischief needs a beer," I tell him.

He grasps my hand. "My queen," he says gallantly and we head toward the beer garden. The battle rages on and Blake fends off a charging warrior with a fell swoop of his staff. We keep walking.

"My hero," I tell him as we step over the fallen, writhing soldier.

We give each other the nerdiest smiles, and my heart feels like it's a big, bright balloon, too large and grand for my chest.

"Hey, is that Ana?" Blake says as we approach the bar.

I look over to see her putting blue body paint on some buff, half naked Avatar. She's giggling and he's flexing, and it looks like she's having the time of her life.

"Is that Kevin and your dad?" I ask, because further down the line of people who want Ana's face slash body paint, there they are. "I didn't know your dad was coming."

"Neither did I," Blake says. "Just as well. Now we can enjoy these beers."

We find ourselves a spot at a picnic table between some wenches who are completely hammered and Neo and Trinity from the *Matrix*, and we drink in the sunshine, talking and catching up over everything that happened during the last week, from family, to our new fame, to book world drama (there's always book world drama).

Two beers in though, and we're both feeling pretty loose.

"Hey, come with me," I tell him, grabbing his hand and leading him from his seat and out of the beer garden.

"Where are you leading me, my queen?" he asks, playfully smacking me on my ass.

"It's a secret," I tell him, glancing up at him over my shoulder. "You know how to keep those now, don't you?"

He rolls his eyes in response.

I take him over to the white cloth tent that Zaphod mentioned earlier and cautiously pull back the curtain. It's empty inside except for an inflatable couch covered with faux furs and royal banners that say Senate of Calgon hanging from the ceiling. I'm not that surprised to find that the place doesn't look used at all. Seems no other maidens have fallen for his proposition.

"Where are we?" Blake asks, his horns nearly grazing the top of the tent.

"The Senate of Calgon," I tell him, leading him over to the couch. "Or the site of every nerd girl fantasy." I sit down and stare up at him, opening my legs wide.

His eyes nearly fall out. "You have a hole in your suit."

"I know that," I tell him. "And I'm not wearing underwear."

"I can see that," he says, practically salivating. "Was this all for me?"

"You get panty lines if you don't go commando," I tell him, beckoning him down with my finger. "And this is a full bodysuit. I'm not taking the whole thing off every time I have to pee."

"Right," he says, not even hearing me anymore. His eyes keep roaming from my bare pussy, over my spandex covered breasts, to my lips and back down again. I feel like he's going to have a convulsion just standing there. "This is seriously the hottest thing I have ever seen in my whole entire existence."

"It's about to get hotter," I tell him as he drops to his knees and runs his hands up my inner thighs, squeezing as he goes, his eyes burning and locked on mine. He's about to dip his head, but I reach up and grab his helmet, taking it off before the horns spear me.

I put the helmet to the side and out of the way. His hair flops forward on his forehead. "Not up for the horns?" he says with a grin.

"Maybe later."

He lowers his head between my legs and I lie back, the

sun streaming in through the parting in the tent door. Out in the distance the battle cries go on, but in here there is nothing but Blake's tongue on my clit, tentative at first, then his mouth opening right over it, gently sucking me in.

I feel the air sucked out of me.

His tongue runs down me in broad, warm licks and I raise my hips, wanting more purchase, more tension, more relief, more of everything.

He places two fingers inside me, holding me open, while his tongue still works, alternating between gentle sucks and languid laps. His teeth raze me at some point and I cry out loudly but the pain has never felt sweeter.

"Come inside me," I whimper as I feel myself getting close, my hands gripping his hair. "Please. I need you. I need to feel you again."

He pulls back, breathless, his mouth red and wet, and looks down at his costume. "You're lucky these are pants, otherwise I'd need a hole too."

"I'd cut it out with my teeth," I tell him.

He gives me an odd look. "I'm not sure if that's sexy or not."

"Shut up and fuck me."

"Yes, queen," he says, bringing his cock out. He moves his body on top of mine and I relish his weight as his elbows plant on either side of my shoulders, pinning me between him. There's little hesitation before he pushes his cock in and I stretch around him, feeling impossibly full. There's nothing else like this. Nothing at all.

I roll my hips under him, pulling him even deeper, causing him to gasp. I've missed those sounds of his. I've missed everything.

We are immediately lost in the silken push and pull of each other, our bodies joined, our souls grappling in lust.

It's so easy with him.

So easy.

He groans and slowly pulls out before sliding back in to the hilt. I close my eyes, pleasure curling down my spine, my legs opening wider.

"Is this a bad time to tell you I'm in love with you?" he whispers against my mouth.

My heart stalls.

I open my eyes and find him gazing at me, his stare so raw and smoldering, like he's giving me all he has, all that he is.

"I suppose there could be worse times," I whisper right back, running my hands through his hair and holding on. "I love you too, you know."

"I didn't know," he says, breaking into a beautiful smile, the dimples deepening on his cheeks. "But I know now. And I won't forget it."

I grin, digging my nails into his ass and shrugging him forward, his cock sliding in deep.

"Take me to Asgard," I cry out. "Or Ragnarok. Or pleasure town, wherever."

"Anywhere you want to go, my peach," he murmurs. "But we're going together."

EPILOGUE

AMANDA

One year later

"Hey, you should sign it Tits McGee," Blake whispers in my ear.

I pause just as I'm about to write my own signature. My eyes slide to him. "What? How did you know about that?"

"Oh, I've learned about a lot of things since your newfound fame," Blake says, leaning in closer. "That your high school nicknames included Tits McGee, Lord of the Geeks, and Sir-Pukes-a-Lot. The last one was pretty explanatory. You know, considering."

I look up at the young woman standing on the other side of the table, waiting eagerly for me to sign her book. I flash her a nervous smile.

This is our first book signing. Blake's father agreed to hold it at Crawford's Books. The store is doing really well now thanks to the new store manager they were able to hire.

Plus there's the celebrity aspect of it all since everyone knows by now who Blake Lovecox really is.

But they also know who Blake Crawford is, just as they know who Amanda Newland is.

It's been a year since *Falling for the Secret Male Stripper* came out. Since then, we've released ten other erotic novels, with one of them, *Slammed by the Single Dad*, hitting the New York Times' list. You can bet Rio thinks she can add that title to her name as well. She's teaching English in Japan now, but she says she introduces herself to people as a New York Times' bestselling influence, which is kind of true when you think about it.

It hasn't been just smut though. True to our hopes and wishes, writing and selling the kinky stuff and finding success in the genre has opened a world of possibilities for us. We both have agents, and we both have our own novels out. *The Land of Tears and Bone*—now retitled *Phenelope*—was just released this month by a major publisher. Blake's sci-fi horror, *Blood Aurora*, was published by a small press two months ago. It's already been optioned for a film, the lucky bastard, even though they say that's never anything to get too excited over since options rarely amount to anything.

But it's hard not to get excited these days. Things are falling into place.

And every day I'm falling more in love with him.

I mean, he's still the man who holds my hair back when I vomit.

Which I did on the way over here this morning, as we walked from our apartment. Right as tourists in a horse-drawn carriage were wheeling past. I think they got photos.

Who knew your first book signing would be so nerve-racking? I was so worried that no one would show up, and then I started worrying that everyone would show up. What if I spelled someone's name wrong? What if someone told me they hated my work? What if I farted? All valid concerns.

But so far it's been going okay, except I almost wrote Tits McGee in this person's book. I slide the open page over to Blake, glaring at him. "If you talk to me while I'm signing, I will seriously write down all the wrong things."

He just flashes those dimples at me and writes down his name in his usual chicken scratch handwriting. At least I'm known as the "neater one."

Even though the signing is only for a few hours, it seems like everyone I know has come in to get something signed at some point. The show of support is amazing, albeit surprising. Sarah and her new husband David stop by, as does Miss Dumas and Heath. Kevin and Angelica briefly pop in on their way to Butchart Gardens for a fun day together.

Though the divorce is old news and she and Blake's dad have gone their separate ways, Angelica and Kevin never ended up moving away. In fact, they moved to a modest house closer to us and even Fluffy is allowed back home. The four of us (minus Fluffy) spend a lot of time together when Angelica isn't working, and we bond over our love of Benedict Cumberbatch. At least, everyone but Blake does.

Speaking of moving on, Blake's dad is also here, putting his disdain for smut aside to watch the money roll in. And let's face it, I know he's proud of his son. But he's not alone. Ana is with him.

Yeah. I guess sparks were flying that day at the LARPing event because when it was Kevin's turn to get made over by Ana, she and his father started talking. Next thing everyone knew, the two divorcees were dating. They can't be more different, and I have no idea what they have in common, but somehow they make it work. They're both happy, that's the important thing.

"I didn't know your parents would be here," Blake says to me as I'm signing another book.

I look up to see my mom next in the line, my dad hovering in the background, talking to Blake's dad. My mom gives me a sheepish wave.

"Mom," I say, not expecting them to be here either. My parents and I have gotten closer over the last year, even though it took a good three months of keeping our distance before we could start again. Now they treat me like an adult (mostly) and I try and act like one (mostly). It's not always easy but it's working so far.

My mom has a copy of our latest erotica, *Sex Bomb*, in her hands and shyly slides it toward me. "It's for your Aunt Sylvia," she explains. She leans in closer and lowers her voice. "You two don't have anything female on female do you?"

"Mom," I admonish her. This is so sweet, incredibly touching but also majorly embarrassing.

"I had to check," she explains with a shrug.

I sign it to Aunt Sylvia and hand it over to Blake to sign.

She hovers at the table. "How about you two come over for a celebratory dinner tomorrow night?"

"If crazy Aunt Sylvia is there, I'm in," Blake says. He looks at me and explains, "I feel she might have some good stories for our next book."

I wrinkle my nose and he gives her the book back.

"We'll be there," I tell my mom. "I'll call you about it later."

She walks off to join my dad and they both wave at us.

"Well, that went well," Blake says with a sigh after the

last of the attendees have been pushed through. "Better than I expected."

"Yeah, well, you got that one woman crying over meeting you," I joke. "And then you had to sign that pair of underwear. And the condoms. And that other lady's breasts. So yeah, it went quite well for you."

"Don't be jealous," he says to me, giving me a cocky smile as we get up and slowly make our way across the store, stretching our cramped hands, arms, and legs. "The time will come when you get to sign breasts too."

We pause among the stacks of books and a thrill goes through me that our own books are in the store here. It never gets old.

But neither does being in love with Blake.

He grabs my arm and spins me around until I'm pinned back against the bookshelf. He brushes his fingers through my hair before placing a soft kiss on my lips.

"What's next, peach?" he asks me softly.

"You mean story idea-wise, or about life?"

"Both. What's our next chapter?"

I link my hands behind his neck and gaze up at him, the love of my life.

"I guess we'll have to keep writing and see," I tell him.

He grins, grabbing my hand, and we walk out of the store and into the sunshine.

THE END

I hope you enjoyed reading Smut! If you're in the mood for another romantic comedy from me, I would suggest the following books to make you blush, giggle and swoon:

\- NOTHING PERSONAL

When her ex-lover and ex-worker, Kessler, ends up being transferred to her office in Honolulu, Nova has to deal with the fact that the very man who broke her heart is now her boss.

\- BAD AT LOVE

Marina and Laz, two best friends who are bad at love and relationships, decide to date each other as an experiment to see what they're doing wrong.

\- THE ROYAL ROGUE

When Princess Stella of Denmark succumbs to a brief affair with the devilishly handsome and arrogant Prince Orlando of Monaco, a man she loves to hate, the last thing she expected was to end up pregnant with his baby. (Coming September 29, 2019)

STAY IN TOUCH

Want to say hello? Get involved in my newest releases or just what I'm up to these days? Check out the links below.

- INSTAGRAM - this is where you'll find me, always, posting about travel, clothes, my dog, island life, paddleboarding, our B&B, books, upcoming releases, my sexy husband, and much, much more. Give me a follow if you need to be entertained!

-MY FACEBOOK GROUP - SUPER SECRET, SUPER SPECIAL! I have giveaways, exclusive access, insights into my life and the writing process, plus tons of fun with a great bunch of like-minded readers. Join today!

-NEWSLETTER - I don't send these out very often (though I am working on that and forever toying with writing a book exclusively though the newsletter) but if you subscribe you'll at least be alerted every time I release a book or have a cover reveal!

- BOOKS - Want easy access to all my books available on Amazon? Just click here and start scrolling!

ACKNOWLEDGMENTS

I've been wanting to write a book about writing since, well, I started writing. And then definitely once I started publishing, either through the magic of self-publishing or through my traditional publishers, Hachette and Simon & Schuster. There's a reason why Stephen King (all hail the King), writes an awful lot about writers—it's what he knows. And it's hard not to write about what's going on around you. Ironically, I've written about a lot of things I didn't know much about (drug cartels, ghost hunters, rugby players) but this (along with Love in English, Where Sea Meets Sky, and Racing the Sun) was so easy to do (in some ways, tough in others). Because I live it (and I live on Salt Spring Island, near to where the book is set). I finally had the chance to write about being a writer.

But it's not just about the highs and lows of the craft. There's an entire world that most people aren't aware of, a crazy, fucked up world of romance authors. I started out writing in the fringe genre of horror romance (The Experiment in Terror Series, go check it out), so I wasn't privy to this world until later and then once I was in it, I was *in it*.

The world of romance authors, bloggers, and readers is equal parts maddening and amazing. It's an underground bubble with daily drama, strife, revenge, pettiness, jealousy, shady tactics, marketing ploys, screenshots, vague-booking, and those fun things that come along with any counterculture (I cut my teeth on Mike Patton fandom, so I know crazy). But it also has the kindest, funniest readers, supportive authors, and passionate bloggers that balance out all the nutty stuff. In the end, these people are my people, and I'm lucky to be part of a world where I get to meet people from all over the globe, where I get to travel for a living, and make long-lasting and very dear friendships.

One thing I have noticed though, and one thing that unites us all, is the label of Smut. Now, "Smut" by definition is a fungus. Not very appealing. It's also the term loosely applied to romance and erotica across most art forms. It's not supposed to be a good label; in fact, most people who throw the term smut around do so in a derogatory manner. But regardless, there is a stigma against romance writers that I was never aware of when I was dabbling in horror romance (or even suspense).

Though this was intended to be a silly, light-hearted read for all intents and purposes, one of the many points of the book was that romance and erotica are nothing to be ashamed of. I've read some erotic novels that are exquisitely layered with beautiful prose and tragic characters (*The Siren* by Tiffany Reiz, go read it now), that are not taken seriously because of the genre. I've also flipped through some poorly-written, here-to-make-a-buck, trope-exploiting smut, and you know what? There's nothing wrong with that either. Whether you're reading to be changed and challenged or reading to escape for a few hours, get off, and maybe make good with your husband, who cares? No one should be judged for what they read, nor should authors by what they write (WHY they write? Well, that's a different topic for another time. I'm not so naïve to think that all writers are in it for the same reasons). Regardless, there is an influential world out there filled with very passionate people, and a little more passion in this world can't be a bad thing.

So thank you to all the readers, bloggers, and authors who wear their desires proudly, and especially to those who have helped support me over the years through my ever-evolving career. I can't tell you enough how important you are to me.

Thanks again to my friends and family for never being ashamed of what I write, whether it's the threesome scene or choking a hooker with barbed wire (Dirty Promises), or public hand jobs (this book and Racing the Sun), anal sex (The Play), or someone getting tortured via tattoo needle to the eyeball (Shooting Scars). Even though I know (and hope) you're all skipping some scenes, the fact you still get excited about each release means a lot after all these years.

Thanks to my lovely husband Scott for letting me see the true dork that he is and for accepting me in my own crazy, nerdy ways (I'm still very proud of reading one thousand National Geographics, my knowledge of dinosaurs, and how I saw X-Men in the theatre six times). Thanks to Kelly for your book trailer and for always being my Tom Hiddleston/Benedict Cumberbatch/Chris Evans/Hemsworth obsessed long-lost sister (pretty sure Amanda is more you than me!). Thanks to Laura Helseth for her proofing skills and Kara Malinczak for her editing. Hang Le for the best cover in the whole world...no really, you outdid yourself! Emma Stone and Sam Claflin for being my muses for Amanda and Blake (they don't know it, but I think they'd approve). Jay Crownover (I actually do know her!). KA Tucker (another lousy Canadian). Stephanie Brown (who still needs a proof of life from Scott). Sandra Cortez and Dani Sanchez (for therapy). The Anti-Heroes. My parents for buying all those encyclopedias and putting up with SO MANY of my obsessions (including everything related to *Jurassic Park*). My in-laws, Wendy and Alan (who isn't even close to the Alan in this book!). And thanks to the people I did lead on night hikes when I was younger, where I would take off with the flashlight and leave them stranded, for not suing me.

Speaking of suing, I have to thank the real Amanda Newland (Amanda N!) and Blake Crawford. I'm sorry, guys, that the book isn't about you (though Amanda, I know one of those nicknames was yours), but I did think your names made for perfect characters! Thanks for letting me borrow them.

P.S. If anyone wants to come up to Vancouver Island and go LARPing with me (it would be my first time), I'll be in my Phoenix costume with a bottle of wine (I legit have worn that costume for Halloween). If that's too far, you can always drop me a line at authorkarinahalle@gmail.com (positive emails only for this lady), or join my author group on Facebook where things are always fun (search: Karina Halle's Anti-Heroes), or follow my Instagram, where you can see my daily updates of living the Blake Lovecox life.

#Nerdgirlsunite #Nervpervs #GeekSmut #NoGimmicksJustSmut

ABOUT THE AUTHOR

Karina Halle, a former travel writer and music journalist, is the *New York Times*, *Wall Street Journal*, and *USA Today* bestselling author of *The Pact*, *A Nordic King*, and *Sins & Needles*, as well as fifty other wild and romantic reads. She, her husband, and their adopted pit bull live in a rain forest on an island off British Columbia, where they operate a B&B that's perfect for writers' retreats. In the winter, you can often find them in California or on their beloved island of Kauai, soaking up as much sun (and getting as much inspiration) as possible. For more information, visit www.authorkarinahalle.com/books.

ALSO BY KARINA HALLE

<u>*Contemporary Romances*</u>

Love, in English

Love, in Spanish

Where Sea Meets Sky (from Atria Books)

Racing the Sun (from Atria Books)

The Pact

The Offer

The Play

Winter Wishes

The Lie

The Debt

Smut

Heat Wave

Before I Ever Met You

After All

Rocked Up

Wild Card (North Ridge #1)

Maverick (North Ridge #2)

Hot Shot (North Ridge #3)

Bad at Love

The Swedish Prince

The Wild Heir

A Nordic King

Nothing Personal

My Life in Shambles

The Royal Rogue

<u>*Romantic Suspense Novels by Karina Halle*</u>

Sins and Needles (The Artists Trilogy #1)

On Every Street (An Artists Trilogy Novella #0.5)

Shooting Scars (The Artists Trilogy #2)

Bold Tricks (The Artists Trilogy #3)

Dirty Angels (Dirty Angels #1)

Dirty Deeds (Dirty Angels #2)

Dirty Promises (Dirty Angels #3)

Black Hearts (Sins Duet #1)

Dirty Souls (Sins Duet #2)

Discretion (The Dumonts #1)

Disarm (The Dumont #2) -

<u>*Horror Romance*</u>

Darkhouse (EIT #1)

Red Fox (EIT #2)

The Benson (EIT #2.5)

Dead Sky Morning (EIT #3)

Lying Season (EIT #4)

On Demon Wings (EIT #5)

Old Blood (EIT #5.5)

The Dex-Files (EIT #5.7)